THE LEGACIES

THE LEGACIES

MICHELLE LARKS

URBAN
CHRISTIAN

www.urbanchristianonline.net

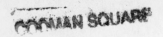

Urban Books
1199 Straight Path
West Babylon, NY 11704

ISBN- 13: 978-1-60162-967-8
ISBN- 10: 1-60162-967-2

First Printing August 2008
Printed in the United States of America

10 9 8 7 6 5 4 3 2 1

Submit Wholesale Orders to:
Distributed by Kensington Publishing Corp.
C/O Penguin Group (USA) Inc.
Attention: Order Processing
405 Murray Hill Parkway
East Rutherford, NJ 07073-2316
Phone: 1-800-526-0275
Fax: 1-800-227-9604

The Legacies is dedicated to the memory my late brother

Roland David Harris, Jr.

(1961–2007)

His life was a testament of God's Grace and Mercy.

Acknowledgements

First, I would like to give thanks to God. He is and will always be the head of my life. I have learned, as I continue to write books, that God has sent many angels my way, much like the heroine in this book. I would like to thank my family; my mothers, father, sisters, brothers, nieces, nephews, and daughters; I am so glad God enriched my life by making me a part of your life.

My friends who have listened to me talk about my books, and those of you who have read manuscripts for me and given feedback: A Million Thanks!

To Joylynn, my editor, thank you for your much-needed guidance, and keeping me on track during this project. I appreciate it. I would also like to send a shout out to the staff at Urban Books and the Urban Christian authors. Tee C., thank you for being an agent and friend. Denise, thank you for sending me an email a year ago offering your assistance; your help has been invaluable.

Radiah of The Urban Reviews, Monique Brunner of The Delta Reviewer, Eleanor of The Black Butterfly Reviewer, Raw Sistaz, Sistah Girlfriend Book Club, Torrian Ferguson, Ella, Tavares, Yasmin of APOOO, Tiffany and The Distinguished Ladies and Gentleman Book Club, Michelle Carswell, *Infinite Magazine*, Ametra of Infini Promoters, Readers Choice Bookstore, Marcus of The Apex Reviewers, Readers Paradise Book Club, Waiting to Exhale Book Club—thank you all for reviewing *Keeping Misery Company* and for inviting me to join you on your radio blog shows, and just plain supporting me. Your encouraging words fill my heart with joy.

To my MySpace friends who supported me by buying a book or left encouraging messages on my page as I waited for *Keeping Misery Company* to be released—thank you!

To my supporters in Bolingbrook, and on my job, as well as Fran, Darlene, Rob and Marlas, Tony, Brenda, Sheila, Pat S., and Pat M., Glen, Kanika, Saundra P., Barbara M., words cannot express how good I feel about your support; you all are so awesome.

Da Book Joint, Peoria Central Library, Plainfield Library, the managers at Barnes & Noble and Walden Books, and Borders bookstores, thank you for allowing me to sign books at your establishment.

Lastly, I have to send a big shout out to my husband, Fred, thank you for being with me every step of the way!

Michelle

Chapter 1

Seventeen-year-old Morgan Daniels-Foster "oohed" and "aahed" as she posed prettily in the mirror. Morgan was about five-feet, nine-inches tall. Her complexion was a deep, dark chocolate. Her looks were striking. Huge doe-shaped eyes and a wide tapering nose made up her facial features. She had a medium build with long legs that seemed to stretch forever. Graceful were her hands and feet.

She lifted her mane of dark, weaved hair off her neck and then released it. The hair streamed like a river down the middle of her back. She finger-combed her bangs. Then she smiled and rolled her neck, tossing her mane from side to side.

Morgan's eyes swept the room until they landed on a pile of designer luggage neatly stacked against one of the walls. Morgan occupied the third story of her mother's gray stone home in the Lake Park community of Chicago.

Morgan's black-and-white-painted space was an open area like a loft apartment. The brownstone's dimensions measured five thousand square feet and included five bedrooms and four bathrooms. The den boasted a wood-burning fireplace and every modern convenience anyone could ask for. The sunken living room was decorated with modern Scandinavian blond furniture accented with earth tones, and the appliances in the silver-and-black-marbled kitchen were state of the art.

The garage provided ample space for four cars Jernell, Morgan's mother had built a small coach house behind the gray stone where her bodyguard resided. Gentrification had yet come to Lake Park, but when it did, the Foster's residence would definitely fit the mold.

Morgan's eyes rested on the partially opened cedar closet door. The inside was almost totally devoid of her belongings. She heard the click-clack of footsteps on the hardwood staircase, which indicated someone was coming upstairs. Morgan's eyes were drawn to the partially obscured figure walking her way.

Lucinda Brown, the Foster family's housekeeper and Morgan's former nanny, stopped in front of Morgan. There were tears in her eyes. "So are you all packed and ready for college?" She walked over to the suitcases and looked down at them. "Make sure you put nametags on all the bags." Lucinda pointed to Morgan's desk. "I put a stack that I wrote out for you over there. I can't believe you're leaving us, Morgan. I remember the day *Jernell* brought you home from the hospital. And here you are all grown up and about to leave for college."

"Well, it had to happen one day," Morgan quipped. "It's not like I'm going that far; just downstate to Bradley. I wanted to go to Howard, but Momma wouldn't let me," the young woman complained. Her nose crinkled in disgust.

"Oh you," Lucinda teased. She swatted Morgan with the dishtowel that was slung over her shoulder.

Lucinda was a honey-colored, big-boned woman. A pair of deep dimples framed her cheeks. She was short in stature, and a pleasant looking woman with medium length brown hair. She was completely devoted to her boss/friend, *Jernell*, and the only child of the house.

"Are you ready for dinner this evening with your relatives and family friends? Your mother is so proud of you that I think she's invited everyone she knows." Lucinda picked up a blouse off the floor and dropped it inside a clothes hamper.

"I guess so." Morgan sighed as she closed the dresser drawers. Then she sat on the side of the salmon pink-and-white-striped canopy bed. The walls were covered with pin-ups of her favorite musical artists: Tupac Shakur, Destiny's Child, Nelly, and her favorite of them all, Sean Puffy Combs. The furnishings in the room included a white oak dresser, an armoire, and a high glass computer desk. Inside a black entertainment center was a high definition television and a Bose CD player along with tons of music and movie CDs. One of the walls was covered from ceiling to floor with mirrors.

A two-cushioned sofa upholstered to match the bedspread and window treatments sat on one wall along with two bean bag chairs. A hutch stored Morgan's porcelain doll collection. Her mother had purchased every Barbie doll produced.

Lucinda stood motionless in the middle of the room. Her eyes dropped to the floor and then focused at Morgan. "Well, you know how that goes. Your mother has gone through a lot of trouble to plan a great evening for you."

"I'm sure she has. Momma has always been generous with her money." Morgan kicked a shoe under the bed.

"You know Jernell has to send her only child off in style. Times have sure changed. I can't believe your mother is hosting what you young folks call a "trunk party." People just called them going-away parties back in my day," Lucinda observed as she shook her head from side to side.

"Hmm, I guess so. Yeah, I'm ready for the tribe. It's too

bad that Daddy's side of the family couldn't join us for dinner today. For once in my life, I wish all my family could get along. I had to go visit Daddy's side of the family last week. Why do I have to suffer because of everyone else's issues?"

"Chile, we all have our crosses to bear," Lucinda remarked. She turned and said, "I have to get back downstairs and check on dinner." She walked to the staircase and headed down.

"Call me when everyone gets here."

"Will do," Lucinda hollered as she walked downstairs.

Morgan walked over to the messy bed and laid down on her stomach with her legs entwined in the air. She really didn't feel like socializing with the relatives. But since she wasn't returning home until Thanksgiving, it was best that she grace the family with her presence.

Jernell had informed her daughter that she could come home sooner if she got homesick. Morgan would be the first person in the Foster family to attend college. Jernell and her sisters, who owned the family business, didn't attend secondary school. Their maternal aunt, who raised Jernell and her siblings, felt that continuing their education was a waste of time since they were expected to work for the family anyway.

Young Miss Foster could hardy wait to leave Chicago and Lake Park to become another anonymous college freshman in the crowd. She thought it would be nice to go somewhere where no one knew her or her story.

Morgan's maternal relatives tended to be loud and overbearing when they gathered together. Someone was always trying to outdo the other one. Music blared from the speakers and the aunts loved to eat and drink their favorite cognac, Martel, as they gossiped. The sisters were generous by nature and would come bearing lavish stacks of gifts.

Morgan's eyelids dropped, and she fell asleep. She awakened half an hour later from a gentle tug on her arm. She opened her eyes and saw her mother staring down at her. Jernell smiled at her daughter, who beamed back at her.

Jernell Foster was a strikingly beautiful woman. Her features showed a mixture of African American and Caucasian. Jernell's complexion was high-yellow. Her nose was small, and she had thin lips.

"The family will be here in half an hour," Jernell informed Morgan. "You need to get up and dressed."

Morgan yawned, rolled over, and then sat upright. She stretched her arms over her head and then covered her mouth, stifling another yawn. "It won't take me long to get ready. I'll hop in the shower and be downstairs in no time."

Jernell scratched the side of her head with a long cerise-colored, gold-tipped fingernail. "Get up out of the bed now, Morgan. Time is running out." Her baby-fine long hair was pulled into a ponytail atop her head.

The doorbell chimed. Jernell walked over to the intercom on the wall and pushed a button. "Who is it?" she asked.

"It's Big Momma. Open that door, gal."

Jernell pressed another button. "I'm on my way down." Her eyes shifted to her daughter. "Big Momma's here, so hurry up and get dressed."

"I'm going to the bathroom now. I'll be down in twenty minutes."

"See that you are." As Jernell walked toward the staircase, Morgan arose from the bed and headed to the shower.

After she bathed and changed clothes, Morgan went downstairs where she found a good few of her family members scattered in various rooms around the house. They snacked on appetizers and sipped either alcoholic beverages or soft drinks. Morgan greeted all of her aunts and cousins in the living room and then walked into the dining room.

The stereo was turned on, as Morgan knew it would be. Aretha Franklin crooned "Daydreaming" softly from the speakers. Yes, her grandmother was definitely in the house; she loved old school R&B music.

"Where's Big Momma?" Morgan asked Jernell, who sat with her sisters in the dining room munching on crab cakes.

"In the den," Jernell replied as she wiped her hands with a cloth napkin. "Go in and speak to her."

"I will," Morgan promised as she walked out the room.

A tall, almost obese, light-brown-skinned woman sat in the middle of the sofa. She wore a mauve and beige floral print dress and a matching head band around her short, coarse black hair. Her face lit up when she saw Morgan and she held out her arms. When Morgan walked over to her and bent over, her grandmother folded her in her arms.

"How are you doing, baby? Are you nervous about leaving home?" Big Momma asked.

"No, I'm fine," Morgan answered Jernell's surrogate mother. She was really Morgan's great aunt.

"Good. Then you'll do fine at college." Big Momma smiled at Morgan. "Come sit by me." She patted an empty spot on the tan and beige micro fiber sofa.

After Morgan sat down, she noticed the gifts lying in and around the steamer trunk that Jernell had purchased a few days ago.

"Momma should have scheduled dinner last week. There's no way in the world I can take that stuff with me. I've already packed for school," Morgan said to Big Momma.

"See, what you're not taking into account is that you don't know what's in those bags and boxes." Big Momma shook her head. "Maybe there's stuff in them that can be sent to you while you're at school at a later date."

"I guess that's true," Morgan replied, shrugging her shoulders. "I'll have to wait and see."

Jernell walked into the room and handed a glistening bottle of Evian chilled water to Big Momma. "Here you go." The cap was half twisted off. Jernell then gave Big Momma a crystal glass with a twist of lemon. "Just the way you like it."

"Thank you, sweetie." Big Momma sat the glass and bottle on the cocktail table on a pair of coasters. Jernell sat down in the wing-backed chair across from Big Momma and Morgan.

The three Foster women sat in the den and chatted about Morgan's freshman year at Bradley University, until Big Momma announced, with a small smile on her face, "I'm hungry! Is the food ready, Jernell?"

Lucinda didn't disappoint Morgan with her choice for dinner. She prepared the young lady's favorite dishes. A coconut cake rested on a glass cake plate in the middle of the massive oak dining room table. The meal was made up of smoked turkey, jerked chicken wings, rib tips, mixed greens, macaroni and cheese, candied yams, potato salad, buttery dinner rolls, and cornbread.

The doorbell rang loudly. Lucinda walked to the foyer to answer it. Brianna, Adrianna's daughter, strolled into the dining room with her mother. Brianna was Morgan's favorite relative, and the cousin closest to Morgan's age.

Adrianna, clad in white pants and a sailor top, apologized, "I'm sorry we're late." She walked over and kissed Big Momma and Morgan.

Brianna walked behind her mother. She carried a big box in her arms. "Hey, everybody! Where should I put this?" She wore a mint green and white capri outfit. Brianna was a pretty biracial young lady. Her complexion was a smooth café-au-lait color, courtesy of her African-American mother and Italian father. She was a little shorter than Morgan; five feet, seven inches tall, and she was thin in build. She has green eyes like her father and a mop of curly, reddish-gold hair.

"In the den. Duh," Morgan told her cousin. She was

wearing a matching capri set. Hers was a different color, fuchsia and white. The cousins wandered off to talk with relatives closer to their age.

A few hours later, the family began to make their exits.

Adrianna stood. "It's time for us to go." Her sisters followed suit and made a mass exodus to the front door. Jernell and Morgan walked with them. As the relatives departed, they exchanged hugs with the new college freshman and promised to write or email her while she was away.

Brianna, in her high-pitched, baby-sounding voice, pleaded with her mother to allow her to stay overnight. "Mommy, can I spend the night with Morgan? Please? You know I'm going to miss her. She's like a sister to me. We're the only two cousins without any siblings."

Adrianna peered at Jernell, who nodded her head.

"Thanks, Aunt Jernell," Brianna squealed. "Can I go to Peoria with Morgan and Auntie? Please, Mommy?"

"Brianna, I don't know." Adrianna's brow puckered indecisively. She put the strap of her Prada purse over her shoulder.

"She's welcome to ride with us," Jernell offered graciously. "I know how much the girls are going to miss each other."

Brianna walked over to Jernell and hugged her aunt's neck tightly. She murmured, "Thank you."

Big Momma was the last to leave. She put a pink shawl around her shoulders. "Call me when you get settled in school," she instructed Morgan.

"I will," Morgan promised after she kissed the older woman's cheek. "Thank you for the gift and I'll see you in November when I come back home."

After the last family member had departed, Lucinda began clearing the dining room table while Jernell and the girls walked upstairs. "Don't stay up too late you two. Tomorrow is going to be a busy day. Just think, one of the Foster girls will finally be attending college. This is a big day for our family," Jernell reminded them.

"We won't," Morgan and Brianna chimed at the same time.

When the cousins walked inside Morgan's loft, she flipped her Bose stereo on and turned the dial to WGCI. Tupac rapped about not being mad at cha.

Brianna flopped on the side of the bed and slipped her sandals off her feet. "I am so jealous. I wish I was going too. You got a lot of money today, didn't you?"

Morgan nodded. She bent over and pulled open a dresser drawer. She reached in and tossed a nightshirt to Brianna, who went into the bathroom to change. Meanwhile, Morgan stood at the mirror wrapping her hair in a silk scarf.

When Brianna returned, Morgan had changed to a green silk nightshirt. She laid on the left side of the queen-sized canopy bed. Using the remote, Morgan turned off the radio and dimmed the lights. The television glowed softly from the corner of the room.

The girls chattered like magpies about the family business and Jernell's expectations for Morgan to head up the business when she finished college. Then Morgan poked her young cousin in the shoulder and said, "Let's go to sleep. I can't hardly wait until it's time for me to go to college. I'm glad you're coming with us. I'm a little scared about leaving home. What if I flunk school or something?"

"Gurl, you don't have nothing to worry about. You were an A student your whole life. Everything is going to go fine. And in another year, I'll be there with you."

Morgan picked up the remote control from the side of the bed and turned the television off.

Before long, she had fallen asleep with thoughts of Peoria and Bradley University dancing through her head.

Chapter 2

Approximately fifteen miles southwest of the Foster's Lake Park home, another teenager was having difficulty falling asleep too. Noah Oliver Stephens had an appointment at Bradley University the following morning to register as a college freshman. He lay sprawled atop his bed on his back with his hands clasped behind his head.

The light-skinned young man was six feet tall and wiry in build. He had a bobbing Adam's apple and a hint of sparse dark whiskers on his chin. His hands and feet were large and he wore his naturally wavy hair in twists. His hair style was his parents' acknowledgement that their only child was a member of the hip-hop generation. Noah was a smidgeon away from being a pretty boy. Instead, he was handsome, in a rugged-looking way, and he always had a smile on his face.

The young man's last day at home differed substantially from Morgan's. His items for his dorm room were packed in cardboard boxes stowed inside his father's azure blue Chrysler mini-van. Noah spent a good portion of his last day home at his father's small storefront church located a few blocks from the family home on the southwest side of the city.

Noah's father, Samuel, and his mother, Gloria Jean, along with the church's mother's board, hosted a going away tea for New Testament Missionary Baptist Church's first son. Quite a few members of his father's congregation took the time out of their day to socialize with Noah and present him with envelopes containing increments of one to twenty dollars.

Following the tea at church, Gloria prepared a family meal for Noah at home. Like Morgan, he didn't plan to return to Chicago until Thanksgiving.

There was a light tap on his bedroom door. The doorknob turned and his father walked into the room, carrying a plate with two thick slabs of chocolate cake.

Reverend Stephens placed the plates on top of Noah's nightstand, then he went back to the kitchen and returned with two plastic glasses of cold milk. He was thin in build like his son, and nearsighted. He wore thick black-rimmed bifocal glasses. The minister's eyes always betrayed his feelings whether he was happy or troubled. Reverend Stephens wore his wooly, graying hair in a small afro.

After he sat comfortably in the desk chair, Reverend Stephens said, "I figured you probably wouldn't get much sleep tonight. Tomorrow is an exciting day for you. Son, your mother and I are so very proud of you. And when you've completed college, then you can go to the seminary in Chicago to prepare to work alongside me at the church."

Noah said in a trembling voice, "You're right, I'm so wound up that I can't sleep." He picked up the fork and cut a large piece of cake and stuffed it inside his mouth.

Father and son sat in comfortable silence until they devoured the last pieces of cake and drained their glasses of milk.

Reverend Stephens set his plate on the desk and put the

glass on top of it. He looked at his only child. Pride and love radiated from his eyes. "You know that you're receiving an opportunity that your mother and I didn't have. Our parents couldn't afford to send us away to college. So I want you to make us proud while you're at Bradley. Soak up as much learning as you can. And, God willing, when you're done in Peoria, you'll come home and work at the church with me as my assistant minister."

"I will, Dad, and believe me, I'm grateful for this opportunity to go on to school and all. I'm just not 100 percent sure that I want to be a minister though, and I don't want to let you down." Noah admitted miserably. His body was hunched forward dejectedly as he sat on the side of bed.

Reverend Stephens peered at his son and stroked his chin. "You know I grew up poor Englewood. I always hoped that I would have something, really anything, like a legacy to pass on to my children. The Lord saw fit to bless your mother and me with just one child, you," Reverend Stephens nodded at Noah. The young man stared at his father, quietly listening to his words.

"Complications arose during your birth and your mother wasn't able to conceive another child, so all of my hopes and dreams fell on you." The minister reached out and patted his son's shoulder. "I don't want you to go away to college feeling like I'm putting pressure on you, son, to follow my in my footsteps. Although nothing would make me happier than to have you work in the church beside me. I just ask that you keep an open mind. I believe that God put you on this earth to minister to His flock, and I think after you finish school, you'll realize what your calling is. Let's resume this conversation when you finish at Bradley and see how you feel at that time."

Noah gulped. His eyes widened with relief, and he sighed. "For real? You mean I can just be a normal person while I'm at college?"

"Noah, wherever you go," Reverend Stephens held his hand out, "you're always a child of God, and don't you ever forget that. There's no reason why you can't enjoy life, too. You're only young once, but I don't want you to lose sight of everything you've been taught here at home and at the church. There is much temptation in the world, and you have to be careful and prayerful at all times."

Noah nodded his head. "I will, Dad." His voice broke. "I could never forget what you and Mom have taught me. I just want to be like other kids leaving home for the first time and not be labeled a preacher's kid like I have all my life. I want to experience life as any other young adult, trying to figure out what I want to do with my life."

Though Reverend Stephens was disappointed, he realized his son was young. Like other teenagers, he felt the strains of peer pressure and a burden to please his family. He sighed deeply. "In the long run, your mother and I only want your happiness, son. But we still want you to be mindful of your Christian teachings."

"I will, Dad, I promise," Noah said entreatingly, leaning toward his father.

"Why don't you try to get some sleep?" Reverend Stephens suggested. "We're getting up pretty early." He looked at the clock. "In another four hours to be exact. So get some shut eye, and I'll wake you later."

Noah laid down on the bed. "I will, Dad. I can hardly wait."

Reverend Stephens closed the door behind him. His feet, encased in slippers, padded softly down the wooden hallway. When he walked into the bedroom that he shared with his wife of more than twenty years, he took off his robe and laid it across a chair in the bedroom.

Gloria turned over in the bed and stared at her husband with sleepy eyes. "Is Noah all right?" she asked in a hoarse tone of voice.

Samuel got into the bed. He turned to Gloria. "Yes, he's fine, just a little nervous about school tomorrow and having second thoughts about following me into the ministry. Where did I fail in raising him, Gloria? From the time he was a small boy, I schooled him and prayed on my knees many a night about our serving the Lord together."

"Sammy, he's still young." Gloria's expression and tone were serious. "Give him time and space to find himself, and trust in the Lord. Our boy will be fine. You received your calling later in life rather than earlier. Isn't that right?"

Samuel pulled Gloria into his arms. "See, that's what I love about you. When my way seems murky, you steer me back to clear waters. I know what you're saying is true, but I worry about Noah being out in the world. There are so many pitfalls for our young black men. They're already the most endangered species on the planet."

Gloria patted Samuel's arm. "Give him the time and space he needs to grow into a man. Where is your faith in God?" she admonished. "It's almost two o'clock in the morning and we'll be leaving soon. There is no doubt in my mind that Noah's future is going to be fine." She kissed Samuel's cheek, and sunk back into the bed. Within a few minutes, Gloria had fallen back asleep.

Samuel closed his eyes, and said a prayer for his son's safety while he was away at school. Sleep finally claimed him.

Gloria awakened a few hours later and removed Samuel's arm from around her waist. She smiled at her husband's light snoring. She rose from the bed and walked to Noah's room, which was across the hall from the one she shared with Samuel. She opened the door and stood in the doorway, watching her son breathe. He was out like a light.

Gloria closed the door and walked down to the end of the hallway to a small beige and black wall-papered bathroom and showered quickly in the ancient-looking, claw-footed bathtub. When she was done, Gloria wrapped her body in an oversized terry towel and returned to the bedroom. She donned a light-weight green and navy blue sweat suit and styled her brown, shoulder-length hair in a French roll. After she finished dressing, she walked down the hallway and into the kitchen to prepare breakfast for her men.

As she stood at the stove scrambling eggs, a tear fell down her cheek. Gloria was bereft knowing her only child was leaving the nest and going out into a secular world. Despite her encouraging words to Samuel earlier that morning, she felt a twinge of sorrow in her heart. Gloria had misgivings about so many things like not seeing her baby on a regular basis. She was terrified because Noah was so good-natured and handsome. He would be an easy mark for the fast girls at school.

Gloria reached up into a pine cabinet, took out a bowl, and scooped the scrambled eggs into it. Then she turned the bacon over in the skillet. After she laid the fork on the stove, she glanced at the clock. It was time to wake up Samuel and Noah.

She'd just wiped her hands on a dishtowel when both men walked into the kitchen. "I was just getting ready to get you up." She beamed a smile their way.

Noah wore blue jeans, a white T-shirt, and newly purchased Nike sneakers. He removed three plates from the cabinet and cutlery from the cabinet drawer. Samuel took a bottle of orange juice and a carton of milk from the refrigerator.

When the family sat down to eat, Samuel blessed the meal. "Father above, we thank you for this meal prepared for the nourishment of our bodies. Bless the cook, Lord. If it's in your will, God, and I know it is, please allow us to deliver Noah to school safely, and for me and Gloria to make it back to Chicago unharmed. These and other blessings, I ask in your son's name and for His sake; amen.

Gloria echoed, "Amen." She dropped her hands to the table and opened her eyes.

Noah pushed the food around on his plate. He was too jittery to eat. Gloria noticed her son's lack of appetite. Her eyes gleamed with sympathy for Noah. "If you're not hungry now, we can get something to eat on the road."

"I'm sorry, Mom," Noah apologized. "Today is the biggest day of my life after graduation, and I'm just a little nervous."

"It's all right, I understand. Why don't you go and finish packing your toiletries in the bathroom." She glanced at the clock again. "We'll be leaving in about half an hour."

"Thanks." Noah hopped from the chair and dashed to his bedroom.

Tears spilt from Gloria's eyes. "I wish God had blessed us with more children, Sam," she moaned to her husband. "Then maybe I wouldn't feel so blue right now. I've taken care of that boy for the past eighteen years. And now I've got to step aside and hope we've taught him well enough to take care of himself."

Samuel reached over and grabbed her hand. "I guess we both got the blues today, Glo. God willing, we'll get through this day." He stood. "I'm going to bring the van from the garage around to the front of the house." He went out the back door adjoining the kitchen.

Gloria sat at the table motionless for a few minutes. Then she stood and scraped the leftovers on the plates into the garbage can and placed the dishes in the sink. She filled a thermos with coffee for herself and Samuel, and then took a couple of cans of 7-Up out of the refrigerator from Noah.

Half an hour later, the rest of Noah's belongings were stowed in the back of the mini-van and they were on I-94 heading to I-55 to take their boy to college.

Chapter 3

Jernell trudged up the stairs to her daughter's quarters. She had on a tangerine colored tank top and stone-washed denim shorts with brass colored sandals on her pedicured feet. Her face was flawlessly made up like she was traveling to a major social event. Jernell stood on Morgan's side of the bed and said loudly, "Girls, it's time to get up. The limo will be here in an hour and a half." She clapped her hands.

Morgan popped up in the bed like a jack-in-the box. She pushed a lock of hair out her face. "It's time." She shook Brianna. "Get up, it's time to go to Peoria."

Brianna burrowed deeper into the bed. Then she turned toward her aunt and looked at her through heavy lidded, sleep filled eyes. "It's too early to get up," she moaned. "I'm still tired."

"Lucinda has prepared a light breakfast for you girls. I suggest both of you be dressed and downstairs in thirty minutes." Jernell's tone indicated that the subject was not up for discussion. She turned and walked out of the room.

Morgan got out of bed and snatched her clothes off her dresser. "I'm going to take a shower. Use one of the bathrooms downstairs, Bri." She looked down at her cousin still nestled inside the bedspread. "Get up, Brianna. You know my momma don't play."

Brianna sat upright in the bed. "Okay already," she replied grumpily. "I'm getting up. I didn't bring a change of clothes with me. So I need to borrow an outfit from you."

"Most of my stuff is already packed," Morgan replied. "I don't have a lot of clothing left in the closet. But go ahead and see what you can find."

As Jernell had requested, both girls were downstairs seated at the dining room table within an hour. They munched on fresh fruit and buttered croissants. While they partook in the meal, the doorbell rang. A middle-aged African-American man wearing a black suit, white button-down shirt, and dark tie with a black hat on his head stood at the entrance. He introduced himself as Mr. Lee.

"I'm your limousine driver. Is there anything you need me to do now?" The man asked politely. He removed his hat and bowed to Jernell.

"You can start loading my daughter's luggage into the car." Jernell pointed to the Louis Vuitton suitcases that Lucinda had brought down from the loft the previous evening.

Mr. Lee appeared to be counting the pieces of luggage. "Is this everything or are there more boxes going with us?" Mr. Lee asked Jernell.

"No this is it. We're just taking luggage with us. We sent boxes through FedEx earlier this week. They haven't arrived at the school yet. They should have been delivered to Bradley yesterday. So we may need to stop at the local FedEx office so that I can fill out a report if they don't arrive in Peoria today."

Mr. Lee put his hat back on his head. "Yes, ma'am." He picked up a couple of the suitcases and carried them outside to the car.

Jernell looked at Morgan. "Do you have your birth certificate and your checkbook with you?"

"Yes, Momma. I'm ready to go." Morgan couldn't contain her excitement. She rocked on the balls of her feet.

"This is so exciting, Morgan," Brianna gushed. She clasped her hands together "I'm so glad Aunt Jernell let me go with you guys."

"I'm glad you're coming too." Morgan smiled fondly at her cousin.

A short time later, Mr. Lee had stowed all of Morgan's bags inside the vehicle. "I'll be waiting in the car," he told Jernell.

"We'll be out in a minute," she replied.

Lucinda walked over to Morgan and put a windbreaker jacket around her shoulders. "This is just in case it gets cold in the limo. I'm going to miss you, baby girl. I know you're going to make me and your mother proud. I'll be here when you come back. Call me when you get settled in your room." Her eyes leaked tears, causing Morgan's eyes to well up as well. The young woman threw her arms around the older woman's shoulders.

Brianna watched them and began sniffling too.

"Okay. Enough with the sob stories already." Jernell picked up her purse off the dining room table. "We've got to go, Luci. I'll call you after I check in the hotel this afternoon. I left the number to the Doubletree Hotel on the counter in the kitchen. I'll be back tomorrow evening or Sunday."

Morgan looked back at Luci helplessly as she and Brianna strolled toward the door. Lucinda blew Morgan a kiss. "We'll talk soon."

Brianna whistled when they walked outdoors. A crowd of people stood across the street gawking at the white stretch limousine Jernell had leased.

After the three got inside the vehicle, Morgan looked at the house. Lucinda stood in the doorway. Morgan waved to her. Luci crossed her fingers and waved back.

"Aunt Jernell, how are we getting home?" Brianna asked. "Can I have one of those bottles of cranberry juice?" She pointed to a mini cooler on the floor.

"The limo driver is going to stay in Peoria overnight at another hotel. Then he'll drive us home tomorrow evening."

"Cool," Brianna responded. "Can I stay in the dorm tonight with Morgan?"

"Yes, you can have a juice, and we'll see about your staying with Morgan tonight. She does have a roommate, you know." Jernell reached down and picked up her bag and removed a manila file folder from it. She put a pair of reading glasses on her nose and then opened the file.

Brianna unscrewed a wet bottle of cranberry juice and took a sip. "*Mmm* this is good." She flecked a few droplets of water at Morgan.

"Girl, watch it."

Brianna got comfortable in her seat, and soon she fell asleep. She snored noisily as her head drooped forward.

The sun beat mercilessly down on the top of the white automobile. They were halfway to Peoria when they noticed a van parked on the side of the median. The hood was raised and white clouds drifted like smoke toward the sky.

"Should we stop and help them?" Morgan asked her mother, pointing at the vehicle.

"I don't know. You can't be too careful these days on the road. There are some sick people in the world," Jernell replied as they slowly passed the vehicle.

Morgan peered inside the van as they passed. She glimpsed a teenaged boy surrounded by cardboard boxes with a miserable expression on his face. "Momma, I bet they're going to Peoria too. Can we stop and give them a ride or something?"

Jernell pressed the button to let down the partition separating driver and passenger. "Mr. Lee, would you back up and see if we can be of any assistance to those people stranded in the blue van back there?"

The driver maneuvered the limousine onto the median and slowly backed up the car. He left the car running and got out of the vehicle.

"Are we there yet?" Brianna asked as she awakened. She rubbed her eyes.

"No. There's a family back there with car problems. I saw a boy in the van with a stacks of boxes. They looked like they were going to Peoria, too."

Jernell pressed the button to roll down the window. Mr. Lee returned to her side of the car.

"Ms. Foster, their van is overheating. The owner has already called AAA. He says someone should be here within another hour. His wife wants to know if her son could ride to Peoria with us. Otherwise, he'll be late for registration. I told her I'd check with you."

"I guess that will be okay," Jernell replied grudgingly. "Tell him to come on." She glanced down at her Rolex watch. "We don't want to be late ourselves."

Mr. Lee went back to the van and returned with the young man. He paused at the open window and thrust out his hand. "My name is Noah Stephens. My family and I appreciate you letting me ride to school with you." He took a navy blue backpack off his back.

"You're welcome. Did you bring anything with you that needs to go inside the trunk? Luggage or boxes? If not, hop in so we can be on our way," Jernell instructed. She opened the car door.

"No, my parents are bringing my stuff with them. I can sit in the front seat with the driver. I don't want to put you through any trouble," Noah answered hesitantly as he shifted the strap of the backpack from one hand to the other. "Should I ride up front with the driver?" Noah asked Jernell.

"Boy, get in here, so we can go on our way." Jernell motioned for the young man to get inside the car.

Noah slid in the seat across from Jernell, Morgan, and Brianna.

Morgan and Brianna's eyes scanned Noah quickly.

He doesn't look bad at all, Morgan thought.

He's kind of cute, in a geeky way, Brianna thought. "My name is Brianna Rizzo-Foster and this is my cousin, Morgan. She's a freshman at Bradley. And I bet you are too."

"You're right." Noah nodded his head. "I'll be starting my first year at Bradley this semester." He held out his hand and shook the girls' hands.

Brianna reached inside her tiny Coach purse and pulled out a green foiled package. "Gum anyone?"

"No. Not for me," Noah and Morgan said at the same time. They stared at each other and tittered nervously.

"What school did you graduate from, Noah?" Brianna asked after she put a stick of gum inside her mouth.

"I graduated from Hales Franciscan. Where did you go?" he asked Morgan.

"I graduated from Jones Preparatory Academy. We got the class of 2002 in the house," Morgan joked. She flipped a lock of hair over her shoulder.

Noah looked at over at Brianna, "and where do you go to school?'"

"I go to Jones Prep and I'm a senior. When I graduate next year, I plan on going to Bradley with you and Morgan. This time next year, I'll be moving into a dorm," Brianna said. She couldn't help but notice the couple eying each other.

Jernell returned her attention to the spreadsheet and its figures. She pulled her laptop computer out of her tote bag.

"So, Noah, where do you go for prom? Do Catholic, all-boy schools even hold proms?" Brianna asked the young man. He couldn't keep his eyes off Morgan. And she was definitely making eye contact in return.

She's fine, and tall, just the way I like a girl, Noah thought. His eyes freely roamed Morgan's lithe body, from the top of her head, down to her long legs. "Uh, did you say something?" He glanced momentarily at Brianna, then back at Morgan.

"Never mind," she replied crossly. "I'm going back to sleep." Brianna pulled a Bulls cap down over her head and folded her arms across her chest. Before long, she was asleep again.

Morgan and Noah conversed for the next hour until the driver turned into the entrance of the campus.

"Oh my God, I can't believe we're really here." Morgan's hands flew to the sides of her face.

Mr. Lee lowered the Plexiglas window. "Young man, you need to call your mother. She asked that I remind you to call her when you arrived here, so they would know where to meet you."

Noah slid his cell phone out of his pants pocket and dialed his mother's cell phone number. His eyes zeroed in on Morgan's. She watched him with amusement.

"Hey, Mom! We're at the school. Are you and Dad back on the road yet? You are? Okay, I'll meet you at the registration hall." He closed the flip phone and smiled at Morgan.

Jernell stuck the papers she'd been reading and her laptop back into her tote bag. "I'm sure you two are probably registering around the same place. Mr. Lee, please drop us off at University Hall. Is that where you're going, young man?"

"Yes, it is," Noah answered eagerly. He pulled the instructional letter from the school out of his backpack. He was ecstatic that he could spend time with Morgan for at least another hour.

Ten minutes later, Mr. Lee pulled the limousine in front of the hall, where a throng of teenagers stood in line waiting to register.

"Oh no. I'm not going to stand in that long line. It's too hot out here for that," Jernell said as she eyed the young people through the tinted glass window. "Brianna, why don't you go inside with Morgan and Noah? If Morgan needs me, you can come back to the car and get me. I've already paid your tuition, room, and board. So all you need to do is get your class schedule and room assignment. Mr. Lee and I might go to FedEx and hopefully get your boxes while you're waiting to register. I called and they are at the facility here in Peoria. Instead of waiting for them to be delivered, we might as well go get them. When we come back, Mr. Lee will be parked in that lot over there." Jernell pointed to her left.

The three teenagers hopped out of the car and took their places at the end of the long line.

Finally, an hour later, the young persons had crossed the threshold and were inside the hall. To Morgan's dismay, the lines inside were rather long as well. Noah and Morgan continued talking to pass the time.

Morgan was drawn to Noah's face. She was captivated by the deep cleft in his chin and his light brown eyes. She thought Noah was fine, with a capital "F." She hoped she and the young man would hook up.

Noah, wasn't immune to the young woman's charms. His eyes traveled over her pretty face and long hair as he tried to decipher if her mane of hair was a weave or not. College life was definitely looking up for the young man. He just knew going to school at Bradley was going to be a blast. He made a mental note to himself to get Morgan's cell phone number before they parted ways. Cupid had definitely shot arrows through their hearts.

Brianna fanned herself daintily with her left hand. "I'm

going to the ladies room and then to the vending machine to get myself a bottle of water. Do you guys want any-thing?"

Noah and Morgan were so engrossed in their conversation that they didn't hear Brianna's question. She looked at them disgustedly and walked away.

An hour later, Morgan was next up in line. Noah stood behind her. A man and woman walked up to Noah. "Mom and Dad, you finally made it." He greeted his parents, and then turned to Morgan. "This is Morgan Foster. Her mother is the one who gave me a ride here this morning. Morgan, these are my parents, Mr. and Mrs. Stephens."

"Pleased to meet you," Morgan said shyly. She shook Samuel's hand and then Gloria's.

"We'll have to thank your parents for bringing our son here," Samuel said as his eyes swept over Morgan.

"There's just my mother with me," Morgan corrected him. "She's in the car waiting for me to finish in here."

"Tell her I said that we appreciate her bringing Noah to school this morning," Gloria responded. She hadn't missed the budding attraction between her son and the young lady. They made what she called "goggle eyes" at each other. Gloria felt perturbed. She noticed Morgan's attire, and it was obvious to her that the young woman's clothing wasn't cheap. Gloria took in the fake hair and what she considered flashy jewelry. What Gloria didn't know was that Morgan's bling bling was the real deal. *Oh, no, this one won't do; she's definitely not a Christian*, Gloria thought. Then she felt a momentary sense of shame. She was judging the young woman without really knowing her.

Gloria and Samuel had agreed to Noah's request that they be called Mr. and Mrs. Stephens during the weekend instead of Reverend and Mrs. Stephens. Noah's mother was itching to re-introduce herself to Morgan using her husband's title.

"Look, I'm up," Morgan proclaimed. She waved at Noah. "I'll see you later." She smiled.

"Make sure you give me your number before you leave," Noah requested of Morgan. "We freshman have to stick together." He held his hand up to his ear, as if he were on the telephone.

"Here comes Brianna. Ask her to give you my cell number. Noah, make sure you call me."

"No problem, I will." Noah watched her sway away.

Brianna carried a bottle of water in her hand. She walked over to Noah. "These must be your parents. You look like your mother." She tipped the bottle toward Gloria.

"You're right." Noah introduced Brianna to his parents, and then his eyes returned to Morgan. He snapped his fingers and pulled his cell phone out of his back pocket. "Brianna, Morgan asked me to get her cell number from you."

Brianna dutifully recited the number. Before long, Noah was standing at another window, pulling his checkbook out of his backpack.

Thirty minutes later, the clerk inside the cage where Morgan stood handed her her dorm assignment and class schedule.

Watch out Bradley, here I come, Morgan thought. Her eyes furiously searched the other cages looking for Noah. He looked over and smiled at her. She grinned in return and motioned with her hand for him to call her.

"Come on, let's go. Brianna grabbed Morgan's hand and led her out of the building, away from her first distraction from college.

Chapter 4

The bright glare of the sunlight assaulted the girls eyes as they exited the building. Morgan was surprised to see there were still so many students lined up outside the hall waiting to register.

Morgan stuffed the key to the dormitory room in her pants pocket. She and Brianna walked to the parking lot to where Jernell had instructed them to meet her. The air was humid, and Morgan put her hand over her bangs to shield her eyes from the sunshine. She looked from left to right, searching for the vehicle. Morgan heard the blast of a car horn. Brianna grabbed Morgan's arm and pointed her cousin toward the limousine.

When she and Brianna got inside the vehicle, Jernell was lying across the seat asleep.

"Momma, wake up! It's official. I'm now a student at Bradley University." She hastily thrust the paper in Jernell's hand.

Jernell sat up and smiled at her daughter's blissful face. "Great. Let's stop by a Kinko's before I leave Peoria and make copies of your paperwork. I need receipts," Jernell said, removing the rubber band holding her ponytail in place. She expertly rewound her hair and bound it back together. She took a tube of lipstick out of her purse and re-lined her lips. "I bet you two are hungry, aren't you?"

Morgan and Brianna nodded.

"Where do you want to eat?"

"McDonald's. Where else?" Morgan laughed. "And I'm starving."

"I prefer Wendy's," Brianna said primly, "but I guess Mickie D's is okay. After all, today is Morgan's day."

After Mr. Lee pulled into the fast food parking lot, he steered the limo into a parking space and lowered the partition. "Do you want me to go inside and order the food or are you going in?"

"I guess we'll eat inside," Jernell answered.

After the women exited the limousine, Jernell handed Mr. Lee money for his noonday meal.

Morgan and Brianna picked up brown trays off the counter. They ordered Big Mac value meals. Jernell had a garden salad and bottle of water. They sat in a booth next to a window. As she ate, Jernell perused Morgan's class schedule. "This isn't too bad. Twelve semester hours. I expect all A's from you this semester."

"But Big Momma said the first semester would be hardest for me," Morgan protested. "And that being away from home will be an adjustment for me. So how about I get B's the first semester and I'll work on A's for the second?" Morgan popped a French fry inside her mouth.

"Just do your best and I'm sure you'll make A's," Jernell replied gravely as she poured more Italian dressing on her salad.

The ladies had finished eating. Brianna slurped the last bit of Coca-Cola through her straw and burped. "My bad, excuse me. That was good. What are we going to do now Aunt Jernell?"

"I guess we'll go over to the dorm. Mr. Lee can bring the bags inside and you two can begin unpacking."

"Great," Morgan replied, enthusiastically tapping her left foot rapidly. "I can hardly wait to see my room. This is so exciting."

"I figure you and Brianna can unpack, while Mr. Lee and I go back to FedEx. It was crowded when we went there earlier, though the customer service person I talked to on the telephone told me your boxes had arrived, they hadn't. If we get enough unpacking done today, then you two can stay here tonight. And that depends on whether or not your roommate arrives today, Morgan. Otherwise, we'll finish up tomorrow and you two can spend the night with me at the hotel. That reminds me, I need to call Lucinda and let her know we made it here safely."

Jernell pulled out her Blackberry palm pilot and dialed her home number.

"Dang, I wish I were you," Brianna exclaimed wiping a bit of sauce off her chin with a napkin. "Morgan, you are going to have so much fun going to school here. You'll be away from your mother. And Western University isn't far from here. I heard some fine boys—excuse me, I mean men—go there. You got it made in the shade."

Jernell ended the call with Lucinda. "Lucinda says hi, and for you to behave yourself while you're at school, Morgan. I told her you'd call her tomorrow. Okay ladies, let's rock and roll."

As Mr. Lee drove through the campus grounds, the girls "oohed" and "aahed" over the surroundings, and before long, the driver pulled the limousine in front of Morgan's dormitory hall.

"Mr. Lee, why don't you start removing the suitcases

from the trunk and bring them to Morgan's room. She's in room 300," Jernell instructed the driver.

"Yes, ma'am," the driver replied. He opened the trunk while the women entered the building.

Morgan felt a rush of giddiness. The lobby looked freshly painted. It was a tan color. An RA or Resident Assistant sat on a folding chair at a desk. In exchange for free room and board, the RA helped the students make the transition from home to college. "What's your name?" she asked Morgan.

"Morgan Foster. I'm assigned to room 300." Morgan's voice and face bubbled with pride.

The young woman looked down at a listing spread on the desk. Her finger moved across the page. She looked up at Morgan. "My name is Dina Watkins and I'm your RA. Your roommate hasn't arrived yet. Welcome to Bradley University." She picked up a packet of pages that were paperclipped together. "This is a copy of the rules and regulations for the dorm. Sign this and return it to me within the next couple of days."

"Thank you, I will," Morgan replied. She wanted to run up the stairway, two steps at a time.

Jernell left the dormitory to return to FedEx after giving her approval of the room. When she and Mr. Lee returned an hour later with Morgan's boxes, Morgan and Brianna hadn't made much headway unpacking the suitcases. They'd spent more time talking than working. Jernell took one look at the room and said, "Okay you guys will bunk with me at the hotel tonight. We'll finish setting up the room in the morning."

Mr. Lee made several trips to the limousine to retrieve the boxes and deliver them to the room.

Morgan was disappointed about staying in the hotel for the night. She longed to stay in her new room and hoped Jernell and Brianna would return to Chicago. Morgan wanted to savor the delight in being away from the gray stone and the pressure of the family's business. She chided herself. *I just need to be patient today. By this time tomorrow, they'll either be back in Chicago or on the way.*

Jernell had reserved a Jacuzzi suite for herself and a double room for Morgan and Brianna. She made reservations for Mr. Lee at a Super 8 Motel a few miles away from the Doubletree Hotel. Twenty minutes later, they were in the elevator headed to their rooms.

"I need to make a few calls to check up on things at home. Let's freshen up and then we'll meet in a couple of hours for dinner," Jernell announced after she walked Morgan and Brianna to their door. She walked over and opened the door to the girls' room.

"Okay. Call us when you're ready to go eat," Morgan replied as her eyes roved her surroundings.

Brianna bounced up and down on the bed closest to the window. The lavender and pink floral window treatments and bedspreads matched. Then she pulled out her cell phone and called her mother.

"Mommy, I love it here at Bradley. I just know that I'm going to have a good time this weekend. Aunt Jernell said to tell you that we'll probably be home tomorrow evening around six o'clock. Morgan's room is nice. But it's a little too small for me and she has to share it with another person." Brianna nodded her head up and down. "Do you think you could get me a room by myself when I come here next year?" Brianna paused to listen to her mother's response. "Okay, Mommy, I'll see you tomorrow. Love you.

"My mother said to tell you good luck next week when you start school," Brianna said to Morgan after she closed her cell phone. She peered at Morgan curiously. Her lips curved into a mischievous smile. "You and that Noah seemed to hit it off pretty good on the drive down here. What's up with that?" She placed her cell phone inside her purse.

"Ain't nothing up yet. But I like him. He seems so nice. I think we vibed. I didn't notice until we got out of the limo how cute he was."

"Hmm, he looks like a geek to me," Brianna commented, cutting her eyes at her cousin and titling her head to the side. She ran her hand through her unruly curls. "But if that's what turns you on, then go for it. Are you going to tell him about the family?"

Morgan looked thoughtful. She took off her shoes and massaged her feet. "We just met today. What are you doing? Testing me? You know the business is one subject that we don't discuss with people outside the family."

"Just checking," Brianna giggled. "Gurl, your nose is so wide open that somebody could drive a Mack truck through it." She held her hands apart.

"Forget you." Morgan waved her hand in the air at her cousin. "What do you want to do?" She picked up the remote control and powered on the thirty-two-inch television. She surfed one cable channel after another.

Brianna answered her cousin with a twinkle in her eyes. "Let's go downstairs and check out the hotel's boutique. I need something to wear tomorrow. Remember, I didn't bring any clothes with me."

Brianna stood and picked the key card up off the dresser. Morgan made sure the door was closed securely behind them. The girls strolled to the elevators.

Once they were inside the boutique, Morgan wasn't really paying attention to the outfits. She impatiently pushed them back and forth on the rack while she waited for Brianna to finish trying on a sundress and a short set. It was close to the time Jernell had set for them to meet for dinner at the hotel restaurant. Morgan pulled her cell phone out of her purse and called her mother.

"Momma, Bri and I are downstairs at the boutique, shopping. As soon as she's done, we'll meet you at the restaurant."

"Don't be too late," Jernell cautioned her daughter.

"We won't be," Morgan promised. Then she disconnected the call.

Jernell stood in the middle of her hotel suite and contemplated her next move. When Morgan called she was about to leave her room and head downstairs to the restaurant. She closed her telephone thoughtfully and walked across the room and picked up her tote bag. She carried it with her to the sofa. When she sat down, she reached inside her Gucci purse for her glasses, put them on, and retrieved the file she'd been working on during the drive to Peoria.

Morgan's cell phone chimed the melody to "I Ain't Mad At Cha." She peered intently at the unknown number on the caller ID. Her heart pulsed erratically. She crossed her fingers hoping Noah was on the other end. "Hello?" Morgan asked breathlessly.

"Hello, Ms. Morgan Foster. This is Noah Stephens. How are you doing?" The sound of Noah's tenor voice in Morgan's ear sent chills up and down her spine.

At that moment, Brianna came out of the dressing room, clad in the aqua and white floral sundress. She executed a model's spin. "What do you think about this dress? Oh, you're on the phone. Who are you talking to?"

"Gurl, handle your business and let me mind mine," Morgan replied sassily. She stepped away from the rack, and eyed her cousin. "I'll be with you in a moment."

"Oh she got business now?" Brianna stalked back to the dressing room. She decided to buy the sundress she was wearing and a couple of other casual outfits. Brianna rolled her eyes. "I wonder if Aunt Jernell would be interested in knowing about Morgan's business."

Morgan glanced at the dressing room. "Hey, Noah. I'm fine. How are you doing?"

"Now that registration is over, much better. I wouldn't wish that process on my worst enemy."

Morgan laughed. "You're right about that. The whole experience was brutal. So which residence hall are you staying in?"

"I'm at Heitz Hall. I don't think it's too far from where you're staying. Didn't you say that your mother had pre-registered you for Harper Hall?"

"Yes, she did. We went by my dorm room. My roommate hasn't shown up yet. I still need to do lots of unpacking. Brianna and I are staying with my mother at the Doubletree Hotel tonight." Morgan's other hand rested on her hip. Her eyes darted back to the dressing room to see if her cousin had finished trying on outfits. Brianna stood in line at the counter. She handed the sales clerk her American Express credit card.

"That must be nice, staying at a Marriot, I mean," Noah commented. "My folks are staying at a non-name-brand motel. We're here now. I thought I saw your limo driver, Mr. Lee, when we passed by the Super 8 Motel."

Morgan nodded her head up and down. "You did. Mom put him up there for the night." She heard someone knocking on a door in the background.

"That's probably my father. We're going to Wal-Mart so I can finish getting more stuff for my room. Do you mind if I call you later?"

"No, that will be fine. I'll talk to you then." Morgan's face brightened like a hundred watt light bulb.

Brianna walked over to her cousin, carrying a bag in each hand. "Uh huh. Look at you. I'm going tell Aunt Jernell." Brianna sang in an off key tone, "Morgan's got a boyfriend."

Chapter 5

At the Pink Flamingo Motel, Noah flushed the toilet and laid his cell phone on the side of the tiny white sink. He yelled to Samuel, "Coming, Dad, I'll be out in a minute." Then Noah turned on the water and washed his hands. When he finished drying them, he stuffed the cell phone inside his pocket. He opened the door and then turned off the light in the bathroom. When he walked into their room, Samuel and Gloria, who had been sitting together on one of the twin beds, jumped up.

Samuel scratched his head and said, "Son, your mother and I decided to go back to Chicago tonight after we go shopping and take you to dinner. I talked to the manager when we checked in and this motel is one of the few in the area that will rent rooms in increments of four hours. So I went for that option. Your mother and I don't really have the money to stay the entire night. Well, we do, but we decided to give the money to you instead. We figured you can use it for school somewhere down the road." The older man looked his son entreatingly.

Noah nodded at his father and stuck his hands inside his pockets. "I understand. No problem."

Gloria smiled at her son weakly, like she was embarrassed by the family's lack of finances as she handed Noah a sheet of paper. "I began making a shopping list of what you need to finish furnishing your room. Take a look at it and let me know if we need to add anything else."

Noah scanned it quickly and gave it back to Gloria. "I'll look at it again when we get in the car."

Samuel walked around the room to make sure he had removed all of their possessions. After he checked out of the motel, Samuel drove to Wal-Mart, which was located about ten miles south of the motel. After they entered the store, Noah asked his mother for the list and the three walked to the linen department. Gloria placed another set of bed linen in the shopping cart. She stocked up on Ramen noodles for her son.

Noah used part of the money the church members had donated to buy a small microwave oven. He also purchased a study lamp, eating utensils, and plastic plates and bowls. After Noah completed his shopping, he had about two hundred dollars left in cash. He planned to put the money into the joint account he shared with his mother.

The young man had worked on a construction crew over the summer and had accumulated a tidy sum of four thousand dollars. Half of the amount was stashed in his savings account. Noah felt like he was in good financial shape. Bradley University had awarded Noah a partial scholarship, which included the room and board fee. The only expense he had incurred was textbooks.

It didn't escape Noah's attention during the drive to Peoria that Morgan's mother was probably well off. He hadn't seen many students arriving on the college campus chauffeured in a limousine.

The Stephens family left Wal-Mart and traveled to

Denny's for dinner. Listening to his parents chat about finances caused Noah's stomach to ache from pressure to succeed at Bradley. The young man realized just how much his parents were sacrificing for him to go to college.

Samuel joked after he finished eating the last bite of meat loaf on his plate. "You see, son, me and your momma, we're just regular folks who grew up in Englewood. It's not one of the best neighborhoods in Chicago, but, to us, Englewood is home. We know with the help of the Lord, you will succeed against all odds."

As dinner drew to a close, Gloria's mood became subdued. Reality dawned on her that her baby wasn't going home with her.

Samuel drove slowly back to Heitz Hall trying to delay the inevitable. He wanted to give his wife a little more time to spend with their son. When the Stephens arrived back at Noah's dorm room, Gloria unpacked Noah's newly purchased items with misty eyes and put them away in the closet.

Samuel set up the microwave oven. After he was done, he plugged the cord from the used television that Noah had brought from home into an outlet on the side of the bed. He turned the television on. Samuel nodded to Gloria, signaling that it was time for them to go. She walked over to Noah and sat on the bed next to him. "I'm going to miss you, Noah Oliver Stephens, starting tonight. Your being at school will be the longest time we've ever been separated."

Noah grabbed Gloria's hand. "I'm going to miss you and Dad, too. Before you know it, time will fly by, and it'll be Thanksgiving and then I'll be home. Hopefully, there'll be someone in the dorm driving to Chicago, so I'll try to get a ride home with him."

Gloria looked at her son sadly as two tears trickled down her face. Samuel turned off the television and walked over to his wife. He pulled her gently up from the bed. "Before you cry a waterfall, Glo, and flood Noah's room, I think it's time for us to go. Our boy will be just fine."

"That doesn't mean I won't miss my baby," Gloria sniffled and wiped her eyes.

Noah reached over on his nightstand and handed his mother a tissue. "Hey, this was supposed to be a happy occasion. I'm starting phase one of building a future for myself. Come on, Mom, don't cry."

"Listen to your son," Samuel teased Gloria as he lovingly watched his wife and son. His arms were folded across his chest.

"Okay, I'm ready. No, I'm really not, but I know we've got to let him go."

Samuel reached inside his pocket and pulled out his wallet. "I wanted to surprise you. I ordered you a Visa credit card in case of an emergency. So try not to use it unless it's absolutely necessary."

Noah took the card from his father and grinned. "Thank you, Dad. I promise I won't use it unless I don't have any other choice."

Samuel held out his hand and gruffly pulled Noah into his arms. "Take care of yourself, boy. We'll call you when we get home."

Gloria began crying earnestly. She hugged Noah tightly and whispered, "I love you, baby. Be careful, study hard, and try to enjoy yourself."

"I will," Noah promised. He rode the elevator with his parents to the ground floor. Then Noah walked his parents to the parking lot. He waved good-bye as Samuel exited the parking lot.

When the van was no longer in sight, Noah walked back inside and ran up the stairs to his room, taking two steps at a time. He went inside his room and shut the door. Noah whooped as he jumped up and down. "In the words of the

Reverend Martin Luther King: 'I'm free at last, free at last. Thank God almighty I'm free at last.' I don't have parents to watch my every move. And most of all, nobody here knows me as the pastor's kid. Hmm, I wonder what Miss Morgan is doing right now."

Chapter 6

Morgan and Brianna were lying on their stomachs at the bottom instead of the head of the bed. The girls lay across from each other in double beds sharing microwave popcorn and watching a pay-per-view movie. Morgan and Brianna's eyes were glued to the screen as they watched one of their favorite movies, *Love Jones*. During the love scenes, Noah's face kept popping into Morgan's mind. She shook her head as if to clear the young man's face from her head.

"Bri, I have something to ask you, and I want you to tell me the truth," Morgan said to her cousin after she swallowed a sip of cola. She set the can on the nightstand.

"What's that? Oh, I bet I know what you want; for me to swear I won't say anything to Aunt Jernell about your crush on Noah."

Morgan sucked her lips and swiveled her head on her neck. She dropped the bag of popcorn and held her hand up. "Gurl, please. That's not what I was going to say."

"Then what?" Brianna looked at Morgan. "Can't you wait to tell me when the movie is over?"

"No." Morgan shook her head from side to side. "We've

seen that movie a million times because you have a crush on Larenz Tate."

"No, cuz, you got it wrong. I'm going to marry Larenz Tate." Brianna tisked as her eyes widened dramatically. "Didn't I tell you he's waiting for me to finish college and then it's on?" Brianna rolled her neck and snapped her fingers. She sat up on the side of the bed and tossed a few kernels of popcorn into her mouth.

"Yeah right," Morgan sputtered with laughter as she sat up also. "Any old way, do you ever think our family could be cursed by God because of the family business?"

Brianna's smiling face turned somber. "Well," she drew the word out, "I don't know about that. We don't really go to church that much. So I don't know about curses and stuff like that. Her eyes darted to Morgan's face. "What do you know about curses and God?"

Morgan shrugged her shoulders. "Luci used to take me to her church with her when I was a kid. I kind of liked going there." Her eyes took on a far-away gaze. "I liked listening to the choir sing, especially at Christmas. The kids in the choir would clap their hands and sway back and forth as they sang." Morgan smiled at the memory, then her face became somber. "The family business is illegal, and I wonder if our grandmother disappeared because God doesn't like what we do. Do you think our grandmother wanted out of the business? Bri, do you think she's alive?"

"Gosh," Brianna's green eyes glittered and grew wide as saucers. "I don't know. Mommy never gave me any details about what happened to our grandmother. Daddy is Italian so my family never went to a black church. We go to the cathedral once or twice a year, usually for Christmas and Easter. Gee, Morgan, I don't know if she's alive or dead. Whatever happened to her is a mystery for sure."

"Sometimes I wish we were just like normal people," Morgan exhaled loudly. I used to like watching families sitting together at Luci's church. Sometime she'd let me go to the children's church and I'd listen to biblical stories. Then when I got in high school, I stopped going to church with her. Daddy makes me go to church when I visit him. He's gotten religious in his old age. I'll admit church has been one of those good memories from my childhood. Every now and then, I question our existence," Morgan said nonchalantly as she picked at chipped nail polish on one of her fingers. "It's not easy being a member of one of the largest drug distribution families in the Chicago, and I don't mean pharmaceuticals either. We're talking weed, heroin, and coke. Major products, as Momma calls them."

"Come on now, Morgan," Brianna countered impatiently as she waved her hand in the air. "We've had this conversation a million times. You know we didn't have any control over who we were born to. It's a way of life for us. At least we aren't common drug dealers on the street. It could be worse," Brianna added in a matter-of-fact tone. She lowered the television volume, sensing that her cousin needed to get some issues off her chest. Brianna gave Morgan her undivided attention.

"That's true. But still, it's embarrassing. What do you tell people when they ask what your parents do for a living? At least you can always truthfully say that Uncle Todd is a lawyer. Sometimes I lie and say Momma is a stockbroker. Don't you feel it's more to life than what our parents do? There are people in the world who have entirely different lives than we do."

Brianna sighed. She sat upright in the bed. "We are who we are, Morg. In our family, the women, not the men, are the breadwinners. It's a business that's been passed down from generation to generation, and there's nothing we can do about it, except make the best of it."

"I don't know . . ." Morgan moaned. "There has to be a better way. Do you know what else I heard?"

Brianna shook her head no.

"That Aunt Joyce had two abortions because the babies were boys and she wanted a girl, Thank God she had Caitlin!" Morgan lowered her tone and whispered to Brianna.

The young girl laughed and leaned back against the bag of popcorn, smashing it. She hastily sat up, picked the bag up, and sat it on the nightstand. "Now that's probably a Foster family urban legend. Where do you get all this stuff from?" She clucked her tongue and wagged her finger in Morgan's direction.

Morgan frowned and replied soberly, "From eavesdropping on Momma and Lucinda's conversations. Seriously, Bri, do you ever worry that the drugs the company distributes might end up in the hands of kids or something? Somehow I feel God wouldn't like that at all."

Brianna looked thoughtful for a moment, then she replied, "No, not really. My mother and father explained to me that sometimes there are positive and negative sides with anything you do in life. But it's not like our family members are the ones on the street selling to kids or anything like that."

"I guess you're right," Morgan said grudgingly, not ready to concede her point. Brianna almost sounded like Jernell.

"Seriously, you need to just concentrate on school and meet you some men. Maybe you need to hang out with Mr. Noah and put the family out of your head. You have four years to experience what can be called a 'normal life'. You'd better enjoy it, because with you being the oldest grandchild and all, you're going to have to take your mother's place one day in the family business."

Morgan nodded in agreement. "I don't know about you, but I'm ready to go to sleep. It's been a long day. Tomorrow this time I'll be in the dorm, hopefully getting to know my roommate or maybe even talking to Noah."

Brianna rose and returned to her own bed. She yawned, "I'm tired. See you in the morning."

* * *

Jernell was sitting in her room at the gleaming polished wooden desk, talking on the telephone to Adrianna, her second-in-command. "How did things go today? Were there any problems?"

"The day has gone smoothly," Adrianna said. "Relax, sis. Don't go looking for trouble, and it won't find you," Adrianna joked.

"Well that's good that nothing has come up since I've been gone."

"Gracious, Jernell! You just left this morning. You haven't been gone twenty-four hours yet. Todd and I can hold down the fort that long."

"You're right, maybe I'm overreacting." Jernell removed the rubber band holding her ponytail. She shook her head. "We've had some difficulty with a couple of the dealers on the west side. I've told Todd a million times that we should just concentrate on the suburban clients and leave the trade in the city alone."

Adrianna replied, "I know, but Todd thinks there's more money to be made and that we should take advantage of the opportunity."

"He's our comptroller and a major player in the company, and I hope for all our sakes that he's right," Jernell replied solemnly. She rolled her neck trying to work a crook out.

"He is." Adrianna tried to soothe her sister's fears. "Let him handle his side of the business. Things will work out fine, and we'll be richer in the long run."

"I hope so." Jernell removed her earring from her ear. "We can't afford any mishaps. The Feds always seem to be breathing down my neck. I've really been worried. I've tried to make this family time for me and Morgan. But I haven't done a good job. I'm glad Brianna came with us."

"Try to spend time with Morgan tomorrow. She won't be home for a while. You're a pro at what you do, and rightfully so. We've been doing our thing for three generations, since Great Granddaddy died and the business passed to Great Grandmother Helena. We'll be fine. Todd has greased a lot of palms. We're good, Jernell. Don't create problems where they don't exist."

Jernell ran her hand through her hair. "I guess so . . . But something just doesn't feel right. I'm getting bad vibes."

"Do you want me to call a meeting Monday with the girls?" Adrianna suggested.

"Yeah, set up something in the afternoon with you, Todd, and our sisters," Jernell requested.

"Will do. Get some rest, and most of all, spend time with Morgan."

"Okay, I'll talk to you tomorrow."

Jernell pressed the disconnect button on her cell phone. She stood and walked over to the mini-bar and removed a bottle of Hennessy. She didn't really drink very much, but her mind told her to be wary, things were not as they seemed. The young woman needed something to help settle her roving mind.

Jernell gulped down a shot of the cognac. It burned her throat going down. She walked over to the radio, turned it on, and set the dial to a jazz station.

The dynamics of the family structure were complicated. The family business was started in the 1930's by her great-grandfather, Mario Santini. He was born in the old country, as he called Italy, and migrated to New York by way of Ellis Island with his parents when he was a child.

A member of a rival mob gang gunned down the patriarch of the Foster clan. His common law wife, Helena Foster, was a mulatto who could pass for white. Helena picked up the reins where her husband left off. The business took off. She hired white men, Mario's affiliates, to front for her dealings with the mob after her husband's murder. And the family prospered greatly under Helena's direction.

Excited by her financial success, Helena decreed the family business should always be run by the oldest female of a new generation when the young woman reached twenty-one years of age. The overseer's husband would act as the head of the family for business purposes, but in reality, the wives would run the company. Another stipulation for women in the family was that they keep their maiden names.

Big Momma, or Darlene, didn't marry nor did she have children. She was second-in-command to Jernell's mother, Pamela. When Pamela disappeared, Darlene took up the reins and never looked back. When Adrianna married Todd, Darlene felt he was the perfect front man for the family, and the couple became Jernell's second in command.

Morgan's father, Rico, was to be Jernell's designated consort and helpmate in the business. The couple became engaged and were nearing the altar when Rico developed a case of cold feet. He announced that he wanted out of the relationship and the business. If Jernell had not been pregnant at the time and nearing Morgan's birth, she would have killed Rico herself. The only reason she allowed him to live was that he was the father of her unborn child.

A month after Morgan was born, Rico pleaded with Jernell to let him raise the child without the family's interference. He planned to move to Cleveland. Jernell coldly refused his offer.

Five years after her daughter's birth, Jernell ascended to the throne. Though Big Momma kept her hand in the pie, Jernell was crowned the official overseer of the family business.

After Rico's defection, Jernell vowed never to fall in love again, feeling that that particular emotion was reserved for the weak. She was young and had her needs. Though she'd taken a series of lovers over the years, no man touched her mind, body, or soul the way Rico had. He still held the key to her heart.

Over the past six months, Jernell had felt misgivings regarding her brother-in-law's loyalty to the family. Usually her instincts were on target.

Jernell stood up. Her face contorted with worry lines. She teetered unsteadily to the bar and poured herself another shot of Hennessy. Imbibing was a taboo in the family.

The overseer couldn't have any vices, drinking, or substance abuse problems. The family also preferred she be single with no emotional attachments, so she could focus on the company, although using sex as means to relieve tension was acceptable. The boss had to be tough, cold, and calculating since many millions of dollars were at stake.

Jernell strolled to the window and opened the drapes. She held the goblet in her hand, swirling the brown liquor with chips of ice and looked at the twinkling Peoria skyline. Unlike Morgan, she'd made her peace with her career and rarely looked back or obsessed about what might have been.

The die had been cast, and after Big Momma explained to the young woman the debacles Pamela had caused during her tenure, Jernell was almost manic in her drive to succeed. Morgan understood emphatically that she'd better follow her mother's lead.

Stumbling against the leg of the desk chair as she walked back to the bar, Jernell swore quietly and set her glass on the top of the bar. She felt woozy and held onto the wall until she reached the bed. She fell on it and closed her eyes. A memory she usually kept at bay darted inside her head. A slice of time when her life changed drastically. The day her mother, Pamela, disappeared.

Jernell remembered the morning Big Momma came to her bedroom and informed her that her mother was gone. Jernell hadn't been the same person since then.

She was sitting at her vanity table brushing her hair with the silver brush Aunt Darlene had given her for her birthday. Preening at her image, Jernell chanted, "Mirror mirror on the wall, who's the fairest of them all?"

There was a knock at her bedroom door. "Come in," she said, laying her brush down on top of the glass vanity.

Big Momma walked into the room and over to Jernell. She stroked the top of her niece's head. "How you doing, baby?"

"I'm fine, Aunt Darlene. There's a dance at school tonight and I'm supposed to go. Momma said that I could."

"Ah, that's what I want to talk to you about." Big Momma pulled the chair from Jernell's school desk and sat it next to the vanity.

Jernell stared at Big Momma with widened eyes. "What's wrong, Auntie?"

"Jernell, I have some bad news. I need you to be a big girl for your sisters. Your mother is gone."

"I know that," Jernell giggled, as she picked up a tube of clear lipstick. "She told me she'd be back home no later than Sunday evening because she had business to take care of."

Big Momma took the lipstick out of Jernell's hand. "Baby, your mother isn't coming back home."

Jernell snatched her hand away from Big Momma's. She felt a chill come over her body, like she was standing unclothed in the middle of Alaska in the winter. She looked fearfully at her aunt. "What do you mean, Auntie, by saying she isn't coming back? She told me she couldn't call me while she was gone and not to worry. She's not dead, is she?" Jernell began shivering.

"We don't know what happened to her, honey. All we know at this point is that Pam has disappeared. We have people out looking for her right now. But so far, we haven't had any luck. I didn't want to say anything to you until we knew something definite. You're a big girl, and I thought we should tell you what's going on."

"Momma wouldn't just leave me and my sisters unless

something was wrong. She has to be dead." The ramifications shook Jernell to the core.

Big Momma took Jernell by the hand and helped the girl up from her seat. She led her to bed, and put her arms around her niece. "We aren't giving up on finding Pam. But we have to make sure the company continues to function. So I'm going to take your mother's place until we can find her. And then when you're ready, you'll take my place."

Jernell began sobbing as though her heart was broken in two. "I don't care about the company. I just want my momma. Please don't let my momma be dead." She laid her head on Big Momma's bosom and sobbed until she was exhausted. The older woman did what she could to comfort the young girl.

From that moment on, Jernell's personality changed. She had been a vibrant, fun-loving pre-teen. After her talk with Darlene, she became serious and silent. She eventually rose to her position as the head of a major drug distribution company.

She followed Big Momma's lead after her mother's disappearance and didn't deviate from her aunt's carefully laid out plans until she met Rico in high school. She thought he was the one, and that together they would lead the company into the next century, but that had not happened.

Jernell wiped away a tear from her eye, and pushed the memory of the past back into the cellar of her mind. She resolved to enjoy the time with Morgan and Brianna and put her qualms about the business aside.

Jernell's greatest wish was to witness Morgan's taking her place triumphantly as the head of the family after her college graduation. She sighed and then hugged one of the big fluffy white pillows and fell asleep.

The jangling telephone sounded the following morning. It was the wake-up call Morgan had requested the previous evening. After she hung up the telephone, Morgan peered over at Brianna who slept through the telephone call. She was curled up like a baby in her bed.

Morgan strode over to the closet and removed her clothing for the day and her underwear from the dresser drawer. Then she walked into the bathroom and pulled her nightshirt over her head. She dropped the cotton material on the floor and picked up a plastic cap from a basket atop the vanity and put it on her head. She turned on the water and then took a shower.

By the time Morgan had departed from the bathroom, she was fully dressed and Brianna had awakened. Her head was propped up on two pillows as she watched the news. "Well, are you ready for your big day?" she asked her cousin.

Dipping her shoulders casually, Morgan nodded. "As ready as I'm ever going to be."

The telephone rang and Brianna picked it up to answer it. "Hello? Oh, hi, Aunt Jernell. What's up? Yeah we're out of the bed and getting dressed." Brianna nodded her head. "We'll meet you downstairs in the lobby in thirty minutes." She hung up the telephone and looked at Morgan. "Well, you heard me; let's get going."

Jernell looked refreshed when the girls met her in the hotel dining room. "I've been up a couple of hours," she confessed. "The hotel has a weight room. So I worked out with the equipment this morning."

The hostess seated the ladies and handed them menus. A few minutes later, a young woman appeared at the table carrying a coffee pot. "Good morning, my name is Beth. I'm your waitress this morning. Would anyone like coffee?"

Jernell nodded her head.

"After the waitress finished pouring coffee in Jernell's cup, she said, "I'll be back to take your orders in a few minutes."

Jernell opened a couple of packets of sugar and poured them into the cup. "Morgan, your father left me a voicemail yesterday. He said something about coming to Peoria to see you next weekend."

Morgan's face brightened. "Cool. I wish he could have come with us yesterday. It would have been nice if both my parents could be in the same place at the same time."

"Don't start with that nonsense," Jernell said to Morgan. She pulled a copy of the local newspaper out of her bag and read as she ate breakfast. The cousins chatted endlessly during the meal.

An hour later, the Fosters left the hotel. Mr. Lee had stowed their luggage back inside the trunk. Jernell checked out of the hotel. She and the girls walked outside to the vehicle.

"Are you sure that you have everything you need?" Jernell asked her daughter. "Do we need to make any other stops?"

"Yes, Momma, I have everything," Morgan said impatiently as she entered the car, which was parked in front of the hotel. "The only stop we need to make is to the school. I'm ready." The young lady tapped her foot excitedly.

Before long, they arrived at the university. While Mr. Lee unloaded Morgan's bags, she and Brianna went inside the dorm and took the elevator up to Morgan's floor. The young woman turned the key inside the lock and pushed the door open. When she and Brianna walked inside, Morgan expected to see her roommate, but she still hadn't arrived. Boxes of items lay on the floor next to the suitcases waiting for Morgan to put them away.

"Unless you need us to hang around, we're going to head back to Chicago," Jernell said after she came into the room a few minutes later.

"Are you saying that you and Brianna aren't staying to

help me unpack?" Morgan asked her mother. "I thought you were staying in Peoria today to help me . . . with the room."

Jernell stood in the middle of the room, with her hands on her hips. "I'm sorry, Morgan. Something came up back home, so I had to change my plans. So no, not this time. Anyway, setting up your room will be a good housekeeping experience for you."

Morgan swallowed back her disappointment. With a smile on her face, she walked over to her mother and hugged her. "I'll see you in November for Thanksgiving."

Jernell's eyes glistened with tears. "I'm going to miss you, Morgan. Do your best, and that's all I ask of you. I'm going back to the limousine. Brianna, be downstairs in ten minutes." Jernell pointed to her watch and then waved to Morgan as she walked out the door.

Brianna opened her tote bag. "Oh, I forgot, I bought a gift for you, actually two of them. She pulled out a five-by-seven framed picture of the two girls and put it inside Morgan's hand.

"I'm going to put this on my desk," Morgan said, in a shaky voice. "Gurl, what am I going to do without you?"

Brianna wiped tears from her eyes. "I hate to sound like Aunt Jernell, but you're going to ace your tests. Knowing you, you're also going to hang out with Noah and have mad fun. Before I forget, I bought you a diary yesterday. So though I'm not going to be around, pretend your diary is me and write down all your innermost thoughts. Then I'll read it when you come home." She gave the burgundy, vinyl-covered journal to her cousin.

"Thanks, Bri. I'll definitely use it. Morgan was touched by Brianna's thoughtfulness. "Dang it, I'm going miss you. I think I'm going to miss you more than anyone else."

"That's because we're like sisters. No, we're closer than

sisters." The two young ladies embraced. Brianna's cell phone chirped.

She looked at the caller ID and answered the phone. "Okay, I'm coming now, Aunt Jernell. Hey, Morg, I've got to go, but I'll call you when I get home." She wiped her nose with the back of her hand.

The girls hugged one more time and then Brianna was gone. Morgan walked over to the window and watched her cousin run to the limousine. Mr. Lee pulled the car out from in front of the dormitory.

For the first time in her life, Morgan was alone. Her wish to become just another face in the crowd had come true. She removed a face towel from one of the boxes and walked down the hallway to the bathroom. She had a good cry in the bathroom stall. She washed her face, returned to her room, and resumed unpacking her belongings.

Chapter 7

After Noah arose bright and early Sunday morning, a sense of guilt clouded his being. He hadn't missed church in more than five years. The reason for his absence then was that he was ill, suffering from the flu. *I guess missing one Sunday won't hurt. I've got to find a church on campus or nearby to attend.* After Noah showered and dressed, he decided to head over to the cafeteria, where he ate corn flakes and milk.

When Noah returned to the dorm, a young man was hanging clothes in the other half of the closet. He paused, looked at Noah, and said, "You must be my roommate. My name is Carlton Fitzhugh." He hung the clothes on the metal rack and then held out his hand.

"You're correct. I'm your roommate, Noah Stephens. Can I give you a hand with anything?"

"No, I've got it. I take it you arrived yesterday?"

Noah walked over to his desk and sat down on the wooden chair. "Yes, I did. My parents drove here with me yesterday morning. You missed registration."

Carl set a twelve-inch flat paneled television set on his

dresser. "My flight was delayed due to a thunderstorm. I flew in from Iowa. I told my father that we could have driven to Bradley, but he had an important business meeting at work and couldn't get away. I called the school yesterday and explained my dilemma, so I rescheduled registration for Monday morning."

"So you're from Iowa," Noah commented, stroking his chin. "I've never been there. Let's see if I remember my geography classes; Iowa is mostly farmland. Do you live on a farm?"

"Are you kidding? My father is a banker." Carl looked horrified. "We live in Des Moines. All of Iowa isn't farmland. How about you? You live in Chicago don't you? Where do you come from, the hood?"

Noah bristled and clenched his fist. "No not quite. Contrary to popular belief, all of Chicago isn't a ghetto." Noah felt guilty, knowing he'd lied to Carlton. Englewood was indeed the ghetto.

"I'm just messing with you. I know that." Carl laughed and held his hands up in surrender. "Des Moines is not too far from Chicago. I've been to the Windy City before. Seriously though, what part of the city are you from?"

"Englewood," Noah exhaled. "I admit it's rough in some areas, but there are still some hardworking, decent people in my neighborhood."

Carl looked at Noah skeptically. "If you say so. I've never heard of Englewood anyway. When my family visited Chicago, we stayed downtown at a hotel on the Magnificent Mile." Carl picked up a box and opened it using a box cutter. The box contained towels and linen.

"Since I already have my schedule, I think I'm going to walk around and get acquainted with the campus, so when classes start next week I won't get lost." Noah stood up. "I'll be back later."

"You don't have to answer to me," Carl smirked, as he

took set of sheets out the box. He began putting the linen on the bed. "I'll see you later."

Noah walked out the room and outdoors. He was agitated that the housing administration had decided to pair him up with a white boy from Iowa. For all Noah knew, Carlton could be a grade A bigot like Archie Bunker from the old television sitcom. Noah also felt self-conscious due to his lack of material possessions. He noticed the expensiveness of Carlton's belongings.

Then Noah squared his shoulders and decided that though he was a minister's son and didn't have lot of expensive things, he knew he was just as good as Carlton, and Morgan for that matter. A smile curved his lips as he thought of Jesse Jackson's famous speech, "I am Somebody." Then the young man pulled a map of the campus out of his pocket. He decided that after he finished his classes Monday, he would pay a visit to the Student Employment Office and try to find a job. He surmised the extra money would come in handy if he planned to hang out with Morgan. Noah also decided to find a local church to attend. Since his dad hadn't pressured Noah about going into the ministry, it was the least he could do. He sat on a bench and whistled a gospel tune as he studied the map.

When Noah resumed walking, he located several buildings where his classes would be held, which were in relatively close proximity to his dorm. He looked down at his wristwatch. It was later than he thought, so he decided to finish his tour tomorrow. Noah continued walking and found himself standing outside of Harper Hall.

He looked up at the building and remembered Morgan telling him she was in room 300. Noah glanced at his watch again. It was noon. He wondered if it was too early to pay Morgan a visit. The young man stood outside the building indecisively.

As if he conjured her up, Morgan walked out the double

doors, wearing a pair of white denim cut off shorts with a white and red top, looking cool as a cucumber. Noah couldn't suppress the grin that covered his face from ear to ear. "Morgan!" he shouted happily.

Morgan looked at Noah and her face broke into a matching smile. The two young people walked toward each other.

"I was just thinking about you," Morgan said. "Did you unpack your stuff?"

"Yes, I did. My roommate arrived this morning. He's a white boy from Iowa. I don't know about him. . . . What about you? Did you unpack?"

"Not really." Morgan's nose was furrowed. "And my roommate still hasn't put in an appearance. Maybe I'll get lucky and have the room to myself. Where are you headed?"

"I just came from scouting the campus so I won't look like a lost freshman when school starts. I took a little tour of the campus to find the buildings where my classes are going to be held."

Morgan punched him in the arm and grinned. "Great minds think alike. That's what I was going to do. Why don't you join me?"

"Don't mind if I do." Noah held his arm out and Morgan grabbed it.

"My first class, Literature, starts at one o'clock. My mother suggested I keep the mornings free. I hate to get up early in the morning," Morgan said as they strolled.

"I'm the opposite," Noah remarked. "I guess it comes from being a . . ." He snapped his mouth shut. He remembered he didn't want anyone to know about him being a preacher's kid.

"A what?" Morgan asked him, puzzled. She stopped walking. "There's a bench over there. Why don't we sit down for a minute? In case you didn't notice, it's a little warm outside."

They sat on a bright-green-colored bench. "Whew, it's

hot." Morgan tugged on the end of her shorts. "Now what were you saying?"

Noah looked away from Morgan. Then he glanced back at her face. "I was hoping when I came to Peoria, I could leave certain parts of my life behind." He waved his hands in the air. "But I guess we can't ever really escape who we are. My father is a minister. I'm a P.K., better known as a preacher's kid."

"Is that all?" Morgan laughed. Then her expression became sad. "There are worse things your parents could be doing than saving souls."

Noah spread his left arm on the top of the bench. "I guess so . . . Still it doesn't feel like it. I'm supposed to use this time away at school to find myself and decide what I want to do with my life."

Morgan couldn't help but notice the unhappy expression on Noah's face. His body seemed to drop. His lips were pursed tightly together. "I feel you. My mother owns her own business, and she's never had much time for me. I understand why on one level, but sometimes I feel neglected. I'm expected to follow in her footsteps and join the family business."

"My dad talked to me before I left," Noah admitted. "He isn't putting any pressure on me or anything, but I know he wants me to come into the church with him."

"At least he isn't pressuring you," Morgan replied wryly. She clasped her hands together. What Morgan really wanted to do was grab Noah's hand. He wore a small class ring on his middle finger. "I don't have a career choice with my mother either. I'm the oldest grandchild and the ownership of the company passes down in succession to the oldest female in the family."

"What kind of company does your family own?"

"An import and export business," Morgan lied smoothly.

She and Brianna had stayed up many a Saturday night trying to come up with an acceptable profession.

"And what does your dad do?" Noah pushed a lock of
hair off Morgan's face. *Hmm, her hair feels like a weave. Mom
would have a fit. I guess Morgan would fit under her fast girls'
category. I like Morgan just the way she is, hair and all.*

"My mother and father aren't together. Actually my dad
is supposed to come and visit me this weekend. He owns a
not-for-profit company in Cleveland, helping inmates find
employment after they get released from jail."

Noah's eyes nodded approvingly. "That's good. At this
point in my life, I really don't know what I want to do. Except I do know that I don't want to be a minister. Don't get
me wrong," he continued, "I will always be involved with
the church in some shape, form, or fashion. I know prayer
works and how a Christian should keep the faith when
times get rough. I just can't see myself leading the people of
the church. When you're brought up in an environment,
it's hard to shake it off entirely.

Morgan pointed to Noah and then herself. "Well, it looks
like we both have four years to figure it out. Are you thirsty?
Let's go get something to drink."

Noah stood, smiled down at her and asked, "Your dorm
or mine?"

"Mine is closest. Let's go to mine. Then when we're
done, we can look for my buildings."

The temperature had risen to nearly one hundred de-
grees. A light sheen of perspiration covered their bodies.
When they walked inside Harper Hall, the chill of the air
conditioner felt like a breeze of fresh air.

"It's a good thing we decided to come to your dorm,"
Noah remarked after they ordered colas and sat at a table in
the cafeteria. "Mine doesn't have air. The room and board
was a little cheaper. Unlike you and probably my room-

mate, I don't have a lot of money. My parents prefer I don't work the first semester so I can focus on my classes and adjust to being away from home. I plan to visit the employment office tomorrow."

"I don't know what gave you the idea I have money," Morgan responded a little crossly. She crooked her finger at Noah, gesturing him to come closer. She cupped her hand around his ear. "I'm going to let you in on a little secret," she whispered. "The person with money in my family is my mother, not me." Morgan moved away from Noah and said comically, "And luckily she shares it with me."

Noah laughed aloud at her antics.

Students began filing into the large room standing in line for lunch, since breakfast was over.

"I hear you," said Noah. "Still I feel poor. . . ."

"As a church mouse?" Morgan teased him with a serious expression on her face.

"Now you know you ain't right," Noah laughed. "I guess I sorta got a chip on my shoulder."

"No, you've got a boulder there," Morgan quipped. "You've got to get over yourself, Noah. We haven't known each other long and yet I sense you're a good person. There is no doubt in my mind that you'll attain any goal you set for yourself."

Noah was pleased as punch at Morgan's remarks, and he couldn't stop a smile from spreading across his face. "I thank you, Ms. Foster, for your kind remarks. I sense you're good people too. Now tell me what classes you're taking the first semester."

The two young people were almost oblivious to the other people surrounding them. They talked about school, their likes and dislikes, and began phase one of the mating game—a.k.a., getting to know each other better.

Chapter 8

"Bye, bye, Aunt Jernell," Brianna said after the limousine pulled in front of her parents' townhouse located in the northern loop area of Chicago. It was four o'clock PM. Brianna began gathering her belongings from the seat beside her.

"I'm coming in with you," Jernell said after Mr. Lee came around to open the door. "I want to speak to your mother."

Adrianna, clad in a mauve-colored, two-piece lounging outfit, opened the parquet wood front door. She was surprised to see her sister. Her eyes rose upward questioningly. "Jernell, I didn't expect to see you today. Come on in."

Brianna raced up the stairway. She paused and said to her aunt, "Thanks for letting me spend the weekend with you and Morgan, Aunt Jernell. I had a great time."

"I'm glad you did, hon'. Morgan would not have had it any other way but the two of us seeing her off to college."

Adrianna looked at her sister uncertainly. "I hope nothing is wrong. Let's go into the den." The sisters walked into a room off the foyer.

"Would you like something to drink?" Adrianna asked

Jernell after she sat on the custom-made, sectional, Italian black leather sofa. She had closed the door behind them.

"Water would be fine."

Adrianna walked to the kitchen to get a bottle from the refrigerator. Jernell looked around the room. Several Annie Lee paintings adorned the wall. The room was painted ivory, and two walls were decorated with floor-length mirrors. There was a black and white marble fireplace, a big-screen television, a stereo system, and two leather reclining chairs in the room. It was the epitome of elegance.

Adrianna returned with two bottles of water and a tray of cheese and crackers. "I didn't know if you were hungry or not." She closed the door behind her after she sat the tray down.

"Thanks." Jernell unscrewed the bottle top and swallowed greedily. After she gulped half of the cool liquid, she put the bottle on the floor. "Where's Todd?" she asked, looking outside the room.

"He's playing tennis as he usually does on Sunday afternoons. Usually Brianna goes with him. Why? What's on your mind?"

Jernell reached inside her tote bag and pulled out Saturday's *Chicago Sun Times*. She opened it to page ten, spread the paper on the table and pointed to a column. "This is what's bothering me, or I should say, Titus Newberry is bothering me. Why didn't you tell me when I talked to you over the weekend that he'd been arrested?" Jernell asked her sister. She was obviously irritated at not being kept in the loop. A frown marred her face, and her lips were pinched with anger.

"Todd and I didn't want to spoil your trip with Morgan. You know you've neglected that child something awful over the years."

Jernell held her hand up. "Don't stray from the subject at hand, Adrianna. And don't you ever criticize the way I've raised my child. Do you understand me?" Her eyes glistened with anger. She looked mad enough to spit bullets.

Adrianna's hand fluttered to her chest. "Okay. I'm sorry. We just didn't want to bother you while you were taking Morgan to school. I planned to talk to you when you called me this evening."

Jernell pointed to her sister. "We can't afford any kind of trouble, Adrianna. You and Todd are supposed to keep trouble from my door. What if this man talks and implicates me or us?"

"He won't." Adrianna reached out and patted Jernell's hand to reassure her sister. "Todd has been in touch with his people. They've assured him that Titus won't say a word. He has good legal representation. I wouldn't worry if I were you."

"See, you're not me," Jernell hissed and rolled her eyes. "I have more to lose than anyone. I don't care what you and Todd have to do to keep that man quiet, just do it. Do you understand me?"

The door opened and the sisters looked at the entrance. Todd strolled into the room wearing white shorts and a white polo shirt. A tote bag was slung over his shoulder and a tennis racket stuck out the top of the bag. "What's happening, Jernell? How is Morgan? Did you get her squared away at Bradley?"

Jernell looked at her brother-in-law frostily from head to toe. Then she rose from her seat and said, "Morgan is fine. Adrianna, remember what I said. I'll talk to both of you tomorrow." Jernell nodded her head toward her brother-in-law. "Todd, I expect you at my office at nine o'clock sharp." She sat her bottle on an end table and returned to the car.

Mr. Lee delivered his client to her house exactly thirty minutes later. She gave him 500 dollars for a tip.

"Thank you, madam. If you're ever in the market for a personal driver, I'm available," Mr. Lee said after he folded the money and put it inside his jacket pocket. He passed her a business card.

"I'll keep that in mind," Jernell replied. She had her own driver. But Mr. Lee didn't need to know her business.

Lucinda opened the door to welcome Jernell home. When Jernell walked inside the house, Lucinda asked, "How did the weekend go? You look tired."

The women walked to the dining room and sat at the table. "Everything went fine. Morgan is set and, in her own words, 'officially a freshman at Bradley University.'"

"That's great. She deserves the best. Her grades were excellent. You know we were lucky that she never gave us a moment of trouble." Lucinda smiled.

"You're right," Jernell said reflectively. "She was a good kid."

"Are you hungry? Can I fix you something?"

"I think I just want a turkey sandwich," Jernell answered. She yawned.

The women walked into the kitchen. Jernell stretched her body before she sat on the tall stool at the dark glass-topped table. The room was painted white and had a navy-blue border along the top of the walls. The table was positioned opposite an oak island with burners atop it for cooking. Stainless steel pots and pans hung from a rack over the island. A huge stainless steel refrigerator was on one wall. A ceiling fan spun a gentle breeze.

Lucinda smoothed mayo on two pieces of rye bread. She paused and asked Jernell, "Would you like the turkey warmed up?"

"No, I can eat it cold."

Lucinda sliced a tomato. She put the slices and lettuce on the bread. She spooned potato salad on a plate and handed it to Jernell, who bit into the sandwich hungrily.

Lucinda removed a fork out of a cabinet drawer and sat it

on the table next to Jernell. "You look like something is wrong," she remarked cautiously. "Is everything all right?"

Jernell put the sandwich down on the plate. She walked to the counter and took a paper towel off the rack and wiped her mouth. "I have a small problem. One of my top clients was arrested Friday and I'm worried about what he'll say or do."

"Isn't that Todd's department? Damage control? Let him do his job," Lucinda advised. "You have enough on your plate as it is." She walked to the refrigerator and removed a can of Coke, and handed it to her friend. Jernell and Lucinda had been childhood friends. Some of Lucinda's family members had been involved in the business.

Lately, Lucinda had been having misgivings about where she was in life and guilt regarding her own past activities. Though she wasn't actively involved in the trade, she knew where the bodies were buried and was Jernell's closest confidant.

The housekeeper was so dismayed by the information that she was privy to that she had sought counseling a few years ago from her mother's minister, Reverend Jefferson. Some days, Lucinda thought she would crack under the pressure of knowing that what Jernell did was wrong, and what she could do to rectify the situation. It frightened her to think that Morgan would one day take over the business and follow her mother's footsteps.

Reverend Jefferson had responded kindly to Lucinda's plight. When she spoke to him, he prayed for her and suggested that she talk to local law enforcement officials. Lucinda was torn between that and her lifelong friendship with Jernell. She hadn't decided what to do about her dilemma. Currently, all she could do was pray to the Lord for guidance. She called the FBI anonymously several times from a payphone and hung the receiver before she could be connected to the correct department.

"That's what's worrying me," Jernell admitted. Dark circles like half moons lay under her eyes.

Lucinda's mouth dropped open. She shook her head from side to side. "No. You don't think Todd and Adrianna are double-crossing you? Do you?"

"I don't know," Jernell said after she sipped from the can of Coke "My gut instinct tells me something is wrong. I talked to Adrianna when I took Brianna home and she assured me everything is under control. I feel uneasy. This is the second time one of my clients has been arrested in the past six months. My gut tells me something is going on. I just don't know what yet."

Lucinda nodded. "If your mind is telling you to be careful, then follow it."

"I will. It may be time for me to call in the troops," Jernell said. "Did anyone call while I was gone?" She devoured the remainder of the sandwich.

"Rico. He wanted you to call him when you got home." Lucinda stood and pushed her chair to the table. "Do you need me to hang around tonight? I was going to spend the night when my mother. She hasn't been feeling well lately. My brother called and asked me to talk to her about seeing a doctor."

Jernell waved her hand. "No. Go ahead see about your mother. Tell her I said hello. Harry will be here in another half an hour. I gave him the weekend off to visit his family. I'll be fine." Harry was Jernell's bodyguard and driver.

"Okay," Lucinda said. "I'm going to call Morgan and then go to my mom's." Lucinda headed into her room to pack an overnight bag. *I must call Reverend Jefferson from Ma's house and see if he can meet with me.* She put clothing into the suitcase.

"I'll see you in the morning," Jernell called after her friend. She finished eating the potato salad.

Jernell put her plate in the sink and walked to the second story of the house where her bedroom was located. She laid her purse on the dresser, then she lay on the bed and stretched out. She closed her eyes. Her cell phone rang. She rose from the bed, reached inside her purse, and pulled it out. "Hey, Rico. How are you doing?"

"I'm fine. I'm just sorry I couldn't get away to see Morgan off to school. How is she doing?"

"She's fine and ready to get into the groove of attending college."

"Good. I'm going to call her later."

"She'll like that." Jernell turned on her left side, trying to find a comfortable position on the bed.

"How are you doing, Nell?" Rico asked.

"I've asked you a million times not to call me that. It sounds so old-fashioned and white," Jernell said with a tinge of annoyance in her voice.

"I don't care what you say. You'll always be Nell to me," Rico teased her.

"Whatever." Jernell activated the speaker on the phone. Then she put the phone on the bed and removed an earring from her earlobe.

"I know this is probably not a good time for you. We've talked about this before, but, baby, why don't you release Morgan from the business? You know that's not what she really wants."

Jernell sat up in the bed. "It doesn't matter what Morgan wants anymore than what I wanted. It's her destiny, fate, or karma, call it what you will. Morgan will take her place as head of the business." Jernell's voice had become glacial.

"It doesn't have to be that way, Nell. Send her to me. She can stay in Cleveland with me. You know I turned my life around. I'm active in the church now. Let her have a normal life here with me," Rico pleaded with Jernell.

"We've talked about this before and the subject is not up for discussion. I'd appreciate it if you wouldn't bring it up again," Jernell stated firmly.

"You're wrong for holding our child hostage to your company. Your family business is dirty. It always has been. Surely you aren't hurting for cash. I'm sure the company has generated enough money for you to start up several corporations. When is enough enough? Don't sacrifice our daughter's life for someone else's dream that could end up destroying the lives of a lot of people."

"Let me refresh your memory, Rico. Let's go back twenty years or so when I explained to you what my family did, and how you were down for it." Jernell's voice rose sharply.

"That was then and this is now," Rico answered just as stridently. "People change, Nell. I'm living proof that it takes faith, faith the size of a mustard seed, for anyone who believes and trusts in the Lord to turn his or her life around. I'm living proof. Give Morgan a chance. It wouldn't hurt you to pray sometimes either."

Jernell continued in her contemptuous wheedling voice. "How soon you forget how we could have taken the company to new heights, instead you punked out. You've already cashed in your favor chip. You asked to be released from your obligations and I let you go. So live your life, Rico, and I'll live mine as I see fit." Jernell hit the bed with her fist. The phone almost fell off the bed. She massaged the sides of her head.

"Nell, I'm talking about our daughter, our only child. Don't do this to Morgan. She deserves better. You know in your heart that she really doesn't want to go into the business. She just wants to please you. Let me show her a different life—a Christian, spirit-filled life." Rico begged Jernell, to no avail.

"I've got to go, Rico. What's done is done. I'll talk to you another time." Jernell clicked the phone off. Her eyes overflowed with tears. She moaned, remembering her own initiation into the family business.

Her mother had lovingly groomed her for the business from the time Jernell could talk. She recalled when she used to stick her pinky finger in the sugar bowl at home. When Pamela asked the child what she was doing, Jernell replied flippantly, *"I'm checking product like Aunt Darlene."*

Pamela looked at her daughter with a dismayed expression on her face. She lightly smacked her daughter's hand and told her not to say anything like that outside of the house.

Back in Cleveland, Rico's heart was troubled. He bowed his head as he sat in the brown leather recliner chair in his den. "Lord, Jernell may think I used up all my favor chips, but she doesn't know I have a Father I can go to, and He will supply my every need, All I have to do is ask and it shall be given." Rico opened his eyes and took his Bible off the end table next to the chair.

He flipped the pages until he came to Psalm 131, and he read; "I will lift up mine eyes unto the hills from whence cometh my help. My help cometh from the Lord which made heaven and earth. He will not suffer thy foot to be moved. He that keepeth Thee will not slumber. Behold, he that keepeth Israel shall neither slumber nor sleep. The Lord is thy keeper. The Lord is thy shade upon thy right hand. The sun shall not smite thee by day, nor the moon by night. The Lord shall preserve thee from all evil; he shall preserve thy soul. The Lord shall preserve thy going out and thy coming in from this time forth, and forever more.

"Lord, take care of my baby. Please don't let any harm come her way," Rico whispered. The fact that Morgan was four years away from realizing her destiny and following her mother's footsteps hit him hard.

Chapter 9

Morgan had returned from the communal shower and put on her pajamas. She was lying in her twin bed on her stomach, writing in her new diary about her first day away from home and meeting Noah. The cell phone that laid on the bed next to her rang, startling the young lady. She smiled when she saw her father's name on the caller ID.

"Hi, Daddy," she greeted him warmly. "How are you doing?" The pen she was holding fell from her hand.

"Good, baby girl. Just sorry I couldn't make it this weekend. How is college life treating you?"

"So far, it's been the bomb. My roommate still hasn't arrived yet. I talked to my RA and asked if I could have the room to myself if she doesn't show up."

"What did she say?" Rico asked.

"She'll let me know next week. I have my fingers crossed."

"Have you met many new people yet?" Rico knew that because of the family's profession that the Foster females didn't have many friends. The sisters became each other's best friends. The same held true for the cousins.

"Yes. I introduced myself to the girls in the rooms next

door and across the hall from me. They seem nice. I think I'm really going to like it here."

"Did you get to spend much time with your mother over the weekend?" Rico probed nosily.

"Not as much as I would have liked. Still, Brianna and I had a good time together. We went shopping then out to dinner and stayed with Momma at a hotel Friday and Saturday night. We rented movies like we were at a sleepover. We had a ball."

"Good. I'm glad you got to enjoy yourself before you buckle down with your studies," Rico hinted not so subtly.

"Me too. I felt a little lonely earlier today. Then I hooked up with a boy I met on the way to Peoria. When we were driving to Bradley, his parents' car broke down and Momma let him ride with us in the limousine."

"You mean your mother brought you to school in a limo?" Rico exclaimed. "Aren't you big time?" he lovingly ribbed his daughter.

"It was fun. We had plenty of leg room." Morgan's voice dropped. "I think our driver, Mr. Lee, had a crush on Momma. He stares at her all the time."

Rico cleared his throat. "I wouldn't worry about it. Jernell knows how to handle herself. Now tell me about this young man you met. Where is he from?"

"He's from Chicago. His name is Noah Stephens, and he went to Hales Franciscan High School. His father is a minister, and he seems really nice. I like him," she confessed shyly. Morgan and her father had always had a close relationship. She spent summers with him in Cleveland. Usually, Brianna joined Morgan during the last week of her vacation.

"Whoa!" Rico exclaimed. "You just got to school. Give yourself time to meet people, and that includes boys. Don't tie yourself down to the first boy that pays attention to you. Although, I have to admit that he has good taste."

"Daddy," Morgan yelled. "I just like him. That doesn't

mean that we're kicking it or anything like that. We're just getting to know each other. I don't have any friends yet, so I think it's a good thing that I have one friend on campus."

"Okay, young lady, time out. I didn't mean to imply anything. I just want you to enjoy this time of your life."

"Because you know what I'll have to do when I finish school, right?"

"Yes," Rico sighed. "You know it doesn't have to be that way. You can always come to me, and we can move away and begin a new life. I'm not married, so it would be easy for me to start over. There are so many things I want to share with you, one being my love of Christ. You know there are no situations that God can't help His children out of, and that includes your mother's business."

"No, I can't do that," Morgan informed her father forcefully. "I'm going to work with Momma. It's all right, Daddy. I'm fine with my future."

"That's what worries me, baby girl, that you don't see anything wrong with your mother's lifestyle," Rico said hauntingly. "It's wrong, Morgan, and it's hurting and tearing apart so many lives."

"Big Momma says we fill a need for people. If they don't get our product from us, then they'll get it from someone else."

"Let's talk about that another time." Rico changed the subject, sensing he wouldn't make any headway with his stubborn daughter that evening. He planned to talk to her earnestly when he visited her over the weekend.

Morgan's phone beeped, indicating that she had another call coming in. "Daddy, I gotta go anyway. Brianna is on the other line. Let me know what time your flight gets in Friday."

"I'll call you Thursday. Love you, baby girl. Take care of yourself," Rico replied sadly.

"Love you too, Daddy. Bye." Morgan pressed a button, and switched over to Brianna. "What's up, gurl?"

"Nothing. I got home a couple of hours ago. Dang, Morgan. I miss you already. If you were home, I could have spent the night with you, or you could have stayed with me."

"Sorry, I can't help you with that one. I thought you said Aunt Adrianna was taking you school shopping tomorrow. You'll be back in the swing of things in no time. Although I have to admit I miss you too, and being at home."

"So what have you been doing?"

Morgan told Brianna that she'd just talked to her father. "Daddy's coming to Peoria and we're going to spend the weekend together."

"That's cool. Let's get to the juicy stuff. Did you see Noah today?" Brianna queried her cousin forcefully.

"Hmm. Maybe I did or maybe I didn't," Morgan admitted coyly. A goofy smile filled her face.

"Gurl, stop playing with me," Brianna wailed. "Tell me what happened."

"Okay. I was just messing with you," Morgan replied. "Yes, I saw Noah. We had an impromptu date earlier, and we walked around the campus to find the buildings where our classes are being held."

"I knew it. I can't turn my back on you before you're on it," Brianna teased Morgan.

"Well, not literally, but I wouldn't mind it," Morgan added quickly.

The girls fell into peals of laughter at the thought.

"Gurl, you nasty. But on the real, you sound as if you really like him," Brianna observed.

"Yeah, I think I do." Morgan nodded as she rolled over on the bed. "I need to call Momma tonight. If my room-mate doesn't show up by the end of the week, I want her to pay the remaining room and board on this room so I can stay by myself."

"Are we setting up a love nest for yourself and Noah?" Brianna teased Morgan.

"What the heck is a love nest? You've been reading too many trashy novels," Morgan replied. "You know I value my privacy. I always had doubts about whether I could live with another person. I never had to share my space with a sibling, much less a stranger."

"It would just be like when I come over and spend the night at your house. Duh!"

"Don't start with me, Brianna. It's an opportunity. And our mothers always told us to be aware of and use an opportunity to our advantage."

"Hmm . . . spoken like the future head of the family," Brianna said. "Is this the same person who was boo-hooing on my shoulder just yesterday?"

There was a tap at Morgan's door. She sat upright in the bed. "Someone is at the door. I've got to go. I'll call you back tomorrow."

"Is it Noah?" Brianna asked, screaming loudly. "You can't leave me hanging. Answer the door and then come back and tell me who it is. Please, Morgan?"

"Gotta go. Later, Bri." Morgan disconnected the call, and pulled her nightshirt down. She pulled the wrap scarf off her head and dropped it on the desk. She walked over to the door and opened it. "Oh, hi, Dina. What's up? Is my roommate here?" She peered outside the room.

Dina told Morgan that her roommate had been injured in an accident, and she wouldn't be attending school that semester. Dina also stated that Morgan could have the room to herself, if her mother paid the remaining fee. Morgan expressed sympathy about her almost roommate's situation. The RA turned to leave, and then she said to Morgan slyly, "I almost forgot, you have a visitor in the lobby."

"Is it a boy? A fine boy?" Morgan asked as she rushed over to the desk, picked up her shorts, and pulled them over her hips. Then she threw on a T-shirt and slipped her feet into a pair of flip-flops.

"I don't know about the fine part, but yes, there's a boy downstairs," Dina answered before she left the room.

Morgan snatched her comb off her desk and began combing out her hair. "Tell him I'll be down in a minute." She squirted a few drops of Tommy Hilfiger cologne over her body. *I bet Noah is downstairs. I wonder what he wants.*

Ten minutes later, Morgan sauntered down the stairway with the poise of a super model. Her heartbeat careened out of control when she saw Noah. He stood up and smiled at her. She walked sedately over to him.

"Is something wrong?" she asked.

Noah grabbed her by the hand as other students watched intently. He led Morgan outside the building. They faced each other silently for a minute.

"No, nothing is wrong," Noah finally uttered. "I'm not usually an impulsive person. More methodical and logical. But I had an urge to see you before I called it a day. I wanted to ask you if we can meet for breakfast in the morning."

Morgan crossed her arms across her chest. "Sure. I mean, yes. I'd love to have breakfast with you."

"I want to share my first day of college with you. You're special to me, Miss Foster, and I'd like to spend time with you and get to know you better."

"I'd like nothing better myself than to get to you know you too, Noah. So far I like what I see," she flirted with him.

"So we have a date in the morning?"

"Yes. What time is your first class?"

"Nine o'clock. Can we meet at eight?"

Snaps; that's way too early for me. "Sure, I'll be out here waiting for you bright and early. Noah, thanks for inviting me. I have a feeling that I'm not going to be as homesick as I thought I would be."

He took Morgan's hands in his and gently kissed her knuckles. Noah said, "I don't think I am either. See you in the morning. Sleep tight, Morgan." His hand caressed her cheek.

"I will." She waved good-bye to Noah. When she went inside the dorm, she floated up the stairs. *Church boy is smooth. He got moves. Thank God one of us knows what we're doing.* Morgan pulled off her shorts, rewrapped her hair, and called Jernell.

Jernell assured Morgan that she'd call the housing office the following morning. Morgan asked to speak to Lucinda so she could tell about her weekend and day. Jernell informed Morgan that Lucinda was away for the night. When Morgan finished talking to her mother, she sat in the middle of the bed with her legs crossed Indian style, and looked for her green-feathered ink pen. After she found it under her pillow, she continued her diary entry for the day.

Dear Diary

Today was my first full day of being away from home. After my momma and Brianna left to go home, I had the blues and cried a river. I really miss Brianna. You see, she's like my sister. I missed Lucinda too and kind of missed Momma. I guess I didn't miss Momma as much because Lucinda really raised me. She's the one who picked me up from school the first day. Momma took me to school, but she was too busy to come back and get me. Lucinda took me to my dance lessons and went to all my recitals. Sometimes my daddy would come from Cleveland to see me dance.

Noah and I just met for the first time Friday morning and I feel like I've known him my whole life. He's so nice and polite. He even pulled my chair out for me to sit when we went to the cafeteria for sodas. When I went to the ladies room and came back to the table, he stood up and waited for me to sit first. When we left the cafeteria he held the door open for me. Noah's face is perfect. I wanted him to kiss me, but I was scared. I don't know if a preacher's kid, as he calls himself, and a drug dealer's daughter can kick it. Our lifestyles are so different. I know he would be horrified at what my mother does for a living. If we do kick it, then I'll have to tell him the truth about my background one day. But right now I just want him to know Morgan Foster, the girl inside me that so few people really get to meet. I'm having breakfast with Noah before I start my classes tomorrow.

I think my daddy doesn't realize I'm a woman and not a girl. I might be a virgin but I get urges sometimes. My body goes haywire when I'm around Noah. I used two days of entries to write all of this. I'm so excited. I'm almost eighteen-years-old, and I think I found the boy of my dreams.
MF

Chapter 10

Lucinda was bent over the spa tub in Jernell's bathroom, drawing water for her employer's bath. She turned on the pure gold faucets and poured vanilla-scented bath salts into the water. Then Lucinda went into the bedroom and gently roused Jernell from a sound sleep.

After Jernell rose from the mahogany sleigh bed and headed to the bathroom, Lucinda returned downstairs to prepare breakfast. The meal included wheat toast, a boiled egg, and two slices of turkey bacon. Jernell's favorite tonic, a power drink, was spinning in the blender. Lucinda couldn't keep her eyes from roaming to the kitchen table where Morgan usually sat before she headed to school.

Lucinda had just poured the drink into a crystal goblet and sat it on the table when Jernell walked into the room. She wore a navy blue and white pinstripe pantsuit with a red tube top. She wore red and silver sandals trimmed with rubies on her feet and red accessories. She picked the *Wall Street Journal* and *Chicago Sun Times* off the counter. Then Jernell sat at the table and spread out the papers and began to read.

Jernell ate her meal as she read the *Wall Street Journal* first. When she was done, Jernell closed it and took a sip of the strawberry-flavored power drink. She then perused the *Chicago Sun Times*. The only sound in the room was the rustling sound of her turning the pages.

"Are you coming home for lunch?" Lucinda asked as she removed the plate from the table. When she glanced at her employer, Lucinda noted Jernell's face was ashen, devoid of color "What's wrong, Jernell?"

But Jernell didn't hear Lucinda's question. An article on page five in the newspaper snagged her attention. Her client was being arraigned at nine o'clock that morning at the courthouse located at Twenty-sixth and California Streets. The article implied that Titus was looking to cop a plea. His doing so didn't bode well for Jernell.

Inwardly, Jernell fumed. She felt Todd should have told her of this latest turn of events. After all, she gave Todd top dollars to use for bribes. It galled her from the top of her head to the bottom of her feet that she had to learn about the possible plea deal from the newspaper. Jernell toyed with the idea of calling one of her sisters to go to court to find out what was really going on and Titus's frame of mind. Then she recalled one of Big Momma's rules. If you want something done right, sometimes you have to do it your own self. She knew that in the cutthroat business that she was involved in, she couldn't even depend on family. It's a dog-eat-dog world, and you have to look out for yourself.

Lucinda broke Jernell's reverie when she said loudly, "Earth to Jernell? Is something wrong?"

Jernell stood up on unsteady legs. "I need to get to the office right away. Luci, I need a huge favor from you. Will you call Bradley this morning and arrange to pay additional room and board costs so Morgan can have the double room? Something has come up that I need to attend to right now."

"Yes, I'll take care of it." Lucinda looked at Jernell worried.

Jernell walked toward the door and stopped. She snapped her fingers. "Tell Morgan that I'll call her later." She walked out the door, pulled her cell phone out of her purse, and quickly dialed a number. "Derrick I'm headed to the office. I'll be there in twenty minutes and I expect to see you there."

By the time Jernell finished the call, Harry had pulled her money-green Lexus coupe out of the garage. He got out of the vehicle and opened the door for his boss. "Where to, Jernell?"

After she got inside the car, Jernell answered, "To the office, *now*." She put Versace designer sunglasses on her face.

Jernell owned an office building on the outskirts of the downtown area of Chicago. The building was located ten minutes from her house. During rush hour traffic, her travel time doubled. She pulled out the *Sun Times* again and reread the article as her stomach churned with anxiety.

Harry made it to the office within twenty minutes as usual. He parked the Lexus in the three-car garage behind the building, and Jernell took her key out of her jacket pocket and unlocked the back door. She waited for Harry.

Jernell and Harry rode the elevator to the fifth floor. He checked the offices carefully before she went inside. When Jernell entered her domain, she noticed a pile of pink message slips on her desk. A flashing red light on her telephone indicated even more messages.

Her secretary, Shari, was due in the office in fifteen minutes. Jernell called out to Harry to start a pot of coffee in the kitchen. She added, "Call Todd ASAP and tell him I want to see him at ten o'clock instead of nine this morning. Derrick should be here any minute. Show him to my office if Shari hasn't arrived by the time he gets here."

"Will do, boss lady," Harry replied. He was dressed in cotton khaki pants and a T-shirt. He wore sandals on his feet. Harry leaned down and removed cups from the dishwasher. Then he opened the window blinds.

Ten minutes later, Derrick Newsom opened the door and walked inside the office. "Good morning, Harry. Is Jernell available?"

Shari had followed him inside the office. She and Harry exchanged greetings.

Harry and Derrick shook hands. Harry said, "Let me check and see what she's doing. Why don't you have a seat?" He turned toward the secretary, "Shari, will you get Derrick a cup of coffee?"

"Sure." Shari took a box of donuts to the kitchen, and set then on the counter. Then she returned to the waiting room with a cup of coffee for the attorney. "You prefer your coffee black don't you?"

"Yes, I do. Thanks." Derrick nodded. He took his cell phone out of his briefcase and began checking his voicemail messages.

Harry returned to the waiting room. "Jernell can see you now," he said to Derrick.

Derrick closed the phone and slid it into his pocket. Then he stood and picked his briefcase up from the floor.

Shari said, "Don't worry about the coffee. I'll bring it to Jernell's office."

"Thank you," Derrick replied. He walked inside the office and found Jernell on the telephone. She gestured for him to have a seat.

Five minutes later, she placed the receiver inside the cradle. "I apologize for the delay, Derrick. I was off work Friday taking Morgan to school and there always seems to be twice as much work to be done when I come back after taking a few days off."

"Not a problem, Jernell. I've penciled you into my calendar for two hours," Derrick replied affably. Shari walked inside the room and handed him a cup of coffee.

After the secretary left the room, the two exchanged small talk. Then Jernell came to the point of Derrick's visit. "I read in the newspaper this morning that Titus Newberry is being arraigned. I thought we had taken care of that problem." Her eyes threw daggers into Derrick's.

He set the cup on her desk and pulled on the end of his tie. "Actually, your brother-in-law was supposed to be taking care of that issue. It appears he dropped the ball."

"I don't pay your firm a half million dollar retainer yearly to hear you tell me that someone dropped the ball, thereby causing me a major problem," Jernell replied in a glacial voice.

"I understand, Jernell," Derrick said in a soothing voice. "I should have been on top of what Todd was telling me. Unfortunately, I was in court working on a major case."

"What is Titus saying to the police or his lawyer? Do you even know that?" Jernell asked. Her body began trembling. *This is not good.*

"Not exactly. But I'll find out." Derrick picked his briefcase up from beside his chair. He took out a pen and yellow legal pad of paper and began writing notes on the pad.

"You do that. I want a report from you by the end of the business day. From now on, I want you to report your findings to me and not Todd." Jernell tapped her knuckles sharply on top of her desk. "Do I make myself clear?"

Derrick nodded meekly. "Is there something you aren't telling me? Why are you so worried about Titus?"

"The paper stated he might cop a plea and his doing so doesn't work for me."

Derrick replaced the cap on the pen he been clutching, and put it inside his shirt pocket. Then he leaned over and placed the pad back inside the briefcase. He stood up so abruptly that his cup rattled in the saucer. "I see your point. I'm going back to my office to make some calls myself. I promise to have news for you by noon."

"Fine." Jernell picked up her telephone receiver, dismissing Derrick.

He put the pad of paper back in his briefcase and hightailed it out of her office. Jernell pushed a button on her telephone. "Shari, I need you to come to my office right now."

"Coming, Ms. Foster."

Shari entered the room and slid into the seat Derrick had just vacated. "Is there something wrong?"

"Was there someone in my office while I was gone to Peoria?"

Shari had been smiling. After hearing the question, she faltered. "Um, let me think for a minute." She paused and then replied, "Just Mr. Rizzo. He said he needed some papers from your cabinet. Should he not have come in your office, Ms. Foster?" Shari could see the fury on her employer's face.

"You can go back to work now," Jernell replied tartly.

Shari closed the door on her way out.

Jernell was seething inside. Todd should not have been in her office unattended under any circumstances. *What was Shari thinking?* Jernell smoldered with rage.

What is Todd up to? What are he and Adrianna trying to do? Do I detect mutiny on the bounty? Jernell twisted a pen in her fingers. *Maybe I should go to court myself. No. That's not a good idea.*

She called Harry on his cell phone. "Do you have a change of clothes here at the office? If not, I need you to go home and change so you can go to Titus Newberry's trial for me this morning. It starts in about an hour."

"I'm changing into a shirt as we speak. Yes, I keep a change of clothes here at the office. I'll go to court and report back to you this afternoon."

"Thanks, Harry. I appreciate it." Jernell put the telephone back in the receiver. *At least someone knows what to do without being told.* She called her secretary. "Shari, hold all my calls."

"Yes, ma'am."

Jernell was bothered by Todd's being in her office, and his not mentioning it to her when she saw him yesterday. What Todd didn't know was that any documentation he saw at her office was doctored. She kept two sets of books. The accurate set was locked inside a safe at the gray stone. She'd bought the building for tax purposes, so the IRS wouldn't have a reason to come to her home.

Harry worked with a contractor and instructed him to build a room beneath Jernell's basement, expanding the crawl space. That's where Jernell kept her private and personal correspondences. No one was privy to the room's existence except Lucinda and Harry.

Jernell returned the phone calls from when she was out of town.

Shari buzzed her boss at nine thirty. "Mr. Rizzo is in the waiting room."

"Thanks, Shari. Please send him to my office." Jernell turned papers face down on her desk and set her face into a neutral expression, masking her true feelings.

"Good morning, Todd," she greeted her brother-in-law. He sat down in the chair in front of her desk. Then Jernell pushed the intercom button. "Shari, please bring me a cup of chamomile tea. Todd, would you like something?"

He shook his head.

"Okay. I'll bring your tea to your office in a moment, Ms. Foster," the secretary replied.

Todd looked at his watch impatiently. "What's on your mind, Jernell? I have another appointment in an hour on the north side."

"Well, you'll just have to wait until I'm done now won't you?" Jernell replied unsmiling.

"Sure." Todd began sweating profusely. "What can I do for you?" He crossed and uncrossed his legs.

"I'd like you to tell me any and all information you have regarding Titus Newberry. What is he being charged with and what can he say to hurt us?" She stared intently at Todd and leaned back in her chair.

"As I told you last night, there's really nothing for us to worry about. I talked to his people this morning and he won't be singing to anyone. I was assured he's going to do the time and keep his mouth shut."

Jernell picked up the newspaper and flung it across her desk to Todd. "The paper doesn't corroborate what you're telling me. It states something entirely different."

Todd began reading the article. "Come on, Jernell." He looked at her condescendingly like she was a child. "You can't believe everything they print in the paper, you know that. I told you we don't have an issue, and that's all there is to it." He clamped his lips tightly together, clearly annoyed by his sister-in-law's questions.

"Okay, Todd. Obviously, that's your story and you're sticking to it." She pointed her ink pen at him and pasted a smile on her face. There was no need to tip her hand until she had all the facts. "Just make sure your information is accurate. I don't want to find out it's not and get blindsided."

Todd smiled magnanimously. Sweat trickled from his armpits. "I've always had your back. Nothing has changed. There's too much at stake for me not to. I'll call you later." He glanced down at his wrist. "Maybe I'll go to the courthouse and check things out myself. Although I'd stake my life on the accuracy of the information I gave you."

"Let's hope it never comes to that," Jernell replied sweetly. "Report back to me later, Todd."

He stood up. "Will do." Then he departed from the room.

Jernell turned on the portable radio that sat on her desk to news radio station 78. She hoped that she could find out what was going on with the trial. To her chagrin, it wasn't mentioned. Then she pulled out her copy of shipments for the evening and debated whether she should cancel the deliveries or not.

Shari knocked at Jernell's door around noon, carrying a tray with a sandwich and salad on it. "You didn't call and tell me what you wanted for lunch, so I took the liberty of ordering out for you." She wanted to stay in her boss's good graces. Jernell paid generous bonuses at Christmas time.

"Thanks, Shari. My stomach was just telling me it's ready to be fed." She cleared a spot on her desk, and Shari laid the tray on it.

Harry rushed into the office and plopped into the chair in front of Jernell's desk.

"That will be all, Shari." The young woman exited the office. "Hold my calls while I'm having lunch."

Jernell reached into the bottom of her desk and removed salt and pepper shakers. She sprinkled the package of dressing provided with the salad and the seasonings over the salad. "Are you hungry?" she asked Harry.

"No, I stopped and got a sandwich before I came back here."

"So what's up with Titus?" Jernell cut up the salad, trying to quell the butterflies darting crazily inside her stomach.

"His lawyers asked for a continuation. So he won't be copping a plea, at least not today."

"Did Todd show up at court?"

"Nope. I didn't see hide nor hair of him."

"Hmm." Jernell looked down at her desk, trying to suppress her anger.

"Was he supposed to be there?" Harry asked. He bent over and retied his shoes.

"That's what he told me. Did you know he was in my office Friday?"

"Shari mentioned it after the fact. I'll talk to a locksmith, and have the locks changed."

"Do that. Okay, Harry, that's all for now. I'll have to wait on Derrick to call me back."

Jernell continued working non-stop until she left the office at four o'clock. She hadn't heard from Derrick yet. After talking to Harry, she decided to have the products delivered tonight per the schedule. During the ride home, she called Morgan, who was excited about having the dorm room to herself.

When Jernell arrived home, Lucinda was downstairs in the basement ironing. Jernell chatted with Lucinda a few minutes before she went upstairs to her room and changed into her workout clothes. She walked down the hall, hit the treadmill, and began releasing tension.

When Lucinda walked inside the room, Jernell was riding the stationary bike. "It's your lawyer. He says it's important." She gave the sweating woman the telephone.

Jernell wiped her moist forehead with the towel draped across her shoulders and took the phone from Lucinda. "Hello, Derrick."

"Good evening, Jernell. I'm sorry it took me to so long to get back to you. I'm afraid the news isn't good."

Jernell got off the bike and sat down hard on one of the mats on the floor. "Why? What's wrong?"

"The judge granted Titus a continuation. But the plea bargain is still on the table. Lucky, I do business with one of the judge's assistants and was able to talk to him after the proceedings this afternoon."

"Derrick, would you just get to the point?" Jernell's left leg began contracting nervously.

"You're being investigated by the city, state, and Feds.

Your office and home phones are probably being bugged. I suggest you be very careful with your business dealings until this blows over," Derrick cautioned his client.

"Humph, you're not telling me something I don't already know. What are they going after me for?"

"None of the agencies has a strong case at this time. They're trying to bolster their weak cases by working together. The Feds are focusing on the warehouses to see what they can find there."

"So is Titus going to cop a plea or not?" Jernell flicked her ponytail over her shoulder.

"I wish I could tell you he's definitely not going to, but it's a possibility. You know you've always said to prepare for the worst. After I finished talking to the judge's assistant, he indicated that he may delay the case until next year for a price."

"Can he legally delay it for that long?"

"Since he broached the subject, I guess he can," Derrick replied guardedly.

"I swear this situation is turning into a catastrophe," Jernell complained. "I'll have Harry get someone to sweep for bugs here at my office and at the house. I keep the books in a safe place. Thank God cell phones can't be bugged."

"At least not yet," Derrick replied solemnly.

"So what else do I need to be aware of?" Jernell asked. Her head began pounding like someone was playing a drum inside it. She rose from the floor and sat back on the bicycle.

"Try to adhere to the measures we just spoke of and lay low. I'm going to put pressure on Titus's people, and make sure he keeps his mouth shut."

"Do that, Derrick. I don't want this to turn into a major problem for me. Do you get my drift? I want this situation taken care of by any means necessary."

"I hear you loud and clear. I'll call you when more information is available."

"Thanks." She disconnected the call and stared thoughtfully into space. *I already have procedures in place to deal with these situations. I pray I don't have to activate any of them. I swear to God, Todd better not be trying to double-cross me. I don't want Brianna to grow up a fatherless child.*

Jernell began pedaling the bike faster.

Chapter 11

By Friday evening, Morgan had managed to get her room into some semblance of order. She'd taped on the walls the pictures of her favorite artists she'd brought from home. She knew the first item on her father's agenda would be to check out her room. She informed Rico when she talked to him the night before that she was treating for dinner and that they could dine in her room. She planned to order a couple of pizzas to be delivered from a local restaurant.

Noah had come to visit Morgan several times during the week when he wasn't studying. They both resided in coed dorms. As she emptied boxes, he took the empty cartons to the trash room. He was impressed by and envious of the extra space she had.

Instead of flying to Peoria, Rico rented a car for the drive from Ohio to Illinois and planned to go to the dorm after he checked in a local hotel. Morgan expected him to arrive around seven o'clock PM.

Earlier that day, when Morgan saw Noah, she had invited him to join her and Rico for dinner. Noah wisely passed on the invitation. He told Morgan that since her father hadn't seen her in a while, it would be best for father and daughter to hang out the first night. He'd stop by her room sometime Saturday to meet Rico.

One of Noah's classmates, Jerome, was a local Peoria resident. He invited Noah to attend a teen meeting that his church was sponsoring the same Friday evening Rico was to arrive in Peoria. Noah hadn't been able to turn away from his Christian roots. Gloria and Samuel were ecstatic. Gloria had told Samuel she didn't expect less from their child and quoted the scripture from Proverbs 22 chapter, sixth verse: *Train up a child in the way he should go, and when he is old, he will not depart from it.*

Morgan's eyes swept the room one last time. She walked over to the extra bed and adjusted the purple comforter. One side hung longer than the other. She had set up the extra desk as a table.

Her cell phone rang. She snatched it up. Dina informed her that she had a delivery waiting downstairs. Morgan snatched her purse off her desk and took two twenty-dollar bills out of her wallet. She pulled the door closed and raced down the stairs. When she arrived on the first floor, Rico was entering the building.

"Daddy!" she squealed, trotting over to her father. She wrapped her arms around his neck.

"How you doing, baby girl?" He grinned and held her close to him for a minute. Rico stood six feet tall. He was the same dark complexion as his daughter. He had dark thick eyebrows, a goatee, and a scar on his left cheek.

His closely shorn hair was starting to gray at the edges, giving him a distinguished look. Despite having gained weight over the years, Rico was still a handsome man. He had a small paunch around his midsection. Morgan was his mirror image. When Big Momma saw Morgan for the first time a few minutes after her birth, she proclaimed that Jernell had spat out a Rico-look-a-like since Morgan didn't have any of her mother's features.

"I'm fine, Daddy," Morgan smiled. "Let me pay the delivery man and then we can go upstairs and eat. Your timing is perfect." Morgan couldn't stop grinning.

As Morgan took care of the dinner bill, Rico watched his daughter. His eyes became misty, full of love for his only child. It dawned on him that Morgan was no longer a girl. She had blossomed into a young woman. He swallowed a lump that rose in his throat.

Morgan picked up the pizza boxes from the RA's desk. "So, Daddy do you want to take the stairs or the elevator?"

"Give me one of the boxes. I'm sure I can handle the stairs. Uh, what floor did you say your room is on?"

"The third."

"That's a piece of cake. Let's go."

As they passed the open doorways of other students, Morgan proudly introduced her father to her fellow dorm mates. Then Rico held the boxes of pizza in his hands while Morgan opened her own door.

"You've decorated your room nicely in your favorite colors: purple and beige," Rico commented as his eyes wandered around the room. "I see you brought some of your posters from home with you."

"Of course, and some pictures too." She pointed to her desk where snapshots of Rico, Jernell, Brianna, and her other relatives sat in multi-colored frames. Her favorite books sat on the other side of the desk.

"Are you ready to eat, Daddy?" Morgan looked up at her father as she sat the pizza on the desk.

Rico's stomach rumbled. "I'm starving."

"Have a seat at that desk, and I'll get some plates and cups."

After Morgan finished setting the plates and cups on the

table, Rico blessed the food. The pair partook of the meal. Morgan ordered two garden pizzas with all the toppings, just the way she and Rico liked.

After they'd eaten, Rico said to Morgan, "Let me see your books and your class schedule."

Rico thumbed through the books and asked Morgan about school.

"I love it here at Bradley, although I miss being at home. Last week was kind of difficult. Noah and I made a pact that we'd help each other through the adjustment period."

Rico frowned and closed the book he was holding. "So you're still taking to him? Haven't you made any other friends?"

"Of course I have. Some friends are closer than others." Morgan looked down at the floor, pretending not to notice the upset expression on her father's face.

Rico's mouth dropped. "You aren't saying what I think you are?"

Morgan stared at her father innocently. She batted her eyes. "What do you mean, Daddy?"

"Nothing." Rico didn't want to put any ideas in Morgan's head.

Rico stayed at the dorm another couple of hours. He and Morgan conversed. At nine o'clock he looked at his watch and yawned. "Your old man isn't as young as he used to be. I'm a bit tired from the drive from Ohio. I'm going back to the hotel and I'll pick you up in the morning for breakfast. Maybe we'll take a trip to the mall, so I can buy something for your room." Rico stood.

"Okay, old man. Go ahead and get your rest and be ready to shop 'til you drop tomorrow. It's on," she teased her father. "I'll walk you downstairs."

The pair walked arm and arm to Rico's car. She waved goodbye to her father. Since the hour wasn't too late, Morgan decided to visit Noah. He'd visited her quite a few times, and she had yet to see his room. She made a U-turn and headed in the opposite direction.

Fifteen minutes later, she stood at Heitz Hall at the attendant's desk and asked if Noah Stephens was in his room.

The young man laid the book he was reading on the desk. He replied, "Noah Stephens. I think he's here. Go on up."

"Uh, what room is he in?" Morgan felt foolish since she'd never asked Noah his room number.

"Room 411," the young man answered. "The elevators are to your left." He stood up and smiled as he watched the young woman walk away.

"Thanks." Morgan's hand trembled as she held onto the stair railing. She began to have second thoughts about her excursion. Suppose Noah didn't want to see her, or what if he was busy. She second guessed herself, thinking maybe coming to the dorm wasn't a good idea after all.

When she arrived at room 411, the door was closed. Morgan lifted her hand and knocked on it. She held her breath until the door opened.

"Morgan, what are you doing here?" Noah asked. He was dressed in a pair of black denim shorts and a black sleeveless tee shirt.

"I was in the neighborhood and decided to drop by. Seriously, my dad just left and I decided to visit you since you'd seen my place and I've never seen yours." Morgan's eyes darted inside the room.

"Come in." Noah smiled. He stepped backward and to his right so Morgan could come inside. "Have a seat on the bed or at my desk. Make yourself at home." He pointed to the left side of the room.

A red, white, and blue comforter was pulled over Noah's bed. Morgan noticed his meager possessions: an obviously used television set and a new white microwave oven. A white alarm clock sat on his nightstand. A small CD player/

radio was set to a gospel station. An old song by the Winans was playing.

A few posters of basketball players were taped to the wall, and a picture of his parents and his prom picture sat on his desk.

Morgan sat on the desk chair. She folded her hands prudishly in her lap.

"I guess my stuff seems scant compared to yours?" Noah's face turned bright red.

"You know we've had this conversation before. I don't judge people by what they have or don't have. What's important to me is that you're here at Bradley getting an education and that you're my friend," Morgan stated staunchly.

A gust of air seemed to dissipate from Noah's lungs. "Thanks, Morgan. I had hoped you'd understand my financial situation, still I wasn't sure."

Morgan stood and walked over to Noah. She grabbed his hands. "I guess you're going to have to spend more time with me, Mr. Stephens. Until you realize I judge people by their character and not by how much money they have in their wallet."

Morgan was wearing a navy blue and beige floral short suit. Noah thought she'd never looked more attractive. Her long slim legs seemed to go on forever. He reached over and caressed her cheek.

Morgan stood on her toes and brushed Noah's lips with her own. He drew back, surprised by her boldness. Then his lips curved into a smile. He put his arms around her waist and drew her body closer to his.

Noah's lips probed Morgan's hesitantly and then hungrily. A fire was lit inside their young bodies. The kiss deepened and seemed to go forever. Noah's arms tightened around Morgan's waist. Her hands lovingly stroked his head.

Then the door opened and Morgan stumbled away from Noah. She smoothed her hair nervously.

Carl walked inside the room. He smirked when he saw Morgan and Noah. "Am I interrupting anything?" He looked at his roommate and then Morgan.

"No. We're just leaving," Noah replied in an irritated voice.

"Introduce me to the young lady," Carl requested of Noah. "Not bad, roomie." He winked at Noah.

"This is Morgan Foster. See you later." Noah grabbed Morgan's hand and led her out of the room.

They walked downstairs with their hands still entwined. When they went outside Morgan said, "He didn't seem too bad to me."

"Don't let his polite exterior fool you. I sense some undertones of prejudice on his part. Sometimes he acts so condescending toward me about his life experiences. He'll end a comment with, 'Do you know what I'm talking about?' Carlton loves to make off-colored jokes, usually about people of color. He really gets under my skin sometimes. Then I have to remind myself that he's a child of God too, and try to forgive his ways."

They walked down the street to Morgan's dorm. The night was clear and starry. Noah dropped her hand and placed his arm around her waist. Morgan told him about her visit with her father. "I definitely want you to meet Daddy. He's cool. He's outgoing and totally different from my mother."

Crickets chirped, serenading them with song. The temperature was hot and humid.

"I'd like to meet him too. But I don't want to interfere with father-daughter time."

"I already told him that I plan to introduce you two. So it'll have to be tomorrow or Sunday before he leaves."

"Okay, I'll come by your room tomorrow. I have an interview at University Hall at twelve noon." Noah shrugged his shoulders helplessly. "I need the money."

"I understand. Just come by to meet my daddy when you finish."

They stood in front of Morgan's dorm. She peered shyly at him. "I guess I should go in."

"Yeah, I guess so. Although I don't want to let you go," Noah said mockingly, like his feelings were hurt.

"I don't want to go either. But we have just enough time for you to get back to your dorm before curfew."

"You're right, Miss Foster." He pecked her lips chastely and squeezed her arm. "I'll see you tomorrow. Hopefully, I'll be able to tell you that I'm gainfully employed."

"You will." Morgan punched him on the arm playfully, then she pulled his body toward her and smothered his lips with hers. "Mmm, just as good as before." She waved at him and switched her hips as she walked inside her dorm.

Noah stared at her, mesmerized. As he walked back to his dorm, when he wasn't smiling from cheek to cheek, the young man whistled a tune.

After she went into the hall, Morgan ran upstairs to her room and peeked out the window to watch Noah until he was no longer in sight. Her first thought was to call Brianna. With a dreamy look on her face, Morgan decided to savor the moment before sharing it with her cousin. She walked to her desk, pulled out her diary, and began to write.

Dear Diary,

Today was one of the best days of my life. Daddy came to see me, and we had a good visit, today that is. I know he's going to start on me about the family business. I wish he would just leave me alone. Working with Momma is something I have to do. Daddy just doesn't understand how it is for me. He's been acting very religious lately. So I know he's going to impart words of wisdom from the Bible.

On a lighter note, I decided to visit Noah's room after Daddy went to his hotel. Poor baby, his parents must really be poor. I admire him for handling his business and improving his life. He's studying engineering. He has scholarships to pay for his education.

I can't believe myself sometimes. I waited for Noah to put the moves on me all week, but he kept me at arm's length. So I had to make the first move myself. His kisses were so hot. I felt like I was going to faint. I wanted to take my clothes off and throw myself on him. I don't know what I would have done after I was naked though. Noah is such a gentleman, he probably would have covered his eyes, or thrown my clothes back at me. I suspect he's not a virgin. That's good, because one of us should know what we're doing. I'm learning by rote.

My classes aren't bad at all. I like the business ones. Maybe that will be my major. I've got to learn all I can to help Momma. I don't think I'll have any problems with my classes this semester. I really like Noah.

MDF

The following morning, Morgan wore denim bib overall shorts and a lilac tube top. She waited outside the dorm for Rico to pick her up so they could go to breakfast. He tooted the horn twice as he pulled up in front of the building.

When Morgan entered the car, her father looked at her outfit disapprovingly. "Aren't you missing some pieces of clothing? Hmm, I need to get you to the mall as soon as possible to buy you some new clothes." He eyed his daughter sternly.

"Daddy!" Morgan wailed indignantly. "I'm dressed like the other girls on campus. Lighten up. Where are we going for breakfast?" She took a vial of perfume out of her purse and squirted a few drops on herself and playfully at Rico.

"Watch it, girl," Rico warned his daughter. "I thought we'd go to IHOP. You can have pancakes and I'll have waffles."

"Sounds like a deal. What else are we going to do today?"

"I already mentioned going to the mall and then maybe after you shop 'til you drop, we'll have worked up an appetite and then we'll go out for dinner. That is, unless you have other plans." Rico glanced at her and then back at the windshield.

"No, not really. Daddy, if you're asking me in a roundabout way if I have a date or something, then the answer is no. But I do want you to meet Noah before you go back home. Maybe he can go to dinner with us?"

Rico didn't miss the breathless way she pronounced Noah's name. Her tongue seemed to caress the young man's name. "You don't leave me a choice in the matter. Okay, Morgan. I'll meet your young man."

She leaned across the seat and kissed her father's cheek. "Thank you, Daddy. Noah is a special friend of mine."

When Rico and Morgan arrived at IHOP, the breakfast crowd had come and gone. A few customers were scattered throughout the spacious dining room. For the most part though, the place was deserted.

Rico studied the menu, although he knew what he wanted. He told the waitress, "I'll have coffee and the Belgium waffles."

The young girl wrote on her pad. She looked at Morgan. "What will you have?"

"I'll have the short stack of pancakes and a large glass of milk," Morgan answered.

Rico stared at his daughter. What's up with the short stack? You could eat two orders of those by yourself!"

"I'm watching my figure." Morgan refused to meet her father's eyes and handed the menu to the waitress.

The young lady took Rico's menu. "I'll be back with your beverages in a few minutes."

Morgan looked at her watch and up at Rico. "It's noon already? Noah is at one of the school cafeterias interviewing for a position," she informed her father and crossed her fingers. "I'm sure he'll get it."

"So the man vying for my baby's heart is broke?" Rico couldn't resist saying.

"Yeah. Noah doesn't have a lot of money." Morgan sighed.

The waitress returned and placed a large glass of milk in front of Morgan. Then she poured steaming hot black coffee in a cup for Rico. Before she departed she said, "Your orders will be up in about ten minutes. Is there anything else I can get for you now?"

Rico shook his head. When the waitress was out of earshot, he said, "Morgan if the boy doesn't have money, how is he going to court you? From what you're telling me, he doesn't have a pot to . . ."

"Do you have to be so vulgar?" Morgan grumbled. "We'll make do. Everything will work out fine between me and Noah."

"Morgan you don't know the first thing about being poor. Your mother has seen to it that you've had access to the best things money can buy. I know she sent you to school with at least one credit card, probably an American Express? Am I right?"

"Daddy, Daddy, Daddy." Morgan *tsked*. She opened her wallet, pulled out a card and waved it in the air. "Momma gave me an American Express card when I started high school. But you're right. She upgraded the card for college. Now I have a platinum card." Morgan had the grace to try to look embarrassed. She looked up to see the waitress returning with their orders and relief flooded through her body. She dropped the card back into her purse

"The food looks great." She picked up her knife and spread butter over the pancakes, followed by a generous pouring of maple syrup. Morgan cut the pancakes into small pieces and put a forkful in her mouth. After she chewed and swallowed she said to Rico, "Um, that tastes good."

"I agree with you."

They ate in silence. When they finished eating, Morgan leaned back in her seat and wiped her mouth prettily with a napkin.

Rico put the last bit of waffle in his mouth and then wiped his hands on the napkin. "Honey, I know Noah is probably your first real crush, but I don't see anything positive from your spending time with him. Your lifestyles are so different. He's a struggling college student, which is probably true for fifty percent of the kids attending school, and you're from money."

Morgan listened to her father speak and shredded a paper napkin as he talked. "Daddy, I've dated before. You're right though, nobody seriously. But I have some experience."

Rico had a point regarding his daughter's dealings with the opposite sex. Most of Morgan's dates in the past were with Jernell's business associates' sons. None had ever touched her heart or body.

"Daddy, don't you remember when you met Momma and how you knew she was the one? I'm not saying Noah is the one for me, but I'd sure like to find out. I'm not a little girl anymore." Morgan chose her words carefully as she looked at her father thoughtfully.

"Sure I do. I haven't forgotten how it is when you're in love or think you are. And that's what makes me afraid for you and the boy. When you're eighteen, you have no fear and think you can conquer any obstacle placed in your path. Trust me. I know too well firsthand that life or love is not easy, especially where your mother's people are concerned." Rico tried to pat Morgan's hand but she pulled away.

"Why should my life be any different from yours and Momma's? Am I not entitled to living my own life, which might include making mistakes? I just know I like Noah, and I'd like to get to know him better."

Rico looked at his daughter sympathetically. "Have you mentioned to Noah what the family business really entails?" Rico held his hand up and shook his head. "No, you don't have to say. I already know the answer to that."

"Then why bother to ask me? You know as well as I do that we can't casually mention what really goes on in the business to outsiders."

The atmosphere between father and daughter was becoming heated.

"For God's sake, Morgan, Noah is a minister's son. There's no way in this lifetime you can justify to him what your mother does for a living. Have you forgotten that you're next in line to take your mother's place? In ten years, and that's assuming nothing happens to Jernell, your life will be a carbon copy of hers. Is that what you really want for yourself?" Rico softened his tone.

Morgan rocked back and forth in her seat. Her face looked miserable. "I don't know . . ." Her face set in hard lines. "Yes I do. I want both love and the business. It can be done; just look at Aunt Adrianna and Uncle Todd. He accepted Auntie for who she was."

Rico took Morgan's hands inside his own, and gently squeezed them. "When you were born, I believed that Jernell and I could overcome our obstacles and make a happy life for you, our first child. But that wasn't our reality. I couldn't stomach the violence and constantly looking over my shoulder waiting for the police to raid a location or go to jail.

"I grew up in the streets of Lake Park. I was a thug, a

gangster, the toughest G you could find. My boys told me how lucky I was hooking up with Jernell. How I wouldn't ever want for any material things because Jernell's family had it like that and everybody knew it. I was content with our life, but when you were born, something changed inside me. That lifestyle was okay for me and your mother since we were born into it.

"But I wanted a better life for you and tried to show you a different lifestyle, which I've tried to do ever since I moved to Cleveland. That's why I'd have you stay with me during the summer. You never even had many friends growing up because Jernell was afraid you'd accidentally say something about her family."

Morgan's voice crackled with emotion. Her face was stony, and, for a minute, she resembled her mother. "Don't criticize Momma and the way she raised me. What did I need friends for, as long as I had Brianna and my other cousins as friends? There's nothing wrong with being close to family members." She began sobbing softly.

Rico leaned over and rubbed her arm. "It's important because you need to learn how to interact with other people. I could understand where the Foster family was coming from because I grew up in the streets and the gang was my family. But Noah hasn't experienced that. How can he accept the family and what they represent? Don't cry, baby. You know I hate to see you cry." He took her hands in his.

Morgan wept silently. Tears trickled from the corners of her eyes. She snatched her hands away from Rico's and wiped her face.

Her father passed her a napkin. "I didn't mean to upset you. I want to give you something to think about before you make decisions that can affect your life and the people around you." He held out his hands. "Your mother wouldn't approve of our having this conversation. I think if you really wanted out of the family, she would let you go." Rico hated rehashing the old conversation with her. But he knew that where there's a will, there's a way. God would see them through this crisis, if that was what Morgan truly wanted. He hoped she would question her lifestyle and make a change. On the other hand, Rico was well aware that the overseer could grant one major defection during her regime. And the sparing of this life was one of Jernell's markers.

"Daddy," Morgan moaned, "you don't understand. Momma lost her mother when she was younger than I am now. Then she lost you. I can't let her down. I just hope that if I ever have to tell Noah about the family that he'll understand. Because, after all, Daddy, love is supposed to be unconditional. I don't want to discuss me coming to live with you anymore. Momma needs me and I'm not going to be the third person who deserts her."

Rico could tell by the unyielding expression on Morgan's face that the words he'd spoken were in vain. His daughter's eyes breathed fire and her lips were tight as prunes. He realized there wasn't anything he could say to change her mind. He shook his head regretfully and waved his hand to get the waitress's attention.

The young woman walked over to the booth and laid the bill on the table. "Can I get either of you anything else?"

"No, we're good." Rico pulled his Visa card out of his wallet.

"I'm going to the ladies' room." Morgan stood and walked down the aisle and around the corner.

When she returned, Rico stood up. He felt guilty for causing his daughter so much distress, although is heart was in the right place. He tried to make amends. "I didn't mean to upset you, baby. I don't want my visit to end on a sour note. "Let's go to the mall, and then I'll treat you and Noah to dinner. How does that sound?"

Morgan's lips trembled. She said, "Good, Daddy. That sounds like fun." When Rico pulled up in front of the dormitory, Morgan flashed him a weak smile and told him she'd see him that evening.

As Rico drove back to the hotel, he couldn't rid his head of a premonition of doom for Morgan and Noah. A minister's son and a gangster's daughter? No way! Sharp throes of foreboding roosted in his stomach. Then his mind meandered to the sermon that his minister had preached the past Sunday. The text was taken from Matthew 7:7. *Ask, and it shall be given you; Seek, and ye shall find; Knock, and it shall be opened unto you.* Rico knew in his heart that, with God, all things are possible. One just has to believe. Pastor Wilson's voice blasted into his mind, he seemed to ask Rico, "Where is your faith in God?"

Rico decided instead of dwelling on the negatives, maybe he should have an open mind to the possibility of a relationship between his daughter and the minister's son. Who was he to say Noah and Morgan wouldn't make it? Time would tell, beginning in a few hours.

Chapter 12

When Noah arrived at the dormitory to meet Morgan and her father, she'd changed into a bubble gum pink and white polka dot sundress and pink sandals for dinner. Sterling silver hoop earrings dangled from her earlobes.

Noah wore a pair of black khaki pants, a white polo shirt, and white Nike sneakers. It was six o'clock and the pair sat on a bench outside Morgan's dormitory waiting for Rico to arrive.

Noah was a perceptive young man, and he noticed that Morgan's mood seemed down. She was unusually quiet while they waited for her dad. "Did you have a good time with your father today? You seem kind of sad."

Morgan smiled at him, although it was a weak one that didn't quite meet her eyes. "It was okay. We caught up on old times." She rose from her seat. "Here he comes now. He's driving the black Ford Taurus." She reached into her pocket, pulled out a pair of sunglasses and slipped them on her nose.

Rico exited the automobile so that Morgan could introduce him to her new friend.

"Daddy, this is Noah Stephens. Noah this is my father, Rico Daniels."

"Pleased to meet you, sir," Noah said after shaking Rico's hand firmly.

"Same here, son." Rico got back inside the car. Morgan entered the car on the passenger's side, and Noah got into the backseat.

"My daughter has told me some favorable things about you, young man. Tell me more about yourself," Rico ordered the young man as he steered the car back to the main thoroughfare.

"Daddy," Morgan whined, "do you have to start on Noah as soon as he gets in the car? Jeez, we haven't even decided where we're going for dinner." She turned to Noah and shook her head helplessly.

"That's okay, Morgan. I'm okay with your dad asking questions. He reminds me of my pops. He's to the point," Noah said gallantly.

"I thought we'd have Indian food. I passed a restaurant on my way here. Is that okay with you, Morgan?" Rico asked.

"That's fine with me. What about you, Noah?" Morgan turned to Noah.

"Sure. Wherever we go for dinner is no problem at all." Inside, Noah felt a twinge of anxiety. He'd never eaten in a Indian restaurant in his entire life. His family tended to frequent soul food or fast food restaurants when they did go out to dinner, and that was rare.

Morgan didn't miss the look of panic on Noah's face. She surmised correctly he wasn't comfortable with Indian cuisine. "How about we go to Red Lobster instead? It's really one of my favorite restaurants. I'd love crab legs for dinner."

"Then Red Lobster it is," Rico said. "Look, there's one up ahead." He pointed. "It's good we stayed on the main road."

Thirty minutes later, Morgan, Rico, and Noah were seated at a large booth. Rico sat across from the couple. Morgan wore a white plastic bib. She cracked open the crab legs, speared the white meat with her fork, and then put it inside her mouth, savoring the taste. Rico and Noah ordered strip steaks and baked potatoes overflowing with butter and sour cream.

The restaurant was crowded with chatting diners. A young couple sat across from the trio, and Morgan watched fascinated as the young woman fed her date. On more than one occasion, the waiters and waitresses walked down the aisles clapping their hands and singing "Happy Birthday."

As the evening wound down, Rico steered the conversation back to Noah. "Now is as good a time as any to finish our conversation from earlier, that Morgan interrupted." He laid his fork and knife next to his plate. "Son, why don't you tell me a bit about yourself?"

Noah removed his napkin from his lap and laid it on the table. "Let me see, I was born, raised, and still reside in Englewood. I'm eighteen years old. My birthday was in May, the twentieth. Most people look down on Englewood as the ghetto, but it's the only place I've ever known.

"My father was born there. After he received his spiritual calling, he decided to stay in the area. My dad tries to help the residents in any way God wants him to."

"Your father is to be commended," Rico interjected, bowing his head. "I work with low income people and ex-felons in Cleveland. It's my way of giving back to the community."

Morgan was impressed by her father's comments. She felt proud of him at that minute.

The waitress returned to the table and asked if she could get them anything else. When they replied no, she laid the bill inside the leather slip on the table next to Rico.

Noah continued speaking after she left. "My mom, Gloria, who my dad calls 'Glo' and 'Glory', was raised not far from where Morgan lives. I'm not exactly sure how Dad and she met. They are secretive about certain parts of their lives. I know they both had rough childhoods, and my mom's was worse than my dad's. She doesn't talk about it much. She works with Dad in the church, and she's working with a grant writer to get funds from the city so she can start some outreach programs at the church.

"Dad worked so hard for his congregation, but he still managed to spend time with me when I was growing up. He introduced me to the basketball court and fishing. We have a great relationship. Actually, I have a good relationship with both my parents."

"That is so cool," Morgan commented, watching Noah with shining eyes.

Rico searched his memory banks to see if he remembered a Gloria from his past. "What was your mother's maiden name," he asked Noah.

"Jones. Gloria Jones."

The name sounded vaguely familiar to Rico. However, the Gloria he recalled wouldn't have married a minister. "So what do you see yourself doing after college? What are you majoring in, Noah?"

The young man grabbed Morgan's hand under the table. "My dad wants me to work in the church with him and Mom. I haven't had a spiritual calling to preach. I'm majoring in engineering. I've always been good in science and math. I'd really like to put my skills and degree to use and earn a living in that field. Like Morgan, I don't have any sisters or brothers. So I feel a lot of pressure to give in to my father's wishes."

Rico nodded. As Morgan had said, Noah was a special young man. He could understand his daughter's attraction. The young man was handsome and had a lot going for him. Rico had a feeling that Noah would attain any goal he put his mind to. "I'm sure Morgan has told you that she too feels pressure to follow in her mother's footsteps."

"Yes, but her situation is different from mine. Her mother is head of a family-owned business. My father struggles to pay the rent on the storefront building he uses for church services. That's one reason I'd like to work in the corporate world: to help my parents financially."

Morgan squeezed Noah's hand. He was doing fine, handling everything her father threw at him.

The waitress returned to the table. Rico picked up the bill and scanned it. "I think management is hinting it's time for us to go. They probably need the table for other diners." He reached inside his jacket pocket for his wallet, then opened the leather bill holder and put his credit card inside it.

The waitress came back to the table one more time. Rico added a tip amount and signed his name with a flourish. Then he looked across the table at Rico and Morgan. "I've enjoyed myself this evening. It does my heart good to see there are still young men around who aspire to a future that includes more than gang-banging and rapping."

Noah sighed with relief. "Thank you, sir. It's been a pleasure dining with you this evening. When you come back to Peoria, I'll have to treat you and Morgan to dinner."

"I may take you up on your offer, but not until you finish college," Rico said. "Are you two ready to go?"

They all stood up, headed for the exit, and went to the car.

Twenty minutes later, Rico pulled the automobile in front of Morgan's dormitory and shifted the car into park. "Can I drop you off at your place, Noah?"

"Daddy?" Morgan's eyes bucked. She looked at her father like he was an alien from another planet. "We're going to hang out a little bit. Aren't you tired or something? Don't you need to go back to the hotel and rest?"

Rico laughed aloud. "I can take a hint. I'll stop over in the morning and see you after I check-out of the hotel." He stuck his hand out toward Noah. "Son, it's been a pleasure. It was nice meeting you."

"The same here, sir. I hope to see you again." He shook Rico's hand briskly.

The couple exited the car. Morgan walked around to the driver's side of the car and kissed Rico's cheek. "Thank you, Daddy. Although I think you were a little rough on Noah at times."

"He showed he could handle it so no harm was done. See you in the morning, baby girl."

"Good night, Daddy," Morgan said as she and Noah waved to Rico.

"Whew." Noah exaggeratedly mopped his brow. "Your dad is tough. I can understand where he's coming from. He loves you a lot, and it was obvious."

"I know. But he still has to understand that I'm a young woman and not a little girl." Morgan poked out her lips.

"I wanted to tell you how pretty you looked earlier. But I didn't know if that was appropriate to say around your over-protective father. "Your chocolate skin is so pretty," Noah stroked her arm. "It feels like velvet."

"You don't look too shabby yourself," Morgan quipped. "I've only seen you in shorts and T-shirts. When you clean up, you look good yourself."

"Aw, shucks. I don't know what to say." Noah put on a country air. "So what do you want to do now? I really have some homework I need to do."

"You mean you don't want to hang with me for a little while?" Morgan lisped with a dejected look on her face. She placed her hand over her heart.

Noah looked at his watch. "Hmm. I guess I can go inside with you for a little while."

Morgan grabbed his hand. "Well, alrighty now. Come on." She took his hand.

They went indoors and took the elevator to Morgan's room. It was Saturday night, and the hall was nearly empty. As they rode upstairs, Noah took Morgan in his arms and kissed her deeply. His tongue eagerly explored her mouth.

When they arrived in Morgan's room, she flipped on the light switch. Noah pulled out the chair to Morgan's desk and sat down. He scanned her music collection, books, and papers scattered on top of the desk while she turned on the CD player. The group 112 sang to the couple. She walked to the mini fridge. "112 is one of my favorite groups. Would you like a pop?"

"Sure, why not? Hey, you write really well." Noah scanned an essay she'd written for her English literature class while Morgan took a can of pop out of the mini-fridge.

"I really enjoy writing. I've always gotten A's in English and composition, classes like that." She handed him a can of Pepsi.

"Cool. You can help me with some of my papers."

Morgan prepared a glass for herself and sat on the bed. She popped open the lid on her can. "You know it'll cost you. Why are you sitting all the way over there? I'm not so big that I take up the entire bed am I?"

"No, I'm fine here. If I sit on the bed with you, I may not want to leave."

"Oh, you're leaving all right. You don't think I'm easy or something, now do you?" Morgan teased him.

Noah walked over to the bed and sat next to Morgan. "Of course not. So how many boyfriends have you had, pretty lady?" He took a sip of Pepsi and stared at her attentively.

Morgan sputtered. "What kind of question is that?"

"I just want to know what I'm getting myself into. Now me, I've had a few girlfriends, nothing serious though. It was murder going to an all-boy school."

Morgan's eyes grew wide, "You mean your dad let you date? With him being a minister and all?"

"Sure he did. I just had to be circumspect about it. You still didn't answer my question, Miss Foster." He tugged the ends of her hair.

"Like you, I've dated some, nothing serious though. My momma kept me on a tight rein. That's one reason I was so gung-ho on going away to school. I'll be eighteen on October the fourth. And before you ask me, yes, I'm still a virgin."

Noah nearly choked on the soda. He began coughing, and Morgan thumped his back a couple of times. When he caught his breath, Noah said. "Somehow I knew you were going to say that. It's cool though." His expression became serious. "I want to be your first everything. But everything happens in due time. Let's not rush things."

Morgan's left foot tap-danced on the floor uncontrollably. *Lord have mercy. I think I'm falling in love with this man-child who I've only known for a week.* She rubbed the cool glass along her forehead. Her body felt warm like someone had stuffed her inside an oven.

She set her glass on the nightstand and took Noah's face between her hands. She kissed his lips with every fiber of her being.

"Whoa, hold on, I didn't mean tonight." Noah gently pushed her heaving body away from his. "There's no rush to do anything tonight, pretty lady. We have plenty of time to get to know each other in every way. I want to share my world with you. That would include going to church." He spread his hands. "The whole nine yards."

Morgan's face felt red. Her body slumped dejectedly. "You don't want me. There must be something wrong with me."

Noah took her hand in his, "Make no mistake about it, I want you. But I want it to be the right time for us. Though it's soon too tell, who knows when our time will come? It may even be on our wedding night. Trust me, in due time,

Morgan, we'll get there." He mussed her bangs. "I need to go back to my room and study. I have a chemistry test Monday morning and I plan to go to church in the morning. Maybe you'd like to go to church with me?" Noah asked Morgan hopefully as he stood up.

Morgan felt slightly mollified by his answer. At least he hadn't outright rejected her. "I have some studying I need to do myself. I'm going to take a rain check on going to church and breakfast, too." The pair had gotten into the habit of meeting daily for their morning meal.

"I understand, maybe we can meet later on tomorrow sometime," Noah suggested. He pulled her up from the bed. "My invitation still stands for you to go to church with me in the morning."

Morgan shook her head mutely. "I promise to go with you soon. But not tomorrow. I'm going to hang out with my dad tomorrow before he goes back to Cleveland."

"Oops, my bad," Noah said. "Walk me to the door. I'll call you when I get back to my room."

"Okay. You sure can give a girl a great brush off." Morgan laughed.

"That was no brush off, Ms. Foster," Noah corrected Morgan. "It's called self-preservation. I have to maintain a B grade point average to keep my scholarship. And I bet your mom is paying your tuition." His eyes narrowed. "Am I right?"

"Right as rain," Morgan replied. She walked out the door with Noah.

"Now," he waggled his finger at her, "you stay here. I'll call you later." Noah wrapped his arms around Morgan, kissed her tenderly, stroked her lips with his pinky finger, and left the room.

Morgan locked the door. Her body sagged against the wood. She fanned her body with both hands. A smile engulfed her face. She couldn't stop grinning. She twirled around the room gaily. Then she stopped and walked over to the CD player and put in a Blackstreet CD. She sang along with the group, "*If you take your love away from me, I'll go crazy.*" Her voice crackled with emotion as she attempted to sing the high notes.

When the song ended, Morgan walked over to her nightstand and removed her diary. She picked up a pen off her desk, then sat on the bed and quickly wrote in the book.

Dear Diary

Today was another one of the best days of my life. Daddy met Noah, and I know he liked him. It was touch-and-go there for a while between me and Daddy. I knew he was going to start in on me about how I should leave Momma and come to stay with him. But I can't. Momma needs me.

Noah and I kissed, and I didn't want him to stop. I think I have the hots for him. Just thinking about him makes me want to squeeze my legs tightly together and wish he were here. He is truly one of a kind. If I had been out with one of the boys from home, he would have jumped my bones without a thought. Noah is different. I feel like he really cares for me.

I didn't talk to Brianna today. I'll have to call her tomorrow. Momma hasn't called me in a couple of days. I hope everything is all right at home. She really sounded tense the last time I talked to her. I hope I never have to choose between the business and love. I don't know what I'd do. I know some of the things my daddy was telling me today were true, but I can't escape my destiny. I wonder what my life would have been like had I not been Jernell Foster's daughter.

Both Daddy and Noah were on my case about going to church. Maybe I will, since it's so important to Noah. I know I should do it for the right reasons and somewhere deep inside of me, I want to walk that Christian walk that Noah talks about sometimes. But what if I can't? I can't change

*who I am. I wonder if it will become an issue between me
and Noah. Like he said, 'only time will tell.'*
MF

The telephone rang a few hours later. Morgan could see
from the caller ID that Noah was calling. She closed the
diary and laid on the bed. "Hi, Noah. What are you doing?
Do you miss me . . ."

Chapter 13

Lucinda laid two slices of bacon on the George Foreman grill that sat on the kitchen counter. The telephone rang. She wiped her hands on a dishtowel and picked up the phone by the third ring. "Hello?"

"Hi, Luci," Morgan greeted her former nanny. "Is my mother home? I haven't talked to her in over a week. Is she sick or something?"

"Hi, baby." Lucinda unplugged the grill; then sat down in one of the chairs pushed away from the kitchen table. "How is school?"

"It's fine. Today is Monday and Thursday is Thanksgiving. I wanted to find out from Momma how I'm going to get home for the holiday."

Lucinda swore softly. She pushed her hair out of her eyes. "It's been a madhouse around here, but nothing for you to worry about. I was suppose to make bus reservations for you last week and forgot to do it. I'll call the bus station today, and if they're full, I'll send Harry to pick you up."

"Geez. I just left home a few months ago and everyone seems to have forgotten about me. Brianna didn't even call me last week. I know something is going on. What is it, Luci?" Morgan's grip tightened on the telephone. She was worried. Jernell didn't call her every day, but she managed to call every other day until two weeks ago.

"Your mother has had some trouble. I don't want you to worry and I think it best that you wait for her to talk to you about it. I can hardly wait to see you. Brianna is on lock down. She had a date last Saturday and missed her curfew." Lucinda loved gossiping with Morgan.

"Well, there's nothing new about that. Brianna has missed her curfew many times."

Lucinda looked outside the kitchen. She lowered her voice. "I'm not one to carry tales, but I heard she was extremely late coming in. She didn't come home until the next day."

"Oh no!" Morgan screamed. "I leave home and everything and everyone seems to be falling apart. I can't wait to get home and straighten you guys out."

"How are your grades? Are you passing all of your classes?" Lucinda grilled the young woman.

"Of course I am. I'm pretty sure I've aced at least half of my final tests," Morgan bragged as she looked at the pile of dirty clothes stacked on her bed. She hadn't done laundry in a few weeks, so washing clothes was on her to-do list before she returned home.

"That's good. I knew you could do it. Look, I've got to go. I'll call you tonight with definite travel arrangements. Okay?"

"Sure, Luci. Tell Momma I said hello and I'll see you guys soon.

Lucinda replied, "I can hardly wait to see you. Have a good day, Morgan."

"I will. Bye, Luci." Morgan hung up the telephone. A frown puckered on her face. "Something is wrong at home," she said aloud. Morgan had one more class that afternoon and then she would be done with school until after the break. Noah planned to ride home with a student in his dorm tomorrow night. He had been hired by the university to work in the cafeteria, which was where he was then. They planned to celebrate the holiday tomorrow evening before he left to go home and after Morgan's last exam. The couple planned to see each other in Chicago if their schedules permitted.

Gloria had already informed Noah that his presence was required at church and that he had to spend time with her and Samuel. Morgan planned to spend time with her relatives.

Morgan gathered her dirty laundry and stuffed it inside an oversized duffle bag. She decided to just take her clothes home and wash them when she got there. When she finished that chore, she pulled two suitcases out of the closet and put them on top of the extra bed. She then sat at her desk and hit the books one final time before her exam Tuesday morning.

She and Noah planned to hang out after Noah finished work for the day. The campus was nearly deserted. Many students had departed for home already.

Finally, at two o'clock Tuesday afternoon, Morgan's last class was over. She stood and put on her black fur trimmed parka. She wished a couple of students happy holiday and put her books in her backpack.

When she got outdoors, Noah stood at the entrance waiting for her. He blew on his hands and stuck them in his pocket. "Hey you," he greeted her. "Are you all done?"

"Yes, I am, and my test wasn't as bad as I thought it would be." She handed him her backpack.

"Brr, it's cold out here. What do you want to do?" Noah asked.

"Let's go back to my room and chill out until it's time for you to go home."

"Okay." Noah took Morgan's hand and they trudged

through the snow to her dorm. It had been snowing all day. Morgan was worried about getting home in the inclement weather.

When they reached the third floor and entered Morgan's room, her cell phone made a racket on the desk where she'd left it in vibrate mode. She ran over to the desk and picked it up. "Hi, Luci. What did you find out?"

"One of your mother's business associates owns a bus charter service. So he's going to come and get you no later than tomorrow afternoon. I know we're cutting it close trying to get you home, but the important thing is that you be home for the holiday."

"My mother is sending a bus to pick me up from school? Why?" Morgan asked. Her voice rose in disbelief.

"Well, not just for you. I called the housing department this morning to see if anyone else needed a ride to Chicago, free of charge, round trip, and so far the number is twelve."

Morgan looked at Noah, who'd turned on the television and was sitting on the side of the bed. Morgan shook her head at Noah. "That was nice of you and Momma. Then I guess I'm set. Where do I meet him?" She gestured for Noah to give her a pad and pen. She wrote down the information Lucinda provided. "Okay, Luci, I'll see you tomorrow."

Noah glanced at Morgan curiously and back at the television. "What was that about?"

Morgan sighed. "If you thought my mother was extravagant about bringing me to school in a limousine, you'll never guess how she arranged for me to go home."

Noah put a finger on his left cheek. "Hmm. Let me guess? She's renting a Lear jet to transport you home?"

"Oh you . . ." Morgan sat on the bed next to him. "She's sending a bus—a charter bus."

Noah's eyebrows rose dramatically. "An entire bus? Just for you?"

Morgan's hands fluttered in the air dismissively. "Well,

not for me solely. Luci called the housing department here at school and they found some students who couldn't afford to go home, so Luci offered them free, round-trip bus rides home."

"Whew," Noah commented, "that's good. At least others can benefit from your mother's generosity."

"So I'll be leaving tomorrow. I'm not sure what time. Hey, why don't you ride the bus home with me?"

"Thanks for the offer." Noah reached over and kissed her cheek. "But I think I'll stick to my plans and go home this evening with James."

"Okay then. You can't say I didn't offer. I'm going downstairs. I ordered Chinese food to be delivered. When I was on the phone with Luci, my phone beeped. I'm pretty sure that was the delivery guy."

"Okay," Noah said. He stood up. "I'll get cans of pop out of the fridge."

Morgan returned to the room several minutes later carrying a large brown bag. "Mmm, this smells good. I ordered kung pao chicken for you and Mongolian beef for me." She set the bag on the make-shift table and removed paper plates from the top shelf inside her closet. While she was doing that, Noah removed the containers from the bag and set them on the table.

Morgan rummaged inside the bottom of one of her suitcases and removed a pair of pewter candlesticks and ivory-colored candles. She sat them on the table. Morgan picked up the remote control and powered off the television. She handed Noah a book of matches. "Light these for me."

Noah looked at Morgan dubiously. She walked over to the CD player and inserted a jazz CD. Noah lit the candles while Morgan fixed both their plates and then dimmed the light on the table/desk.

Noah said a short blessing and then he asked her, "What's the occasion?"

Morgan unfolded her hands and looked across the table at Noah. "No special reason, just because." The expression on her face revealed her feelings and how special Noah had become to her.

Noah's eyes telegraphed back to Morgan the same message. He passed her a container of noodles. "I think I like just-because occasions; we'll have to continue doing this. Now what is this called?" He held the container toward Morgan.

"Noodles. Just plain noodles."

"Once again you have me at a disadvantage. I've never had Mexican food and this is the first time I've ever had Chinese."

Morgan winked at him. "Thai is pretty close to Chinese. Tell you what, we'll have to broaden your horizons." She picked up a chopstick, maneuvered a few strands of noodles around it, and gently guided the sticks into Noah's mouth. "I've been wanting to do that since I we went to Red Lobster that time with Daddy. The woman sitting across from us was feeding her significant other." She scooped noodles into her own mouth.

"That tastes good," Noah replied after he swallowed the tasty morsels. Morgan fed him a piece of her beef. He tried using his chopsticks, but he couldn't coordinate them correctly. "I give up." He picked up a plastic fork that Morgan had left lying next to his plate.

He openly stared at Morgan as if he were captivated by the sight of her loveliness. The dim glow of candlelight heightened her features. She decided after being at school for two months to have the weave removed from her hair. Morgan found a stylist who cut her thick hair into a short, easy to manage bob, which made her look even younger and her eyes look larger.

Morgan was clad in a coral angora sweater and a burgundy leather skirt. She wore short, two-inch heeled boots. "Sexy," came to mind when Noah gazed at her.

"Oh, I want to read you a poem I wrote about you." Morgan stood and searched through a stack of papers on top of her desk. She turned and faced Noah. "It's called, *What You Mean To Me*." She proceeded to read.

> *"What are you doing to me?*
> *Blowing my mind,*
> *'Cause you stepped into my life*
> *Right on time*
> *I can't get enough of you*
> *and the special things you do,*
> *Making me feel pretty*
> *and fine.*
> *Yes, you're blowing my mind.*
> *The touch of your lips*
> *Against mine*
> *Ignite a fire that ravages*
> *my body*
> *I can hardly wait*
> *'Til we come together*
> *In that special way,*
> *You know what I mean."*

Noah stood up. He whistled and cheered, rotating his fist in the air. "Ms. Foster, you got mad skills, I'm impressed."

Morgan bowed and then curtsied. "Thank you, thank you."

Noah took her hand and pulled her in his lap and caressed her face. "I feel special. No one, not even a girl in elementary school, has written a poem for me. I didn't even get a roses are red violets are blue, one. You'll have to give me a copy of it so I can save it."

"Good, I'm glad you like it. I've never shared my poetry with anyone else but you." She dropped her head shyly.

"Then bring it on. I'll be a willing audience," Noah promised as he nibbled on her neck.

"I hope we can hook up during the holidays, otherwise I'm really going to miss you," Morgan said after they'd dined. They sat on the bed and listened to music.

She took a sip of Pepsi, put the can on the nightstand, then stood and put Mary J. Blige's album, *What's The 411*, in the player.

Noah stood up and held his arms out. "Can I have this dance?"

"I didn't know that P.K.'s danced," Morgan exclaimed as she wrapped her arms around Noah's waist. "Isn't that a sin or something?"

"There's a lot about us P.K's that you don't know," Noah shot back. "And I'm going to give you plenty of time to learn about this one." He spun her around.

"Oh, I see you got skills," Morgan said as the song ended. When the next tune came on, her feet segued into a two-step movement. She snapped her fingers, and began stepping. To her surprise, Noah didn't miss a beat. He moved in tempo with her. "My goodness, I didn't know you could step too?"

Noah grabbed her hands and they matched each other movement for movement. "In my freshman year of high school, my father decided to let me go to parties and sports events at school after I whined about how I wanted to be a regular kid," Noah said. "I saved my money, and bought a used CD player, so between that and the radio, I learned to dance. I guess my mom used to dance back in the day, because sometimes she'd come into my room and show me some old school moves." Noah smiled at the memory.

"Then I made the mistake of telling a friend of mine that my father was a minister and there went the invitations to parties. I was crushed, but I kept dancing. Stick around, there's a lot to be learned from this church boy."

They danced, kissed, talked, listened to music, kissed some more, and sang the lyrics to most of the songs. A couple of hours later, Noah told Morgan it was time for him to go.

"I wish we could stay like this forever," Morgan sighed.

"Me too," Noah said regretfully. He took his jacket off the back of the chair. "But this break is only for a week and a half. Hopefully, we'll get a chance to met during the semester break. Anyway, we'll be back next Sunday. Time will fly like an eagle."

Morgan grabbed the collar of his jacket and pulled him to her. "I don't want you to see any other girls while you're home."

Noah's eyes widened. "Who me?" An innocent look traversed his face. He pointed to his chest and shook his head from side to side. "Not me. I'm smart enough to know when you find a good woman, you hold on to her. I've never been a dummy." He pulled her into his arms. "I know the same holds true for you."

"Noah, I . . ." Morgan experienced a fit of shyness. Her face dropped down to the floor.

"Me too. I know what you mean. Take care of yourself, Ms. Foster. I'll call you when I get home."

They kissed good-bye until Noah pushed her way. "I've got to go, lady. You be good, and I'll call you tonight."

Chapter 14

"Hello? Is anyone home?" Morgan yelled after she turned her key inside the lock of the gray stone and stepped inside the warm house on Wednesday evening. Aromas from the kitchen wafted through the house.

Lucinda's footsteps clacked across the marble flooring. She flew to Morgan and gathered the young woman in her arms. "Welcome home, baby." Her face exuded pure joy. "Don't you look grown up? Take off your jacket." Lucinda helped Morgan take off her garment like she did when Morgan was a child. "Oh, you had your weave removed." She eyed Morgan closely. "Your hair looks cute. The new look becomes you."

"Thank you, Luci. I'm thinking about getting streaks." Morgan self-consciously ran her fingers through her hair. She hung her jacket in the closet and rubbed her hands together. "Where's Momma?" she asked Lucinda

"She's still at work. Are you hungry? Let me fix you something to eat. You know I started Thanksgiving dinner Monday. I fixed one of your favorite dishes for dinner tonight. Come in the kitchen with me." Lucinda took Morgan's hand and steered her down the long hallway to the kitchen at the front of the house.

Morgan strolled to the stove and began opening the lids of the pots and skillets. "Oh, you fried catfish and made lasagna. Thanks, Luci."

"There's coleslaw in the refrigerator." Lucinda nodded toward the appliance. She opened the door to the oven, pulled back the foil, and checked the turkey.

Morgan washed her hands, took a plate out of the cabinet, and loaded her plate with food. She sat at the table while Lucinda bustled around the kitchen. "So what is Momma doing that she isn't home this time of night? I thought she'd be here to welcome me."

Lucinda shrugged her shoulders and shook her head imperceptibly. She then got a glass of cold water from the sink faucet. "I just know that Jernell has had some problems. I don't want to say the wrong thing. It would be best for her to tell you what's going on. She'll be home soon."

They could hear the sounds of the garage door lifting. "I bet that's her now," Lucinda said. She and Morgan looked at the door leading to the garage. Morgan hopped out of her seat.

Jernell walked into the kitchen and brushed snowflakes off her black sable coat. Then she looked up and saw Morgan. Mother and daughter walked to each other and hugged.

"Welcome home, Morgan. You look so grown up." Jernell looked over her daughter.

"That's the truth," Lucinda agreed. She put a large pot on the stove to cook the collard greens in.

"What did you do to your hair?" Jernell patted the top of Morgan's head.

"I decided to take the weave out. I couldn't find a hairdresser in Peoria to fix my hair the way I wanted. This style is easy for me to maintain. I like it. Come have dinner with me, Momma," Morgan urged her mother.

"I'd love to, Morgan, but I need to make a couple of calls first. Give me twenty minutes and I'll join you. Lucinda, hang up my coat for me." Jernell walked out of the kitchen and downstairs to her office in the basement.

"Something is definitely up," Morgan said after her mother left the room. She and Lucinda chatted for about an hour while Morgan waited for her mother to reappear. When Jernell didn't return after another ten minutes Morgan told Lucinda, "I'm going to call Brianna. I'll be in my room."

Morgan ran up the stairs. Her room looked exactly as she had left it, except that the stuffed animals that Rico had given her for her birthdays since she'd been born had been removed from her bed. She laid down on the bed and spread the comforter over her body. She snuggled under the covers and sniffed. The comforter smelled Downy fresh. She picked up the telephone receiver from her nightstand and dialed Noah's number. She decided to call him first and then Brianna.

"What's up, beautiful?" he asked, smiling broadly.

"I got home a couple of hours ago. Momma was still working. I chatted with Luci a little while."

"How is she doing?" Noah asked. Samuel and Gloria watched him in fascination. They'd never seen their son speak intimately to a female. "Hold on a minute," he told Morgan, covering the receiver of the telephone. "I'm going to take this call in my room," he informed his parents. Then Noah walked rapidly to his bedroom and closed the door behind him.

"I'm back," he told Morgan.

"How are your parents doing?" Morgan asked as she turned on the television set.

"They're fine. My mother cried when she saw me."

Morgan and Noah talked a while longer. He invited her to join his family at church on Thanksgiving. She declined, explaining the family was meeting for dinner at Big Momma's house. She told him she planned to visit his father's church one day soon, maybe during the summer break from school. Then Morgan told Noah that she needed to call Brianna, and asked that he call her later.

Morgan eagerly dialed Brianna's cell phone number. "Hey, Brianna."

"What up, cuz? 'Bout time you came home for a visit," Brianna greeted her cousin.

"It's a good thing I did. Someone has to keep an eye on you and help keep your butt out of trouble."

"Now that was foul. You ain't right," Brianna joked. "I guess you heard what happened. Momma came down hard on me like a ton of bricks. I've been on lockdown. It seems like forever. Usually, I can usually talk Daddy into helping me out of jams with Mommy, but this time he wouldn't budge an inch."

"Bri, what do you expect? You stayed out all night. Come on. What did you think was going to happen?" Morgan scolded her young cousin.

"I thought my parents would chalk it up to me being a teenager, sowing my wild oats. What really happened was that I was having a good time at a party. You know, smoking a little weed, drinking a little wine, and I lost track of time."

"When did you start smoking weed?" Morgan asked Brianna disapprovingly. "You know that's a no-no in our family."

"Since you've been gone to school, I've been bored. I really missed you Morgan," Brianna said morosely.

"Why didn't you hang around our cousins close to our age; Cydney, Karen, or Jasmine? They're not that much younger than you or me. At least being with them would have kept you busy and out of trouble."

Brianna sucked her lips together. "The problem is that they're younger than me. I prefer hanging with older girls not younger ones. Geez, Morgan. They're more sheltered than we were. Plus, you didn't seem to have much time for me since you've been at school. Since you've been kicking it with Noah, you kicked me to the curb," Brianna complained.

"Brianna, I was at school." Morgan's eye fluttered upward in frustration. "College is not like high school. The classes are harder, so I have to study longer hours. And yes, I spent time with Noah. I tried to call you throughout the week. But most of the time I was busy hitting the books. Anyway, we'll see each other tomorrow and everyday while I'm here. I promise to talk to Aunt Adrianna at Big Momma's tomorrow. Maybe she'll let you stay here until I go back to school," Morgan tried to console her cousin. "Look, I hear someone coming up the stairs. It's probably Momma. I'll call you later." The cousins disconnected the call. Morgan looked up to see her mother entering the room.

Jernell had changed into a red, lacy, floor-length nightgown and robe. Her hair was loose and hung over her shoulders. Morgan couldn't help but be impressed at how youthful her mother looked considering she was almost forty years old.

Morgan scooted across the bed so Jernell could sit down. "You look so pretty, Momma. I hope I look that good when I get to be your age."

"I guess there was a compliment somewhere in that statement," Jernell joked. "How is school? Did you pass all your classes?"

"School is wonderful, and yes, I'm pretty sure I passed everything."

Warning bells went off in Jernell's head. The only time a teenager said school was great was when he/she were involved with someone of the opposite sex. "So have you met anyone? Any boys?"

"Remember the young man we gave a ride to when you

were taking me to school? We've kind of been seeing each other. You'd like him. He's really nice," Morgan said dreamily, holding her pillow to her chest.

Okay. This is worse than I thought. Jernell looked at Morgan pensively. "You're still a virgin aren't you? And if you're not, I know you're taking precautions."

Morgan felt a flush infuse her body. If she had been a white girl, she knew her cheeks would have turned a blushing red. "Of course I'm a virgin, Momma. And I know how to take care of myself."

"You'd better. I'm not supporting you and a bastard child. I had you out of wedlock, and I wouldn't wish that misery on anyone."

Tears stung Morgan's eyes. She felt diminished; like her birth was a mistake and her mother regretted having her. A tear rolled down her cheek.

"I didn't mean it the way it came out, Morgan." Jernell reached over and hugged her daughter. "You were the best thing in the world to happen to me. I just don't want you to go repeat the mistakes I made when I was growing up. Looking back in retrospect, I should have married Rico, but I was too immature to know it at the time. Forgive me if I hurt your feelings."

Morgan sniffed. "Thanks, Momma. What's going on with Brianna? I talked to her on the telephone and she sounds like she's out of control. She implied that it was my fault because I went away to school."

"Don't let her lay that guilt trip on you," Jernell advised. She clasped her hands around her legs. "I think she's just going through the terrible teen stage."

"Momma, what's going on with the business? You haven't called me much over the past few weeks. Is everything all right?" Morgan asked. Her expression was serious.

"As far as business is concerned, we'll talk about it after the holiday. I want you to enjoy being home."

"Thanks, Momma. I'd love to have Noah over to the house before we go back to school."

Jernell's eyes narrowed. "We'll see about that. Since I haven't seen you in a long time, I'd really like us to spend quality mother-daughter time together."

Mother and daughter talked for hours. It was the longest conversation Jernell had with her child in a long time. Morgan felt delighted, glad to be home.

Chapter 15

Noah sat with Samuel and Gloria at the kitchen table. They'd just finished eating a late dinner. Samuel had been called away for an emergency regarding a church member and had just returned home. Gloria couldn't keep the joy she felt in her heart from radiating through her eyes. She greedily drank in the sight of her boy. "Do you want something else to eat, Noah? Let me fix you another plate."

"No, Mom." Noah shook his head from side to side. "I'm full. Those care packages you sent me during the first semester came in handy. Thank you again, and please keep them coming."

"It was my pleasure." Gloria glowed happily. "I made a pound cake for tomorrow. I can cut you a slice now. If you'd like, we can eat a bit of Thanksgiving dinner right now instead of tomorrow, the actual day." She stood up.

"No, Mom. Sit down. That's not necessary. I'm good."

The small kitchen felt warm and cozy. Steam hissed from the old-fashioned radiator. The yellow and green curtained windows were fogged up. The room was painted pea green.

A maple kitchen table with six chairs sat in the middle of the room. A green stove and refrigerator sat on opposite walls. Yellow ceramic canisters were lined up side by side on the white counter.

Gloria had prepared a pot roast along with white pota-toes, green beans, and macaroni and cheese for Noah's homecoming meal. They were eating the leftovers from Tuesday night when Noah arrived home. A glass of his fa-vorite childhood drink, cherry Kool-aid, rested next to Noah's now empty plate.

"That meal was great, Mom. I'm stuffed," Noah said.

Gloria and Samuel exchanged conspiratorial looks. Glo-ria almost motionlessly nodded her head encouragingly at Samuel. Then she bowed her head toward Noah. The cou-ple was still taken aback at their son leaving the room earlier that day to take a phone call privately.

Samuel coughed and then he nervously cleared his throat. "Son, who is 'beautiful'?"

Noah looked at his parents perplexed. Then understanding dawned on his face. He snapped his fingers. "Oh, I'm sorry, I was talking to Morgan." His parents looked at him with baffled looks on their faces. "You remember, I told you about her. Morgan Foster? The girl I rode to Peoria with when the car broke down." He peered at his parents intently.

"Hmm. So you really like her?" Gloria queried her son.

"Yes, I guess you could say that. We're tight." Noah ex-plained.

"Tight as in what?" Samuel asked, wasting no time get-ting to the matter that was really on his and Gloria's minds. "Do you love her or think that you're in love? Are you hav-ing sex with her? Define 'tight' for me."

Noah laughed uneasily, feeling like he was on the hot seat. His parents eagerly hung on to his words. "Tight just means we're close. If you want to put a label on our relationship, then I guess you could call her my girlfriend, although she's more than that. I like Morgan and I like spending time with her. We're taking things slow. That's all."

"So you're not having sex with her?" Gloria couldn't stop herself from asking her son.

"Mom." Noah looked at his mother aghast. "If we were, then that would be our business. But no, we're not at this time."

Gloria looked at Noah alarmed. Her son saying not at this time implied the couple would be at some time in the near future. Noah hadn't ever been forthcoming with his parents regarding his feelings about a member of the opposite sex, and his mother felt a tinge of jealousy.

She was used to being the sole female in her son's universe and now she had to share him. God forbid. Gloria rose from her seat and rubbed her forehead. "I have a headache. I'm going to lie down. Sam, I want you to try and talk some sense into your son. I know he didn't have the nerve to say 'not at this time'. Humph," she muttered under her breath. "Noah we plan to be at church at nine o'clock on in the morning to begin serving dinners to the homeless. I'll see you tomorrow."

"What's gotten into her?" Noah watched his mother walk into his parents' bedroom.

"She's just worried about some hoochie mama taking advantage of you and feels like she's been replaced in your affections."

"Worried about me for what?" Noah slid his chair away from the table and folded his arms across his chest.

"In Glo's eyesight, you're her baby and I think she feels like she's losing you to Morgan."

"Why would she think that? Mom is my mother and Morgan is my girlfriend. She's far from being a hoochie mama. My relationship with both of them is different."

"I hear you, son, You know that and so do I, but some-times mothers don't think logically when it comes to their children."

Noah sighed. "I guess I'll have to spend extra time with Mom while I'm home for the holiday."

"That would be good. You are still going with us tomorrow, Thanksgiving day, to church aren't you?" Samuel asked his son openly.

"Of course I am. Why would you ask me that question?"

Samuel leaned forward in his chair. "Well, you might be spending the holiday with Morgan and her family for all we know." He held his hands out. "Just checking."

"Okay, I catch your drift. No. I plan to spend Thanks-giving at church for service and feeding the hungry, like we have in the past. I'd like to thank the members who attend service tomorrow for sending me money this semester. I know it was a huge sacrifice for some of them. The extra cash helped out a lot in addition to what I make in the cafe-teria."

"Good. They're trying to do what they can to help a Christian soldier fight the war against illiteracy. We figure with the things you've learned in college, you can share with our young men at church. Perhaps mentor a couple of them. I also wanted to mention it's not too soon to think about your plans for the summer."

Noah expelled a gust of air loudly. "What I'd really like to do is stay at school and work. Caterpillar is one of Peo-ria's largest corporations and they're offering a summer in-tern program to Bradley students. Dad, they pay quite well."

Samuel took a toothpick out of the holder on the table and stuck it in his mouth. "Sometimes life is not about the money one makes, son. It's about your spiritual soul and the deeds we do here on earth."

"Dad," Noah said, his voice breaking emotionally. "I

understand that. But I hate seeing you and Mom struggle so hard to make ends meet. I'd like to contribute to my education and make life easier for you two. If I just work summers during college, that will give me an opportunity to give back to you . . ." Noah paused when he saw Samuel shaking his head.

"That's not necessary. Our Father above provides for all of me, and your mother's needs. We're fine. I need you to get your educational and spiritual life together." Samuel's chin jutted out defensively.

"Dad, trust me, both are okay. I told you I've been attending a church on a regular basis in Peoria, and I'm involved with the music, and teen ministries." Noah stood up and pushed his chair up to the table. "I'm going to call it a night since we're getting up early tomorrow morning for church."

Samuel stood and placed his hand on Noah's shoulder. "Okay, son. I'll see you in the morning."

When Noah returned to his bedroom, he felt troubled by the conversation he'd had with his father and mother. Noah closed the door behind him and sat on the bed looking out the window. Englewood hadn't changed much since he'd left for school. From his vantage point, Noah could see the winos congregating on the corners and across the street from them stood the drug dealers. Loud music blared from car speakers as drivers passed the house. Sometimes it seemed to Noah that the life his father carved out for himself was overwhelming. There was only so much one person could do and people only changed their behavior when they wanted to. Noah sensed there was too much wrong in his community and it would to take too much effort from his father to correct the wrongs.

Noah felt ashamed. The sometimes illegible checks Noah received from some of the church members was a blaring reminder that his father had and continued to do good in the neighborhood. His small congregation had expanded to more than one hundred people. Gloria was looking into a grant from the city or government to get money to buy the church building.

When the family arrived at church Thanksgiving morning, Noah felt a sense of pride when many of the parishioners told him after the service how proud they were of him. Noah went to the basement of the church and dished stuffing on plates at Old Landmark Church of God and Christ. A stream of homeless people filled the small space awaiting their turns for food. Gloria had never been more proud of her son.

While Noah distributed food at the church, Morgan and the Foster family spent the day at Big Momma's house. One of the Foster family traditions was Big Momma hosting the Thanksgiving holiday.

Lucinda and Big Momma's staff prepared a feast worthy of royalty. The meal included turkey, pork roast, fried chicken, and chitterlings. Lucinda prepared greens, lima beans, yams, stuffing, corn on the cob, and several desserts. Big Momma's dining room was so large that it had two dining tables instead of one.

The adults were seated at the main table, the young people sat at the smaller table, and the children ate in the kitchen.

The weather was frigid in Chicago and everyone was dressed to the nines in their warmest Sunday best. Most of the women had on various types of fur coats when they arrived. Their daughters wore fur jackets with matching head bands around their newly coifed hair.

Morgan regaled her cousins with tales of her college experience at the smaller table.

Jasmine asked, "Are there a lot of fine boys at your college?"

Brianna exclaimed, "Ha, like she would know. Morgan don't know. She already has a boyfriend. I can't ever catch up with her."

"Does Aunt Jernell know?" Cydney's eyes grew large like small saucers and darted toward her aunt and back to Morgan.

"You know you can't hold water," Morgan complained to Brianna. She looked at Cydney. "Of course she knows. My momma and I don't have any secrets."

"Not yet, you don't," Brianna interjected. "I can't wait to go to Bradley."

"I hadn't thought about going to college," Karen said shyly. She was the quiet, plump cousin of the bunch.

"You should go away to school. It's the best way to get away from home," Morgan whispered. She continued to hold court for her cousins.

The family had welcomed the college student home with open arms. By the time the evening was over, Morgan had talked Adrianna into allowing Brianna to spend the rest of the weekend at her house.

Morgan and Noah didn't hook up during the school break due to conflicts in their schedules. Gloria made sure she kept her son busy with church activities the entire time he was home.

The young couple pined for each other. Still they managed to burn minutes on their cells in addition to chatting on the land phones lines. Being apart only deepened their relationship. They shared a joyous reunion when they returned to Bradley.

Morgan's grades were good, as she had predicted. She earned three A's and two B's. Noah received all A's.

Life was good for the couple over the next four years. They fell deeply in love. Both of them eventually realized that love is a give and take and that someone has to compromise sometimes. Eventually, Morgan began going to church with Noah. She didn't attend services every Sunday, but she made sure she went with him at least twice a month and Noah was so proud of her for doing so.

Then Noah and Morgan's love, like Job's life, was severely tested. Morgan still had not shared with Noah the truth regarding the nature of her family's business. That omission hovered over their lives, like a vulture waiting to pounce on a carcass. Morgan sensed correctly that Noah was going to pop the question at the conclusion of college. Guilt from not coming clean with Noah spun Morgan's emotions into a tizzy. Their once golden lives were poised to fall apart like a building demolished by a wrecking ball.

Chapter 16

Time flew by like a thoroughbred horse running the last lap at the Kentucky Derby. The date was April 1, 2006. Morgan had rented an apartment when she returned to Bradley the previous year to begin her third year of college.

She and Noah were scheduled to receive their sheepskins in May. School was almost over and she was slated for her ascension to the family throne in September. Another Foster family edict was that the chosen one go on a long vacation before giving up all rights to a normal life.

The telephone rang. Morgan smiled when Brianna's name appeared on the caller ID. She snatched the receiver from the cradle. "Hey, gurl. What's up?"

"Hi, Morg. I'm frazzled. I feel like I have a million and one things to do before my wedding next month." Instead of attending Bradley University with Morgan, as Brianna had vowed to do, she decided to attend a historically black college. She made Howard University her alma mater instead. She met a young man named Terrence Greer while attending school in D.C. and proclaimed he was the one. Brianna was a brain and had finished college in three and a half years, instead of four. Her young man had proposed last New Year's Eve, and her extravagant fall wedding ceremony was right around the corner.

"I bet you do. Who would have thought you'd get married before me? Remember how jealous of Noah you were during my freshman year of school?"

"Please. Let's not dwell on the past. That happened a million years ago," Brianna scoffed as she eyeballed two samples of purple material for her bridesmaids' shoes. "You have to admit, it was good karma that I met Terrence. Remember how you and I fell out because of a stupid fight about my parents and your mother, and I decided to go to Howard for college instead of Bradley?" the young woman mused.

"What do you need me to do?" Morgan asked as she sat on the floor. Her back was pressed against the sofa. Morgan was going to be Brianna's maid of honor.

"I have a huge favor to ask you. Can you possibly come to Chicago this week so you can get measured for your dress?" Brianna crossed her fingers. She knew she'd waited until the last minute to contact Morgan.

"Sure. I can do that. I need to pay Momma a visit anyway." Morgan nodded her head.

"How is your mother doing?" Brianna nervously twisted the phone cord between her fingers."

"She seems distracted. Momma is busy as usual. I sense she's wracked by tension. Whenever I ask her if anything is wrong, she says no," Morgan confessed anxiously.

"I'm sure Aunt Jernell is fine." Brianna was glad Morgan couldn't see her face. She was sure it was a tell-tale red hue.

"So where do I go to try on the dress?" Morgan asked. She heard the door opening and looked up to see Noah walking inside. She blew him a kiss with her free hand. He winked at her and mouthed, "Hi, beautiful."

"To a boutique on the north side. I'll email you the address.

Sasha, the seamstress, does beautiful work. I need you to do this so I can check that task off my list and try to maintain my sanity. Make sure Sasha shows you a copy of my dress. It's to die for. It's a copy of an original Vera Wang design."

"Then I'm sure it's beautiful," Morgan told her cousin. "What else is new?" Noah squatted down next to Morgan and eased her body away from the sofa and massaged her shoulders.

"Nothing. I've got to run. Someone is calling me." Brianna moved the phone away from her ear and peered at the caller ID. "That's the caterer." She disconnected the call.

Noah pulled Morgan up from the floor into his arms. "Who was that on the telephone?"

"The bride-to-be, who else?" Morgan replied wittily. "I need to enter her on *Bridezillas* on the WE network. Brianna is too much. She's going to drive both of us crazy before her wedding day."

"Oh, you'll survive the wedding. I have confidence in you." Noah kissed the tip of Morgan's nose. She put his arm around her neck.

"Speaking of weddings . . ." Noah reached into his pants pocket.

Morgan pushed his hand away from his pants and jumped up off the couch. She stood up so abruptly that one would have thought a pack of bees were swarming after her. She rushed into the bedroom and shut the door soundly behind her.

Noah rose and sped down the hallway behind Morgan. He knocked on the door and then twisted the doorknob. The door was locked. He waited for Morgan to open the door, but she didn't unlock it immediately. His body rested against the wall. "Morgan, it's okay. I'll understand if you're not ready yet. I'm ready to take the relationship to the next level, and I thought you were too."

There was silence from the bedroom. Noah paced the

length of the hallway and back more than a few times before Morgan finally unlocked the door.

When Noah entered the room, the first thing he noticed was Morgan's reddened eyes. It was obvious she'd been crying.

After many days and nights of soul searching and prayer, Noah had decided to take a position with Caterpillar after he graduated. He'd been offered a position as a structural engineer. Noah hadn't told his parents about his plans yet. Morgan wasn't even aware of his decision. He planned to tell her after he proposed.

Noah walked over to Morgan. She sat on the edge of the bed. "What wrong?" he asked as he knelt on the floor before her, taking Morgan's cold hands in his own. Then he sat on the bed beside her.

Morgan's eyes spewed tears. She looked so solemn. She stood up and walked over to the dresser. Her arms were out-stretched as she said, "Noah, I need to talk to you. There's something I need to tell you." Her teeth chattered as if her body was engulfed in a feverish chill. She kept her face averted from Noah's gaze.

Noah's cell phone rang loudly, shattering the moment. He rose from the bed and pulled the phone out of the case attached to his belt and flipped the phone open. "Hi, Dad. How are you doing?" He paused and staggered backward, nearly falling down. His face blanched white as snow as he fell into the bed. "What did you say, Dad? Okay. I'll be home as soon as I can." He closed the phone, sat heavily on the bed, and covered his eyes.

Morgan stared at Noah. Furrows of worry crisscrossed her forehead. "What happened? What did your dad say?"

Noah licked his lips nervously. His voice broke. "Dad said my mom was in a car accident. She's been hurt badly. It doesn't sound good and he wants me to come home as soon as I can."

"Oh, baby," Morgan exclaimed. She walked over to Noah, sat next to him on the bed and hugged him. "Let's go."

Noah looked at her through deadened, lifeless eyes. He looked terrified. "I can't move. Morgan, I feel paralyzed. I can't imagine life without my mother. I used to call her, 'My Morning Glory' when I was a child." Noah looked like a little boy.

"Let me make some calls. I can get us home in a few hours." Morgan patted Noah's shoulder and stood up. She went into the living room and called Jernell and explained what happened.

"I have a pilot on standby in Peoria. I'll make a call and he'll be ready to fly in half an hour," Jernell said. "I'm sorry to hear the news about Mrs. Stephens. I'll call a limo service to pick you and Noah up from the airfield and transport you to the hospital as soon as possible," Jernell promised.

When Morgan finished the call with her mother and walked back to the bedroom, Noah was still seated on the bed in a state of shock. He sat there frozen while Morgan threw some of their belongings in an overnight case.

Twenty minutes later, the doorbell rang. Morgan flew to the door and told the driver they'd be downstairs in five minutes. She had to help Noah up from the bed. He had shut down emotionally, still shaken by his father's call.

Twenty minutes later, they were airborne in route to Chicago when Noah's cell phone rang again. He took it out of his jacket and stared at it hypnotically, fearing the worse. Morgan took the phone from Noah's shaking hands and answered it.

She peeked at the caller ID. "Hello, Mr. Stephens. No, he's not doing too well. How is Mrs. Stephens doing? We just left Peoria and we should be in Chicago within an hour and a half. We'll come to the hospital as soon we can." She closed the phone and stared at Noah, who stared at her expectantly. His eyes were glazed over.

"It's all right." She took his hand in hers. "Your mother . . . she's, uh . . . still here. He just wants you to hurry and get to the hospital."

An hour later, the plane made its descent to a private airstrip owned by one of Jernell's business associates. Noah stared out the window of the plane until it landed. Jernell had dispatched a limousine to meet them at the airfield. They rushed to the waiting vehicle. Before long, the driver dropped the pair off at the entrance to the University Of Chicago Hospital in Hyde Park.

Noah's gait was unsteady as they walked through the entrance of the hospital. Then, his step picked up when he saw his father waiting near the emergency room. Morgan sat down on one of the plastic chairs in the waiting room, discreetly allowing father and son to talk alone.

Noah could tell by the pain emitting from Samuel's eyes that the prognosis wasn't good for his mother's recovery. The minister hugged his son tightly as if he couldn't bear to let him go.

"She's in cubicle three, son. You need to go see your mother," Samuel told Noah.

"Give me a minute, Dad." Noah walked over to Morgan. She stood up and clasped him to her body tightly.

"Are you going to stay here with me?" he asked Morgan.

"Of course I am. I'll be here as long as you need me. Hurry up and go see your mother. I'll say a prayer for her recovery." Though Morgan's walk with Christ was still in its infant stage, with Noah's gentle probing, the young man had taught her to pray. He started her off with the simple prayer, 'Now I Lay Me Down To Sleep.' Morgan discovered that praying was second nature to Noah. At the conclusion of a school or work day, Noah suggested the couple read the *Daily Word* devotional together. During Morgan's moments of indecisiveness about revealing the truth of her family activity to Noah, she would always remember him saying to her. "Morgan, with God, all things are possible, taken from Matthew 26:19."

Morgan had been trying to convince herself for months that the statement was true and that Noah would accept her, baggage and all, when she decided to bare her soul to him. She certainly hoped the scripture would be applicable for Gloria's recovery. Morgan felt that nothing short of a miracle would do.

"Thank you, Ms. Foster," Noah croaked out. A lone tear trekked down his face. He went back to where his father was standing and the men walked together behind the double doors.

Morgan pulled a tissue from her purse and dabbed at her eyes. Then she walked outside the building and pulled her cell phone out of her purse and called Jernell. Morgan brought her mother up to date on the latest turn of events. "Thanks, Momma, for helping us to get home so quickly."

"I'm glad I was able to help." Jernell kicked off her shoes and spun in her chair at her office, facing the window.

"I think Noah's father took him to see his mother so he could tell her good-bye."

"Do you need me to come there or do anything else?" Jernell asked her daughter. She took off her reading glasses and rubbed the bridge between her eyes.

"No, not right now. I'm not sure what time I'll be home. I'm here for the long haul." Morgan walked a few steps away from the building.

"Okay, call me if you need me to do anything," Jernell said.

"Will do." Morgan disconnected the call, wondering how Noah was doing. She went back inside the building, found a vending machine and bought a cup of coffee. When she returned to her seat, she glanced at the doors to the emer-

gency room, and her hands began shaking. Morgan almost
spilled the coffee. After she drank the strong coffee, she
closed her eyes. *Lord, I'm not real good at this praying stuff.
Sometimes I think I don't sound right when I talk to you through
prayer. I ask that you please lay your healing hands on Mrs. Stephens
today.* "Amen," Morgan whispered.

When Noah walked inside the cubicle, the first thing
he noticed was the whooshing sound of a machine and a
tube connected to the side of his mother's mouth. Her eyes
were closed and she looked near death.

Noah's eyes overflowed with tears and his step faltered.
He brushed tears away with one hand and held on to Samuel's
arm with his other.

There seemed to be a million tubes attached to Gloria's
body. To Noah, they resembled tentacles. The men walked
over to the bed to be closer to Gloria. Samuel stood on one
side of the bed and Noah on the other. Noah groaned and
took Gloria's cold, lifeless hand in his own and patted it over
and over. Samuel caressed his wife's cheek.

Gloria's face was unscathed, but the upper portion of her
body was encased in white bandages, stained with blood.

Noah looked at the respirator. It seemed the machine was
the only thing keeping his mother alive. He felt faint as if all
the air in his body had been turned inside out. The young
man threw himself on the side of the bed and wept uncontrollably.

Samuel cleared his throat loudly and stoically brushed
tears from the corners of his eyes.

"Oh, Mom," Noah groaned aloud. He repeated 'Mom'
over and over as if it were a litany.

Samuel allowed his son time to grieve for his mother. He
walked over to the other side of the bed and patted the top
of Noah's head.

With tear-stained eyes, Noah looked up at his father and whispered hoarsely, "What happened?"

Samuel took a deep breath. "She was driving to church from the grocery store and someone hit her broadside. The accident was bad. Her car was totaled. God help us."

"Has she awakened?" Noah looked up at his father.

"Yes, she did earlier. She asked for you."

Noah began crying again. "Mom, wake up. Please talk to me. Mom, don't leave me. I need you. Mom, I love you so much."

A nurse walked into the room and checked the respirator and the medicinal bags attached to the I-V stand.

She nodded soberly at Samuel and Noah and left the room.

"Is she going to wake up?" Noah asked Samuel as he watched the rise and fall of his mother's chest.

"She might. She had a powerful urge to see you. The doctors don't know everything." Samuel tried to swallow a lump that had risen in his throat. "Only our Father above."

An orderly brought two chairs inside the cubicle and placed them on opposite sides of the bed. Samuel and Noah began their long vigil into the night.

The doctor and nurse were in and out of the room continuously. After consulting with another specialist, the emergency room doctor decided to transfer Gloria to the intensive care unit. While they prepared her for the move, Noah went out to the waiting room to see Morgan.

She jumped up out of her seat, when she saw him come through the double door. "Is your mom all right?" Morgan nervously twisted her hands together.

"She's hanging in there. They're moving her from the emergency room to intensive care. She suffered a lot of internal injuries." Noah and Morgan sat down in the chairs.

"Noah, I'm so sorry. I know how close you and

Mrs. Stephens are. Do you need me to call anyone? Are you hungry?" She clutched his hand tightly.

"No. I don't have an appetite. I don't know how long I'm going to be here. You can go back to school if you need to."

"No." Morgan vehemently pooed-pooed the suggestion and waved her hand in the air. "We have more than enough credits to graduate. I'll stay here until we both go back to Peoria."

"Thanks, Ms. Foster. I appreciate it. I'm going back to check on Mom." Noah stood up.

"Okay," she nodded. "I'll be here."

When Noah returned to the cubicle, only Samuel remained in the room. "Let's stop and get Morgan and head over to the intensive care unit. It's on the other side of the building," the father informed his son.

The men went to get Morgan and then had to wait another half an hour to enter Gloria's room. Samuel and the doctor spoke in hushed tones. Noah impassionedly watched them as he stood outside the glass window to Gloria's room. His heart ached. He figured one didn't have to be a rocket scientist to know that his mother's injuries were life-threatening. The nurse motioned that he could enter the room.

Noah glanced back at his father and the doctor. Samuel was vigorously shaking his head at whatever the doctor was explaining to him as Noah walked inside the room. The nurse explained that he could only stay for fifteen minutes.

"I understand." Noah walked over to the bed. Gloria stirred briefly. She opened her eyes and saw Noah. Her eyelids fluttered and her mouth curved into a smile.

Noah took her hand inside his own and held it tightly as if he were clinging to the side of a life raft. "Mom, don't leave us. Please fight this. Stay with me and Dad. We need you . . ." His voice choked up and words failed him.

Gloria opened her eyes and a lonely tear trickled from her left eye. Her hands fluttered upward. She stroked Noah's cheek. "I love you, son." Her voice sounded weak and reedy.

Noah's eyes widened. He looked outside the glass window and gestured for Samuel to come to the room immediately.

Samuel flew into the room. The doctor followed on his heels.

"Mom, don't talk," Noah begged. "Save your strength." He shook his head rapidly from side to side.

"No," Gloria coughed. "I don't have much time. Noah, I love you more than life itself. Promise me something. Promise me that you'll go into the ministry with your daddy."

Noah nodded mutely.

"Glory." Samuel's voice sounded strangled. "Don't worry about that. We have to concentrate on getting you well." He held his wife's hand tightly in his own.

"I have to say this, Sammy. God knows I love you, and I know the Lord is going to take me home with Him soon. Take care of my baby." Her voice trailed off. She closed her eyes and then opened them again. "Tell Noah about our old lives. He needs to know where we came from. Sammy, I thought I had more time. I wanted to tell him in my own way."

Samuel raised Gloria's hand to his mouth and kissed it. "Don't worry, Glory. I'll take care of it." Tears streamed down Samuel's face.

Noah's gaze traveled over his mother's prone body, as if to memorize her features so that he could pluck them out of his memory bank another day.

Gloria turned to face her son. "Take care of your father. Stay with him and work with . . ." Her body arched up from the bed. Gloria's eyes rolled to the top of her head. Machines began beeping.

Noah looked anguished. Nurses ran into the room.

"No!" Samuel held his hand up. "Don't resuscitate her. Those are her wishes."

Dr. Sherman shook his head. His expression was grim.

"We're going to stay here with my wife until the end," Samuel vowed.

Gloria looked at Samuel and Noah one more time, and she smiled. Then she turned, expelled a long sigh, and was gone.

Noah swore that later he could feel her spirit leaving him and his father behind. He dropped Gloria's hand and clutched his midsection. Noah howled, "Mom!" He sobbed aloud.

Samuel walked over to his son and gathered him in his arms. Then with a quiet dignity, he asked the doctor, "Can we stay with her a little while longer?"

The doctor nodded. "Give us a few minutes to straighten up in here. Come back in ten minutes or so. Is there anyone we can call for you? We have a chaplain on-site."

Samuel replied, "No, we're fine. I can take it from here." He turned and attended to Noah, who refused to leave his mother's side. Samuel took his son's hand like he was a toddler and led him back to the waiting room.

When Morgan saw Noah and Samuel's slumped shoulders, she knew the worst had happened. She jogged over to Noah and grabbed him by the waist. "Baby, I'm so sorry." Noah continued to sob. Morgan choked up and cried with Noah.

Samuel led the young people to a row of seats near the back of the waiting room. He and Morgan managed to get Noah to sit down. The young man rocked in his seat. His grief was a terrible sight to behold.

Noah's face was red and his eyes had shrunk into slits

from crying. Noah's voice was hoarse. His hands shook. He looked drained from sorrow.

The young man and Morgan sat welded together until Dr. Sherman came to the waiting room and told them they could go back to Gloria's room.

Morgan hadn't ever experienced the death of a loved one. Her stomach felt squeamish. She squared her shoulders as Noah leaned on her.

After they walked into the room, Morgan's eyes flew to Gloria's body. She sighed inwardly with relief. Gloria looked at if she were asleep. Noah stood between Morgan and Samuel, and they walked over to the bed. They gazed at Gloria quietly. Samuel smoothed her hair down.

"I have to believe she's in a better place. Away from pain, trouble, and strife. She's in our Father's house. I'll see you in the morning, Glory." Samuel bent and kissed his wife's cheek. "I'm going to make some calls. I'll be back shortly."

Morgan nodded.

Noah was in a place where nothing and nobody mattered except his Morning Glory. He didn't know how he was going to keep living without his mother. Words from a song, "Earth has No Sorrow that Heaven Cannot Heal", slipped into his mind. A wave of sadness seized his body. He bowed his head and cried on Morgan's shoulder. Her heart ached for Noah. She stroked his arm and sobbed along with him.

Chapter 17

Gloria Jean Stephens's untimely passing was a difficult time for her son and husband as Morgan had expected it to be. Morgan called her mother around two o'clock in the morning, nearly eight hours after Gloria was admitted to the hospital. The young woman asked her mother to send Harry to the hospital to transport Noah, Samuel, and herself home.

Morgan wanted to stay at the Stephensses' house and hold Noah in her arms the rest of the night. She longed to hold his body close to her own and kiss away his tears—anything humanly possible to alleviate his pain. Morgan was aware that Samuel was a minister and wouldn't approve of her being with his son anywhere near a bed.

Noah and Morgan had been living together in her apartment for the past school year. They hadn't consummated the relationship, although both were sorely tempted at times. Noah was adamant that when the couple came together that they would be husband and wife. As far as Samuel and Gloria knew, their son still resided on campus in a dormitory. Noah knew he could only get away with his parents not knowing the truth of his living arrangement because of cell phone technology. They could always get in touch with their son when they dialed that number.

Noah spent the remainder of the week after his mother's death with a dazed, confused expression on his face. He found himself looking at the doorway to the kitchen, Gloria's favorite room in the house, as if he expected his mother to walk into the room and he could wake up from the bad dream his life had suddenly become.

To cope with his grief, Samuel threw himself into preparing Gloria's funeral arrangements, leaving Morgan to deal with Noah's sorrow as best as she could

It rained cats and dogs the day of Gloria's home-going services, which Samuel scheduled on the Saturday morning following her death. When Noah awakened that morning, he thought, *The sky is crying. It's dark and gray like I am.*

Jernell, Brianna, and the rest of the Foster clan sat en masse on the rows of seats behind the immediate family. Morgan's father flew in from Cleveland to support Noah.

Rico's flight was delayed due to the weather. He arrived at the church at the end of the wake. The pulpit and aisles of the church were filled with beautiful floral arrangements of roses, lilies, and mums as well as loving testaments to the first lady of the church.

The line of people ahead of Rico moved quickly to view Gloria's body. And a few minutes later, Rico was almost at the head of the line. He walked over to the front row of folding chairs where he shook Noah's hand and hugged Morgan. Rico thought, *It's a shame Noah had to bear such misery.* He inched closer to the plain wooden coffin. A bleeding heart arrangement made of red and white roses laid on the closed portion of the casket.

When Rico saw Gloria's face, his mouth dropped and his face became pale. Morgan didn't miss her father's shaken expression and neither did Samuel. The minister was seated on the pulpit. Noah missed the byplay. He was distracted as he accepted condolences from the mourners.

Rico stood for a minute next to the casket and tried to compose himself. Then he walked to the back of the church and sat down heavily on the seat. He broke out into a cold sweat, pulled his handkerchief out of his jacket pocket and mopped his brow.

Morgan twisted her head and looked back at her father, wondering why he had such an unusual reaction to Noah's mother. The Fosters were acquainted with Noah's parents, but Rico hadn't been introduced to them yet.

After all the mourners had viewed Gloria's body and returned to their seats, the morticians closed the casket. Gloria's funeral began.

Samuel's associate pastor, Reverend Smith, opened the service by reading First Corinthians 15:51-2 verses. He read, "Behold, I will shew you a mystery. We shall not all sleep, but we shall all be changed. In a moment, in a twinkling of an eye, at the last trump: for the trumpet shall sound, and the dead shall be raised incorrigible, and we shall be changed. May the Lord have a blessing on the reading of His word. Father God, I come to you this morning, asking you to begin the healing process for the Stephens family. Touch Samuel and Noah's hearts, for they know that our first lady has just transitioned to the next step. She has traveled on the road that we all have to go down one day. Help Pastor Stephens, his son, and our church to be strong in the days that lie ahead. Let the church say, amen." The mourners responded accordingly.

The white collared, royal blue robed choir of about twenty members stood when the organist nodded at them. They sang A and B selections, "Peace Be Still" and "Walk With Me Lord." The small church was packed to the hilt.

The abundance of love for Gloria was evident as each person stood on the dais and spoke her praises.

Suddenly, there was a loud outburst from the rear of the church. The ushers tried to quiet a group of people who'd just walked into the church.

Noah turned his head and looked over his shoulder with a concerned look on his face.

An older, heavy-set, dark-skinned woman wearing blue jeans and a red tattered sweater beneath a black leather jacket stumbled up the aisle. She tottered to the casket with outstretched arms. A motley crew of people followed her and they began wailing Gloria's name. Noah rose from his seat and looked at his father questioningly.

The woman stood in front of the casket and rubbed the outside of it. "My, baby" She turned and faced the congregation. "That's my baby in there. Gloria Jean." She fell on to the top of the coffin and began sobbing profusely.

Samuel streaked from the pulpit and attempted to remove the woman and the other people. He whispered to the woman, "Susie, this is not the time or place. Don't do this today. Can you respect my wishes and your grandson's?"

The associate minister walked down from the pulpit to assist Samuel. "We're in the middle of a service. Would you please have a seat so we can proceed?" he asked the unruly crowd.

"But that's my daughter. I loved my Gloria." Susie Jones slid to the floor. Samuel helped her up, and he and Reverend Smith escorted the group to the foyer of the building.

The choir director rose from her chair and motioned the choir to stand and sing another song.

Noah's face whitened like he'd seen a ghost. He sat back down in his seat and stared questioningly toward the back of the church. Morgan reached over and pressed his arm. She whispered in his ear, "Let your dad handle this situation."

"But she said that she, she was my grandmother. My mother said her mom and dad had passed and that she was an only child." The mortified young man kept turning toward the back of the sanctuary. He wanted to get up out of his seat and see the people up close and personal.

"Why can't I sit up there with your son?" Susie cried to Samuel. The stench of alcohol stung the minister's nostrils. "That's my baby up there. I'm part of this family. We should all be sitting up there in the front."

"It's too late to have everyone move to other seats. The service has already started. Please sit back here, Susie. Would you do that for Gloria?"

Reverend Smith talked to the usher, who requested the people on the next to last row give their seat to Gloria's long-lost relatives. As fate would have it, they were seated across from Rico. He kept his face averted from the Jones family.

By the time Samuel returned to the pulpit, the choir was finishing the third musical number. Samuel walked to the microphone, adjusted it, and said, "Amen. I apologize for the interruption. The service will proceed as noted in your program."

The funeral continued without incident. Rico scurried out of the church at the conclusion of the service. The mourners left the church and returned to their cars, slowly following the black hearse carrying Gloria's body as it traveled to her final resting place: Evergreen Park Cemetery.

By the time the crowd returned to the church for the repast, it was two o'clock in the afternoon. The sisters of the church had already set out the food. When Samuel went into the basement, he saw Gloria's family sitting at the head table, much to his dismay. They'd begun eating before the rest of the people were served.

"I tried to get them to wait for everyone else," Sister

Barnes whispered to Samuel. "There wasn't anything I could do."

Susie wiped her hands on her pants and walked over to Samuel. "You put my gal away real good, Sammy. It looks like you and Gloria did well for yourself. I want to meet my grandson. He's all I have left of my baby now."

"Susie, why don't you come to our house one day this week?" Samuel suggested tactfully. "How about you visit us tomorrow or the next day? This has been a trying time for both myself and Noah."

"There he is," Susie said. She left Samuel and walked over to Noah, who was standing with Morgan. Susie took Noah's face in her hands. "You look just like my girl. Boy, I'm your grandmother, Susie Jones." She threw her arms around his neck and nearly smothered him with her fervent hug. Noah almost gagged from the loud floral perfume that didn't quite mask her musty body odor and the smell of booze.

"Are you hungry?" Susie asked Noah. "I can fix you a plate." She turned away from him, and spied Rico out the corner of her eyes. "Rico Daniels, is that you?" Susie yelled. Her eyes bucked wildly, and she reared back on her heels. "It's like old home week up in here. Rico don't act like you don't know me." Rico had tried to slip back into the church after he returned from the cemetery unnoticed by the Jones. Being around them brought back unpleasant memories. He was unsuccessful in his attempts to avoid them.

Rico turned and walked toward the loud woman. "Er, hi, Susie."

"Boy, give me a hug. It's been years since I seen you." She stepped back and looked at him from head to toe and then the older woman threw herself into Rico's arms. "My poor baby is dead. I read about it in the paper. I bet Sammy gonna get a lot of money from that accident. And I bet that Gloria had insurance. Sammy gonna get paid."

Noah looked at Morgan. She shrugged her shoulders helplessly. They walked away from Susie and went to sit at an empty table.

Susie hadn't noticed that her grandson had left. She continued talking to Rico. "I guess you heard about Gloria, too. Huh? Y'all stayed in contact all this time? That was nice, Rico. You always looked out for my girls." Susie sniffled as she clutched Rico's arm.

"This whole scene is so unbelievable," Noah whispered to Morgan. "There's a set of my relatives here that I haven't met until today—the same day we buried my mother." He loosened his tie. "I need to go outside for a minute and get some air." Morgan and Noah stood up and walked outdoors.

Samuel sat at one of the tables drinking coffee. He watched Rico converse with Susie.

Rico had never been more embarrassed in his life. Gloria's mother was a loose canon, and there was no telling what might come out of her mouth. "We can play catch up another time, Susie. Today is Gloria's day."

"Say, did you ever get married to that stuck-up Foster girl?" Susie asked Rico. "That was the best move you ever made in your life, hooking up with her and her money. It got you out the ghetto. I always told Josephine that she should have stuck with you and how you were going places."

Rico shook his head. "Josie and I had crushes on each other when we were ten years old. How is she doing?"

"The drugs got her. She been dead for nigh on five years," Susie said in a quaking voice. "Two of my girls is already gone." She rubbed her nearly dry eyes.

"I heard them Fosters rolling in dough. You done good, Rico."

"Look, Susie, I've got to go." Rico turned away from the older woman. "We'll, talk again soon." He sped off, looking around the room for Morgan and Noah. *I have some explaining to do*, he thought.

Rico headed over to Samuel's table to offer his condolences. Susie stood up and went to the kitchen area, where she got another chicken leg to eat. It was her fifth piece of chicken. Then she returned to her family, sat down, and finished eating. When she pointed toward Rico, the Jones family looked his way and waved.

Rico decided to introduce himself to Samuel after he couldn't find Morgan and Noah. He sat across the table from Samuel and held out his hand. "I don't believe that we've met. I'm Morgan's father, Rico Daniels. I'd like to offer my sympathy for your loss."

"Thank you," Samuel murmured, swallowing hard. "I thought you recognized my wife when you went to view her body. And I would have known you were Morgan's father because she looks just like you."

"Yes, I recognized Gloria and I was shocked." Rico still looked stunned. "She and I grew up on the same block. Gloria was like a little sister to me. I'm sure you can see from her family's behavior that she didn't have an easy life growing up."

"My wife and I didn't keep any secrets from each other," Samuel commented. He took another sip of coffee. His hand trembled as he sat the cup down on the table.

One of the sisters of the church walked over to Samuel. "Can I get you anything to eat, Pastor? I know you must be hungry."

"I'm fine, Martha. I'll eat something later," Samuel replied.

"If you change your mind, just let me know."

"I will."

She walked back to the serving table.

"Like I was saying, Mr. Daniels . . . ," Samuel continued his conversation with Morgan's father.

"Please call me Rico," Morgan's father quickly interjected.

"My wife and I didn't keep any secrets from each other. I knew about her family. Gloria chose to keep that part of her life a secret from Noah. I begged her to tell him the truth about her background. Secrets always seem to rear their heads at the wrong time. But it will be okay. I'll explain to Noah about his mother's life."

"I understand completely where you're coming from. There are parts of my life I'm not proud of that I'd like to keep hidden myself," Rico commented dryly.

"That's true of all of us, even we men of the cloth sometimes," Samuel said feebly. He closed his eyes for a moment and massaged his eyelids. "It's been a long day. I plan to stay a little while longer and then Noah and I are going home. Morgan is a wonderful girl. I know you're proud of her."

"That I am." Rico stood up, sensing the minister had run out of steam. Samuel suddenly looked tired and sad.

"I'm sure we'll see each other again." Rico thrust his hand toward Samuel.

"No doubt."

Rico passed Susie's table. She waved. "Come by and see us sometime, Rico. We live in the same area."

Rico nodded. He walked over to Morgan and Noah, who'd returned from outside. He sat at his daughter's side. "I'm going to cut out, Morgan. I'll be in town until Monday evening. I'll call you and we can meet up."

"Sure, Daddy. So you know Noah's maternal family?" Morgan gazed at Rico so strongly that her eyes seemed to pierce his body.

"Yes, I grew up on the same block as your mother, Noah. It's a small world." He rose from the seat, "I'll see you two later." Rico departed after kissing his daughter on the cheek, and patting Noah's shoulder.

"What a strange, long day this has been," Noah said. He looked over at Samuel. "I wonder if Dad is ready to go home. I just want to stretch out on my bed and close my eyes for a few hours."

Morgan laid her hand on Noah's back and rubbed consolingly. "You're almost done here. Why don't I go ask your dad if he's ready to go?"

"Thanks, lady." He watched her sashay over to Samuel. She bent over and whispered in Samuel's ear that she and Noah were leaving, then she strolled back to Noah.

"He's not quite ready yet. I told him that we'll see him later at the house."

Noah stood and looked around the room. He took Morgan's hand and they walked outside to the waiting limousine. Morgan's body quivered from the tension of the day. She sensed that Samuel and Noah would have a long father-son talk that night, due to Gloria's relatives' appearance that day.

Chapter 18

Several hours later, Morgan closed the door to Noah's bedroom after checking on him one more time. She'd just finished washing dishes and stacking them in the drainer. Samuel walked out of his bedroom.

"I'm going home now, Reverend Sam. I know you need time alone with Noah." She put the dishtowel on the rack and picked her purse up off the kitchen table. She looked at Samuel sympathetically.

"Thanks for all your help today, Morgan." Though Samuel was close to Morgan's father's age, today he looked wizened, like he'd aged twenty years since Gloria's death.

"Tell Noah that I'll call him later. We plan to go back to school either Tuesday or Wednesday; whenever he's ready." She walked to Samuel and kissed his cheek.

Samuel walked Morgan to her car and came back inside the house. He felt suffocated with grief. The tiny house was a reflection of life with Gloria. He turned off the light in the kitchen. He then went into the living room, sat on the sofa, and opened his Bible.

He fell asleep and later awakened to Noah's gentle touch

on his arm. "Hmm. Did I fall asleep?" Noah sat on the sofa beside his father. Samuel asked, "How you holding up, son?"

"I feel numb. I keep expecting Mom to come out of the kitchen and tell us dinner is ready. Or listen to her singing hymns while she's doing her chores." Noah put his hands over his face and wept.

"I know what you mean, Noah. I feel the same way too. Gloria was a good woman. The Lord wanted her on His right side, and it was much too soon for us."

The men sat in silence. Noah turned to his father. He licked his lips and asked hesitantly, "So who were those people at the funeral today?"

"Those are your mother's people: her mother, Susie, and her sisters, Lawanda, and Phyllis. She had an older sister named Josephine. I don't know where she was today. The men with them were Gloria's brothers, Norman and Vincent."

"So how come I didn't know about them until today?" Noah queried his father. "I don't understand."

"You know that your mother didn't like to talk much about her past. I begged her from time to time to tell you about her upbringing. It seems to me when people try to hide from their past, it always has a way of resurfacing. The Joneses were a rough bunch. They drank heavily and sold and used drugs. They were gangbangers, even the girls."

Noah looked horrified. His eyebrows rose and his forehead wrinkled. "Are you trying to tell me that my mother was involved in stuff like that?" He shook his head vigorously from side to side.

Samuel sighed heavily. "Yes, but not all of it, and not just your mother. I was too. When Gloria and I were teenagers, we both did things we weren't proud of. We got into trouble and had criminal records. We had the same parole officer and that's how we met."

"You broke the law?" Noah shied away from his father.

His body sagged against the back of the couch. His eyes radiated specks of pain.

Samuel nodded and reached out to pat his son's arm. "Gloria was convicted of shoplifting and I was guilty of grand theft auto. They were our first offenses, and, by the grace of God, we were paroled and only had to do community service work."

"I don't believe this." Noah jumped off the sofa. He turned to face Samuel and stared accusingly at his father.

"Why don't we talk about this another time?" Samuel suggested, holding his hands out entreatingly to the young man. "Today might be just a little too emotional for this talk."

"No. I want to discuss it right now." Noah's voice seemed to drip with venom.

"Okay. Whatever you want." Samuel held up his hands in surrender. "Son, why don't you sit back down?"

Noah sat on the chair across from the sofa. He folded his arms across his chest and glared at his father.

"Gloria and I did our community service at a Baptist church. We did menial chores like sweeping and cleaning up the place. The minister always took time to talk to your mother and me about religion and how God forgives all sins. A year later he baptized us both. We eventually found low-paying jobs, but we still attended services at the church. The minister married us. Then the Lord blessed us with you five years later. When you were two years old, the Lord called me into service, and I've been serving my God since then."

"That's all well and good, Dad, but why didn't you and Mom tell me about your families and your backgrounds?" The people Noah had met today left a sour taste in his mouth.

"Your mother wanted you to make something of yourself and she knew that would be impossible around her family. There was always some drama with them as she explained to me later. She decided your extended family would be the members of the church. And she wasn't so wrong, was she?" Samuel shifted his weight and settled more comfortably on the sofa.

"What about your family, Dad? Should I expect any other relatives to fall out of the woodwork?" Noah asked sarcastically. He'd never spoken to Samuel in that tone before.

"No. My mother only had one child, me, and she died after I was arrested." Samuel's voice broke. "I began hanging in the street when I was thirteen years old, hustling for a living."

Noah rubbed the top of his head. "What you're telling me is unbelievable. You and Mom had a whole other life and didn't say a word to me about it."

"We were wrong; I admit it. But not telling you doesn't mean Gloria and I didn't love you. Your mother loved you more than anybody in the world. She turned her life around. We both did, and I'm not ashamed of our past. Son, please come back over here and sit on the couch with me." Samuel pleaded with his son.

Noah reluctantly rose from the chair and sat on the sofa a few feet away from his father.

"I'm sorry you had to learn of your relatives the way you did. It didn't occur to me that they would show up today. But don't discount the good deeds your mother has done." Tears filled Samuel's eyes. "I don't know how I'm going to make it without her. I've been with Gloria almost thirty years."

Noah's heart felt heavy. Though his father presented a strong front for him, Noah knew he was suffering. He knew his mother would want him to try and move past what he'd learned today and be there for his father. Noah moved closer to his father and the men cried together for the beautiful, unconventionally special woman they'd lost.

* * *

Morgan returned home to an empty house. Jernell wasn't at home and Lucinda was spending the weekend with her relatives.

The young woman changed into a pair of jeans and a top. When she finished, she called her father. After they exchanged greetings, Morgan, took the bull by the horns and asked her father, "Daddy, just how well did you know Noah's mother?"

"Quite well. Gloria was like a little sister to me," Rico replied. "I was shocked to learn she was Noah's mother."

"I'm sure you were, and the expression on your face showed just how surprised you were," Morgan murmured. "Mrs. Stephens was a nice woman. It's hard for me to associate her with those people at the church today. I guess she had an unusual past. She came off as very conservative."

"Gloria had a rough life. She's a true testament to how people can change, Morgan, despite adverse beginnings. And from what I can see, Gloria did. Even you can turn your life around, baby girl. It's not too late. God doesn't have a timetable as to when people should make a change."

"Daddy, don't change the subject." Morgan had a false tone of bravado in her voice. "Let's not go there. My future is set."

"Anyway, I was floored to see that Gloria was married to a minister, your boyfriend's father. It's a small world."

"That it is," Morgan seconded. "Poor Noah," she sighed. "I hope he can get through this. He was so close to his mom."

"His father seemed strong, so I know Noah will be fine in time. So are you ready for graduation and what's going to happen after that?" Rico asked.

"Of course I am. I've been working with Momma since my sophomore year of high school, at least going over some of the accounts. I'm amazed by how much money she's accumulated over the years."

"Have you talked to Noah yet about the business? What does he plan to do after school?"

"I was trying to tell him when Reverend Samuel called to say Mrs. Stephens had been injured. I really don't know what I was going to say to him. Though he hasn't said anything about it, I know Noah really wants to stay in Peoria and work for Caterpillar. They made him a good offer. But that may change with his mother's passing."

"That would be a problem for you, wouldn't it?" Rico asked his daughter gently.

"Well, his plans aren't definite. I know he's going to propose to me and I know before he does that I need to tell him the truth about the family or break things off."

"Can you really walk away from your relationship?" Rico asked. He hoped his daughter wouldn't do that. He figured Noah would be his daughter's last shot at a normal life. That was assuming Jernell would let her go. His stomach careened upside down at the thought of Jernell refusing to do so.

"I've spent many sleepless nights trying to figure out what I'll do if it comes to that. I pray that I won't have to." Morgan closed her eyes as if in prayer and then opened them.

"So Noah isn't going to follow his father's footsteps and become a minister?" Rico asked curiously.

"Well, he hasn't really said anything about it," Morgan admitted. "I'm 100 percent sure that he would have said something to me if he decided to go that route."

"Do you think his mother's death might push him towards the ministry?" Rico couldn't resist asking his daughter. That question had been haunting Morgan's mind since the day Samuel called with the bad news about Gloria.

"That's definitely a possibility. I can't lie to you, Daddy. He was so close to his mother and I know they talked before she passed, although Noah hasn't said a lot about it. We also haven't had a chance to spend a lot of time alone since we've been home."

"I hope everything works out for you, baby girl," Rico murmured softly. "Noah is a good man. You two were lucky to have met each other."

"Yeah," Morgan smiled. "If his father's car hadn't over-heated on the way to Peoria, who knows whether we would have hooked up or not? I've got to go, Daddy. Brianna is going to stop by soon to talk about the wedding. Call me next week."

"Sure, I will," Rico promised. "Tell Noah he's in my thoughts and prayers."

"I will. Bye, Daddy." Morgan hung up the telephone. She looked up as Jernell walked into the room and sat on the gold chaise. "Mom, when did you get home?" Morgan asked.

"Not too long ago. I heard you on the telephone and waited until you finished your call. I really like what you've done to your space," Jernell remarked, looking around the room.

Morgan had redecorated the loft area after her twenty-first birthday last year. It was now the apartment of a young lady instead of a girl. She purchased new bedroom furniture, and asked Jernell to install a kitchen area in the loft-like space. In addition, Morgan bought a brown leather couch and love seat and marble cocktail and end tables.

"How are you doing, Morgan?" Jernell noticed circles around Morgan's eyes. To her mother, Morgan looked like she was wrestling with a huge dilemma. Jernell could fully sympathize with her child.

"I'm okay, Mom. I just finished talking to Daddy. You and the family left the service early. Noah's relatives on his mother's side put in an appearance. Guess what? They knew Daddy."

"Is that so?" Jernell asked, leaning forward on her seat. She'd crossed her shapely legs comfortably.

"Yes. Did or do you know them? Mrs. Stephens's maiden name was Jones. Daddy said they grew up on the same block."

Jernell closed her eyes, trying to place the name. "Yes, I remember a family named Jones." Jernell opened her eyes and Morgan noted the surprised look on her mother's face.

"They aren't people you do business with, are they?" Morgan asked timidly. She held her breath waiting for Jernell's answer.

Jernell thought carefully about how to respond to Morgan's question. How easy it would be to lie to her daughter and allow her to continue living her fairy tale existence just a little longer. On the other hand, Jernell cursed herself for not grooming her sooner on that aspect of the business. Her conscience wrestled with her. Morgan was a big girl now, and it wouldn't hurt for to be aware of the pitfalls associated with being the head of the family. Jernell felt it was a curse, and burden most of the time. She knew she had to be sure Morgan was capable of handling the responsibility before she handed the reins of the business over to her.

"Uh, Momma, did you hear me?" Morgan asked Jernell again.

"Yes. I have done business with the Jones family in the past. But not for a long time. More than likely they may have gotten product from me, but I don't deal with dealers directly." Jernell stared at Morgan, trying to gauge her reaction.

Morgan's face dropped. She looked up at her mother. "Do they know you?"

"There's a good possibility they do. I'm sure they've heard of me. I didn't associate with many people back in the day. Not everyone is privy to my actual function within the business, they just knew me as Big Momma's daughter."

Morgan sighed audibly. She hadn't yet assumed her role as overseer, and complications had already arisen.

"Graduation is around the corner. Next month right? You don't officially start taking over the company until the beginning of next year. I wanted to see what you thought about me booking a European cruise for you as your graduation gift, and if I should make reservations for two. You have talked to Noah, haven't you?" Jernell's eyes seemed to penetrate her daughter's like sharpened stiletto knives. Morgan looked away.

"I was going to tell him the day his mother died. I'll talk to him when we go back to school." Morgan's stomach ached like it was tied in knots. "I'll let you know next week about the cruise."

"No rush. But you need to take care of your business soon."

"I will, Momma."

Jernell stood up. "I have some business to handle myself. I'll talk to you later." She walked over to Morgan and patted her arm. "Don't worry so much, everything will work out the way it should."

Morgan nodded feebly. After Jernell departed, Morgan lay on the bed, with one hand flung over her closed eyes. Thoughts danced in her head about why life had to be so difficult. She knew Noah was upright and moral and she wasn't sure if he'd accept her family's lifestyle. Morgan chewed her fingernails as she wondered if Gloria had spoken to Noah about going into the ministry before she passed. The young woman felt like she was being torn into two parts. One part of her couldn't let her mother down, and the other part of her didn't want to lose Noah. She wondered if love really conquered all obstacles, as she nibbled on her lower lip, with worry. She closed her eyes. Inside her head, she silently asked the Lord to help her with her dilemma.

Chapter 19

Morgan and Noah's graduation was scheduled a week and a half away, on a Sunday afternoon in mid-May. Morgan called her mother after she returned to the campus from Gloria's funeral and asked her to hold off making reservations for the cruise. Brianna's wedding was about a month away. The young woman was head-over-heels in love with her fiancé. He was the sole topic of Brianna's conversations. She had become a nervous wreck trying to tie up loose ends for the wedding. Though she and Morgan remained close, each woman was immersed in her own life.

When Morgan returned to the apartment after her last and final class, she checked the answering machine. There weren't any messages awaiting her attention.

She went into the bedroom and changed into a pair of denim cut-off shorts and a midriff shirt. The day was unseasonably warm for May. She poured herself a glass of lemonade and took it outside to drink on the patio. The warm breeze ruffled the ends of Morgan's hair. She pushed her bangs off her forehead and put the glass to her forehead as she tried to cool off.

She and Noah were stuck in an impasse. A week after they returned to Peoria following Gloria's death, Noah informed Morgan that he planned to join his father in the ministry. The couple went round and round with the issue, which led to their first major disagreement. They still hadn't found a way to return to the warm intimacy they'd shared before Gloria passed away.

Noah entered the apartment twenty minutes after Morgan did. He saw Morgan sitting on the patio and waved to her. She returned the gesture anemically.

She continued to sit under the umbrella table. Noah joined her several minutes later after he changed into a pair of shorts and a sleeveless T-shirt. Noah sat in the chair opposite Morgan's. He took in her serene face.

As she gazed upon Noah, Morgan thought, *He's no longer the slender man/child I met four years ago.* Morgan's breath stopped for a minute from loving and fearing Noah.

"I'm surprised you're out here and not inside with the air conditioner on," Noah remarked. He fanned himself with his hand.

"Sometimes fresh air is good for you. We sit in air-conditioned rooms all day long," Morgan replied. She kicked her sandals off.

Noah lifted his hand and gently pulled Morgan's face toward his own. He smiled at her. "I'm not going to give up on you or our relationship, Morgan."

"I'll never give up on you either. But I'm not sure I'm cut out to be a minister's wife," she replied sadly.

Noah took her hand in his and kissed it. Morgan began sobbing and drew away from him. Noah pulled her body out of the chair and onto his lap. "Shh. We can do this if you'd only give us a chance."

Morgan felt overwhelmed, like her being was being pulled into two pieces. When Noah announced his intention to join Samuel at the church, she had felt that was the end of their relationship. Morgan felt she had no other choice except to end the relationship. She thought it would be kinder to let Noah assume it was because of his decision to join the clergy.

"If only it were that easy," Morgan wailed. "Noah let, me go. I can't be a minister's wife. I just can't do it." She pounded on his chest.

Noah held her in his arms and caressed her hair while she bawled like a baby. After the emotional tempest passed, Morgan's eyes were puffy and she looked bereft; like she was lost in a maze and couldn't find her way out.

Then Noah surprised Morgan and said, "What if I don't go into the ministry? We could stay here in Peoria and make a life together. What do you think about that, lady?"

Morgan's heart rate accelerated uncontrollably inside her chest. She covered her face with her hands and began crying anew. "Oh, Noah, I love you so much. I should have told you something a long time ago. I was hoping to spare you."

Noah continued stroking her hair. He paused. "Told me what?"

Morgan stood on weak, shaking legs. "We need to talk inside." Noah rose from his seat and followed her inside the apartment.

The two young people sat down silently beside each other on the sofa in the living room. Noah was bewildered. He'd never seen Morgan look so grave, and it made him feel nervous. "What is it, Morgan? You're not sick or something are you?" he asked her solemnly. "I know there's not another man in the picture. Is there? You haven't been yourself since we came back from Chicago."

"Oh, if only it were that simple . . . ," Morgan groaned. Her eyes were dilated with tears. "Please don't hate me, Noah. I can live the rest of my life with us not being together. But I just don't want you to hate me."

"Aw, woman, there's nothing you say or do that would

ever make me hate you. I'm in this relationship forever and a day. I love you, Morgan. I've told you that at least a million times and there's nothing or nobody in this world that can change that."

Morgan sobbed softly. She rocked back and forth in her seat. *I need to find the words to tell him the truth. Do I have the strength to do this? I love Noah so much. He's my soul mate. On the other hand, I want to do the right thing by my mother. I feel so conflicted. God, I don't know what to do. Please help me.*

Noah's expression became sober. He realized that whatever Morgan had to say to him was dire. Maybe she was dying or something of that nature. That was the only reason he could think of to justify her strange behavior.

Morgan moistened her lips. They felt dry as a wasteland. She moaned and then said almost inaudibly, "Noah I haven't been totally honest with you about my family."

"What haven't you been honest with me about?"

Lord please don't let him leave me. Make him understand. I couldn't stand living without Noah in my life. Please God, if you're listening to me right now, please let Noah stay with me. "My mother's business isn't really an export or import one. She's a distributor," Morgan gulped. Beads of moisture gathered on her brow.

"And what does she distribute?" Noah asked forcefully. He sat up erect in his seat, hoping Morgan wasn't going to say what he suspected she would.

"Drugs . . ." Morgan whispered. "My family distributes drugs." She clasped her shaking, sweaty palms together.

Noah looked at Morgan puzzled, like she was speaking a language he didn't understand. Her voice seemed to come from a far-off place. "Drugs?" he repeated.

Morgan nodded.

Understanding dawned in Noah's eyes as they widened in astonishment.

Morgan felt paralyzed with fear. Her hands and legs felt heavy and numb. She nodded her head and tried to answer Noah's question. "Yes, drugs as in cocaine, heroin, and others I probably don't know of. You name it and we distribute it."

Noah jumped up from the sofa like his pants were on fire. He stumbled over to Morgan who sat inertly like she was a statue. He pushed the cocktail table away from the sofa and dropped to his knees on the floor before her. "That's crazy. Your mother wouldn't do anything like . . . No. Morgan, please tell me that what you're saying isn't true. That's not the business you're planning to take over from your mother?"

Morgan nodded her head jerkily like she was a marionette on a string. "Yes, I am," she said in a low tone of voice. "I don't have a choice. It's my legacy. Just like yours is working alongside your father."

Noah took Morgan's ice-cold, trembling hands in his. "No, baby. You don't want to do that. You can't. It would be against everything we believe in. We've talked many times as we watched the news together about how drugs have destroyed our communities, and our people. You wouldn't do anything to perpetrate that injustice. You don't have it in you." As Noah reminisced about those conversations, he remembered how he was the one railing against the influence of drugs, especially in economically-challenged Englewood, and how Morgan would become strangely silent, or find a chore that needed to be done immediately.

"Noah, I'm my mother's daughter. Momma has been grooming me to take the reins from her my entire life. Like you, I have to follow the life she has carved out for me."

Noah looked at Morgan, and she could feel disapproval emit from his body like a blast of chilly air. "You mean this is something you want to do? Please tell me this isn't what you want. I know you couldn't. Morgan, we can start a new life together. Don't do it, baby, I beg you."

"We can't, love." Morgan shook her head. "What would happen to your father? All he has is you. There's nothing we can do about the hand fate has dealt us, except follow our destinies."

Noah stood up clumsily. He grabbed Morgan's arms and lifted her up from the sofa. He felt an urge to shake Morgan like a rag doll until she came to her senses. He blinked his eyes rapidly as if he didn't recognize the woman standing before him, but his heart told him that it was his Morgan, the woman he'd fallen deeply in love with over the past four years. Morgan had listened to his hopes and dreams and encouraged him when he felt weak and couldn't go on. She had his back when his mother died. She had lovingly comforted him when he told her how awful he felt about his mother's relatives and Gloria and Samuel keeping secrets from him. And now she had betrayed him in the worst way by revealing that she was poised to take over a drug empire.

Noah felt like his world had been flipped upside down multiple times. "Do you realize the ramifications of what you're about to do, Morgan? If you were caught, then you'd spend the rest of your life in prison. Don't you think the price is too high? Is distributing drugs worth throwing your life away? Distributing drugs is not your God-given destiny."

Morgan reached out and caressed Noah's face. She babbled, "No, you don't understand how it works. I would never be in a position to take a fall. My mother told me that she has procedures in place to deal with those kinds of situations. The business has been in existence for many years, and it's like a well oiled machine."

"You sound like you've been brainwashed. Is this what you learned from your mother all these years? Morgan, what your family does is morally wrong." Noah pulled away from her grasping hands.

"It doesn't have to be that way, Noah. We do good things with the money too. My family contributes to many charitable organizations. We could rule Chicago, you and I." Even as she said the words, Morgan knew there was no way in the world Noah was going to agree or see the situation her way. What she feared most in the world was coming to pass.

"I can't do it, Morgan. I'd rather work with my father in that little storefront church than work with you or even associate with you. Your money is tainted and it's hurting our people in the worst way." He dropped her hand like it was a hot potato.

"Noah, please don't go," Morgan pleaded with him as she tugged on his arm. "Why don't you think over what I'm saying for a few days? Don't decide right now. Please don't let this tear us apart. I love you." She began kissing his face.

Noah pushed her roughly away from him. "There's nothing to think about, Morgan." Noah voice dripped finality. "We talked about the life from which I was born, my mother's family, and how I had to come to terms with accepting it. Not only was I embarrassed by the Jones family, but my faith was sorely tested. Now, you want me to willingly put myself at risk for something like distributing drugs. I don't think so." He looked at her dolefully, and tears streaked down his face. "I'll always love you, Morgan Foster. When you're ready to come back to your senses and face your true destiny as a child of God, you know where to find me. You know I'll be praying for you night and day. The Lord will eventually show you the way." He kissed her cheek and went into the bedroom and began packing his belongings.

Morgan slumped on the couch and slid to the floor. She cried and beat the carpet with her fists. She had taken a gamble and lost. She cried softly as she listened to the closet door opening and closing and then the click of Noah's suit-

cases from his bedroom just feet away from where she lay.
Her eyes were nearly swollen shut from crying. She didn't
look up when Noah returned to the room.

Noah set his bags down near the door. He laid the key to
the apartment on the cocktail table. "I'll be waiting for you,
Morgan. I know in my heart that you'll realize the error of
your ways, and, with God's guidance, we'll get it right the
next time. I love you and God loves you, baby. Don't you
ever forget that." He opened the door, and it closed behind
him.

Morgan wanted to get up from the floor and run out the
apartment and block Noah from leaving the building. She
longed to drop to her knees and beg him to stay. Her mind
flirted with the idea that she wouldn't go into the family
business. It would pass to Brianna after her anyway. Morgan's soul was torn with misgivings. Under no circumstances, could she let her mother down. But what if she
became her mother? That thought had never factored into
her thoughts until now. Noah had told Morgan many times
that no matter what happened in life, that God would never
forsake her. She recalled his words and wondered: where
was God now? Like many people experiencing a crisis,
Morgan was so caught up in her dilemma that she couldn't
feel or hear God.

She stood. Her head ached almost as bad as her heart.
Morgan stumbled into her bedroom and pulled her diary
off the top shelf of the near empty closet. Her hands shook
as she wrote.

The Void In My Heart
oh how it hurts
like someone
has scalded my heart
he's gone
and taken away

my reason for living
I want to scream
tear out my hair
how can I go on
without you in my life
please don't let it be
love don't hurt me
come back to me
I need you so

Morgan sat upright on the floor, wiping away another tear. She stood and walked woodenly to the dining room and removed her cell phone from her purse. She walked back to the living room, sat back on the floor, and decided to call Noah. His phone rang five times and she was routed to voicemail. She tried calling Noah over and over in fifteen minutes intervals. She still got the same results. She dropped the phone on the carpeted floor, finally giving up after two hours of calling Noah without any luck.

Then Morgan lay back on the floor inertly. Her hand picked up and grasped the cell phone as if it were a life line to Noah. Her other arm was wound across her heart as if to stymie the palatable pain that vowed to snap it in two.

The only sounds in the room were the tick-tock of an old grandfather clock she found at a garage sale, her ragged breathing, and hiccups. Morgan lay on the floor lifelessly until darkness fell. From time to time, she'd raise her head and glance hopefully at the door. She prayed valiantly against all hope that there would be a knock at the door. She'd jump up and open it and find Noah standing on the other side. Instead there was silence.

Later, Morgan roused herself to dial Brianna's home tele-phone number. She received a tone indicating that the line was busy. Morgan decided to call Jernell. Her mother didn't answer the cell phone, and, once again, Morgan was routed to voicemail. It seemed everyone was busy living their own lives, and Morgan was relegated to mourning the demise of her relationship with Noah alone.

The Lord, indeed, doesn't forsake His children. When life seems to be at its lowest point and all hope is gone, God steps in, and unravels the mess our lives become so we can learn who's really in charge of our lives.

Chapter 20

A short time after midnight, Morgan fell asleep from sheer mental and physical exhaustion. When she awakened a few hours later, she sat up rapidly and said in a gravelly voice, "Noah, are you here?" She didn't hear a response. Morgan rose from the floor and walked into the bathroom, and her reflection in the mirror over the sofa frightened her. Morgan thought she looked like she'd lost her mind. Her face bore smatterings of the desolation. Dark circles punctuated her deadened eyes. Salty lines and tracks of her tears smudged her cheeks. Her mouth drooped miserably.

Morgan walked back to the living room and dialed Brianna's number again. It was still busy. She tried calling her mother. The phone didn't ring, instead her call was routed immediately to voicemail like the telephone was powered off. *Has something happened? Where is everyone tonight?*

Fear mushroomed through her soul. *What else could go wrong today?*

Morgan laid the cell phone on the cocktail table. She spied Noah's key laying on top of it. She picked it up and hurled it toward the patio door with all her might. The impact made a hideous sound. Morgan's cell phone rang, startling her.

She snatched it up and peered at the caller ID, hoping it was Noah on the line. But it wasn't.

"Hello, Lucinda. What's going on? I've been trying to call Momma and she's not answering."

If Morgan thought life couldn't get any worse, she found out how mistaken she could be. Lucinda sounded tense. "Morgan, we need you to come home immediately. Don't ask any questions. Just get here as quickly as you can."

"Why? What's wrong, Luci? Where's my mother?" Morgan's hands began to tremble.

"We can't talk on the telephone. I need to talk to you in person. Your mother needs you." Lucinda's voice quivered emotionally.

Morgan sensed that something was terribly wrong. "Okay. I'll be there as soon as I can. Why can't Harry pick me up?" She put her hand on her chest, trying to quell her shattered nerves.

"Morgan," Lucinda said warningly. Her voice sounded stern. "Don't ask any questions. Just come home." She disconnected the call.

Morgan legs felt loggy. She rose from the floor and walked slowly to the bathroom. After she washed her face, she changed clothes, her fingers felt clumsy when she buttoned her shirt and pants. She looked around the apartment sorrowfully when she locked the door. Then Morgan hopped into her black BMW convertible. Before long, she was headed north on Interstate 55, driving close to eighty miles per hour.

Morgan tried desperately to ignore the voices in her head telling her that something was wrong at home. Her face crumpled with grief when her mind wandered to Noah.

Two and a half hours later, Morgan exited I-55 onto Lake Shore Drive. Within ten minutes, she exited at Thirty-ninth Street. When she turned onto Lake Park Boulevard, police cars were lined up and down her mother's street. Several unmarked cars were parked in the driveway of the gray stone. Morgan's heart thumped erratically inside her chest. Her left hand flew to her mouth. She debated whether to park or keep driving south when she saw Lucinda wearing a pair of dark glasses, standing near the end of the block. Hordes of people were clustered on the street watching the police officers going in and out of the house.

Morgan drove the car slowly as she peered at the house and Lucinda. She steered the car to the next block and parked the vehicle. Her breathing became shallow, and she began hyperventilating. She had never been more frightened in her life. She heard a rap on the passenger side window and looked up to see Lucinda motioning for her to open the car. Morgan pressed a button to unlock the door.

Lucinda slid into the passenger's side. She looked a wreck. Her hair was pulled back off her face and was covered by a scarf. "Thank God you came."

"What's going on back there?" Morgan turned and pointed to her mother's house.

Lucinda put her hands over face. "They took your mother to jail a few hours ago. I'm not exactly sure what happened. But what I do know is that Terrence, Brianna's fiancé, is involved. I had a chance to talk to Harry for a hot second. I was away from the house. Before Harry left he said Terrence is not who we think he is."

"What do you mean?" Morgan's brow wrinkled. Her mouth gaped open as she breathed loudly.

"Terrence is a undercover narcotics agent. All this time he pretended to love Brianna, he was setting her up to get information on the family. They arrested your mother and Todd earlier. I heard that no-good uncle of yours is trying to cut a deal in exchange for immunity." Lucinda's voice choked up.

"I, I, I," Morgan stuttered. "Momma told me that couldn't ever happen. She has measures in place for situation like this. Is she going to prison? Oh my God." Morgan's head pounded like someone was beating bongo drums inside of it.

"I really don't know," Lucinda replied. "You can't go home. I'm sure at some point they'll want to question both of us. If there is somewhere you can stay until this blows over, then I think you should go there. Truthfully, I don't know how long all of this is going to take. Look." Lucinda and Morgan turned to look behind them. Trucks from television stations began converging on the block. Reporters were there from all the Chicago media stations—channels 2, 5, 7, 9 and Fox.

"Go," Lucinda instructed Morgan. The young woman fumbled as she tried to insert the key back in the ignition. She finally started the car and accidentally stepped on the gas pedal instead of the brakes. The vehicle roared down the street. "Where are we going?" Morgan asked as she drove south. A few people stared at the car as she passed them and pointed. "Oh, no," Morgan moaned, "we're in serious trouble aren't we?"

"Yes. I'd say so. Our worst fears have happened, or as my ma says, 'the chickens have come home to roost.' " Lucinda's hand flew up to the side of her face. She wiped away trickles of sweat that rolled down her face and tears from her eyes.

Morgan returned to the Lake Shore Drive Expressway. She drove a few miles north to the beach surrounding Lake Michigan and turned off the car. "What are we going to do?" she asked Lucinda.

The housekeeper sat in an almost comatose state beside Morgan. "Huh? What did you say?"

"Where do we go from here? We obviously can't go home."

"Do you think you can stay at Noah's house until you can talk to a lawyer? Call Noah and ask him to call his father and ask if you can stay there. I'm sure he'd be more than happy to help you."

When Lucinda said Noah's name, a geyser of tears fell from Morgan's eyes. A sob escaped her mouth. "Noah and I are . . . I can't call Noah or stay with his father," Morgan finally said in a tiny voice, wiping her eyes with the back of her hands.

"Morgan. I'm so sorry." Lucinda understood what Morgan couldn't say. She moved over in the seat and hugged Morgan's shoulders.

"I don't know what to do! I can't go to Brianna's. What about Big Momma?" Morgan leaned against Lucinda's side. The young woman struggled as she desperately tried to find the strength to go on. Morgan began gasping like her lungs were depleted of air.

"I wouldn't advise you go there either. Big Momma is being investigated, too."

"Brianna must be beside herself with grief," Morgan said unhappily. "We've both lost the men we love."

"What happened between you and Noah?" Lucinda asked Morgan as she turned away from the window.

"I told him about the business." She flung out her hand. "Not about the inner workings." She shook her head. "He proposed last night, as I knew he was going to at some point." Morgan bowed her head. She looked at Lucinda defensively. "I had to tell him something. I asked him to join the family with me. It's a good thing he didn't."

The women sat in the car for another fifteen minutes.

"I guess we'll have to go to my mother's house I hate to take you there, but I can't think of any place else to go that's safe."

"What do you mean you hate to take me there? Where does your mother live, Luci?"

"My mother lives in the projects, someplace that you've never been. There's simply nowhere else to go right now."

"Well, it's not like Lake Park is the Gold Coast of Chicago. If that's the only place you can think of us for us to go, then we don't have a choice." Morgan lifted her chin. "What's the address?"

"It's on Ninety-fifth Street, over west." Lucinda gave Morgan instructions.

Forty-five minutes later, Morgan parked her conspicuous vehicle on Ninety-fifth Street. She locked the doors and set the alarm with the keyless remote after she and Lucinda had exited the car.

Morgan trembled a bit from shock and exhaustion as she looked around. Lucinda was correct when she said the projects didn't resemble her block in Lake Park. However, Morgan was aware that a few blocks south or north of the street her mother lived on probably looked similar to where she was then.

Dirt, instead of emerald green grass, was part of the landscaping in front of the two-story project housing. Debris cluttered the walkways. When they passed the space between buildings, the scent of marijuana was overwhelming.

A few children ran back and forth in front of their houses playing, although it was way past their bedtime. A group of teenaged boys ogled her as they walked to Lucinda's mother's house. Morgan understood why Lucinda was reluctant to bring her to this neighborhood.

"Don't worry. No one will bother you," Lucinda whispered.

They walked another block and Lucinda knocked on a faded lime green door. The paint was peeling. A heavyset woman, built sturdily like Lucinda, opened the door a crack and peered narrowly out the slit. Then, she opened the door wider when she saw her daughter's face. "Gal, where you been? That darn phone been ringing all day."

Lucinda and Morgan walked inside the small dwelling. The aroma of greens, corn bread, and fried chicken greeted their nostrils. The younger woman's stomach filled with delight, reminding her that she hadn't eaten for hours. "You two can introduce yourselves." Lucinda walked to the kitchen to use the telephone.

"Well, go on in and have a seat." Lucinda's mother ushered Morgan into the living room. The furniture was worn, but clean. Lucinda's mother held a dishtowel in her hand. She looked at Morgan kindly. "Excuse Cinda's manner's, I'm her ma, Mabeline Smith. Is you hungry?" The woman wiped her hands with the dishtowel and extended a hand to the exhausted-looking young woman.

Mabeline was a tall mountain of a woman, almost six feet tall and wide. Her dark hair, woven with streaks of gray, was pulled back into an untidy bun. Lucinda had inherited her mother's large eyes. The older woman wore a pair of enormous dark blue jeans and a black and white checkered shirt. Size eleven tennis shoes covered her feet.

Morgan clasped the woman's hand and said, "I'm Morgan Foster. And yes, I'm hungry."

"Oh, I know who you is." Mabeline smiled back at the young woman. "Heard a lot about you over the years. I'll be back in a minute with a plate for ya."

"Thank you, ma'am!" Morgan replied subdued. She looked around the room. It was neat and clean. The carpet on the floor had raveled around the edges. The cinderblock walls, once painted white, were now a dingy gray.

An old sofa that Morgan remembered from her mother's basement about five years ago sat on a wall beneath a picture of a black Jesus Christ, Martin Luther King, and John F. Kennedy.

An old glass cocktail table leaning to the left was in front of the sofa. Morgan sat in the corner of the room in a chair matching the sofa. Brass lamps sat on tables next to the chairs. An old étagère stood upright on a wall. Pictures of family members were placed on the shelves.

Mabeline returned to the room with a plate full of food. She handed the plate to Morgan and went back in the kitchen. She came back with utensils. "What do you want to drink?" she asked Morgan.

Morgan shook her head. "This is too much food for me. Water would be fine."

"Eat what you want," Mabeline instructed Morgan, "and leave what you can't eat." She brought a tall, pink plastic cup filled to the brim with cold water from the kitchen. The ice-cubes clinked when she sat it on the table. Mabeline sat on the sofa and stared at the young woman.

Morgan's stomach growled aloud after she put a forkful of greens in her mouth. She ate the entire plate of food. Butter dripped down her hand as she demolished the corn bread. She licked her fingers.

Mabeline chuckled and shifted her immense girth comfortably on the sofa "I guess you was hungry. Do you want some more?"

Morgan covered her mouth, and then she belched loudly. "Oops. Excuse me. I'm full. I guess I was hungrier than I thought. Her eyelids dropped from fatigue. "Where's Luci?" she asked Mabeline, yawning.

"Still on the phone. Would you like to lay down?" The older woman rose from the sofa with a speed that belied her weight, and stood in front of Morgan's chair.

Morgan stood up and felt light-headed. "Yes, I'd like to lie down."

Mabeline led Morgan to her bedroom and the young woman fell across the bed and into a deep sleep.

When Morgan awakened a few hours later, her head lay in the crook of her cramped left arm. She sat up and rubbed her arm. The sun's ray peeked through the half-opened blinds on the window. Morgan shook her head as if clearing cobwebs. She rose from the bed and walked over to the mirror and patted her tousled hair down on her head.

She took her cell phone out of her purse to check if she had any messages. Morgan had forgotten to bring the charger with her from Peoria, so the phone was dead. She dropped it back inside her purse, walked back to the bed, and folded the quilt someone had laid across her legs. When she walked out the bedroom, she could hear the audio of the small television coming from the kitchen. Morgan paused to listen.

A newscaster said, "Jernell Foster was arrested at her palatial Lake Park Home. The Feds picked her up after indictments were sworn out in the federal court of Illinois. Ms. Foster is charged with possession of illegal substances with intent to distribute. The DEA has alleged that Ms. Foster is one of the largest distributors of drugs in the Midwest, possibly as far reaching as the entire United States."

The reporter paused dramatically. "The case was broken by the unwavering efforts of DEA Agent Terrence Greer. Ms. Foster is single. She has a daughter graduating from Bradley University next month. The daughter's whereabouts are still unknown. Darlene Foster, Ms. Foster's aunt, is also wanted by police for questioning."

Morgan crept into the kitchen slowly. Her ears seemed to burn from listening to the reporter's words. Her eyes flew to the television set in time to see Jernell being led from the gray stone with her hands bound behind her back. Her head was bowed. Morgan grabbed the edge of the counter to keep from sliding to the floor.

Lucinda and Mabeline raced to Morgan's side. Each woman took one of Morgan's arms, led her to the table, and into a chair.

"Oh God, this is the unbelievable," Morgan sobbed. "What's going to happen to Momma and Big Momma? Am I being charged with anything? Maybe they're going to put me in prison too." She dropped her head to the table, sobbing wildly.

Lucinda bent over and gathered Morgan in her arms.

"Hush, Morgan, it's going to be all right. You've got to be strong. I talked to Rico last night. He's on his way from Cleveland now. He should be here soon. We're going to get a lawyer for you. Everything is going to be all right."

Morgan looked up at Lucinda. Her eyes were wet and glassy. "How can you say that, Luci? You don't know. No one knows. I need to talk to Brianna and find out what happened. I can't believe she told Terrence anything that would incriminate Momma or that Uncle Todd is cooperating with the police. You can't trust the media. They'll say anything to boost their ratings." Morgan shook her head stubbornly.

Lucinda and Mabeline exchanged worried glances over Morgan's head.

Mabeline walked to the counter and turned the television off. "Child, I'm a tell you like I told Cinda. This is a situation that you need to turn over to God." She looked at Lucinda and Morgan. "Give me your hands, both of y'all." Mabeline, Lucinda, and Morgan stood in a circle, each one clasping the other's hand tightly.

The older woman closed her eyes and bowed her head. "Father in heaven, I stand here grateful for the many blessings you've given me and my family. Today, Lord, I ask you to please stop by my house this morning and lay your healing hand on Cinda and Morgan. Your children done forgot in times of trouble, how you promised to take care of us. Lord. You said you'd never leave us alone.

"Only you, Father, can make a way out of no way. Hallelujah!" Mabeline stomped her foot. "Help them, Lord. Help Morgan as she faces her trials and tribulations, I know, Lord, when you're done working with her, she'll be a stronger woman, able to let go and trust you to guide her way. Give her strength, Lord, for what lay ahead." Mabeline squeezed Morgan and Lucinda's hands tightly. "And she will know how wonderful your grace and mercy are. These blessings, I ask in your son's name. Amen." Mabeline dropped Lucinda and Morgan's hands. "Let go, and let God." The older woman went to sit on the couch. Morgan returned to the chair she'd sat in, taken aback by what had just happened.

Lucinda said, "Thank you, Ma. We needed that. But now we have to focus on what lies ahead for Morgan." She took a chair from the dining room table and pulled it next to Morgan. She put her hands on each side of Morgan's face and gently pulled Morgan's face toward her own. "Morgan, this is a difficult time for all of us, but you can't fall apart, not now. Too much is at stake. I talked to Harry and he's been in touch with your mother's lawyers. So far, the police just want you to come in for questioning. You haven't been charged with anything. I suggest we wait for Rico to get here and figure out what to do next.

"Harry said the situation isn't good for your mother and aunt right now. I'm going to try and go see Jernell tomorrow. She's going to court tomorrow for an indictment hearing. Try to keep it together, Morgan, and like Momma said, rely on God. I know it's hard to figure out right now, but He'll keep you strong." Lucinda let go of Morgan's face and hugged her again.

"I'll try to, Luci, though I can't promise anything. I feel like my life is falling apart right before my eyes. The day before yesterday I was happily in love. Then I told Noah the truth about the business, and he leaves me. Now Momma and Big Momma are in jail. I don't know if I can take anymore." She began rocking back and forth in the chair.

Lucinda looked at Mabeline. "Ma, I have some sleeping pills in my purse. Take Morgan back to the bedroom and give her two of them."

Mabeline nodded. She went to the sink and filled a glass with water. Then she went to the bedroom and returned with Lucinda's purse. She handed it to her daughter. Lucinda removed two pills from a small vial. She gave them to Morgan and Mabeline handed her the glass of water.

Morgan swallowed the pills and drank the water. She stood and followed Mabeline docilely to the bedroom like a sleepwalker. When she lay on the bed, Mabeline shut the door.

Morgan squeezed her eyes tightly together and said over and over like a mantra, "Please, let everything that's happened be a dream. When I wake up please let all of this be gone." Then the pills took effect a few minutes later, and Morgan was out like a light.

Chapter 21

Noah spent the night on the lumpy sofa bed at his friend Jerome's apartment, oblivious to the news unfolding in Chicago. He awakened close to noon with his body aching from tossing and turning. He shaded his eyes from the glaring sunlight that flooded the living room. His head felt like someone had hit him with a 2x4. He felt the remnant of a tension headache that wouldn't quit. He and Jerome had stayed up the better part of the night praying and discussing what Noah could do about his dilemma with Morgan.

"Jerome, are you here?" Noah called out feebly. When he didn't hear an answer, the young man went into the bathroom to relieve his bladder. After he was done, he washed his hands and strolled into the kitchen. The mere act of walking seemed to painfully jar the young man's head.

Thoughtfully, Jerome had left a pot of coffee on the stove. Noah reached into the cabinet and removed a cup and saucer and poured himself a cup of java.

He walked back to the living room, turned the television on, and sat down.

Noah gingerly sipped his coffee. The sound was turned

low on the set. Using the remote control unit, he turned up the volume. The young man's mouth dropped open when he saw Jernell's face on the television. The cup slipped out of his hand and hit the floor.

"What the heck?" he said. "That's Morgan's mother. What's going on?" Noah listened to the segment. When it was over, he looked between the sofa cushions for his cell phone. It wasn't there. He finally found it in his jacket pocket. He hurriedly ripped it out.

He checked his messages. Morgan had called many times since he had left the day before. But she hadn't tried to contact him after midnight last night. He wondered if she was all right.

Noah called his father's house hoping Samuel hadn't left for church yet. His tense body sagged with relief when Samuel finally answered the phone.

"Dad, it's me. Have you seen the news? What's going on?"

"Son, the news about Mrs. Foster is the biggest scandal to hit Chi-town in a long time. It sounds like Morgan's mother is involved in the drug trade. She's in court as we speak, probably being indicted for the charges against her. We'll have to keep Morgan's family in our prayers. I know God will see them through this tribulation."

"Have you heard from Morgan?" Noah gripped the phone tightly.

"No," Samuel replied, confused. "Isn't she there with you? I hope that girl doesn't get caught up in all this mess."

"Uh, we had a major argument yesterday, and I left her. I spent the night with a friend of mine. Um, you know what I mean." Noah wasn't ready to go into details with his father about what had happened.

Samuel shook his head. Unbeknownst to Noah, Samuel and Gloria assumed Noah and Morgan were playing house when they learned that Morgan had rented an apartment in Peoria. What the older couple didn't know was the young people had been practicing celibacy. Morgan had her room, and Noah had his own. "Gone where, son? If she's not there in Peoria with you, then she has to be in Chicago. I think you need to get here as soon as you can. Morgan is going to need the prayers and support of all the friends she has."

The older man put the phone receiver in the crook of his neck, took his breakfast dishes off the kitchen table, and put them on the counter. He turned on the hot water, filled the dishpan, and then transferred the dishes into it.

"We had a serious disagreement. I haven't seen her since then."

"Son, what would cause you to leave her like that? Did she know what happened to her mother at that time?" Samuel poured the excess coffee from the pot into the sink. Then he put the coffee grounds into the garbage can.

"Well, to be honest, she'd just told me the truth about her mother and the family business. Morgan actually thought we were going to get married, and I was going to join the company. I was so shocked that I didn't know what to do. I started to call you and talk to you about what happened, but I was too shocked. I thought you would judge her harshly and think me a fool for falling in love with Morgan. I told her yesterday that I loved her, but I couldn't condone what her mother did for a living. I asked her to think about the situation a little longer. I realized later that eventually that she'd make the right choice. Now look what has happened. I just want to talk to Morgan and make sure that she's all right. From what I saw on the television, I'm sure she's not home."

"You're probably right about that. Son, I thought you knew that you could talk to me about anything. Your mother and I always suspected something wasn't right with Morgan's mother's business when we saw how well she lived. When we went to Ms. Foster's house for Morgan's twenty-first birthday party, we noticed Mrs. Foster didn't seem to have many friends at the celebration—that mostly her family was there. We didn't get to meet Morgan's father because he came to the party after we'd left. I sensed Gloria may have known Mrs. Foster from the old days, although she never said anything to that effect. You know how your mother was about her past. Sometimes, she'd say Morgan reminded her of someone she knew a long time ago, but she never said who.

"The whole thing is unfortunate. But you can't totally blame Morgan for being confused about her family's activities, considering her background. The news reporter said her cousin's fiancé is DEA. You should have heard that young man bragging on television during one of the press conferences. He was talking about everything he has on the family. There was a picture of Morgan from high school in the newspapers today."

"Lord, have mercy. This situation is worse than I thought." Noah ran his hand through his hair. He had parted with his twisties after his sophomore year of college. "I'm on my way home. If Morgan calls you, then tell her I'm on my way to Chicago."

"I will, son." Samuel hung up the telephone. He wondered if Morgan would try to get in touch with him. "Naw, I doubt it," he said aloud. He departed the house, got in his car, and headed to church. As he drove he said, "Lord, take care of Morgan and her family as they go through this difficult time. Father, help Morgan to understand that she only has to trust in you, and you will direct her path. Lord, we mortals don't always understand why misfortune comes knocking on our door. That's not for us to know. But, Lord, with your abundant grace and mercy, I know Morgan and her family will get through this, and become the people you intended them to be. Father, keep my son safe as he drives here from Peoria. These blessings, I ask in your son's name, Amen." Samuel had become fond of the young woman. He had prayed for her when Noah had told him that she had begun her spiritual walk with the Lord. Once Gloria got over her initial jealously of Morgan, she developed a deep affection for the girl.

In Peoria, Noah sat on the couch staring at the television. Then he called Jerome.

After his friend answered his cell phone, Noah blurted out, "Man, I need to borrow your car. You know most of the time, I use public transportation, or Morgan's car. I don't have a vehicle, and I need to get to Chicago fast. I know you need your car yourself, but I have an emergency at home. I may not be back for a few days."

"I assume this is about Morgan?" Jerome asked. He was at work and paused entering data on his PC. "Go handle your business. I asked Zandra to pick me up for work this morning, so you wouldn't be stuck at my apartment since we don't have public transportation in the 'burbs. I can get by without my Jeep until you come back to Peoria. Be careful and take your time driving home. I left the key for you on the top of my dresser. Hey, man, I'm pulling and praying for you and Morgan. Be safe, my brother."

"Thanks, J. I really appreciate it." Noah hung up the telephone. He jumped off the sofa, showered, dressed, and followed Morgan's route to Chicago.

Morgan's head felt fuzzy when she awakened several hours later. For a few seconds, she didn't know where she was. She tugged the sheet around her waist. Lucinda had probably removed her shoes and thrown the quilt back across her legs. Morgan sat up on the side of the bed. Then, remembrance of yesterday's events clicked into her memory bank. Everything that happened the day before wasn't a dream as she'd hoped. Instead, her life had become a living nightmare.

Her mouth felt gummy, probably from the medication.

She swallowed a couple of times. Morgan rubbed her upper arms. Lucinda came into the room with Rico trailing behind her.

"You're awake," Rico said. "We were just coming in here to wake you."

"Have you talked to Momma?" Morgan asked drearily. She raised her arms to hug Rico.

"I talked to her lawyer, Ms. Collins. Jernell wants to keep you out of the fray as much as possible," Lucinda answered, leaning against the dresser.

Rico sat on the bed beside Morgan. "Unfortunately, we don't know if we're going to be able to do that." He handed his daughter the *Chicago Sun Times*.

Jernell's mug shot had made the front page. She was glaring at the host of media personnel gathered around her as they thrusted microphones into her face.

Morgan scanned the article. When she turned the pages, her own face stared up at her. "Oh no! I'm in the paper too?" She handed the newspaper back to her father.

"Have you talked to Aunt Adrianna? How is Bri?" Morgan's voice sounded shaky. Her hands shook. She put them under her thighs.

"Adrianna isn't taking any calls and neither is Brianna," Lucinda answered. "Jernell's arrest has kind of split the family apart, and right now, everyone is fighting about who'll take Jernell's spot."

"How do you know this?" Morgan asked.

"I've talked to Harry. He's been keeping me posted. He's going out of town tonight to handle some business for your mother."

Rico patted Morgan's arm. "Everyone is going to be examined like a bug under a microscope until this situation is resolved."

"And I guess that includes me," Morgan murmured in a flat tone of voice.

Rico sighed heavily. "Yes. I'm sure it does. Lucinda told me you talked to Noah yesterday. And he didn't take the news of your mother's profession very well?"

"That's putting it mildly. He looked at me with loathing in his eyes. Like he didn't know who I was." Morgan's voice sounded strangled. Tears gushed from her eyes.

"Come on, Morgan. It was a lot for him to take in. Noah is a fine young man. He's a Christian and fair-minded. I don't think he'll desert you in your time of need, regardless of the circumstances."

"I beg to differ. You didn't see how he looked at me." Morgan's sinuses became clogged, and she sniffed. "What am I supposed to do now?"

"Your mother's lawyer recommended another criminal attorney in her firm. I made an appointment with him this afternoon. Unless there's hard evidence implicating you in wrongdoing, we don't think you're going to be charged with anything. The police simply want to talk to you. Lucinda and I will go with you to see them."

"Meanwhile, your mother's house is off limits to you. And Jernell's accounts have been frozen," Lucinda added.

"She has other accounts doesn't she?" Morgan inquired. Her eyes darted between Rico and Lucinda.

"Jernell has a Swiss account, and a couple of accounts in Belize, and the Bahamas," Lucinda answered. "Your mother had tight measures in place in case something like this happened. Harry should be back in Chicago in a few days."

"Was Uncle Todd aware of Momma's procedures?" Morgan asked point-blank.

"No, just me and Harry. She felt she could only trust us," Lucinda answered. "So now you're a wealthy woman. Jernell has set up many accounts in your name. Some since you were born. Before Harry left, he was in the process of transferring some of the money to an emergency account here in the states so you wouldn't be left penniless."

"This is so unreal," Morgan said. She closed her eyes for a moment. "You've been a true friend to my mother, Luci."

Lucinda couldn't meet Morgan's eyes. She looked beyond the young woman, out the window and nodded.

Rico looked at Lucinda guiltily. Morgan's head was bowed so she missed the exchange between her father and old nanny. Lucinda shook her head warningly at Rico. Morgan didn't know the true dynamic of Rico, Jernell, and Lucinda's relationships when they were teens.

"Can you make some calls, Luci, and find out if I can visit my mother today?" Morgan rose from the bed to go to the bathroom.

Rico said to his daughter, "I know you feel like the weight of the world is on your shoulders, and what has happened seems like your worst nightmare. Just remember that God is always with us. He sees us through the storms in life. What you are going through may seem like an earthquake, high on the Richter scale. Still, God is here even in the midst of this difficult time. Just try to keep the faith."

He and Lucinda walked back to the living room. Mabeline was sitting on the sofa. The television was turned down low. Lucinda sat beside her mother. Rico sat in the same chair as Morgan had the day before.

"Is she up?" Mabeline asked her daughter. Lucinda nodded. "I think you need to tell Morgan the truth," Mabeline proclaimed. She folded her huge arms across her chest.

"Tell Morgan the truth about what?" Rico asked as he looked between the two women.

"Ma, it's not your business. Let me handle this," Lucinda protested. A frown marred her face.

"The child is hurting. Imagine how she's gonna feel if something personal comes out. The girl is going to feel like she ain't got nobody."

"Ma," Lucinda warned her mother.

Mabeline waved her hand. "Keep pussyfooting 'round

and next thing you know, it's gonna be on the news or in the papers. Secrets are harmful. They only hurt people. I know Reverend Jefferson done told you that. You gotta make your peace with God, and that child in the room." The older woman snapped her mouth shut, stood, walked into the kitchen, and began banging pots and pans.

Rico stared at Lucinda long and hard. "What is she talking about? It can't be that old stuff. It happened a long time ago. Nothing would be gained from bringing it up."

"Ma is talking about something else that happened a very long time ago. Not what you're thinking. We don't need to get into it right now, Rico. I promise we'll talk when the time is right." Lucinda tried her best to mollify Rico's feelings. She could tell from the look on his face, he'd drop it for now, but not for long.

Chapter 22

Rico left Mabeline's house half an hour later feeling disgusted with Jernell for putting his daughter in such an ugly situation and afraid of what might happen next. He was put out with Lucinda for not telling him what her mother referred to when they were in the living room. He also felt he was backsliding as a Christian, since he couldn't find forgiveness in his heart for what Jernell had ultimately caused. Rico knew he had a lot of praying to do about his shortcomings.

He drove his car to the nearby discount store to buy Morgan an outfit to wear to the meeting with her lawyer, Gilbert Franklin. He glanced at his watch. They were due downtown in two hours. *How did things spiral out of control so fast?* he wondered. Morgan's graduation was scheduled for the next weekend. He'd already called Bradley after Jernell's story broke on television and requested her degree be mailed to his office in Cleveland.

Rico's cell phone sounded. He picked it up from the passenger seat. The number didn't look familiar to him. "Hello."

"Mr. Daniels, this is Yolanda Collins. I'm Jernell's lawyer.

I was able to schedule a short meeting between my client and her daughter this afternoon. I know Morgan has an appointment with Gilbert in a couple of hours. So when she's done talking with him, you can take Morgan to the jail located at Twenty-sixth and California. That's the facility where Jernell is being held."

"I'll do that," Rico replied tersely. "How does it look for Jernell?"

"Mr. Daniels, I can't discuss my client's case with you without her permission. She asked that I tell you to do everything you can for Morgan."

"Thank you, Ms. Collins. I'll have Morgan at the California address as soon as she's done with the police." Rico angrily disconnected the call. Everything that happened was Jernell's fault. Her greed had gotten everyone in a predicament that they might not be able to get out of. Rico feared there was a possibility that he might be investigated as well. He realized that from his work in the legal system that the questions Morgan faced could lead to charges being filed against her.

Thank God Harry was able to transfer funds to Morgan's account. If Morgan's indicted then at least I can post bail immediately.

While he waited at a stoplight, Rico rubbed the bridge of his nose. He thought he was prepared for this day if it ever came to pass, but he wasn't . . . not really. Too much was at stake. He prayed he and Lucinda where making the right decisions regarding Morgan's legal woes. The stoplight changed to green and the driver in the car behind Rico honked his car horn impatiently.

When he arrived back at Mabeline's house, Rico handed the bag of clothing to Lucinda to give to Morgan. "Tell her to hurry up. We have to be downtown soon."

Lucinda nodded and walked to the bedroom.

"Too many secrets," Mabeline lamented as she sat on the sofa and pointed at Rico. "Them secrets gonna take all of us down, and most of all, that gal. Lord, please have mercy on us all."

Rico's voice rose, spilling over with frustration. "There are too many things going on right now. Lucinda and I are trying to tend to them as best we can. Would you please stop the babbling, and let us handle things as we see fit?"

"In case you forgot, Rico Daniels, this is my house. I can say what I darn well please." Mabeline got up from the sofa and stalked into the kitchen. Rico could hear her grumbling for the Lord to give her strength as she opened and closed the refrigerator door.

Thirty minutes later, Lucinda and Morgan came out of the bedroom. Morgan wore a conservative looking navy blue dress, with white lace around the collar and the edges of the short sleeves. The garment hung on her frame because it was a size too large for her. Lucinda had changed into a dark pantsuit along with a white blouse.

Rico jumped up from the chair. He pulled his car keys out of his jacket. "Let's go," he said crankily.

The trio walked quietly to the car. Rico opened the back door for Lucinda and the front door for his daughter.

Morgan was silent during the trip downtown as she gnawed nervously on a hangnail. Rico and Lucinda were quiet, too. Thirty minutes later, Rico parked the car in the public parking lot a few blocks from the lawyer's office and turned off the car. Morgan turned to her father, scared out of her wits. Her face paled. "Daddy, I'm not going to jail, am I?"

"Morgan, try not to jump to any conclusions," Rico said calmly, although he was as apprehensive as his daughter. "The lawyer will be able to answer any questions we have. Try to calm down, baby. Everything is going to work out fine. We've got to trust in God."

"You can't promise me that for sure; can you?" Morgan's voice rose hysterically with fright.

Lucinda exited the backseat and sped to the front passenger side of the vehicle. She opened the door and nearly pulled the young woman out of the car. She put her arms around Morgan. "Come on now. Calm down. You know that your dad and I are not going to let anything happen to you. I promise that." Morgan's body quivered like a wounded bird in Lucinda's arms.

Rico got out of the car and pushed Lucinda's door shut after he closed his own. "Let's get this over with," he said gruffly. Lucinda went back to the rear of the automobile to get her purse. They quietly walked the couple of blocks north to the attorney's office.

Ten minutes later, Rico, Lucinda, and Morgan sat on a dark leather sofa in the reception area. A woman walked out of the lawyer's office door. "My name is Anne Baxter. I'm Mr. Franklin's paralegal. He'll be with you in just a moment." She was dressed in a conservative ash-gray suit, and an ecru-colored blouse. Can I have Judith, our receptionist, bring you coffee or any other refreshments?"

"No, we're fine," Rico said. Morgan crossed her legs to keep them from shaking.

"Let me know if you change your mind. I'll be back to escort you to Gilbert's office in five minutes.

Lucinda was the calmest of the three persons seated in the reception area. She picked up the latest issue of *Time Magazine* and scanned through it.

Ms. Baxter, as she had promised, ushered them inside Gilbert's office within five minutes. She shut the door behind them.

Gilbert's blue eyes peered over a pair of silver wire frame glasses that had slid down his nose. His black hair was slicked back with gel. The attorney was tanned and of medium build. His nose was large and crooked. Gilbert rose from his chair and dropped a gold cross pen on his neat dark, mahogany desk. He greeted Rico with a handshake, then Lucinda, and last, Morgan.

He opened a manila folder that laid on his desk and quickly read it. He looked across the desk at Morgan and folded his hands in a triangular shape in front of him. "Before we get started, Ms. Foster, let me put your mind at ease. So far, you haven't been implicated of any wrongdoing from the police's investigation. Though it's still fairly early on in their fact-finding process, I don't anticipate a change in your status as far as the investigations are concerned."

Morgan was so relieved that she nearly fell out of the chair.

Lucinda turned to Morgan who sat sandwiched between her and Rico and smiled. "See, I told you not to worry." Her lips twitched, "Thank you, Jesus."

"So what is it exactly the cops need to talk to Morgan about?" Rico asked. Although he didn't show it, Rico was relieved that some of the tension of the past few days was finally allayed.

"Almost everyone in the Foster family is being investigated to see what role they played in the alleged drug distribution ring. The focus has been on Jernell." Gilbert glanced down at his notes and then back at Morgan, "Also, her brother-in-law, Todd, and aunt, Darlene Foster." Gilbert pushed his glasses up on his nose. "Your aunts, your mother's sisters, are scheduled for interviews, too. My guess is since Morgan has been away attending college, the police will accept that she doesn't share any culpability."

Morgan looked sick like her stomach was upset. Everyone in that room except the lawyer was aware that she'd been privy to sensitive information regarding the business.

Morgan held her breath, and then exhaled noisily. She looked down at her hands folded on her lap. "What would happen—and this is just hypothetical—if it were to come out that I was more heavily involved?"

"Jernell suggested that you invoke the Fifth Amendment,

and I concur with her advice. She's instructed us to keep you out of the dispute at all costs."

"But won't the police think I'm guilty if I do that?" Morgan looked up at Gilbert. Beads of sweat roosted on her forehead.

"No," Gilbert stroked his goateed chin. "What they'll think is that you're trying to protect your mother. Keep in mind that when you make your statement to the investigators, that I will be there with you. So if I feel you're getting into murky waters, I'll intervene." Gilbert advised Morgan in a soothing tone of voice. "You're not in this alone."

Rico cleared his throat and asked Gilbert, "Can you tell us what's going on with Jernell? Or is that information confidential?"

Gilbert pressed the intercom button on his phone and said, "Judith, would you call Yolanda and ask her to join us?"

"Yes, I will," Judith answered. She disconnected the call.

Ten minutes later, Yolanda Collins strolled into the room. She was an African-American woman with a no-nonsense look on her plump brown face. She appeared to be all business. She was dressed in a black and white pin-striped suit and a white silk blouse. Black onyx earrings decorated her earlobes and she wore a matching bracelet on her right arm. There was a folder tucked under her arm. She sat on a black leather sofa to the left side of Gilbert's desk. "What can I do for you, folks?" she asked crisply.

Rico spoke up. "I talked to you earlier. I'm Morgan's father. You said you were going to talk to Jernell to see if she was okay with us discussing her case with you."

Yolanda shot Rico a piercing glance. "Yes, I remember talking to you, Mr. Daniels. Jernell has agreed to my talking to you, but only in generalities. What are your questions?" Her eyes swept over the group.

Lucinda sat up in her seat and held her hand up like she was in school. "What exactly is Jernell being charged with?"

"The media was correct in their reporting that time," Yolanda responded ruefully. "The main charge, and there are other against Jernell, is possession of controlled substances for distribution. What complicates matters is that the FBI is involved."

Morgan stomach roiled. "Is it true that my Uncle Todd is cooperating with them?"

Yolanda nodded her head. "Unfortunately, that seems to be the case."

"Then that doesn't bode well for my mother. She will certainly be found guilty," Morgan cried. Her knuckles had whitened from her tight grasp on the chair handles.

"As we speak, my team and I are working the best defense possible for your mother. Don't worry, young lady. Allow me and the other lawyers here at the firm do our job."

Morgan rolled her eyes up toward the ceiling and shrugged her shoulders skeptically.

"Now, I suggest you get over to the precinct where Jernell is being held before visiting hours are over for today." She stood up and pulled three business cards out of her pocket. "Call me if you have any further questions."

Gilbert rose from his chair also. "I agree with Yolanda. You need to get going to make it before visiting hours end. I believe you all have my number. Call me if anything comes up. I would also suggest you find some place to stay where you can avoid the media frenzy." He pointed to the high-definition television set in the corner of his office.

Lucinda gasped when she saw television crews assembled outside her mother's house. "Goodness gracious! How did they know where my mother lives?" She turned to the lawyer. She was open-mouthed and her eyes were riveted to the screen.

Gilbert replied cynically, "You'd be surprised what people will do for money, especially if the amount is high enough. More than likely, someone saw an opportunity to better his or her financial situation in your mother's neighborhood. They made a call and *violà*, the media descends."

Lucinda shook head in wonder at the mob of people surrounding her mother's home. "Excuse me. I need to call my mother."

Gilbert nodded his head sympathetically. "Just tell her to say, 'No comment,' or better yet, not to open the door. If you're lucky, they'll leave soon."

Lucinda pulled her cell phone out of her purse and dialed her mother's telephone number as she walked out the door.

"Is there anything else I can do for you?" Gilbert asked. "Try not to worry, Morgan. I'll be with you every step of the way."

"No. That's it for now. We'll be in touch if we have any more questions," Rico answered. He took Morgan's arm and they walked out of the office.

They found Lucinda standing near the bank of elevators. She snapped her flip phone shut. "Ma is not happy about this latest turn of events, to say the least. My sister, Gwen, is coming over to take Ma to her house." Lucinda looked at Rico. "Where are we going now?"

"We're going to Twenty-sixth and California so Morgan can see Jernell. We'll think of someplace to stay later," Rico promised.

The bell rang, indicating that the elevator was arriving. They stepped into the car and rode down to the first floor.

Morgan felt like butterflies were fluttering inside her stomach. She would see her mother in a matter of minutes at jail. Would this bad dream never end?

Chapter 23

The correctional facility located on Twenty-sixth and California wasn't as crowded as Rico feared it might be. About five people stood in line before Morgan to see their loved ones. Lucinda and Rico decided to wait downstairs in the lobby area while Morgan visited her mother.

Morgan felt a tinge of discomfort being at a jailhouse and seeing her mother alone. After her father and Lucinda had left and she had been frisked by the prison officials, Morgan wished that she had asked Rico to stay with her. But of the three of them, Morgan was the only one on her mother's visitor's list.

Lucinda pressed Morgan's hand tightly before she and Rico left. "You'll be fine. Rico and I will wait for you down here. Visiting hours end soon, so you won't be here long." She tried to soothe the young woman's rattled nerves.

After Morgan emptied her purse, she was escorted to meet Jernell.

She found a seat at a metal table near the door. Her body was racked with tremors. She folded her hands on the table before her. Her face burned. She sensed that the guards were whispering about her. The two men kept glancing her way.

Eons seemed to go by before Jernell walked inside the room. She wore an orange jumpsuit and had cheap-looking white sneakers on her feet. Her ponytail was intact. One of the guards unlocked the handcuffs binding her hands together. Jernell rubbed her wrists. Then she walked over to the table and sat down in the seat across from her daughter.

Morgan rose awkwardly from the chair, which made a clattering noise when she accidentally bumped into it. She leaned over and hugged her mother.

"Hi, Momma," Morgan said timidly after she sat back down. "How are you doing?"

"I've certainly had better days," Jernell quipped weakly. "No, really I'm okay."

"Gosh, Momma, I can't stand to see you here, looking like that." Morgan's eyes brushed over her mother's body. She put her hands to her mouth to stifle the sobs that threatened to tear from it.

Jernell patted Morgan's hand. "Don't worry about me. I'll be fine. Yolanda is one of the best lawyers in the city that money can buy. If anyone can get me out of this predicament, she can."

"I just can't believe all of this is happening to us. Terrence is not who he says he is and everyone is saying Uncle Todd is going to testify against you. This whole situation has been a disaster," Morgan exclaimed. She wiped her eyes.

Jernell casually took a pack of cigarettes out of her pocket. She removed a Virginia Slim 120 from the pack and lit it with a match.

Morgan looked at her mother aghast. "Momma, what are you doing? You don't smoke." Her voice faltered.

Jernell took a drag on the cigarette and exhaled. "I do what I can to pass the time in here, and don't worry, Todd won't be testifying against me or anyone."

"That's not what Mr. Franklin said," Morgan interjected.

"I don't care what anyone is saying, Todd won't be testifying against me, now or anytime soon." Jernell blew a smoke ring toward the ceiling.

"Okay, Momma, if you say so. I just came from talking to Attorney Franklin and your lawyer, Yolanda. They both seemed confident you can beat this."

"Humph," Jernell tapped the ashes from the cigarette onto the floor. She looked over at the guard. "Can you please bring me an ashtray?"

The female guard, whose hand never seemed to leave the hilt of her weapon, used her walkie talkie and requested an ashtray be brought to the room. Another guard eventually walked to the table where Jernell and Morgan were sitting and put the receptacle on the table.

"Thank you!" Jernell replied mockingly. She stole a look at Morgan. Until that point, she had avoided looking in her daughter's face.

"What can I do to help you?" Morgan asked tensely. Her voice rose from strain. Her eyes drank in her mother's face.

"Nothing," Jernell finally replied. She put out the cigarette and lit another in its place. "I'm doing everything in my power to keep you out of this." She lowered her voice and looked around the room, then back at Morgan. "You don't know anything about that part of my life. Do you understand me?"

"Yes, Momma." Morgan swallowed hard. The young woman unsuccessfully tried to hold back the sobs that eventually emanated from her mouth. She made mewling sounds like a baby.

Jernell clumsily patted her daughter's arm. "Morgan, please stop it. Crying isn't going to help the situation. I'm the one with the most at stake. You don't see me bawling. You're going to have to try and be strong. Your father and Lucinda will help you. And you have Noah. If I can't beat this, and I know I will, at least you'll have a shot at a some- what normal life. Isn't that's what you've always wanted?"

"You know, Momma, when I went to Peoria that was all I wanted at that point in my life." Morgan sniffed and fum- bled in her purse for a tissue. "I realize now that my life will never be normal. I wanted to be like other girls and enjoy the same experiences they did. I understand now that kind of life won't ever be in the cards for me." Morgan blew her nose and then balled up the tissue in her hand.

Jernell shrugged her shoulders. "My life hasn't ever been normal either. I'm sure Big Momma thought she was doing right raising me the way she did, like I did with you. I wish I could have spared you everything that's happening now, but it's out of my hands." She tapped the cigarette on the corner of the ashtray.

"But Uncle Todd . . ." Morgan began. She snapped her mouth shut when she saw the murderous look that covered her mother's face. Fire seemed to emanate from Jernell's eyes.

Jernell raised her hand and shook her head warningly. "There are some things we can't discuss while I'm here. Questions of that nature, I suggest you direct to Yolanda, and I'll write you back. We may have to use that method of correspondence for a little while."

Morgan looked into her mother's eyes and saw pain. Morgan nodded her head and said, "I'm so sorry, Momma. I wish things could be different and we were at home chillin' . . . Just hanging out."

"There's nothing for you to be sorry about, Morgan. What's done is done. I just have to concentrate on picking up the pieces of my life at this point."

"Visitation ends in five minutes," the guard announced. He looked pointedly at Jernell and Morgan.

"Anyway," Jernell stubbed out the cigarette, "you have Noah. He seems like a fine young man. I know he'll be there for you. Who knows? Your life may turn out more normal than you could imagine." She stood up and gestured to the guards that she was ready to go back to her cell.

Morgan walked around the square table and threw her arms around her mother. Jernell pulled slightly away from Morgan. "Just remember," she whispered into her daughter's ear, "everything I've done has been for you. Keep your head up, and never let them see you down." She turned to the guard, held out her hands, and winked at Morgan. The guard cuffed Jernell and led her away.

Morgan watched her mother walk back through the door through blurred eyes. She tried to stand up and couldn't. Finally, she held onto to the side of table with her head dropped down. A few minutes later Morgan walked slowly out of the room. Her step was slow, like she was an arthritic older woman.

Morgan's shoulders were slumped forward. *I forgot to ask Momma if she wanted me to bring her anything the next time I visit.* Morgan's body quaked, and she rubbed her upper arms briskly. *What am I thinking? Momma will be out of here before no time. After all, like she said, she has the best lawyer in all of Chicago.*

When the elevator descended to the first floor, Morgan saw Lucinda. She sat on a bench turning the pages of a newspaper, which was spread out on her lap. Rico was slumped on the seat beside her. His head lay against the back of the bench, and his eyes were closed.

Lucinda rose. The paper slid to the floor. Rico opened one eye and jumped up. "How did it go?" he asked Morgan when she stopped in front of them.

The young woman shook her head morosely. "It was rough seeing Momma like that. It drove home the fact that she's really in jail. When you see that stuff on television, it doesn't seem real." She waved her hands. "It was like I was watching a movie or something. But seeing Momma sitting at that table still trying to be tough, wearing an orange jumpsuit, kind of messed with my head. . . . and my heart." Morgan's hand fluttered over her chest.

Lucinda slipped her arm around Morgan's waist, and the young woman laid her head on Lucinda's shoulder.

Rico said to his daughter, "You've got to pull it together and trust in the Lord. I know I keep saying that over and over. . . . This is only the beginning."

"I know," Morgan murmured softly.

Fifteen minutes later, they returned to the parking garage and entered the car. Rico put the key in the ignition to turn on the automobile and then he stopped. "We need to figure out where we're going to stay tonight. Your mother's house is out," he turned and said to Lucinda.

Morgan said, "I wish I could go back to Peoria and barricade myself in my apartment."

"Uh, Morgan, I called your landlord and asked him to send your belongings to my house in Cleveland. Obviously with everything that's happened, you won't be going back to Bradley."

Morgan sat erect in the seat. "It would have been nice if you'd talked to me first."

"I apologize. But it seemed the right thing to do at the time. So where are we going, ladies?"

Morgan stroked her brow. "All those years of hard work and I can't even walk across the stage to get my degree. What a waste." She peeked first at Lucinda, then at Rico and said, "I want to go see Big Momma."

"I don't know if that's such a good idea!" Lucinda exclaimed vehemently. "She has her own problems to deal with right now."

"Please, Daddy?" Morgan sounded like a small child. "I feel unsettled. I need to try to understand what happened to bring our family to where we are today."

"I guess so, but just for a little while." Rico started the

car. "We need to decide where to go to rest. You also have a big day in front of you tomorrow, in case you've forgotten, young lady."

"I understand. How could I forget? Although Momma is optimistic about the outcome of all of this, I don't quite share her enthusiasm. I feel like she was putting on a brave front for me anyway. There are two more things I need to do, not necessarily both of them tonight. I need to talk to Big Momma and Brianna. I am going to do so with or without your help," Morgan warned Rico.

"Okay, let's take things one step at a time. We'll go to Darlene's now, but only for a little while." Rico changed lanes and sped up to the corner of the street. He turned and headed south. "Seeing Brianna can wait for another day." He turned on the radio, which was set to a news station. When they heard Jernell's name mentioned, Rico quickly turned from the news station to V103.

"You didn't have to do that, Daddy," Morgan commented. She turned her head and looked out the window. "Maybe I should listen to what being said about Momma."

"There's such a thing as overkill and that's what the media is doing now," Rico commented. Lucinda chattered about nothing in particular as Rico drove on Lake Shore Drive back to Lake Park.

He exited the expressway and braked at a stop sign. Rico turned on his right turn signal and eased the car onto Darlene's block. He pulled the vehicle in front of a ten-foot-tall black iron gate surrounding Darlene's property. It slid open. Whereas Jernell's house was a three story gray stone structure, Darlene's abode was an original brownstone that she had restored fifteen years ago.

"I think it's best that Lucinda and I wait for you in the car. I don't think I can stand being in the same room as Darlene right now." Rico shifted the car to park. "Morgan, please don't stay inside too long. Your appointment with the cops is early in the morning."

Morgan unlocked the car door. "I won't. She swung her legs out of the car and pushed the door closed. As she walked the length of the driveway, Morgan fought a battle with the jitters and lost. She thought the odds were against her, having a normal conversation with Darlene. All of her life, Morgan had loved and respected her aunt. She also recalled how her aunt would viciously berate Jernell if she felt her niece had done something wrong. Morgan's stomach felt pinpricks of apprehension about her conversation with Darlene. She wondered if her aunt would criticize her too. The young woman walked to the ornate front door and pressed the lit doorbell. Loud chimes sounded inside and out.

Chapter 24

Much to Morgan's surprise, Darlene answered the door herself. She expected Big Momma's housekeeper, Louisa, to admit her into the house.

When Darlene saw Morgan standing on the front step, she pushed the door open and moved aside. "I knew it was a matter of time before you showed up," the older woman said brusquely. "Come on in."

Morgan stepped over the threshold and shivered. A flash of the fairy tale, "Little Red Riding Hood" popped in her head and Big Momma became "the Big Bad Wolf." "How you doing, Big Momma?" Morgan leaned over and kissed the older woman's cheek.

"I'm fine. Ain't nobody and nothing ever held Big Momma down, and they ain't gonna start today. Come on, let's go into the den." Big Momma led the way.

Big Momma gestured to the white fur, custom-made sectional sofa. "Have a seat." She sat in a red leather recliner and picked up a snifter filled with Old Granddad whiskey. Big Momma crossed her legs delicately. "Can I get you something? You hungry?" She picked up the remote control and muted the sound on the big screen television.

"No. I'm good." Morgan sat primly on the sofa. Her eyes wandered around the room and stopped on an oil painting of Big Momma when she was about Morgan's age. She was dressed in a white diaphanous dress and wore a glittering tiara on her head. Her head rested on her hands which were encased in white gloves. It seemed like a relic from another era.

The living room was large and spacious, painted eggshell white accented with exquisite dark woodwork. One mirrored wall boasted a bar that was the length of the wall. Behind the bar were shelves full of every type of liquor imaginable.

Aretha Franklin wailed from the CD player. "You know I like me some 'Retha," Big Momma smiled. "Especially 'Respect.' So what bring you here, Morgan?" Big Momma turned to her niece and gave Morgan her undivided attention.

"I just came from the jail, seeing Momma." Morgan swallowed hard when she said "jail," and her eyes dropped. Then she looked up, and stared at her aunt. "What's going to happen to her?"

The older woman took a sip of the whiskey and swallowed, adroitly avoiding the question. "How is Jernell doing?"

"She says that she's fine. But I don't believe her. If I were in her predicament, I think I'd die."

"Jernell is a big girl. She understood what she was getting into and the risks involved in assuming the reins of the business."

Morgan sucked her teeth. She chose her words carefully. "Big Momma, you sound so cold. You claim to love my mother like your daughter. Don't you care that she might have to go to prison for the rest of her life?"

Big Momma put the glass on the end table nearest her chair. She clapped her hands. "That was priceless, Morgan. You're young and still in the process of being trained. It's obvious you still have a lot to learn. Or should I say, you did have a lot to learn. What's unfortunate about all that's happened is that Adrianna and her offspring didn't choose their mates well. There will be repercussions, but don't think for a minute that our life and business won't continue."

Morgan looked confused "How? With Momma behind bars?"

Big Momma snickered and sipped the golden colored liquor. "Jernell was lax in teaching you your life lessons. We have contingency plans in place to deal with almost all situations. If Todd has talked to the Feds, which is a no-no, he will pay dearly for that indiscretion. And Jernell will more than likely have to do some time. But the family has markers out to some people in high places that we can call in. Jernell won't be too old when she gets out."

Morgan couldn't believe what her aunt had said. Her body became flushed. "You're right. Apparently I did have more to learn. So what happens to me?"

"Jernell didn't finish training you. Since you never really started, then you're out. I'll take over running the business until Jernell is released or we find a suitable replacement."

Morgan had been holding her breath. Her body relaxed, and air escaped her lungs like a deflated balloon as her brain processed the information. She felt relief, then a profound sense of sadness. *Lord, what was I thinking? How could I have been so blind? I gave up so much—Noah, the man, I love—for what? This?*

"I can see Jernell was going to have her work cut out with you. You're soft, Morgan, like your father. Your mother spoiled you. Did she ever get around to telling you exactly how the business was started?" Big Momma was obviously enjoying her niece's discomfort.

Morgan just stared at Big Momma intently, "Well, um, she said my great-grandmother, she started, um, started the business," she stuttered, ill at ease.

Big Momma shook her head from side to side and took another swig of whiskey from the snifter. "I didn't think so. Officially, my grandmother, Helena, started the business along with her common law husband, an Italian named Mario Farina. Helena fled to Chicago to escape a loveless marriage to a sharecropper in Arkansas. We never knew his name.

"She ended up finding work on the north side of the city as a housemaid for the wife of a mobster. That's how she caught the eye of Mario. He was one of the mobster's associates. They said Mario was crazy about Helena."

Morgan felt a sense of disgust and inquisitiveness as she listened to Big Momma's story.

"Helena was the family's first Big Momma. She had two girls by Mario, my momma, Rosalee, and another girl they named Maria. Now Mario was good at what he did. He was an enforcer with a violent streak, and he was able to eventually break into the drug trade. He was the brawn behind the family operation and Helena was the brains. They ran a profitable business until a rival gang took out Mario.

"Helena wasn't about to let all that cash line somebody else's coffers. Like any other astute businesswoman, she had made a few contacts of her own. After Mario was killed, Helena decided to go into business with the owner of a nightclub, with mob ties, named Grady Reed.

"It was rumored Grady was part of the black mafia. Under Helena and Grady's regime, the business grew by greater leaps and bounds. Helena began grooming Rosalee to take over. The mob didn't bother Helena as long as she had a front man and she paid her hush money like she was supposed to.

"Rosalee never married, but she managed to do her family duty and produce two girls, me and Pamela. We never knew our father. Pam was older than me by a year. Pamela's downfall was she fell in love with a two-bit hustler named Roscoe. He had a gambling problem and loved the ladies a little bit too much. Needless to say, he was an embarrassment to the family and he died at an early age." Big Momma cackled aloud as if she knew something that nobody else did. "And that, my girl, is how the family business began, mothers teaching their daughters how to become entrepreneurs. Rosalee was beautiful. I'll have to show you pictures of her one day.

"Momma told me Helena always told her to never underestimate the power between a woman's legs." Big Momma grabbed her crotch.

Morgan felt the entire situation was bizarre. Big Momma was sitting in her living room talking to her in such a vulgar and calculating manner. She stared at her aunt, flinching from her presence like Big Momma was the serpent in the Garden of Eden.

Morgan tittered nervously. Her hand fluttered over her throat. The young woman was becoming increasingly uncomfortable. She thought Big Momma was going to comfort her. Instead, she was babbling about what she perceived as the good old days.

Big Momma pounded the side of her recliner with her fist. "There's a lot you still don't know. The women in our family run the business with the expertise of any Fortune 500 CEO."

"What does that have to do with me? Especially now?" Morgan asked naïvely.

"Gal, that's your legacy. It's who you came from. I knew when I heard you was messing with that church boy that you wasn't going to cut it. Jernell told me to be patient and that she could whip you into shape. But what your momma didn't understand, or maybe it's something she turned a blind eye to, is that toughness is not something that can be taught. It's what's in here, and here." The older woman pointed to her head then to her heart.

"Do tell me more," Morgan replied drolly. Her body began shaking again.

"To keep the business functioning and make sure the good ole boys get their piece of the pie, we need a front man to do that part. Personally, I think the overseer is more effective without emotional entanglements. Men are a necessity solely for begetting. We need them so we continue birthing our girls. We had high hopes for Rico and then he turned tail on us."

Morgan ignored the slur against her father. "So how do Uncle Todd and Aunt Adrianna fit into all of this?" Morgan asked puzzled.

"You don't think we just let the overseer run amok and do what they want, do you?" Big Momma smiled cynically. "That person has to be accountable for their actions to the rest of the family. You can think of us as the board of directors. If there's any hint of wrongdoing, the overseer can be replaced. I guess you could say Adrianna and Todd didn't agree with the present regime." Big Momma's face crinkled with smiles. She hooted aloud.

"So you are saying it was because of greed? Could I get myself a soft drink?" Morgan pointed to the mini fridge behind the bar.

"Help yourself. You can pour me another drink while you're up." Big Momma handed Morgan her snifter and tried not to snicker at the sight of Morgan's shaking hands as she poured a generous helping of the amber liquor into the glass. Then she took a can of Coke out of the refrigerator.

Morgan handed the glass to Big Momma. Then she sat back down on the sofa. The younger woman's face was pale from horror and anger. Jernell hadn't been completely honest about the family business.

"I think that fool, Todd, persuaded Adrianna to go for the

power for herself or he had his own agenda, perhaps for Brianna. I don't see Adrianna as the mastermind behind what happened. Jernell and I have been keeping a close eye on Todd. But something slipped through the cracks." Big Momma's face hardened like cement. She swallowed more whiskey. A drop trickled down her chin. "And he's going to pay."

"But, but, he's Brianna's father." Morgan's hand grasped the can so tightly that she dented it.

"His might be the sperm that participated in her birth, but he's a traitor. And Big Momma don't suffer fools lightly."

Morgan's heartbeat became irregular. She shook her head from side to side, looking dazed. This whole day had been a series of dreadful events. Sitting there talking to Big Momma seemed to top it off. Her lungs felt smothered like she was drowning. She began gasping. She was unable to catch her breath.

Big Momma set her snifter on the table. She stood and walked over to Morgan, and sat heavily on the sofa beside her niece. The younger woman recoiled slightly from her aunt like a snake had bitten her.

"Well, be that way. I was just gonna try and help you." Big Momma moved away from Morgan. She held out her hand and let it fall by her side. "I know this is a lot for you to understand, Morgan. I don't dislike you or anything. But for you to have been the one, you had to know the whole story of who we are and what we came from. Just like any other family or business, there's a lot of infighting, but the business is bigger than that. It will always survive."

Morgan's eyes, dampened with tears, were lifeless. She stood up and her body tottered She rubbed her sweaty forehead. "Big Momma, I've got to go. Daddy is waiting outside in the car for me. I just wanted to see how you were doing and see what you thought about Momma's chances for the trial." Morgan bumped into the table and the can tipped over. "I'm sorry. I've got to go."

She blindly ran for the front door. She fumbled with the lock, opened it, and flew out the house with her arms flailing like a swarm of bees was at her back.

Morgan tripped over a large stone that was part of the landscape in front of the driveway. She fell to her knees and wept.

Big Momma walked to the door and closed it. From the window she watched Rico jump out the car and assist his daughter. The older woman went back into the den. "Louisa," she bellowed, "come in here and clean up this mess."

She sat in her recliner, picked up the remote control and turned up the audio on the CD player. She closed her eyes, and hummed to Aretha singing, "Riding on the Freeway."

Rico's car tires squealed as he pulled out of Big Momma's driveway. Morgan was still breathing loudly and rocking back and forward rapidly as she sat in the backseat with Lucinda. Tears rained from her eyes.

Rico yelled, "What did she say to you? Morgan, baby talk to us." He glanced in the rearview mirror.

Lucinda put her arms around Morgan's shoulder. "Shh, don't cry. She can't hurt you."

Morgan broke into another round of tears. "Yes, she can. She told me she . . . Oh my God," the young woman repeated over and over, between deep breaths.

"Let's get out of here," Lucinda murmured softly. She pulled Morgan's head onto her shoulder.

"And go where?" Rico yelled, frustrated. He punched the steering wheel after he pulled the car into a parking space.

"I don't know. . . . Don't holler at me," Lucinda cried as she stroked Morgan's hair.

They sat in silence for some time. Then Lucinda snapped her fingers. "I think I know where we can go. Jernell has a condo downtown in Marina Towers. Harry told me she transferred the deed to Morgan's name for her graduation. Let's go there. I can't think of any place else to go."

Rico shifted the car gear. "Then we'll go there.

By the time Rico left Lake Shore Drive and was driving north on Michigan Avenue to Dearborn Street, Morgan had fallen asleep. The young woman moaned occasionally. Lucinda instructed him to park in front of the building and then she went inside. She returned to the car fifteen minutes later, triumphantly, with the key to the condo.

Rico roused Morgan. She could barely walk. Rico took one arm, and Lucinda took the other. They walked inside the building and took the elevator to the twelfth floor.

Rico slipped the key inside the lock, and they went inside. The apartment was in immaculate condition.

"The bedroom is this way." Lucinda pointed to a closed door. She and Rico laid Morgan down in the bed. Lucinda pulled the door closed. Then she and Rico returned to the living room.

"What a day," Rico complained. He went to the bar and poured himself a glass of orange juice. Then he loosened his tie and sat on the peach and green sofa. "With everything that's going on, I forgot to go to Sprint today to get a new charger for Morgan's cell phone. I thought, under the circumstances, that I'd have the number changed too. I'm sure there's a store somewhere around here. I'll go out later and see if I can find one."

Lucinda nodded. "You're right. This has been some day. The sad thing about all of this is that it's just beginning. I don't know if Morgan will be able to withstand the strain." Lucinda went into the kitchen and returned with a bottle of water for herself.

"She doesn't have a choice except to cope with the issues at hand, Lucinda. Morgan is going to have to dig deep inside, and, with God's grace, I know she'll find the will to keep going." Rico looked around the two-bedroom condo. The décor was classy, like Jernell. It was decorated with modern glass furnishings and African art. He walked to the floor-length window and peered outside at a view of the starry Chicago skyline.

"We're going to need all of the grace and mercy the Lord can spare right now, because the body and mind can only absorb so many shocks at one time, Rico. I'm really worried about her." Lucinda stood, walked to the television and turned on the television to the WGN News, Channel 9.

A banner ran across the bottom of the screen that read late breaking news in the Jernell Foster trial. Terrence stood at a podium and read a prepared statement. "New developments have arisen in the investigation of Jernell Foster. The remains of a body were discovered beneath the garage of the drug queenpin. The remains have been transported to the Cook County coroner's office."

A female reporter waved her hand. "Do you think the body can eventually be identified?"

Terrence nodded his head. He wore an unkempt black suit and a white shirt. "No doubt. We have some of the best forensics experts in the country at our disposal. It's just a question of when. Are there any other questions?"

Volleys of questions were shot his way. He answered them and promised to give everyone an update the following day.

Rico turned off the television and rubbed the space between his eyes. He looked at Lucinda and said, "Let's try to keep this new development from Morgan as long as we can. When it rains, it pours. What else can possibly happen today?"

Chapter 25

Later that same afternoon, Noah parked Jerome's Jeep Cherokee in front of his father's two-story house. He hopped out of the car, flung the gate open to the silver chain link fence and ran up the gray cement stairs two at a time. He impatiently thrust his key into the lock and opened the door.

Samuel was sitting in the living room reading when Noah walked in. The men exchanged greetings. "Son, I'm glad you're home," Samuel said. "Before you ask, things are not going well for Morgan and her family right now. I'm sure Morgan needs you more than ever. Try not to worry, and know that God is at work even in the midst of troubles." The minister sighed and sat down on one of the kitchen chairs.

"What else has happened? Morgan isn't in jail, is she?" Noah braced his body as if expecting the worst. "I've been trying to call her, but she hasn't been answering her cell phone. My calls have been routed to voicemail."

"No, she hasn't been arrested. Praise God." Samuel exhaled noisily. "But the remains of a body were found in her mother's garage. The officials haven't said who it is yet."

"Is it a man or a woman?"

"At this point, they haven't said."

Noah leaned back in his seat and rubbed the top of his head. "That's horrible. Has Morgan tried to get in touch with you?" Noah asked his father hopefully.

"No she hasn't. I'm praying for her and her family. It's a tough situation for anybody to be in. Still, we can find comfort in knowing God doesn't put more on any of us than we can bare. Are you hungry? I was just fixing myself dinner; nothing fancy though."

"No, I'm not hungry." Noah jumped up from his seat and paced the confines of the small room. "I called Morgan's apartment complex manager before I left Peoria to see if anyone had seen her. The manager told me that Morgan's father called yesterday to cancel her lease and asked her to forward Morgan's belongings to Cleveland."

"Well, she's not in Cleveland if that's what you're thinking. She's definitely somewhere here in Chicago. They've announced on the news that she's meeting with the cops tomorrow for questioning. Maybe you should try to call her cell phone again?" Samuel suggested. He rose from his seat and walked to the wooden cabinet over the sink and removed a plate. Then Samuel took a fork and knife out of one of the cabinet drawers. He strode to the stove and spooned portions of food onto his plate.

"I tried before I came in the house and I'm still getting routed to voicemail. I knew that she would turn to her father and Lucinda. I don't have telephone numbers for either one of them," Noah lamented.

Samuel sliced a fried pork chop into bite size pieces and put a bite inside his mouth. He'd prepared mashed potatoes and corn as side dishes. "Check the telephone book son. Maybe Lucinda is listed."

Noah walked to the pantry, and removed *The White Pages*. He sat down and laid it on the table. He opened then closed it. "No, that won't work. Lucinda lives with Jernell. She's a live-in housekeeper. It doesn't matter, because I don't know Lucinda's last name anyway."

"Then there's nothing you can do except wait for Morgan to call you. It's in the Lord's hands now." Samuel said a prayer and devoured his meal. He glanced at Noah. His son sat listlessly at the table. The fork dropped from Samuel's hand, clattering to the table. "I have an idea." He nodded his head up and down.

"What's that, Dad?"

"Deacon Elijah at the church works for the police department. Maybe we can call him, and see if he can find out which station Morgan will be questioned at tomorrow."

"Hmm. That's not a bad idea. Why don't you call him now?" Noah asked. A tingle of hope surged through his body.

"Okay, I'll do that after I eat."

Noah drummed on the tabletop, waiting anxiously for his father to finish the last forkful of fried corn. It seemed to take Samuel twice as long as normal to eat.

Finally, the older man put the last kernels of corn in his mouth. Samuel wiped his mouth with a napkin, stood, and put his plate in the sink. He turned on the hot and cold water faucets.

Noah stood up hastily. "Are you washing dishes now?"

"Yes, I always wash dishes after I eat."

Noah waved his father away. "Let me do that for you while you call Brother Elijah."

"Okay, son. "Samuel wiped his hands on a dishtowel. "I'll be right back." He walked into his bedroom.

Noah squirted green dish washing liquid into the dishpan and turned on the hot water. He longed to go to his father's bedroom and listen to the conversation. He put the dishes in the dishpan and let them soak for a minute. Noah kept glancing down the hallway to the bedroom.

Finally, Samuel returned to the kitchen, holding a piece of paper in his left hand. His reading glasses hovered on the end of his nose. Samuel peered at the slip of paper. "Luckily, I was able to get a hold of Brother Elijah. He told me that Morgan will be questioned at the first district precinct station located at Twelfth and State Streets tomorrow morning at nine o'clock."

Noah reached for the paper Samuel handed him. Then the older man removed his glasses. "If I were you, I'd try to be there by ten o'clock. That way you can catch her as she's leaving."

"That's exactly what I'll do." Noah stuck the scrap of paper inside his shirt pocket. "Dad, would you do a favor for me and say a prayer for Morgan? She needs all the help she can get."

"Sure I can, son." The older man closed his eyes and folded his hands in front of his chest. "Father, we come to you this evening, asking that you wrap your arms around your child, Morgan, as she faces adversity. Lord, you never promised that our way would be easy, but we know that if we trust in you, and allow your spirit to guide us, everything we do will turn out the way you planned. Lord, thank you for allowing my boy to make it safely home this evening. God, I ask that you put strength in Noah's body and mold his heart so he can help Morgan in the way you see fit. God, all praises to you as we wait on your divine guidance. These and other blessings I ask in your son's name. Amen."

Noah opened his eyes, "Amen." He echoed Samuel sentiments ardently.

Chapter 26

When Morgan awakened the following morning, she turned over on her left side in the king-sized bed. The young woman squeezed her eyes shut, as if she were reluctant to face the day. She raised one eyelid, then the other. Morgan glanced at the clock on the nightstand. It was six o'clock AM. She closed her eyes and lay motionless in the bed. Her legs were tucked against her body in a fetal position.

The events of the past few days enveloped Morgan's body and spirit heavily like an eider quilt. She thought about her appointment later that morning. She was scheduled to meet with the detectives regarding her involvement in her mother's business. She was still worried about being arrested. And how she was gong to cope if the worst happened. Thoughts of that nature eddied in and our of her mind like white waters rushing along a river. Most of all, Morgan missed Noah and the life she'd thrown away for the wrong reasons. She wondered if he had tried to call her. Morgan closed her eyes and prayed to God for forgiveness.

She stretched her legs, turned over, and laid on her stomach, debating if she should get up. She rose from the bed and picked up her purse from the top of the dresser. She rummaged inside the bag looking for her cell phone. It wasn't there. She could visualize Big Momma's mocking face in her mind from the night before, and Jernell, clad in the orange jumpsuit, and how her ponytail swayed from side to side when the guard led her back to lockup with her hands cuffed together.

The situation was almost too much for the young woman to bear. A tear rolled from the corner of Morgan's eye. A knock sounded at the door. She hastily wiped the tear from her eye and said, "Come in."

Lucinda turned the doorknob and walked into the room. She wore a wrinkled terry robe, which hung an inch beneath her knees and was carrying a cup of coffee. "I thought you might be up. How did you sleep last night?"

Morgan waved her hand from side to side. "Like a log. I think I was exhausted from everything that happened yesterday, with the lawyers, Momma, and then Big Momma."

Lucinda nodded kindly to Morgan and handed her the coffee. "Your dad and I went out last night and picked up a few personal items for both of us. He bought a charger for your cell phone, and it's in the dining room. Sprint changed the number like you requested. You and Jernell are close to the same size so you can probably wear something in her closet. There's a twenty-four-hour cleaner in the building, so Rico took his suit there. It should be ready in a hour. I can wear what I wore yesterday. I'm going to try and go by my mother's this afternoon and get some of my clothes."

"I wish I could go home." Morgan heaved a sigh. "On second thought, maybe not. If we're going to stay here for a while, then I need to go shopping myself."

"I'm sure we can do that after your meeting this morning. I'm going to shower and dress and then I'll fix us breakfast. You still have time if you want to relax a few more minutes." Lucinda headed to the door. She peered at Morgan. She hated to see the young woman looking so glum. *Lord, give her strength*, Lucinda thought as she walked out the room to begin preparing for the day.

Twenty minutes later, Morgan rose from the bed. She looked around the bedroom. She walked over to the dresser and opened it. Lingerie with the price tags still attached to it lay nestled in a jasmine sachet inside the drawer.

Morgan strolled into the walk-in closet. Dresses and pantsuits were hung on padded hangers. A rack of shoes rested on one wall. Jernell's feet were half a size larger then Morgan's. *Well it seems I don't have to go shopping after all. I might as well use Momma's stuff. She probably won't be . . .* Morgan felt guilty about her negative thoughts.

After a thorough inspection of the closet, Morgan went to the bathroom. A coral colored Jacuzzi spa tub sat in the middle of the spacious room. Morgan checked in the cabinet beneath the his-and-her sink and found Victoria's Secret bath salts. She turned on the powerful jet stream and waited for the tub to fill. When the tub was finally filled with water, Morgan shucked off her clothing and eased her body inside the tub. She felt refreshed when she was done. Curling and flat irons were on top of the sink counter. Morgan powered on the curling iron.

After she bathed and dressed, Morgan put on a white blouse, black skirt, black pumps, and a black and white cardigan sweater she had found in her mother's closet. She went back to the bathroom and applied light makeup to her worn face. She curled her hair and walked to the kitchen/dining area.

Lucinda stood at the stove turning over bacon in a black skillet over the stove. Rico sat at the glass-topped table, checking e-mails from his palm pilot. Morgan kissed his cheek before she sat across from him at the table.

"You're looking better this morning," he observed, smiling at his daughter, although his stomach was still upset. He and Lucinda still hadn't told Morgan about the corpse found in Jernell's garage. They stayed up half the night trying to figure out who the person might be, but had come up empty-handed. They were at a loss.

"I'm still nervous about my appointment this morning," Morgan said as she spread butter on a slice of toast. Lucinda set a plate with bread and eggs in front of Morgan. "But I've got to do it so I might as well get it over with."

"Do you want any meat?" Lucinda asked Morgan. She held the fork poised in the air.

"Yes, one piece, please," Morgan answered. She tackled the food hungrily, like she hadn't eaten in days.

Rico looked on amused. "I'm glad your appetite is returning. I'd say that is a good sign."

After the three finished the meal, Rico said a prayer for a favorable outcome with the detective. Half an hour later, they took the elevator down to the parking garage. Rico drove in circles down one floor after another and exited onto the street.

The condo wasn't far from the police precinct. By the time they were walking toward the building, a horde of media personnel descended upon the them.

Rico told the reporters, "No comment," as he and Lucinda struggled to get Morgan inside the building.

Gilbert stood inside near the revolving door. When he saw a deluge of people around Morgan, Rico, and Lucinda, he rushed outside. He pulled Morgan firmly by the arm and steered her inside. He repeated over and over to the eager reporters as they thrusted microphones in his face, "My client has nothing to say at this time."

Eventually, Rico and Lucinda got inside. "Whew, that was a circus!" Lucinda said, patting her mused hair.

"I'm sorry about that mishap," Gilbert apologized. "We assumed incorrectly that public interest was focused on Jernell. Obviously, we were wrong. "Morgan, if you're ready, we'll head up to the tenth floor. Remember, we can always take a break from the questioning for you to consult with me if you'd like."

Morgan nodded. Her stomach fluttered like moths were darting around inside.

"Just like yesterday, Lucinda and I will be down here waiting for you when you finish." Rico squeezed his daughter's arm comfortingly. "Everything is going to be fine. God's got this."

Lucinda nodded in agreement.

Morgan and Gilbert stood before a bank of elevator cars. "I'm sure that ordeal outside threw you a bit off kilter. Don't let them get to you. I apologize again. I should have anticipated that."

"It's okay. What happened wasn't your fault." Morgan's voice sounded shaky to her own ears.

They exited the elevator and made a left down the hallway. Detectives' names were stenciled on the glass-paneled door.

Gilbert held the door open for Morgan. She looked increasingly uncomfortable. They walked to the reception desk. "We have an appointment with Detective Simmons," Gilbert informed the older white woman.

"Have a seat over there." She pointed to a row of brown wooden chairs. She pushed a button on the telephone. "I'll call and let him know that you're here."

Fifteen minutes later, Detective Simmons walked from the rear of the room and greeted the pair. "Follow me," he instructed Gilbert and Morgan. He led them to a small cubicle.

An unused pad of paper lay atop a table surrounded by three chairs. "Can I get you a soda or coffee?" he asked Morgan and the attorney.

They sat down and Morgan shook her head no. Gilbert said, "I'll have a cup of coffee—black. No sugar."

Ten minutes later, the detective began speaking. "I'd like to record Ms. Foster's statement if that's okay with you, counselor?" he asked Gilbert.

The lawyer peered at Morgan. She'd been silent since they entered the room. She nodded hesitantly.

Detective Simmons was African-American and wore his hair in a short afro. He said in a no-nonsense, deep voice, "My partner, Luke Jennings, may join us later. He had just received an important call when you arrived."

The officer removed an ink pen from his shirt pocket. He then took off his suit jacket and laid it on the back of his chair. He uncapped the pen and opened the pad. He turned on a small tape recorder and identified himself, Gilbert, and Morgan. Then he recited the date and time.

"Ms. Foster," he began, "I'd like to assure you that, at this time, we have no probable cause or evidence to hold you. What we're interested in learning is what part, if any, you played in your family's business. What can you tell us about your mother and aunt's goings-on as they relate to your mother's corporation?"

Morgan had practiced her answers while she soaked in the spa that morning. She knew her future depended on how well she answered the officer's questions. She prayed that she sounded credible. "Well, since I was a child, I was taught that my mother ran an import and export business."

Detective Simmons checked his recording device then he looked up at Morgan. "And what type of merchandise did she sell or import through the company?"

Morgan laughed nervously. Gilbert looked at her warningly, "Electronics," she answered modestly, and dropped her eyes.

"When did you become aware that she actually moved illegal substances?"

"To my knowledge, my mother has never moved any illegal substances." Sweat gathered under Morgan's bangs. She clasped her hands together and moved forward in her chair.

"So, you've never, ever heard anything to that effect?" The detective rephrased the question.

"I never heard any rumors like that, so I never asked my mother any questions about that kind of stuff." Morgan crossed her fingers, fudging the truth.

Gilbert nodded approvingly at her answer.

"Come on now, Ms. Foster. You lived in a mansion, and your mother wasn't married. Didn't you wonder where her income came from?" the detective grilled Morgan.

"Not really, I mean," Morgan stammered, "that I focused on my schoolwork and kept to myself." The young woman's clammy hands shook. She kept them laced together on her lap. "I couldn't tell you what many of my classmates' parents did for a living. So I didn't have any point of reference. For the most part, I mostly associated with my cousins, and they had nice homes and clothing too. Because my mother was the president of the company, I just assumed she made more money than everyone else." She anxiously tapped her heel on the carpeted floor.

The detective's expression became grim. His voice held a hint of exasperation when he asked Morgan, "So you're telling me that you never discussed any of your mother's activities with her? At any time in your life?"

"No . . . not really," Morgan answered wide-eyed. She wanted to close her eyes and block out the detective's face.

"Well, that's not what your uncle told us." The officer's voice became menacing. "He said you're heavily involved."

"My uncle didn't reside with us. So he really has no way of knowing what went on in my mother's home. And I've been away at college for the past four years. The only thing I've been heavily involved in is preparing to graduate." Morgan's voice sounded stronger, though her eyes were sad.

Detective Simmons grilled her unmercifully for another

hour. Morgan's voice would falter at times, then she'd recover her resolve, glancing at Gilbert from time to time.

Finally, after what seemed years to Morgan, the officer turned off the machine. "That will be all for now, Ms. Foster. We may call you back in for questioning at a later date."

"So, I'm not being arrested?" Morgan asked. She relaxed. Her body felt so weak that she had to suppress an urge tumble to the floor, curl up into a ball, and go to sleep.

"No, that's it for now." He stood up, nodded his head, and departed from the room.

Gilbert stood up and turned to Morgan, peering at her compassionately. "You look beat."

Morgan stood. Her legs felt like limp noodles. "That was difficult. Did I do all right?"

"Let's go. We'll talk outside," Gilbert informed her. He took her arm, and they walked out of the cubicle, to the elevator. The lawyer pressed the down button.

As they waited for the car to arrive, Morgan tried to gauge the detective's reaction to her answers. She assumed she did okay and that if there had been a problem, Detective Simmons would have detained her.

Gilbert and Morgan exited the elevator. Lucinda and Rico walked to them.

"How did it go?" Rico asked tensely.

"I think she did well under the circumstances. The detective said he'll be in touch if he needs her for any further information." Gilbert nodded at Morgan."I think it would be in Morgan's best interest if we leave from the basement exit to try and avoid the crowd outside," Gilbert suggested. "Lucinda, I'm sure you'll be eventually called in for questioning too, along with Jernell's other employees."

The four people returned to the bank of elevators and rode down one floor. When they arrived outside, Rico said hesitantly, "Uh, Gilbert, can we talk to you for a minute? We didn't tell Morgan the latest development."

"And what would that be?" Morgan turned and asked her father dryly. She crossed her arms over her chest.

"I thought you and Lucinda had told her," Gilbert commented as he transferred his briefcase from one hand to the other. He looked at Morgan. "The police found the remains of a body in your mother's garage buried under the concrete."

"Who is it?" Morgan asked, feeling alarmed.

"The coroner will be running tests. They haven't been able to identify the body yet," Gilbert replied, frowning slightly at Rico and Lucinda.

"I tell you, my life is going from bad to worse. The police don't think Momma killed someone, do they?" Morgan scrutinized Gilbert's face. Pings of pain tumbled through her head. She massaged her forehead.

"No, they don't, not at this time. The body has apparently been in the garage a long time. So I suggest we wait until the tests are concluded before we jump to any conclusions," Gilbert suggested.

"If you hear anything regarding the body or anything else, then please let us know," Rico instructed Gilbert.

"Will do. By the way, where are you folks staying?" he asked.

"In the Marina Towers. Not too long ago, Jernell transferred the deed to Morgan's name. It's okay for us to stay there, isn't it?" Lucinda asked.

"The Feds have seized Jernell's house, and of course, the warehouses, so those places are off limits for you right now. The disposition of the property she owns outright will depend on the outcome of the trial. I'll be in touch with you all as information is available. I know in light of everything happening, saying this may sound insensitive, but try to have a good day. Especially you, Morgan." Gilbert turned to look at his client.

"Same to you," Morgan replied in a sing-song voice.

They departed the parking garage and walked to their cars. Gilbert's car was parked a couple of blocks away from Rico's. He waved good-bye to the trio.

As Morgan turned to open the car door, she heard someone calling her name. She pirouetted around and her ear honed in on the voice. Her mouth curved upward with pleasure when she saw Noah walking rapidly, almost running, toward her. Even though she wore four-inch pumps, Morgan raced down the street to meet him.

When they were about a few feet apart, Noah stopped and held out his arms. Morgan flew into them. He held her in his arms tenderly. His arms tightened around Morgan neck like a vise, as if he couldn't bear to let her go.

Morgan wound her arms around Noah's neck. "You came back," she murmured against his chest between sobs. "I am so glad that you came back to me."

Lucinda looked upward and silently whispered, "Thank you, Lord."

A grin, like a burst of sunlight, covered Rico's face. "I knew that young man wasn't going to desert Morgan," he said. "God granted us one of those little miracles we needed."

Noah's hand lovingly stroked Morgan's hair. "I'm sorry for leaving you, baby. I should have stayed and talked to you instead of leaving the way I did."

"No," Morgan moaned as her hand caressed Noah's face, "it was my fault. You were right about everything. I didn't understand it then. I just didn't want to let Momma down. I'm all she has. And after these past few days, I realize now that I wasn't really cut out for that kind of life. Noah, will you forgive me?"

"There's nothing to forgive, Morgan. I'm here now. The Lord brought us back together, and that's all that matters." He turned her face up and kissed her lips hungrily.

"Well, Lucinda, our work here is done. I'm sure Noah will make sure Morgan gets home later," Rico smiled. His hand dropped to his side. He'd shaded his eyes to watch his daughter and Noah.

"Yes, we're done for now. The cavalry has arrived. Noah's being here will ease Morgan's load a bit. But Rico, we can't fool ourselves, we still have a long way to go before this ordeal is over," Lucinda commented. Worry lines, like thread, were etched across her forehead.

They continued to converse as they walked to Rico's car.

Noah and Morgan looked up and waved to Lucinda. Rico tooted his horn as he drove by them. The young man took Morgan's hand in his, and they strode to his vehicle.

"When did you get here?" Morgan asked Noah, looking at him shyly as they walked down the street.

"As soon as I learned what was happening with your mother. I didn't have any way of getting in touch with you. I tried to call, but you never answered your phone."

"My cell phone was dead," Morgan explained. She reached down and brought Noah's hand to her lips and kissed it. Then she said, "I didn't bring the charger with me when I left Peoria. Daddy bought me a new charger yesterday evening, and he had the number changed. How did you know I would be here this morning?"

Noah put his arm around Morgan's waist. "One of the deacons at Dad's church is a policeman. He tipped us off to which station you'd be at this morning. I was camped down here at eight o'clock this morning, hoping to catch up with you."

"Thank God he gave you the information. I needed you so badly." Morgan's voice became husky. "I was trying to adjust to life without you, and I wasn't doing too well," Morgan complained. "A big piece of my heart was missing: You."

Noah patted his chest. "I brought it back to you, baby, and I ain't going nowhere."

They walked around the corner to Jerome's car and got inside.

"What are you going to do about school and graduation?" Morgan asked. She rolled down the window. Her life, just a few days ago, seemed very remote and far away.

"If I didn't tell you before, I'm here for as long as you need me. The important thing for me to do now is take care of you, and do what I can to ease your burdens."

Morgan looked at Noah forlornly. "You can't do that, Noah," she protested. "You have to go back to school. Graduation has always been so important to you. You're the first person in your family to earn a degree. It wouldn't be fair to deprive your father of seeing you walk across the stage to get it because of my troubles."

"Don't worry about my father. He understands." Noah started the car. "Where to, Ms. Foster?"

"I'm so tired. I just want to go somewhere where I close my eyes and sleep. And when I wake up, I'll see you there with me. I wish everything from the past days few would just go away. I don't want to wake up and find out that being with you today was a figment of my imagination," Morgan said morosely.

"Trust me," Noah placed Morgan's hand on his cheek. "I'm here in the flesh. God sent me here to keep an eye on my lady. I think I know a place where you can lay your head. It's not a five-star hotel or even in the best part of town. But I guarantee, Morgan, that you'll be safe from harm there. And when you awaken, I promise I'll be there."

"Where is that place, Noah? Does such a place really exist?" Morgan's nose crinkled in wonder.

"Sure it does. I'm talking about my dad's house. So far, the media doesn't know about our relationship. It would be the perfect place for you to get away from the maddened crowd."

Morgan nodded her head thoughtfully. She pulled her cell phone out of her purse and called Rico. She told her father that she'd be back at the condo later.

Noah drove to the Dan Ryan Expressway. Then he steered the car on the entrance ramp and headed south. He looked over at Morgan. She'd fallen asleep. Her body was slumped against the window. Her grip on Noah's hand had loosened.

He peered at her from time to time as he drove. He felt better that some of the worry lines he'd seen etched in her forehead had disappeared.

Noah parked the car in Samuel's garage instead of on the street. He made a right turn into the alley. Then he used the remote to raise the garage door. Noah backed the vehicle into the garage. He turned off the car and turned to gaze at Morgan. He hated to rouse her. She looked so peaceful. He gently pressed her shoulder. "Morgan, we're here," he said softly.

She opened her eyes and smiled. "You're still here." She sat upright in the seat and reached out to touch his face.

"We're here. Let's go inside, baby."

Noah walked around to the passenger's side of the car and opened the door. When Morgan exited the vehicle, he hugged her again.

They walked to the back door and up the stairway. Noah unlocked the door and opened it. "Dad, are you home?" he yelled. There wasn't an answer. "I guess we have the place to ourselves then." He turned to Morgan. "What do you want to do?"

"Go back to sleep," she yawned, covering her mouth. "I'm still tired."

Noah led her to his bedroom, which was still decorated the same way it had been when he was a teenager. "Why don't you rest in here?"

"Okay." Morgan walked over to the twin bed and sat on the side of it. She bent over, removed her shoes, laid down, and closed her eyes.

Noah walked to his closet and removed a red blanket from the shelf. He spread it over Morgan's legs. "Sleep well, love. Everything is going to be okay."

Jernell lie on her back on the top bunk in the jail cell with a pair of earphones on her ears. One of her hands was beneath her neck. Her eyes were closed, but she wasn't asleep. A guard walked to her cell and banged lightly on the bars with a nightstick. "You have a visitor," he informed the prisoner.

Jernell sat up quickly. "Is it my daughter?"

"No, it's your lawyer."

The guard opened the cell door, then she shackled Jernell's hands behind her back. The guard led her to an interrogation room. Yolanda sat at the desk, reading notes she'd made inside a folder.

"To what do I owe this visit?" Jernell sat down and massaged her wrists. "Did everything go alright with Morgan today? Is she okay?"

"As far as I know, Morgan is fine. Gilbert says she did a good job this morning. I'm here on another matter."

"What's happening now?" Jernell's right eyebrow arched up.

"Did you happen to watch the news last night?" Yolanda asked her client.

"No. Why?"

"As I told you, the police are still digging around your house. They found the remains of a body buried beneath your garage, and from all accounts, it looks like it has been there for a long time."

Jernell closed her eyes. Her mouth dropped open. She

swayed back in the chair as if she were going to faint. She opened her eyes and asked Yolanda. "Did you say a dead body, as in skeleton?"

"Yes, I did. The remains have been transported to the coroner's office. They're going to start testing soon. They plan to have a report available within a week or two. So I thought I'd come talk to you to find out if you knew of any reason someone's remains would be found on your property."

"Well no, not really. Although . . ." Jernell's voice weakened, "my mother has been missing for years. Big Momma told me and my sisters that she may have left us because she didn't want any part of the family. The story always seemed kind of fishy to me, because I know my mother wouldn't have left without her children." Jernell sucked in air. She looked colorless. Her hands grasped the side of the table tightly.

Yolanda sat her pen down on the table. "Do you think there's a possibility that the body could be your mother?"

Jernell gazed off into space. She looked back at Yolanda and shook her head, "I don't know. It could be . . ."

"I have to ask you this, Jernell, and I know it will be painful for you to hear. Could your aunt have had anything to do with your mother's disappearance?" Yolanda's eyes dug tunnels into her client's.

Jernell waved her hand impatiently. "I don't know . . . No, what am I saying? Of course not. Big Momma loved my mother and me and my sisters. There's no way she would have hurt Momma. My mother was her older sister. Big Momma looked up to her. They didn't have any other siblings. It was only the two of them."

"Stranger things have happened. And the family business was very lucrative."

Jernell jumped up from her seat. The guard rapped on

the window. Jernell sat back in the seat. "Don't try to cross me up, Yolanda. I know what you're doing, trying to play one family member against the other."

"That's not true," Yolanda protested. "My job is to help you beat your criminal charges and get you out of here." The lawyer held out her hands. "I have no ulterior motives. You know I have to ask you these questions in case they become an issue during your trial."

Jernell looked horrified. "The cops don't think I had anything to do with this, do they?"

Yolanda didn't answer for a minute. "The body was found in your garage. Based on that fact alone, you're going to be a suspect. I would suggest we let the coroner complete the tests, then we'll take it from there."

"Is that it?" Jernell rose from the chair.

Yolanda stuffed her folder and pad back into her briefcase. "Yes, that's it for now. I'll keep you apprised of any new developments."

Jernell walked toward the door. She paused and placed her hands on her hips. "So, Morgan did okay, huh? Gilbert doesn't foresee any problems down the road for her?"

"He said she stuck to her story, that she really didn't know much and has been away at college. The detective tried to trip Morgan up a few times by telling her that Todd and your niece, Brianna, told him otherwise. The fact that Morgan has been away attending school the past four years was a huge factor in her not being charged as an accessory or worse. If this brouhaha had occurred a year from now, it would be a different story for your daughter." Yolanda stood and put the briefcase strap on her shoulder.

"I always taught my girl that timing is everything. I'm glad she's out of this. So the Feds will probably concentrate on me." Jernell looked at Yolanda seriously. "So what does it look like for me? Do you think I can beat this?"

Yolanda looked away from Jernell uneasily, "I don't like to predict the outcomes of trials. I'm optimistic, and I'll do my best to get you off."

"Hey, Yolanda, I can read between the lines," Jernell replied. She walked to the door and rapped on it. Then she turned to face Yolanda. "Just do your best, that's all I ask of you."

Yolanda stood, strolled over to Jernell and laid her hand on her client's shoulder. "Of course I will. I didn't mean to imply that the situation is dire. It's hard to say what will happen. Todd spilling his guts to cop a plea hasn't helped matters. All I can say is that we have an uphill battle on our hands."

Jernell's lips tightened. "I've been in tighter spots. Just do your job and everything will work out fine."

As Yolanda departed from the facility, Jernell held out her wrists so the guard could cuff her. Then the woman led her back to her cell.

Chapter 27

Morgan awakened from a restful sleep. Her eyes traveled along the walls in Noah's room. Pictures of his favorite sports heroes from bygone days were still taped to the blue walls. An old wooden bookshelf desk laid on one wall. The bottom shelf held quite a few books and Bibles. The room was small—a mere fraction of the size of Morgan's room at the gray stone.

The young woman pulled the blanket up to her nose and inhaled Noah's natural scent. She felt comforted. A boom box sat on the old oak scarred dresser. The matching chest of drawers sat on the wall opposite the dresser. Morgan wondered if she'd ever go back home to live. *Probably not.*

Morgan sat up in the bed. Then she stood and walked to the bookcase and picked up a red leather-covered Bible with gold lettering on the outside. She flipped through the pages until her eyes rested on a verse, Second Thessalonians 2:16 verses: "May our Jesus Christ himself and God our Father, who loved us and by His grace gave us eternal encouragement and good hope, encourage your hearts and strengthen you in every good word and deed." *Amen Lord, I need en-*

couragement, hope, and strength. Please grant me all three. She closed the Bible, and put it back inside the bookcase. She walked to the dresser and peered at her reflection in the mirror. The ends of her hair flew in opposite directions. She looked in her purse, found a comb, and repaired her hair. After taking a deep breath, Morgan followed the voices she heard coming from the kitchen.

Samuel bounded up from his seat, walked over to the young woman, and hugged her. "Praise God, you're here. You look like you're doing okay. Young lady, Noah and I have been very worried about you and praying for you."

Noah sat at the kitchen table. The telephone book was opened in front of him. "I was just looking for a restaurant so we could have some food delivered. What do you have a taste for? We can go out to dinner if you'd like." Noah smiled at Morgan.

"I don't think so; not with my face in the newspapers. I'm not choosy. Anything you have here would be fine," she answered as she sat at the table. Morgan clasped her hands together on the tabletop.

"I could go to the grocery store and bring something back here to cook," Samuel suggested, looking from Noah to Morgan.

"Oh no, Reverend Sam, I don't want to put you through any trouble," Morgan protested. "Really, I can eat whatever you have here."

"I didn't go grocery shopping this week. So I don't have much in the house: lunch meat, hot dogs, and peanut butter and jelly." Samuel looked abashed. He dropped his head to the floor.

"You know what? I haven't had a peanut butter and jelly sandwich in a long time." Morgan's stomach rumbled. "That would be fine with a glass of milk."

"Then peanut butter and jelly it will be." Noah stood. "I'll fix it for you."

"And I'll pour you a glass of milk," Samuel volunteered.

A warm feeling suffused Morgan's body at the sight of the two men catering to her. "While you're doing that, I'm going to call my dad and Luci."

She returned to the bedroom and called Rico. After Morgan talked to Rico, she spoke to Lucinda.

"I'm glad you and Noah have been able to put your differences behind you and get back together," the older woman commented.

"It's a start," Morgan agreed. "Reverend Sam says we've had divine intervention in this case."

"I'll agree and defer to the minister on that one," Lucinda remarked, laughing. "You're so blessed that Noah came back to you."

"I know it, and I don't plan to ever let him leave me again," Morgan vowed. She and Lucinda talked a while longer. She then told her former nanny good-bye. Morgan closed her cell phone and grinned.

When she returned to the kitchen, Noah had prepared her sandwich. "Lucinda thinks there is a chance I may be able to go the gray stone in a few days and get some of my clothing," Morgan informed the men. Then she wolfed down the sandwich. She smiled prettily at Noah. "Would you make one more sandwich for me? I've been pigging out since I came back to Chicago. I guess it's due to nerves." She greedily gulped the milk. Noah and Samuel looked at her. Amusement danced in their eyes.

When Morgan finished eating, she wiped her hands and mouth on the napkin that Samuel had placed next to her plate.

"Morgan, I'd like for you to do something for me," Samuel said. He walked to the den and returned with his Bible. "Whenever you're feeling low, and like you have no one, or no place to go, I want you to remember the Twenty-third Psalm. Noah, would you recite it for her, son?"

"I sure will, Dad," the young man replied. He closed his eyes and said, "The Lord is my shepherd. I shall not want. He maketh me to lie down in green pastures. He leadeth me beside the still waters. He restoreth my soul. He leadeth me in the paths of righteousness for His name's sake. Yea, though I walk through the valley of the shadow of death, I will fear no evil. For Thou art with me; Thy rod and thy staff they comfort me. Thou preparest a table before me in the presence of mine enemies. Thou anointest my head with oil; my cup runneth over. Surely goodness and mercy shall follow me all the days of my life; and I will dwell in the house of the LORD for ever."

"Amen. I want you to always remember, whenever we face battles that we're not alone," Samuel said to Morgan. "Pay special attention to the verse; thy rod and thy staff they comfort me. God always has you under His protection."

"I will, Reverend Sam," Morgan promised with shiney eyes. She took his hand in hers and squeezed it.

Several minutes later, Noah asked Morgan, "Now what do you want to do? Go back to the condo or stay here?"

"I can't impose on you and your father indefinitely," Morgan objected.

"Young lady, think of my house as your house," Samuel protested, holding up his hand. "You're welcome to stay as long as you'd like. Just don't try any funny business under my roof. You catch my drift, don't you?"

Noah and Morgan knew exactly what the older man meant. They nodded and Samuel left the kitchen.

"Actually, I'd like to go see Bri," Morgan declared. "I'd like to find out how she's doing. Maybe she can tell me what's happening with her father."

Noah rubbed his chin. "Are you sure about that? Seeing your aunt and cousin might exacerbate the situation. After all, your cousin's father is responsible for your mother being in jail," he said openly.

Morgan sighed softly. "Despite all that's happened, we're still family. I owe it to myself to find out what went wrong, even if it hurts me. Plus, I know Bri is hurting too, and she needs me."

"Have you talked this over with Lucinda and your father? What do they think?"

"We talked a little bit about it yesterday," Morgan admitted. She rubbed her eyes. "Seeing Brianna is something I've got to do."

"Then let's go. But be prepared for the possibility of more heartache, Morgan."

"I am," she replied grimly.

Samuel sat writing at his desk inside the same den. He looked up when Noah entered the room. "What's up, son?"

"Morgan has an errand to run. I'm going to take her there, and then we'll be back later."

"Okay, I'll see you when you come back."

When Noah returned to the living room, Morgan had her purse under her arm. "Let's go," she said simply.

"No problem." They left from the back door and headed to the garage. Noah started the car and drove north.

There was little conversation during the drive. The mood inside the car was somber. Noah turned on the CD player and BeBe and CeCe Winans's voices flooded the interior of the car as they sang "Addicted To Love."

Butterflies resumed waltzing inside Morgan's stomach. The closer Noah got to Adrianna's house, the tenser the young woman became. Her fingers nervously thumped the console between the bucket seats. Brianna had opted to stay home with her parents instead of renting her own apartment while she was home at the end of the semester from college. It made sense to the young woman since Adrianna played an active part in helping with the wedding preparations.

Noah and Morgan sat in bumper-to-bumper traffic on

the Dan Ryan Expressway that Wednesday evening in May, due to a White Sox game. Morgan gave Noah directions to the house as they got closer to their destination.

Noah had a hard time finding a parking space near the townhouse. He circled the block three times until he saw a midnight blue Lexus coupe exiting a parking space. Noah steered the car into it. He shut the car off and turned to Morgan. "You don't have to do this, you know. Sometimes it's best to let go and let God handle this in His own time instead of taking matters into your own hands."

"I need to know everything that went wrong with my family, Noah."

"Do you want or need me to come inside with you?"

Morgan shook her head and opened the door. "I'll be back as soon as I can."

"I'm praying for you, baby. I know God is going to be there every step of the way. You know I have your back if you need me."

"I know you do. I'll meet you back here as soon as I can."

Morgan exited the car and walked midway down the block. She reflected on how most of her life, she couldn't wait to come to the townhouse, to spend time with three of her most favorite people in the world. Brianna's home was Morgan's home away from home, and now she dreaded the visit like the plague. She wondered why her life had to change so drastically and hoped she was doing the right thing by coming to see her cousin. Morgan drew in a lungful of air and expelled it.

Before Morgan could ring the doorbell and give herself time to steady her shaky nerves, the door flew open. Adrianna held a crystal goblet of clear liquor in one hand. She stepped aside to allow her niece entry. Smirking at Morgan, the older woman said, "What are you standing out there for?" She raised the glass in her hand. "Come on in."

After Morgan stepped inside the door, she leaned over

and kissed Adrianna's cheek. Morgan inhaled a whiff of sourness from her aunt's body, mingled with the scent of alcohol. "Hi, Aunt Adrianna. How are you doing?"

Adrianne swept her hand in the air. The liquor sloshed out of the glass and spilled on her fingers. Morgan watched as her aunt licked it. "How do you think we're doing?" She pointed at the boxes strewn around the nearly empty room.

"What's going on here?" Morgan asked. Her eyes widened in surprise as she surveyed the room.

"We're out of here." The usually flawlessly dressed Adrianna wore a pair of soiled forest green sweat pants and an equally grimy matching top. She rose on the balls of her feet and tethered on the pair of high heel mules she wore on her feet. Her hair resembled a bird's nest.

"There's a card table and chairs in the dining room. We can go sit in there," Adrianna suggested as she staggered to the adjoining room.

Morgan sat on the edge of one of the padded chairs. "Where's Brianna?" she asked her aunt as she looked directly into the older woman's face.

Adrianna's once smooth complexion was littered with unsightly bumps. Crow's feet danced around her red, blurry eyes. "She's here somewhere." Adrianna burped. The sour scent of gin wafted from her aunt's mouth, aggravating Morgan's nostrils. "Oops, I'm sorry," Adrianna hiccupped. She covered her mouth.

Brianna ran down the staircase. "Oh, it's you," she said to Morgan tautly. She strolled into the room and circled around her cousin's body. Brianna's arms were crossed belligerently over her chest. She glared at Morgan hostilely.

"Uh, Brianna, are you all right?" Morgan asked, concerned about her cousin's attitude.

"I don't feel too well." Adrianna rose shakily to her feet. Her gait was unsteady. She clutched her abdomen as she walked to the bathroom.

"Does it look like I'm all right?" Brianna hissed at Morgan. She clenched and unclenched her fists.

"I know this is a bad time for all of us. I just don't understand why you seem to have an attitude against me," Morgan lamented with her hands outstretched. "I wasn't even in town when all of this went down."

If Morgan thought Adrianna looked unkempt, Brianna's appearance was even worse. Her hair was piled untidily on top of her head, resembling a stringy dry mop. Her eyes radiated hatred. She wore an olive colored tank top and a pair of khaki cut-off jeans with an uneven hem. She looked and smelled like she hadn't bathed in days.

Morgan felt as if she'd stepped into a house of horrors and the person she was facing was an alien. She wanted to grab Brianna by the shoulders and shake her until the Brianna that she'd known and loved returned.

"It was your mother that got us into this mess," Brianna yelled. Her breath reeked like she hadn't brushed her teeth in days.

"I beg to differ," Morgan countered as her voice rose. "Your father is the reason all this has happened."

"Daddy didn't do anything wrong. He was only trying to protect the family. He tried to work with your mother, but she had her own agenda," Brianna yelled as she walked menacingly toward Morgan.

"I think you'd better back off me," Morgan said heatedly. She thrust her hands in front on her body.

Brianna's face turned red. She hesitated and then moved away from her cousin. "Do you realize that I'm the laughing stock of Chicago? By now, everyone in the city knows Terence used me to advance his career. Daddy is tucked away at a safe house and Mommy has nearly lost her mind. Then you have the nerve to come here acting like little Ms. Innocence, asking how we're doing. How do you think we're doing?"

Brianna yelled. She burst into tears and fell to her knees on the floor. She covered her face with her hands.

Morgan stood and rushed to her cousin's side. She knelt on the floor beside Brianna. She gathered the young woman in arms. The women sat down on the floor, clung to each other and cried together.

Many minutes elapsed, then Brianna pulled away from Morgan and sniffed. "I wish I were dead. I hate Daddy for what he's done, and I hate Terrence even more." She began rocking back and forth. Her face was screwed into a fierce scowl. Brianna wiped her eyes.

"Have you talked to Terrence since all of this happened?" Morgan ventured to ask.

"He called a couple of times. I didn't take his calls. What can he say? My life is ruined. All of our lives are ruined. Aunt Jernell is in jail. Mommy feels guilty because Daddy is trying to cut a plea deal and she knows that will strengthen the case against your mother. She's been drinking since your mother was arrested. I just don't know . . ." Brianna's gaze dropped, and her voice trailed off.

Morgan noticed her cousin's fingernails were bitten to the quick, and the big diamond ring she'd sported on her left ring finger was missing.

Despite everything that had happened, Morgan empathized with her cousin and her aunt. "Things aren't going too well for me either, Brianna. I feel just as bad as you do. My world feels like a globe spinning around. I went to visit Momma yesterday and she was wearing an orange jumpsuit like you see criminals on television wearing." Morgan's eye's brimmed with tears. "Momma was trying to put on a brave face for me, but I know being in jail has to be killing her."

"We were the original BAPs," Brianna laughed harshly. "Rich, young, and beautiful with successful lives ahead of us. Now those lives are gone like a poof of smoke." Brianna snapped her fingers. "Daddy is going into the witness protection program. Mommy wants me to come with them, but I don't know what I want to do. I don't have anything to live for, Morgan.

"The Feds have seized our accounts. We're broke. I guess you are too." Brianna pushed a stray strand of hair out of her face. "All we have is our clothing and what you see here. Mommy sold most of our possessions to raise bail money for Daddy, even though it wasn't necessary since he opted to go into the witness protection plan. Have you talked to Big Momma? I don't understand why she isn't helping us."

"Didn't your parents have some money saved?"

Brianna snorted. "Gurl, you know we lived high on the hog. We don't even have a car. It was impounded due to the case." Brianna rubbed her brow. "Where are you staying? Have the police talked to you?"

"Yes. Detective Simmons interrogated me this morning. The ordeal was brutal."

"Detective Williams was the officer who talked to us. He's been here three times already."

"I'm staying with Luci and her mother," Morgan lied. She didn't want Brianna to go off on another tear about her staying in a condo on the lakefront while she and her mother suffered.

"You know I was always jealous of you," Brianna admitted to Morgan. "You were the chosen one. I knew you really didn't want the power like I did. If only I had been born before you. But I guess that's all a moot point now. No one will be running the empire."

"Maybe it's for the best." Morgan patted Brianna's arm.

"Don't you dare say that." Brianna pulled away from Morgan. "We've never been poor a day in our lives. Everyone knows who we are. What do we have to look forward to now?"

"Bri, you're smart. We'll survive. You're done at Howard.

I know you already have enough credits to graduate. Maybe the Lord wants us to just become just regular people."

"That's what you wanted for yourself, Morgan. It's not what I wanted, not by a long shot." Brianna had a far away look in her eyes. "I can't believe Big Momma hasn't called or come here." A look of fright crossed the young woman's face. "You don't think she would try to do something to hurt Daddy do you?"

"No, I don't think so." Morgan was grateful her complexion was dark. She knew had her complexion been lighter, that Brianna would see her blushing, and sense that she was lying. "Don't forget Big Momma is being investigated too."

"You're right. She's probably taking care of her own business. So what are you going to do now, Morgan?"

Morgan looked down at her feet. "I don't know. I told Noah the truth about our family. He was going to propose, and we broke up. Then when he heard what happened to Momma, he rushed from Peoria to be with me. He's parked outside waiting for me now."

"See, that's what I mean." the corners of Brianna's mouth turned down. She smacked the heel of her palm on the floor beside them. "You've still come out on top. I don't have anyone or anything."

"You'll always have me." Morgan patted the younger woman's hand. "Terrence just wasn't the one. We're young, Brianna. You'll meet someone else one day, and everything that happened will become an old memory. You'll see."

"Not soon enough," Brianna murmured. "Do you think life will return as we knew it?"

"No, I think those days are long gone," Morgan replied honestly. "Hey, it can't get any worse than this.

The cousins continued to talk. Morgan tried her best to raise her cousin's spirits. Brianna was in a bad way.

An hour passed before Morgan bade her cousin good-bye. As they stood at the door, Morgan promised Brianna that she'd come back and visit her. Though Morgan had put on a brave face, she was worried about her cousin and aunt. All she could do was hope things would work out the way God planned. Like Samuel had told her, "He has love in His heart for everyone."

When she arrived at the car, Morgan found Noah asleep. She smiled before she tapped on the window to wake him. She realized after her dismal discussion with Brianna, that her load was lighter than her cousin's. Maybe Reverend Sam was right in saying that God was in the blessing business. After all, she had Noah, Rico, Lucinda, and Samuel, and now it seemed God, too, was in her corner.

It had taken a spate of misfortune for Morgan to accept that there was a God. After she got into the car, Morgan looked at Noah and said, "There's something I want to share with you . . ."

Chapter 28

The public assumed incorrectly that Big Momma would be indicted along with her niece. That wasn't the case. Law enforcement officials couldn't find charges to pin on the older women. Jernell became edgy from being locked up after Yolanda's petition for bail was denied. She advised her lawyers to do whatever was necessary to have the trial expedited.

Yolanda and her team strategically decided to place Jernell's fate in the hands of a judge, requesting a bench instead of a jury trial. Doing so would shorten the time that would have ensued with a jury selection. To complicate matters, the coroner's office hadn't yet released their findings regarding the remains from Jernell's garage, even though the autopsy had been completed. Yolanda assumed the hold-up was due to political shenanigans, to help the Feds bolster their case.

Three months later, on a mid-September Monday morning, Jernell's trial was scheduled to begin.

As Yolanda had feared, a few days before the trail, the coroner's office, after stonewalling her attempts to get a copy of the autopsy report, held a press conference at Stroger Hospital to announce their finding regarding the body from Jernell's garage. Local news channels interrupted their regular programming to broadcast the results.

Dr. Sloan blinked rapidly from flashing cameras as he stood at the podium in the hospital. He announced in a solemn voice, "The body found in Jernell Foster's garage has been positively identified as that of her mother, Pamela Foster."

Pandemonium arose in the conference room at the hospital as reporters waved their hands and notebooks in the air. Flashbulbs went off.

Morgan was sitting in the living room at the condo. Lucinda sat on a chair next to her. Morgan looked at Lucinda and shook her head wretchedly. "When will this drama end? My life can't get any worse, can it?

Lucinda murmured, "God willing, it won't." The older woman crossed her fingers.

The next morning the *Chicago Sun Times* headline shouted the latest news:

Bitter Rivals, or Loving Mother and Daughter?

The grisly remains found at a Lake Park mansion on the southeast side of Chicago have been identified as those of Pamela Foster. The woman vanished from her South Side home, the same home in which Jernell Foster resides, more than twenty years ago.

The disappearance of the Foster woman wasn't reported to the authorities, a spokesperson for the Chicago Police Department commented.

A close relative, wishing to remain anonymous, said their family member disappeared under suspicious circumstances.

Pamela Foster is the mother of alleged queenpin, Jernell Foster. The younger Foster woman faces multiple federal and state charges of money laundering and possession and distribution of controlled substances. The U.S. Government has also filed RICO charges for tax evasion. If convicted, Ms. Foster could spend the rest of her natural life behind bars.

Detectives of the eleventh precinct attending the press conference at Stroger Hospital yesterday, said they plan to investigate Jernell Foster's possible involvement in her mother's death.

Yolanda Collins, Mrs. Foster's attorney and a member of the Smyth, Hollingsworth, & Ellis Law Firm, scoffed at the detectives' assertions that her client played any part in her mother's demise. Ms. Collins was quoted as saying, "My client was a child at the time of her mother's disappearance. She was devastated by what she perceived as her only parent's desertion. My client is innocent, and we'll prove that the allegations against my client are false. Mrs. Foster is also suffering a beating by the press."

Thomas Levy, spokesperson for the Cook County Coroner's Office, stated the elder Mrs. Foster was a victim of foul play. The cause of her death resulted from a single gunshot wound to the back of her head. Ms. Collins asserted during her own press conference that the findings bolster her client's innocence.

The police are researching another anonymous tip regarding the ownership of the murder weapon. They refuse to divulge details of the case at this time, citing the investigation is ongoing.

Jernell Foster's sensational trial is slated to begin Monday, October 15, 2006 in the honorable Judge Malcolm Henry's courtroom.

The date was a few weeks before Morgan's twenty-second birthday.

Chapter 29

The spectators in Judge Walter Henry's courtroom stood as the dark-robed, white-haired judge made his way to the bench. The trial of the United States of America and the City of Chicago versus Jernell Foster was in session.

All of Chicago was abuzz about the court proceedings. Never in the city's history had a woman been charged in connection with such an infamous crime. The stories took a prominent position in the newspapers for months. You couldn't open a newspaper without finding Jernell's face inside. *Court TV* petitioned the court to telecast the trial, but Judge Henry denied their request.

Jernell, according to the media, was a woman of ill repute and therefore, everyone affiliated with her was guilty by association.

Lucinda was subpoenaed as a witness by the prosecution, much to her chagrin. She sat on a bench outside the courtroom waiting for her turn to testify. Morgan, Brianna, Big Momma, and other family members were seated a few rows behind Jernell. The star witness was none other than Todd.

He wasn't in court today, but would testify later during the proceedings.

"You may be seated," Judge Henry said, peering at the sea of faces in front of him. The press was out in full court.

The female members of the Foster family were dressed in black dresses, hosiery, and shoes. They wore large rimmed designer sunshades on their noses to shield their eyes from inquisitive stares.

"You may begin your opening statement," Judge Henry instructed the state. A team of four attorneys sitting at the table opposite Jernell were eager to bring down the most notorious female drug distributor in Chicago's history.

The Foster women listened—fascinated at times and horrified at other points—as the female, blonde prosecutor painted a grim picture of Jernell Foster.

The defendant sat in her chair stoically, not giving a hint of her emotions. She was dressed conservatively in a black Calvin Klein knit dress and matching jacket, stiletto heels, and dark hosiery. Jernell's hair was styled in her signature ponytail.

Morgan and Brianna sat beside each other, shaken to the core at how the state portrayed their mother and aunt. Jernell, the state claimed, was a manipulating criminal, a mastermind with no regard for morals or the law. The cousins occassionally clutched each other's hands tightly.

"It's a good thing Aunt Jernell isn't having a jury trial," Brianna whispered to Morgan. "If they heard a whiff of that stuff, they'd have no problem convicting her."

The bailiff frowned warningly at the young women.

Yolanda Collins rose from her seat dramatically. She held an ink pen in her hand that she used as a pointer. It was her turn to rebut the state's allegations. She painted a rosier picture of Jernell, citing how she raised her child alone and was misguided by a family business gone awry.

When Yolanda finished her opening remarks, the judge struck his gavel upon the bench and announced succinctly, "Court is in recess for lunch. I expect everyone back in an hour."

Jernell made eye contact with Morgan as the guard led her away. Yolanda and her team of attorneys from the law firm walked behind their client.

"I guess we should go get something to eat," Morgan said. Her stomach felt unsettled. She didn't know how Yolanda could counter the accusations made against Jernell, especially since most of them were true. The young woman had to keep reminding herself that no one in authority was privy to that knowledge.

The cousins decided to get a sandwich from a vending machine located in the building. They were aware that the media would pounce on them like a tiger in the jungle if they ventured outdoors. The rest of the afternoon passed slowly, as did the rest of the week.

Lucinda was scheduled to take the witness stand the coming Monday morning.

Noah had planned to go to court that week. He and Rico planned to rotate attending the trial to support Morgan. Samuel needed Noah's help with a project the week of Lucinda's testimony, so Rico drove from Ohio to go to court with Morgan.

Monday morning arrived and the housekeeper/nanny was up. "Do you swear to tell the truth, the whole truth and nothing but the truth, so help you God?" the bailiff asked Lucinda.

"I do." She held up her left hand, trembling in her seat.

"Please state your name for the record," the state's attorney, Rose Maxwell, instructed Lucinda.

Lucinda answered in a tinny voice. "Lucinda Yvette Brown."

"Is that Ms. or Mrs. Brown?"

"Ms."

"Please speak up Ms. Brown," Ms. Maxwell requested. "Would you tell the court how you know the defendant."

"Yes. Jernell and I have been friends since we were little children. Our mothers grew up with each other and went to high school together."

Ms. Maxwell glanced at the judge then back at Lucinda. "Ms. Brown, would you say that you and Jernell are best friends."

"I consider Jernell one of my closest friends," Lucinda answered tentatively, not sure where the attorney was going with the question.

"That being the case, would you say that you were aware of the defendant's illegal activities? Like her drug business?"

"No, I didn't and don't have any knowledge of Jernell's business dealings."

"Come now, Ms. Brown, you've known Mrs. Foster since you were a child, and your mothers were close friends. You expect me and the court to believe you weren't privy to your friend's activities?" Ms. Maxwell's left eyebrow lifted skeptically.

Yolanda Collins jumped from her seat, "Objection, your honor. The prosecution is badgering the witness."

"Your objection is noted and overruled. I'll allow the testimony. Ms. Brown, please answer the question," Judge Henry ruled.

Lucinda unconsciously crossed her fingers together. "No, I didn't have any knowledge of Jernell's business activities. I was an employee in her house. Our conversations were always of a personal nature, never business related," Lucinda lied.

Ms. Maxwell walked toward the prosecutor's table. She paused and studied a note pad. "Ms. Brown, what did your duties entail in Ms. Foster's home?"

"I cooked, cleaned her house, and was Jernell's daughter,

Morgan's, nanny until Morgan went away to college." Lucinda's eye jumped to Morgan.

"Do you have any children of your own, Ms. Brown?"

"No." Lucinda's eyes dropped to her lap.

"Have you ever had any children, Ms. Brown?" Ms. Maxwell's eyes bored holes into Lucinda's. She paced back and forth. Then Ms. Maxwell stopped in front of the witness stand.

"Uh, I don't understand. . . ." The color in Lucinda's face drained. She closed her mouth and looked down at the floor.

"Do I need to repeat the question, Ms. Brown?"

Lucinda didn't say anything. It was obvious she was uncomfortable with the line of questioning. She shot a pleading look at Jernell.

"Ms. Brown, you must answer the question," Judge Henry instructed Lucinda.

"Okay. Yes I had a child. The baby died," Lucinda answered morosely.

Ms. Maxwell looked down at the paper she held in her hand. "What year was your child born, Ms. Brown?"

Lucinda closed her eyes, then she reopened them. "In 1976."

"Isn't that the same year the defendant's child was born?"

Lucinda looked uneasy. She crossed and uncrossed her legs then moistened her dry lips. She looked as though she wanted to bolt from her seat. A tear trickled from her left eye. "Yes, it was," she managed to say.

Ms. Maxwell walked to the prosecution table. She picked up a sheet of paper. Then she returned to the witness stand. "Ms. Brown, I have a statement from Betty Carson. She was employed as a nurse at the University of Chicago Lying-In Hospital. She worked there in 1976. The same time you and Jernell were admitted to have your babies. According to hospital records, you and Mrs. Foster were pregnant at the same time and gave birth on the same day. Is that true?"

Morgan looked at Lucinda compassionately. She didn't know Lucinda had a baby who died.

Jernell leaned over and whispered in her attorney's ear. Yolanda said from her seat, "Your honor, I'd like to request a sidebar. The defense wasn't aware of the evidence Ms. Maxwell is introducing today."

"We'll take a short recess. I'd like to see both you and Ms. Maxwell in my chambers." The judge rose from his seat. The two lawyers followed him to his office.

The bailiff handed Lucinda a tissue.

Poor Lucinda. I guess the attorney is really bringing back sad memories, Morgan thought. She looked over at Big Momma who stared at her niece pityingly. "What do you think those questions were about?" Morgan whispered to Brianna.

"I don't know," Brianna replied. "Look, the judge is coming back."

"I've decided to allow the line of questioning to continue. Ms. Maxwell, you may go on."

"Thank you, your honor," the attorney smiled. "Ms. Brown, you testified that your child died. Need I remind you that you're under oath? What really happened to your baby?"

The door to the courtroom opened and an older woman walked inside, dressed in a nurse's uniform. She appeared to be in her mid-fifties. She sat in the back row of the courtroom.

Jernell turned to look at the woman and gasped. Lucinda looked as though she was about to swoon. The spectators in the courtroom began to chatter.

"Order in the court!" Judge Henry banged his gavel. "Ms. Brown, please answer the question.

"I-I-I-my baby didn't die."

Ms. Maxwell looked at Lucinda triumphantly. "Is your child here in the courtroom today?"

Lucinda sobbed. She covered her face and nodded.

"Would you please point out your child, Ms. Brown?" Ms. Maxwell eagerly went for the jugular.

Lucinda felt numb as tears trickled down her face. Her body shook uncontrollably. She could barely raise her hand. Her finger trembled as she pointed to Morgan.

Morgan's face felt hot, she felt faint. Her body sagged. She shook her head from side to side in disbelief. *Please don't say I'm your child, Luci. Please. Please. Please. Don't let this happen to me. Not today, and not this way.*

She jumped from her seat. Morgan flung her head from side to side. "No, that's not true!" she yelled. "Lucinda is not my mother." She looked over at Ms. Maxwell. "You'll stop at nothing to smear my mother. Haven't you done enough to hurt our family? Oh God, please don't let it be true." Morgan clutched her abdomen, glowered at Lucinda and Jernell, and then fled from the courtroom.

Reporters, snapping photographs, followed Morgan's mad dash out of the courtroom.

Brianna was as stunned as everyone else by Lucinda's testimony and Morgan's outburst. Her mouth gaped open as she watched Morgan flee the courtroom. After she regained her composure, Brianna jumped from her seat and flew out of the room to find her cousin. Rico, who had been sitting by in the back row of the courtroom, had a dazed expression on his face. He made a weak attempt to stand up then staggered and fell back into his seat.

"Order in the courtroom!" Judge Henry struck his gavel upon the desk so hard that it nearly broke. "Court is adjourned today. We'll resume tomorrow morning at nine o'clock. Ms. Brown, may I remind you that you're still under oath. I expect you to finish your testimony in the morning."

Lucinda's head was bowed. She sat paralyzed in her seat. Her legs refused to work, and it took her a few minutes to stand. Camera men sped over to Lucinda, snapping her picture. When she passed by Jernell, the woman sat in a state of shock at the table. Lucinda mouthed. "I'm so sorry, Jernell. You know I would have gone to my grave before I hurt you or Morgan."

Jernell frowned at Lucinda. Then she stood and the guards cuffed her once again.

"I'll see you at the facility," Yolanda advised Jernell. She stood and quickly put paper inside her briefcase. She said to her team, "I'll meet you at the office in an hour," then she departed. Damage control of the utmost was needed for tomorrow's session.

Lucinda ran out of the courtroom. She looked to her left and right for Morgan, but the young woman wasn't anywhere in sight. She saw Rico sitting on a bench with his head dropped into his hands. Rico was so dismayed by the latest revelation that he could only make it to the bench and no farther. He seethed with rage as he tried to gain his composure and wait for Lucinda to come out the courtroom. Rico knew he had to go to find Morgan, but at that moment, his mind was mired on finding out the truth about what happened twenty-two years ago.

He looked up and saw Lucinda. Rico rose from his seat, walked to her, and took her by the arm, forcefully leading her out of the courthouse.

Rico continued to hold Lucinda's arm in a hard grasp as they walked to his car. He finally released her when he reached inside his pocket and flung the attendant a ten-dollar bill. He and Lucinda walked to his car. He opened the passenger's door for the woman. Lucinda had become mute. Her worst fears had materialized before her eyes.

Lucinda got inside the car. She rocked back and forth, and keened aloud. "God, I'm so sorry. Please let Morgan forgive me."

Rico got inside the car and slammed the door as he closed it. He turned and pulled Lucinda's face harshly toward him. "What just went on in there? You told me that our baby died. Cindy, please tell me that you didn't give our baby to Jernell! Naw, you wouldn't do something as foul as that."

"Rico," Lucinda began. She put her hand on Rico's arm.

The man was inflamed with anger. The look on Lucinda's face told him the truth. He pushed her hand off his arm.

"I didn't have a choice," Lucinda cried. "It was a conspiracy. I never should have gotten involved with you, knowing you were Jernell's man. Big Momma found out about us, and she was livid. The family had plans for you and I couldn't come in the way of that.

"Jernell never knew about us or that my baby was yours. I let her think my boyfriend, Corey, was my baby's father although we had broken up. Somehow, Big Momma found out about us. I don't know how. She threatened to kill me, Rico. What could I do? You can't think that I would have willingly given our child away?"

Rico recoiled away from Lucinda. His eyes clouded over with disgust that burst from his eyes. "Luci, you should have given your life for our child. Don't you think I would have?"

Lucinda pleaded with him frantically. "Please, let me finish telling you what happened. Rico, hear me out. You, yourself, know Jernell had problems throughout her pregnancy. She was ordered to stay on bed rest for months. She was a high-risk case. The doctor told Big Momma that she might miscarry.

"Jernell felt sorry for me when she found out I was pregnant, too. She talked Big Momma into paying my hospital bills. We both went into labor at the same time. Jernell went to the delivery room before I did. After I delivered Morgan, I stayed in recovery for a while. When the orderlies finally wheeled me to my room, Big Momma was sitting in the chair next to my bed. She told me Jernell had lost the baby. She had a boy."

Rico rested his elbows on the steering wheel and dropped

his head in his hands. Lucinda touched the sleeve of his jacket.

"Big Momma told me Jernell was sedated. They hadn't told her about the baby yet. And that's when Big Momma told me that she wanted to take my baby and give her to Jernell. I was in pain and full of medication. I looked at her like she was crazy, not sure I'd heard her correctly. When Big Momma repeated what she wanted to do, a cold blast of terror filled my veins. I told her no.

"Then she reached inside her purse and pulled out a pearl handled twenty-two-caliber pistol. Rico, Big Momma pointed it at me and told me that I could do either of two things. One, I could play hero and die, and she would take the baby for Jernell. Or two, I could give her the baby willingly. Big Momma said she'd have Jernell hire me as her housekeeper and I could be around the child as she grew up. She cocked the hammer of the gun and asked me which would it be, choice A or B."

"Why didn't you tell me what happened, Lucinda? We could have gone away together. You never gave me a choice," Rico implored Lucinda. Tears hovered in his eyes.

Lucinda closed her eyes and rubbed them. "Rico, I wanted to. But she made me sign a statement saying that I'd never reveal the truth to you or Jernell. I'm scared of Big Momma, Rico. I think she's crazy. I tried to tell Jernell that so many times, but she couldn't see it.

"I signed the papers she gave me. I didn't want to, but I didn't have any other choice. I wanted to live. If I couldn't claim my baby, then at least I'd be around her. I love Morgan. I wouldn't do anything to hurt her. Did you see how she looked at me before she left the courtroom? Lord, please forgive me." Lucinda began weeping again.

Rico punched the steering wheel. The horn wailed and then stopped. "Lucinda, you should have told me what happened. Maybe we could have done something. Right now, we've got to find Morgan. I should have followed her when she left the courtroom, but I was too stunned by what I heard." He turned on the car and put it into drive and screeched out the parking lot.

Brianna walked through the courthouse again looking for her distraught cousin. There wasn't hide or hair of the young woman. After she exited the building, Brianna tried calling Morgan on her cell phone. She shrugged her shoulders helplessly when she was routed to voice mail. The young woman decided to go home, assuming that her cousin would call her when she was ready to talk.

The object of everyone's concern sat in the back of a taxicab and sobbed wildly without restraint. The cab driver adjusted his rearview mirror and asked, "Miss, are you all right?"

The driver made a right turn, pulled into a grocery store parking space and shifted the vehicle to park. "Miss, where do you want me to go? I don't know where to take you."

Morgan continued to weep. Fifteen minutes later, she managed to choke out, "Just head south." She wiped her eyes and moaned softly to herself. Several minutes later, Morgan gave the driver an address.

Twenty minutes later, he pulled in front of her destination. "That will be thirty dollars."

Morgan fumbled in her purse and pulled out two crisp twenty dollar bills.

"Say, ain't you . . ." the cab driver began.

Morgan quickly jumped out of the cab and walked to the building. She opened the door and walked inside. Passing through another set of doors, she went inside the dimly lit small sanctuary and sat on a folding chair at the rear of the room. The only visible color was the sunlight streaming through the multi-colored stained glass windows.

The hushed atmosphere seemed to calm her shattered

nerves. The door opened and closed. Morgan's head was bowed and she didn't look up to see who came in. Instead, she felt a presence beside her.

Samuel reached out and touched Morgan's shoulder. "What's wrong, Morgan? Are you all right, dear?"

"Oh, Reverend Sam! No, I'm afraid that I'm not," Morgan wailed. "I just came from the morning session at court. Remember you told me that my life couldn't get any worse? Well it did," Morgan snorted. "I found out that Jernell is not really my mother and that Lucinda is my biological mother. Both of them lied to me."

Samuel reached into his lapel pocket, pulled out a white handkerchief, and handed it to Morgan. She wiped her eyes.

The kind minister said, "I know you've gotten devastating news once again. Try to keep your head up and your heart open. You see, child, the Lord never said that our way would be easy. But make no mistake, God doesn't put more on us then we can bear."

"He has this time," Morgan cried out as tears crawled from her eyes. "Everyone in that courtroom, especially my aunts, looked at me with horror in their eyes. My so-called mother couldn't even look me in the eye. Lucinda got caught. She had no choice but to come clean. If the trial hadn't happened, she never would have said anything."

"Then, God wanted you to learn who your parents really are today, on this day, Morgan. Everything that happens in our lives happen for a reason. Perhaps it was simply time."

"Why would a loving God want to destroy me with news like that? I feel drained and empty. I don't know who I am. I don't even know who my father is. Who knows what other secrets Lucinda has been keeping," Morgan complained. She dabbed at her eyes again with the crumpled handkerchief that she twisted in her hand.

Samuel put his arm around Morgan's shoulders. "You

know, the first thing you need to do is talk to Lucinda and your father. Circumstances are not always what they seem. But trust in the Lord, Morgan. Let Him direct your path, and, most of all, talk to your parents. Before you jump to any conclusions, wait to hear their side of the story. Will you do that for me?"

"I can't make you any promises." Morgan shook her head vehemently. "I don't know. I feel intense anger toward everyone I thought I could trust. My father said he and Lucinda would protect me while my mother was in jail. Some job they did." Her lips twisted together in a downward slash.

Noah strolled into the sanctuary carrying a stack of Bibles. He did a double-take and the books nearly slid out of his hands when he saw Morgan talking to his father. She looked shaken.

The young man hurried over to where they were sitting and placed the Bibles in the empty chair next to his. "Is court done for today already?" He glanced at his watch and sat down next to Morgan. "What's wrong? What happened in court?"

Samuel quickly explained to Noah what Morgan had told him. Morgan continued to sniffle.

Noah took the young woman in his arms and held her while she wept. He stroked her head. "Shh, baby. It's going to be all right." Noah continued holding Morgan in his arms until she stopped sobbing.

"I'm going to take her to our house, Dad. I'm glad you were here for Morgan," Noah informed Samuel.

"Son, I couldn't do any less and call myself a minister. Morgan, I want you to think hard about what I told you. Situations in life are tests sometimes and those tests can be about facing our worst fears and overcoming them. You're facing so many issues, and that means Satan has been busy. But even through your adversities, I want you to try to believe and trust in God. He'll comfort you and give you peace. That I can promise you."

Noah stood and helped Morgan out of her seat. She stared at Samuel mutely and shook her head. The young man led Morgan outside and almost had to put her inside the car. He drove home quickly. Morgan had shut down. She stared blindly out the windshield of the car.

The garage door yawned open as Noah pulled inside the two-car structure. He got out of the car, walked around to the other side, and lifted Morgan from the car.

She twined her arms around his neck and shuddered violently. Her body twitched.

Noah set Morgan on the top stair next to him. Her body sagged against his while he unlocked the door. Noah kicked it open and carried Morgan to the bedroom. He laid her down gently in the bed. She turned and faced the wall. Noah slid on top of the bed beside her and put his arm protectively around her waist.

"Come on, Morgan. I know finding out the truth about your mother was distressing. Still, isn't learning the truth best for you in the long run? Just think if you hadn't found out, you would have been fulfilling a destiny that wasn't your burden to carry in the first place." Noah continued talking to Morgan, caressing her back.

She turned over in the bed and stared at him. Then Morgan held out her arms. "Make love to me, Noah. Please. I just need to feel you next to me to remind me that I'm a person, and that you love you me." She snaked her arms around Noah's neck and began kissing his lips.

Noah sat up quickly. He pulled Morgan's arms from around his neck, and pulled her into his arms. "Come on, baby, we don't have to do this. You know that I love you. I don't care who your momma or daddy are. I love the woman you are inside." He caressed her cheek.

"There is no woman inside," Morgan said woodenly. Her

arms dropped back to her side. "That woman doesn't exist anymore." Her head flipped from side to side. "I don't know who I am. The lies I've been fed all those years—and for what? How dare Lucinda and Jernell perpetrate that lie. Didn't they feel they could tell me the truth? Am I that horrible?"

"Neither one of us knows the answers to those questions. Only one person does and, Morgan, you're going to have to talk to her. Not today, not now, but when you're ready to hear the truth."

Morgan's eyes became watery. "I feel so low. Noah, why don't you want me? I want to feel you inside me and your heart beating next to mine, I want to feel your love. Is that too much to ask for?"

"The timing isn't right, Morgan. We don't have to make love for you to know I love you. I am crazy about your long beautiful legs and your tiny waist that I can almost put my hands around." He gently touched her leg. "And the curve of your breasts drive me wild. Your smile can light up a room." He took her hand in his. "Woman, I love you with every fiber of my being. When we come together, it won't be because I'm trying to make you feel better about yourself. It will happen because we both want to, and after we're married. I love the total package, Morgan. I love what's in here." He gently touched her head. "And what's there." Noah put his hand over her heart.

Morgan lips formed into a tiny smile. She took Noah's hand and kissed the palm.

Noah tousled Morgan's hair. "We are going to be married one day in the not-so-distant future. And you better believe when it happens, you won't be able to keep me away from you, all of you." His eyes swept over her body. "I love you, Morgan. My feelings will never change, and I hope you realize that. You were there for me when Mom passed. I realized how pompous and selfish I must have sounded that night when you told me about your family when we were in Peoria.

"I shouldn't have run away from you. Instead, I should have stayed and trusted in God to work our problems out. During my drive here to Chicago, it hit me that you didn't have it in you to run your family business. I should have stayed in Peoria and talked to you until you realized the truth."

"I think I would have done it anyway if Momma hadn't been arrested," Morgan confessed. Her head dropped ever so slightly. She didn't want to see the look on Noah's face.

"No. You didn't even have to make the choice, because God made the decision for you. You running the family business wasn't meant to be."

"Maybe," Morgan conceded thoughtfully as she chewed her lower lip. "I always felt so sorry for my momma, Noah. Even though she was the head of the family, Momma really didn't have anybody except for me. She didn't allow herself to be close to anyone except Aunt Adrianna. And look what happened? I wanted Momma to be proud of me and be happy. She always looked worried, or she was on the phone taking care of business. Momma never relaxed or looked happy."

Noah nodded. "Your mother made her choices and she had to live by them. I imagine she wasn't in a good place, always having to look over her shoulder and anticipate what was coming next. But your mother, with all the adversity she has faced, is still a child of God, and He will help her when she'd ready to see the light."

"I guess all of that doesn't matter since she isn't my mother anyway." Morgan's voice faltered. She began crying again.

Noah laid her down on the bed. He slid next to Morgan and held her in his arms. He talked to her softly, reassuring her that he loved her, until she calmed down and fell asleep.

He thought, *Lord, in your infinite wisdom, you decided it was time for my Morgan to learn her mother's identity in court today. Morgan, doesn't realize it yet, but it was a blessing that set her free. Father, give Morgan peace and let the healing begin.* Noah kissed the side of her head.

While Morgan slept, Noah continued to pray for peace for her. Life isn't always straightforward. As fate would have it, more misfortune lurked around the corner, waiting to pounce.

Chapter 30

Yolanda sat perched on the edge of the cold steel chair in the interview room, waiting for the guard to bring Jernell into the room. She scratched a few notes on the legal pad that lay flipped open before her. The hinges of the door creaked noisily, and Jernell walked into the room.

She looked pale, as if all the blood had been drained from her body. Her eyes were red. Jernell bore little resemblance to the haughty defendant from the courtroom that morning.

Jernell folded her wobbly hands together on the table. She looked beyond Yolanda's shoulder.

"How come you didn't tell us about Morgan?" Yolanda began aggressively. "The prosecution drew blood with that testimony today. I asked you many times, Jernell, if there were any secrets that might be revealed that might hurt you, and you told me no."

"I didn't know myself until today," Jernell whispered. Her voice sounded raspy. "Whatever went down those years ago has Big Momma written all over it."

Yolanda backed down a bit, "I'm sorry about you having

to learn the truth about Morgan and your baby the way you did, Jernell. But we still have to stay focused on your trial and try to get you acquitted. Morgan's maternity being revealed in court today struck a huge blow at your credibility. The news reports have painted you as a cold schemer who would lie and take someone else's child as her own.

"When I leave here, I'm going back to the office so my team can rethink our strategy. Jernell, is there anything else you haven't told me? Do you know anything about that corpse found in your garage? I just don't want any more surprises." Yolanda held up her hands pleadingly toward Jernell.

"I don't know anything about that corpse. Although I have ideas about what may have happened, I don't want to share them with you at this time." Jernell sighed heavily. "Yolanda, I want you to try and work out a plea bargain for me. I want to plead guilty to some of the charges. This trial is turning into a farce. Too many lives are being impacted, including Morgan's." Jernell looked directly into Yolanda's face. Her expression was stony, like her mind was made up and there was no going back.

"I don't know that we can do that." Yolanda looked at her client in disbelief. She hadn't seen that one coming. "The judge usually sticks to the agenda we've set up front. Jernell, are you sure you want to do that? It seems so drastic." Yolanda uncapped the pen and wrote more notes.

"Yes, I'm sure. I want you to at least try. I don't want to cause Adrianna or Brianna any more pain. Everything I did was for my child. Isn't it ironic that my baby died and no one bothered to tell me? Do you know how that makes me feel?" Jernell looked up at Yolanda. "I am devastated about losing the baby I never knew. And Morgan being Lucinda's child is going to take some getting used to.

"Maybe Todd entering the witness protection program is for the best. He and Adrianna can go away maybe, put all

this stuff behind them, and find some happiness. I don't
have anything to live for at this point. I'd rather do the time.
I guess even to the end, that I want what's best for the family." Jernell shook her head as she smiled sardonically.

Yolanda twisted the pen she held in her hands. "As your
lawyer, I'd advise you to think about your decision further.
We have to go back into court tomorrow anyway. The judge
may or may not grant your request." Yolanda closed the
pad. "Think about what you want to do tonight. Don't
make a decision based on emotions. I'll see you in the
morning." She stood, picked up her briefcase, and patted
Jernell on the shoulder. Yolanda put the legal pad and pen
inside the case and locked it.

Jernell stood and flipped her ponytail over her shoulder.
"I'm not going to change my mind. Goodnight, Yolanda."
She walked to the door and knocked on the window. The
guard entered the room to escort her back to her cell.

Yolanda left the building and walked to her car. Her cell
phone rang. She answered the call. "Gilbert, what's up?
What did you say?" Yolanda stopped dead in her tracks.
"I'm on my way to the office." She disconnected the call.
"Well, Jernell, I'd say your decision may be out of your
hands and mine."

Brianna sat on a folding chair in the dining room of her
house. She was in a catatonic state of incredulity. Her father's contact for the witness protection program, Mr. Riley,
had come to the house thirty minutes ago and informed
Adrianna and Brianna that Todd was dead. He'd been poi-
soned.

Brianna felt numb and shook her head in denial. She
muttered to herself, "No, my daddy can't be dead. I talked
to him this morning after I came back from court."

Adrianna had fainted upon hearing the news. As Brianna
tried to revive her mother, Mr. Riley's words circled around

her mind. *I'm sorry to inform you that your husband and father is dead.* The phrase rushed like a torrent of spring water down a mountainside inside the young woman's head.

Brianna rubbed her mother's hands and then gently patted her face. When her mother still didn't awaken, Brianna went to the guest bathroom and moistened a towel. When she returned to the dining room, she dabbed Adrianna's face.

"No," the older woman moaned as she began to come to. She looked at Brianna's teary face and then up at Mr. Riley. She shook her head. "Tell me it's not true, that my Todd is not dead. He couldn't be. No, it's not true." Adrianna fell on the floor and thrashed about on the carpeting. She screamed "Todd" over and over.

Mr. Riley tugged at the ends of his blue and red striped tie. He looked uncomfortable. "Is there someone you can call? Is there anything I can do to help?"

Trying to muster as much dignity as she could, Brianna said, "I'd say that you've done enough for one day, Mr. Riley. Please see yourself out. I'll take care of my mother myself."

Mr. Riley departed quickly. Brianna heard the door shut behind him.

Adrianna was beset with grief. She rocked back and forward on the carpet, tearing at her hair.

Brianna knelt beside her mother on the floor. "Mommy, please don't cry. Don't do this to yourself. Mommy, please." She tried to gather her mother in her arms.

Adrianna pushed Brianna away from her and then crawled on all fours and stood up with her hands outstretched. "Todd, where are you?" She walked rapidly from one room to another.

Brianna sat with her legs splayed out before her and cried without restraint. When she stopped, she watched her mother walking from the kitchen to the powder room, still calling her husband's name. The young woman stood and walked over to her mother. She pulled Adrianna's arms. "Mommy, he's gone," she said in a shaky voice.

Adrianna slapped Brianna so hard that the young woman's head reeled backward and the imprint of her mother's hand was seared on her face. "No, don't say that. Your father isn't gone. He's going to come walking in that door any minute, and everything will be okay. I'm going to the door to wait for him." She walked in an unsteady gait and then stood at the door like a sentry.

Brianna looked at her mother through watery eyes. She dropped to her knees, bowed her head, and bawled more.

Adrianna put her hands over her ears to block the unearthly sounds coming from her daughter.

Chapter 31

Morgan's cell phone rang. Noah looked down at Morgan. She was still asleep. The young man rose from the bed and took the phone from Morgan's purse and answered it. "Calm down, Brianna. What did you say? Oh no. I'll tell Morgan. We're on our way."

Morgan stirred in the bed. She sat upright. "Who was that?" She rubbed her eyes.

"It was Brianna. She has bad news," Noah answered gravely. He walked over to the bed and sat beside Morgan.

"What did she say?" Morgan asked fearfully. Her throat tightened. She unconsciously began rubbing her upper arms.

"It's bad, Morgan, real bad. Your uncle is dead."

"You're lying," Morgan accused Noah. "Uncle Todd couldn't be dead. He was in protective custody." The young woman rose from the bed. Her movements were clumsy. "I've got to go to Brianna. I know she needs me." She walked to the desk and picked her purse.

Noah took the purse from Morgan's hands and took her

hands inside his own. "Please, before we go, I'd like to say a prayer for Brianna and your aunt. Morgan nodded and closed her eyes.

Noah said, "Lord, you said in your word, Come unto Me, all ye that labor and are heavy laden, and I will give you rest. Father above, the Foster family needs your strength and comfort right now. All they have to do is hold onto your unchanging hand, and know that you will fix it. The song says, weeping may endure for a night, but joy will come in the morning. Lord, let my sister, Brianna, and her mother know that joy will come in the morning. And, all they have to do is lean on you to make it through this tough time. These blessings I ask in your son's name. Amen."

She and Noah left the house. He drove to Adrianna's house as quickly as the speed limit allowed. Noah crookedly parked the car in front of the house. He and Morgan rushed out of the car. When they walked up the last step, Brianna flung the door open, and the pair followed her inside.

Adrianna sat on the floor in the living room, pulling her hair with her thumb in her mouth.

Brianna looked like death warmed over. Her complexion looked waxy. "I can't get her to get up. She's been that way since Mr. Riley left," Brianna muttered helplessly.

"Maybe you should call an ambulance, Brianna," Noah suggested.

"No, I can't do that to Momma." Brianna swayed back and forth.

"Come and sit down." Morgan led her cousin to a folding chair. Noah went to the kitchen and returned with a glass of water for Brianna. Brianna took the glass in her trembling hand.

Morgan knelt in front of Brianna. "Bri, we've got to call someone. Aunt Adrianna obviously isn't well. What do you think about calling her doctor? She can't stay this way."

"I don't know what to do," Brianna said softly. "Morgan, my daddy is dead. What am I going to do?" She dropped the glass on the hardwood floor, and it shattered into pieces.

Morgan took Brianna in her arms. The two women cried while Noah went to the kitchen to find supplies to clean up the glass and water.

A few minutes later he said, "Morgan, we need help here. Maybe you should call your dad. He'll know what to do."

"No," Morgan hissed. "I don't know that Rico is my father."

"Babe, just let me call him and ask him to come over and help." He looked at Brianna. "Unless your cousin wants to call an ambulance or your aunt's doctor . . ."

Morgan felt torn. She wasn't ready to face Rico or Lucinda, but she knew she had to put her feelings aside to get help for her aunt. "Okay," she said begrudgingly, "call him. I don't want to see Lucinda though."

"Maybe you should," Noah suggested. "It would help the situation to get everything out in the open."

"After you call Daddy, I'll call my aunts. Maybe one of them can help Aunt Adrianna. Make the call, Noah."

Noah went to the kitchen and called Rico on his cell phone. Morgan's father simply said that he was on his way.

When Noah came back into the living room, he told Morgan, "Your dad is coming."

Morgan walked to the powder room and called her aunts. None of them answered the phone. Morgan was so taken aback that she didn't think to leave voicemails. She tried calling Big Momma too, and the call was routed to voice mail. She returned to the living room, depressed.

Brianna sat on the floor. She appeared to be in a trance and Adrianna wasn't faring much better. She'd call Todd's name periodically, then stick her thumb back into her mouth.

Morgan stood at the window. Her arms were folded

across her chest. Noah stood behind her with his arms entwined around her waist.

They watched Rico park his car across the street. He and Lucinda raced to the house.

Noah opened the door. Lucinda walked inside first. She looked at Morgan guiltily then she walked over to Adrianna. She tried to lift the woman from the floor. "Rico, would you give me a hand?" Lucinda asked.

"Noah and I will get her up." Rico stood at Adrianna's left side and Noah at her right. They managed to ease the prostrate woman up.

Adrianna slumped against Rico's body. "Do you know where Todd is? I can't find him."

"Come on, Adrianna, let's go upstairs. We'll help you look for him."

Adrianna pouted like a small child. "Do you promise? I have to find Todd now." She pointed at Brianna. "She tried to tell me something bad happened to Todd. But I know that's not true. He's here in this house somewhere. I just can't find him." Madness lurked inside her eyes.

Noah and Rico supported almost all of Adrianna's weight as they walked up the staircase to the second floor. Lucinda followed them.

Brianna's head was bowed between her legs. She still wasn't communicating.

Morgan sat grimly in the folding chairs waiting for the trio to return. And they did thirty minutes later.

"I found a bottle of sedatives in your mother's medicine chest," Lucinda said to Brianna. "We got her to take two pills. Maybe that will calm her down. I think you need to call a doctor though. Adrianna is in bad shape . . ." Lucinda's voice faltered.

Brianna didn't acknowledge Lucinda's suggestion.

Rico walked over to Morgan and whispered, "Maybe you

should try to get Brianna to lie down. It wouldn't hurt for her to take a couple of sedatives too."

"I'll see what I can do," Morgan replied disparaging to her father. She walked over to Brianna and talked to her for a few minutes. Then Brianna and Morgan went upstairs.

"How is she doing?" Lucinda asked Noah, referring to Morgan.

"Not good. But we know Morgan is made of strong stuff. Sometimes she doesn't realize it. I think as time goes by that she'll come around. Right now she's hurt and confused. She isn't really sure you're her father, Mr. Daniels."

"I can put her mind at ease on that issue. I'm definitely her father," Rico growled.

Noah looked embarrassed. He held his hands up. "Hey, I'm not questioning you. There's a lot happening in her life right now. Mrs. Foster on trial," he gestured toward Lucinda, "the courtroom revelation, and now this."

Rico looked ashamed. "I understand. I know I have some tall explaining to do."

"Me too," Lucinda murmured softly.

Morgan returned from the second floor. "I managed to get Brianna to take the pills. Both she and Aunt Adrianna are finally asleep." The young woman rubbed her hands together. She went into the dining room and returned with another folding chair and placed it next to Noah.

"I called my aunts earlier and no one has returned my calls," Morgan observed. "You would think they would have bust down the door by now to check on their sister."

"I think they aren't sure how to react with Todd providing evidence of the family activities," Lucinda said softly.

Morgan glowered at Lucinda, then she looked at Rico. "Are you my father?" she asked him austerely. Morgan held her breath waiting for his answer.

"Of course I am," Rico said angrily. "You didn't have to ask me that question."

"I had to be sure." Morgan clasped her shaking hands together. "So you got Jernell and Lucinda pregnant at the same time?" The young woman shook her head sadly. "You never mentioned the doggish side of your personality before, Daddy."

"Yes. I got both women pregnant. It's not something I'm proud of, but it happened. I was just as shocked as you were when the truth came out this afternoon. Lucinda had told me our baby died."

Morgan looked at Lucinda disgustedly. "You didn't even bother to tell Daddy the truth about what happened? Did Momma know what about the switch? I'm assuming that's what happened."

Lucinda coughed and dropped her eyes, feeling ashamed. "No one knew the truth except for me and Big Momma. It was her idea. I had no choice except to go along with what she asked."

"What did she do? Hold a gun to your head?" Morgan asked sarcastically.

"Actually, she did," Lucinda clasped her hands tightly together to try to stop them from trembling.

"I don't believe you," Morgan rolled her eyes at Lucinda.

The older woman reached down for her purse that was on the floor. She pulled a document out of it and passed it to Morgan.

Morgan quickly scanned the letter. It was the contract that Lucinda had made with Big Momma. Lucinda had kept a copy in a safe deposit box at the bank in case something unforeseen happened.

After reading the letter, Morgan stood and handed it back to Lucinda. "Tell me what happened," she said to her biological mother.

"Jernell never knew what happened between me and Big Momma. You know that we were best friends while we were growing up. What you didn't know was that your grandmother Pamela and my mother, Mabeline, were also best friends. My daddy was in the drug trade. He was a lower level dealer. The Foster family felt it was safe, me and Jernell being friends, sort of like birds of a feather.

"Rico was my boyfriend in eighth grade, then he started to get into trouble. By the time he was fifteen years old, he had changed and was a hard-core gang banger. I know none of this is new to you, Morgan, since Rico has discussed his past with you. My daddy didn't want me hanging around Rico. He felt he was a loose cannon and out of control." Lucinda peeked at Rico, and he nodded for her to continue.

"Those same qualities my father didn't like in Rico, Big Momma loved. Your father and I broke up by the time we started high school. Still, we'd get see each from time to time, and somehow we always seemed to end up in bed. I loved Rico, but to appease my father, I dated other guys."

"You were aware of this?" Morgan asked her father.

"Yeah, we knew we shared something special. But it seemed like the timing wasn't ever right and her father really disliked me. I met Jernell during my sophomore year of high school, right before I dropped out, and we hit it off. But there was something about Lucinda that always drew me back to her."

"Spare me the love story, Daddy. So you cheated on Jernell with Lucinda or vice-versa?" Morgan snapped.

"Lucinda and I, uh, we came together while I was with Jernell. I was young and thought I was "the man" getting two girls pregnant at once. At that point in time, I was content being with Jernell. I knew Big Momma had plans for me, and I planned to fulfill them, until Big Momma ordered a hit on Lucinda's father," Rico said remorsefully, folding his hands together. He looked outside the room with a distant look in his eyes, as if he'd been transported to another time and place.

"She made me watch it. His money had been coming up

short for some time. I'd never seen a man beg for his life before. He pleaded with Big Momma to spare him. She gave the order for him to be executed, and she had him shot by one of her men in cold blood. Seeing that happen and knowing it was Lucinda's father made me realize that the life she had carved out for me with Jernell wasn't going to happen. I knew if I got out of that situation, it would be time for me make some major changes in my life.

"When Lucinda told me she was pregnant, we made plans to run away and leave Chicago. I was going to save up the money I made from Big Momma, then things started moving fast. The next thing I knew Big Momma had ordered the hit."

Rico's tale was as intriguing as a movie. "Then Jernell told me was she having a baby a few weeks later. I knew my fate was sealed then. I decided the best thing for me to do was join the family and take care of Jernell and the baby. I felt so guilty about knowing what happened to Lucinda's father, and the part I almost had to play in it, that I stopped seeing her. When I heard Lucinda was in labor, I went to the hospital the next day to see her, and she told me our baby died at birth. That was the end of our relationship." Rico's eyes darted between Lucinda and Morgan's faces. Noah listened with a stoic expression on his face.

Lucinda looked horrified when she learned Rico had been present for her father's murder. She pressed her hands over her mouth.

Rico looked at his daughter beseechingly. "But after you were born, Morg, I couldn't go through with it—being a part of the family. I talked to Jernell and we decided to hold off getting married and telling Big Momma of my decision. I knew if I didn't marry Jernell that my life would be in danger. I knew too many of the family secrets. When you were about three months old, Jernell went to Big Momma and begged her to spare my life."

Morgan looked from her father's face to Lucinda's. She felt they were telling the truth. Her stomach muscles contracted harshly when she thought about what she'd almost gotten herself into. The young woman knew she could never be as ruthless as Big Momma. She wondered if Jernell was cut from the same cloth.

"I never meant to hurt you, Morgan, or you, Rico," Lucinda interjected dolefully. "Big Momma held the upper hand. I was just satisfied to be a part of your life and watch you grow up. I knew I could never tell you or Rico the truth without severe repercussions from Big Momma. Please forgive me. You don't know how many times I've prayed to God for Him to forgive me too." Lucinda held out her hands and looked at Morgan imploringly.

"I need time to think about all of this," Morgan finally shook her head and said. "I can't promise anything right now."

"I understand," Lucinda said gratefully. She wanted to hate Rico for the part he played in her father's death. But she knew she had to let it go. During her counseling sessions with Reverend Jefferson, he always emphasized forgiveness. The scripture the minister recited to Lucinda during the last time they met was Hebrews, eighth chapter, twelfth verse, "I will forgive their wickedness, and will remember their sins no more, says the Lord." The words stuck in Lucinda's mind.

"I'm going to check on Brianna and Aunt Adrianna." Morgan rose from the chair, and walked up the stairs.

Noah, Rico, and Lucinda watched Morgan walk up the stairs. Each hoped and prayed that the storm was over and that the healing process could begin. But was the tempest over?

Chapter 32

Brianna had hosted a memorial service for her father at her parents' townhouse the day before his burial. Lucinda prepared food and Rico rented folding chairs and tables. Brianna tried to remain upbeat, showing home movies of her mother, her father, and herself. She spoke of her father in loving terms to Morgan, Noah, Lucinda, Rico, and a few of Todd and Adrianna's friends and associates.

Morgan broke down when Brianna put on a video of a family trip to Disneyland. Jernell had always been too busy to take her own child on vacations, so Adrianna and Todd always took Morgan along with them on their trips, gladly. Morgan realized that as heinous and cowardly as she considered Todd to be for turning on her mother, that he was still Brianna's father, Adrianna's husband, and he had played a major role in her life.

Following the service, Noah dropped Morgan off at her condo. Then he departed for home. When he walked inside the house, he found his father on the telephone in the den talking to a church member. Noah went into the kitchen and poured himself a glass of water. He waited in the kitchen until Samuel finished the call, then he went to the den, and sat on the couch.

"Hi, Dad. How are you feeling?" Noah asked his father, unloosening his tie.

"I'm good. I just got off the telephone with Sister Patrice, and we were discussing the guest choirs for the musical Sunday night," Samuel added.

"Thanks for going to the memorial service last night and for supporting Brianna and Morgan, Dad. They were really touched," Noah remarked. "Are you hungry or thirsty? Can I fix you something to eat?" He stood up.

"No, son, I'm not hungry." Samuel shook his head. He made a notation on the notepad on his desk. "You don't have to thank me for supporting the young ladies. I've grown fond of Brianna. Morgan is like a daughter to me, or should I say daughter-in-law? What's happening with you?"

"I'd like to talk to you," Noah stammered nervously as he sat back down.

Samuel took off his reading glasses and laid them on the desk. "What's up?"

"Dad, I need to talk to you about my calling."

Samuel stared at his son. "You have my full attention." He folded his hands together on the desk.

Noah hesitated and began speaking, "Dad, the last thing I want to do is disappoint you. I really love and admire you. I've tried hard all my life to do everything I can to gain your respect and trust."

"And so you have, Noah," Samuel nodded. "Just tell me what's in your heart."

Noah leaned forward in his seat. "Dad, I don't think I'm cut out to be a minister." The young man sighed heavily. "Don't get me wrong. I am and will always be a child of God. I will continue to assist you at church in any capacity you need me, except that of being a minister."

Samuel's heart felt heavy, but he had known deep inside

that there was a good possibility that Noah wouldn't go into the ministry with him. The young man's heart was in the right place, but he lacked the passion and fire of one having a calling. Samuel chose his words carefully. Though the older man had prodded Noah about speaking during one of the church services, Noah had yet to attempt to preach a sermon since he decided to go into the ministry. "Why do you feel that way, Noah?" Samuel asked his son gently.

"I really feel bad about what happened with Morgan, all the tribulations she's faced." Noah dropped his head, and then he looked back up at his father. "And most of the time I didn't think to pray for her as she was going through her crises. I didn't try to counsel her. Instead, I just reacted to the circumstances. Later, after I returned home, I could think of so many things, after the fact, that I should have said and didn't." Noah shook his head regretfully. He crossed and uncrossed his legs.

"Did you ever stop to think that maybe you reacted the way you did because you were so close to the situation and had an emotional tie to Morgan?" Samuel probed his son gently. "Being a minister certainly comes with experience, maybe you should give yourself more time, before you give up."

Noah rubbed his chin, and flashed his father a weak smile. "I know what you're saying," Noah waved his hand. "And to be honest, I thought that might be the problem, I was too close to Morgan to effectively counsel her. But when I'm alone in the still of the night, I know in my heart that I decided to go into the ministry because Mom wanted me to and not because that was what I wanted." Noah exhaled heavily, he felt a sense of relief about confessing his feelings to his father, and then guilt, because he knew how much his parents wanted him to join his father.

Samuel's eyes glinted disappointment for a second. Then he put his feelings on the back burner in order to help his son. "You're right, Noah, you should have a calling, or at least a strong desire, to serve the Lord, and make sure it's for the right reasons and not because it's what someone wants you to do."

"Dad, I've wrestled with my decision day and night. I try to walk in the way the Lord wants me to, but a calling, it's just not there . . . Sometimes I feel like a pious fool. I used to get on Morgan about her walk with the Lord, and here I was lacking myself." Noah dropped his head disconsolately.

Samuel stood up and walked over to the couch. He put his hand on Noah's shoulder. "Don't beat yourself up too badly. Your walk in faith has been different from Morgan's. She's really just getting started. You've been at this a long time."

Noah looked up at Samuel and nodded.

"I don't think you came off as pious. After all, you told me that you and Morgan read daily devotionals together. She would go to church with you at least twice a month, sometimes more. Son, I'd have to say what you did was a good start. Morgan, like everyone else walking that Christian journey, will have to go it alone at times. Her tests will not be yours and vice-versa."

The older man sat on the couch next to his son.

"So you're not terribly disappointed in me?" Noah looked at his father hopefully.

"I could never be disappointed in you. You're a man, and I have to trust that me and your mother's upbringing was sufficient for you to make decisions even if I don't necessarily agree with you. You've brought nothing but joy to me and your mother's lives. When the doctor laid you in my arms, I knew parenting wasn't going to be easy since I didn't grow up with a father myself. Still, you made is so easy for me." Samuel consoled his son.

"Thank you for saying that, Dad." Noah reached over and grabbed Samuel's hand and shook it. "I won't be going to the seminary, at least not now. I'd still like to work with you at the church on different projects. I'd like to try my hand at fundraising, that was really Mom's baby. The membership has outgrown our church home and I'd really like to do whatever I can to help us get a new building."

"You know, when your mother and I started the church, we didn't have many members at all, maybe a total of five. Every Sunday after church, I'd come home and read Matthew, chapter eighteen, verse twenty: 'For where two or three are gathered together in My name, there am I in the midst of them.' That simple verse brought me comfort, and I knew when the Lord was ready, there would be more people attending service. And one day there was. I had to let go and let God, like you've got to do regarding your decision to go into the ministry. Always remember, son, God is in control. If that's where He wants you to be, it will happen. Of that, I have no doubt." Samuel smiled at his Noah.

Noah nodded his head, "Thank you, Dad, for being so understanding."

"Of course, son, I could do no less." Samuel pulled Noah to him and hugged the young man.

Brianna's father, Todd Rizzo was laid to rest the next day rest at a suburban cemetery. The only people in attendance at his burial were his daughter, Morgan, Noah, Lucinda, Rico, and Samuel. Todd was estranged from his family. His parents disowned their son when he married out of his race. Adrianna had been hospitalized in a mental facility. On her good days, she waited patiently for Todd to return home.

Brianna's father was buried beneath a huge maple tree. A bench was placed nearby for visitors. The October morning was sunny, a perfect Indian summer day in Chicago. There wasn't a cloud in the clear azure sky.

The young women wore black dresses, and veiled hats. Brianna parked a pair of dark sunshades on her nose to hide her red swollen eyes. Samuel spoke about Todd and prayed at the burial site. When he finished, Brianna walked to the gaping hole in which her father was to be interred and dropped a rose inside it.

As they turned to leave the cemetery and return to the limousine, Terrence walked up to Brianna. "I am so sorry, Brianna. I know I'm the last person in the world you want to see right now. You wouldn't return my calls, and I just had to extend my condolences."

Brianna took off her shades and stared aghast at Terrence's brazen audacity, his actual presence at her father's burial. "Haven't you done enough harm to my family? Just leave, Terrence. Go!" She pointed her shades toward the exit.

"Brianna, please . . ." Terrence fell backward as Brianna slapped his face soundly. The imprint from her hand was burned into his light-complexioned face.

"You're not wanted here, Terrence, I'm going to ask you one more time to leave." She unzipped her purse and pulled out her cell phone. "If I have to call someone to throw you out of here, then I will."

Terrence stepped away from Brianna. He held up his hands in submission. "I'm sorry about the way everything happened, Bri."

Brianna put her glasses on her nose and walked away from Terrence. Morgan and Noah walked slowly behind her. Lucinda, Rico, and Samuel brought up the rear.

Morgan walked faster, catching up to Brianna. "He certainly had a lot of nerve showing his face today."

"That's the truth." Brianna sucked her teeth and rolled her eyes. "I want to thank you and Noah, and your parents . . ."

Morgan waved her hand impatiently.

"Let's keep it real, Morgan, that's who Lucinda and Rico are, your parents. Reverend Sam has been especially helpful. I told him that I just might come to his church service one Sunday. I don't want you and Noah to feel obligated to babysit me today. I'm going to have the limousine drop me off at the hospital after I go home and change clothes, then I'm going to visit Mommy. You guys can all ride with me back to my house, so you can get your cars."

Morgan and Brianna hugged. "I love you, Brianna. You're still my little sister."

"Girl, you're my ace, my sister, girlfriend, and my cousin all rolled into one. You'll always be my cousin, and thank you, Morgan, for having my back."

They strolled back to the limousine with their arms entwined around each other's waist. Brianna turned, looking at her father's grave one more time and blew him a kiss. "I love you, and I'm going to miss you, Daddy." She got inside the car. Morgan, Noah, Rico, Lucinda, and Samuel followed suit.

When the driver returned to Brianna's house, Rico said he'd take Lucinda and Samuel home. Morgan waved goodbye to them when Rico drove by. She hugged Brianna before she went inside the house to change clothes. Morgan and Noah walked down the street to his silver Honda Civic that Samuel had given him as a graduation gift. Samuel explained that Gloria had been saving for a car for Noah since he went off to college. Jerome and Zandra had picked up Jerome's car the Sunday after Noah came to Chicago following Jernell's arrest.

"Where to, pretty lady?" Noah turned and asked Morgan.

"Let's go to the beach and park. I just want to chill for a minute."

"Your wish is my command." Noah smiled. He drove to Lake Shore Drive, then he steered to the entrance ramp and drove until he exited at Thirty-first Street.

"This has been the craziest time," Morgan remarked after Noah parked the car. She put her left hand over her eyes. "I am so tired. Mentally, I'm drained, and physically, I feel like I could sleep for a year."

"You've faced some very complicated situations, Morgan. I'm not surprised you're tired. I think you should wait awhile before you get on with your life. Take it easy for a while. Do you feel like walking? It's such a beautiful day."

"Sure."

Noah exited the car and walked to the passenger's side to open Morgan's door.

The beach was nearly deserted. It was Wednesday, and still fairly early in the afternoon, so people were still at work. Noah took Morgan's hand as they walked along the shoreline.

"Harry has been in touch with me," Morgan said off-handedly.

Noah nodded. "Speaking of Harry, I'm still in shock about Mrs. Foster going to prison. Who would have thought she would cop a plea deal and get life in prison? My dad and I thought without your uncle's testimony that the case against her would be dropped and she could walk away. So what did Harry want?"

"He wants to meet with me next week to give me information on how to access the accounts Momma set up for me." Morgan nodded. They stopped walking.

"How much money are you talking about?" Noah asked Morgan casually.

She turned to Noah and said, "A lot. We're talking about millions of dollars. I'm not sure if I should keep the money or even what to do with it," Morgan admitted. "I'd like to use some of it to help Brianna. She doesn't have anything. I outright own the condo downtown, as well as other real estate around Chicago and other states."

"I thought all of Ms. Foster's assets were seized and frozen when she was arrested. I know they won't give them back since she was convicted of multiple felonies," Noah said.

"From what I could tell, she transferred most of her assets to my name when I turned twenty-one. What they seized was the property she had in her name: the gray stone, warehouses, and a few other properties."

"Just when I thought I was marrying a poor woman," Noah teased Morgan, "then I find out you're richer than I imagined."

"I guess that saying money can't buy happiness is true. I may have money, but look at what came with it." Morgan shrugged her shoulders. "The people I thought were my family really aren't. My aunts and their families act like I never existed. Momma is going to be in prison for a long time. I can't say that money brought me or her happiness."

"What do you think you might do with the money?" Noah slid his arm around Morgan's waist. They resumed walking.

"I'd like to do something good with it. Maybe rebuild your father's church and make sure Bri and Aunt Adrianna are taken care of for the rest of their lives. I was thinking about donating monies to charities. Maybe I could start a couple of foundations."

"You have that much?" Noah whistled in amazement. Morgan nodded shyly.

"Those are good suggestions." Noah nodded approvingly. "I think you should keep your mother and father in mind when you start writing those checks. They appear to have been victims of circumstances more than anything else."

"I know." Morgan nodded. She tightened her grip on Noah's hand. "I'm still trying to adjust to the idea of Lucinda being my mother. At first, I wanted to just give away the money, change my name, and make a fresh start. I know a lot of people would look at the money as being tainted. But after further thought, I'm leaning toward doing some good deeds with the money. What do you think?"

"I think if you want to change your name, I have the perfect replacement for you."

"Now what would that be?" Morgan placed her finger along her cheek. She snapped her fingers. "It wouldn't be Stephens, now would it?"

"Of course that's what I'm talking about. Morgan Stephens has a nice ring to it. How does it grab you?"

Morgan looked up in the air pretending to think about Noah's question. "It sounds fabulous. Now, Mr. Stephens, are you proposing to me or something?" Morgan put her hand over her heart.

"Not here, but most definitely, I plan to when the time is right," Noah promised. He leaned over and took her in his arms and kissed her.

"Hmm. I love you, Noah." Morgan's voice broke, full of emotion.

"I know, Ms. Foster. Let me tell you a secret. I love you too."

They walked over to the large stones that lined Lake Michigan. Then they and sat down together, basking in each other's presence without an emergency to pull them apart.

Noah stood and picked up a couple of stones. He tossed them into the blue water. Then he sat down next to Morgan. "I have a job interview next week!"

"Is that so?" Morgan asked joyously. "With what company?"

"U.S. Steel. One of my fraternity brothers called and told me about it. I sent him my resume last week. My interview is scheduled for Tuesday at nine o'clock."

"Noah, that's wonderful. I'm sure you'll get the position."

"Thank you for your vote of confidence. I feel optimistic about it." He grinned.

Morgan poked Noah in the arm. "You majored in engineering, so you knew you were guaranteed a job. Do you have regrets about not joining your father as a minister at church?" Morgan felt guilty, as if Noah had based his decision on her feelings.

"Just a little bit," Noah admitted. He arose and stood in front of Morgan. He took her hands in his. "He didn't say that, but I saw the light in his eyes dim for a minute. We left things with me serving as chairman of the Board of Trustees and in any other capacity Dad needs me. We need a bigger church home, so I've been giving some thought to doing some fundraising."

"Well, you know I'm good for a big donation," Morgan quipped.

Noah laughed heartily. "I kind of figured you'd say that."

"Noah, can I ask you a question?" Morgan looked away from him.

"Sure. What's on your mind?"

"Do you think you could still love me if I don't become a Christian of the same caliber as you and your dad? I mean, your mother was the first lady of the church. I know expectations for you and Reverend Sam are high. I wouldn't want to do anything to jeopardize your reputations."

"You know what, Morgan? People come and turn to God for different reasons, sometimes it's because of circumstances, like a tragedy or someone is terminally ill. God wants all of us to acknowledge Him. With some people, it takes a little longer before they begin their spiritual journey. I believe if your heart is good and you're sincere, God will know. You just have to surrender your will, and let Him lead, and your ways will become clear."

Morgan wrinkled her nose. "You're starting to sound

more like a minister every day. Maybe you do have a calling. I just don't want you to have any regrets about me or us."

"Trust me, Ms. Foster, I've already talked to God about you. We're just waiting on you to surrender to Him, and there's no doubt in my mind you will. As they say in church, 'let go and let God'. We'll be fine."

Chapter 33

Big Momma stood in her bedroom closet selecting outfits to pack for a long-overdue vacation. With all the family drama that had ensued over the past months, she felt now was the perfect time for a Mediterranean getaway. She owned a cabana in Aruba.

Al Green was singing "Love and Happiness" from the speakers of the stereo in the corner of her bedroom. She popped her fingers to the beat and crooned along with Al. She stepped to the left then to the right. Loosened pink curlers on her head, bounced to the beat.

Clothes were strewn about the room and bureau drawers stood open. A few items lay haphazardly inside a set of luggage lying on the floor on the side of the bed.

As Big Momma removed a canary colored sundress from the clothes rack, a rap sounded at her bedroom door. Spotting a fuchsia sleeveless pantsuit in the rear of the closet, she removed it and ignored the sound.

"What do you want, Louisa?" she yelled out as she stepped out of the closet when she heard the door open. The sight of her housekeeper followed by two detectives holding their badges caused Big Momma to drop the outfits from her hand. They slid to the floor.

She pulled her robe tighter around her body, and with a dark frown on her face asked the pair, "What are you doing here?" She looked angrily at Louisa.

"Madame, I couldn't stop them," Louisa tried to explain. "I tried to alert you on the intercom, but you didn't answer." Louisa nervously wrung her hands together. Her eyes nearly popped out her head as she watched one of the detectives pull out a pair of handcuffs from his pocket, while the other read Big Momma her rights.

"Mrs. Foster, you have the right to remain silent, anything you say, can and will be used . . ." The Caucasian, middle-aged officer recited the Miranda from rote.

The other officer, an African-American woman in her late twenties, advanced toward Big Momma, holding up the handcuffs.

The older woman stepped away from the woman. "What do you think you're doing?" Big Momma yelled. "You have no right to barge up in my house. Do you have a warrant?"

The man removed the document from his jacket pocket.

Big Momma didn't have on her glasses so she couldn't read the print. "What am I falsely being accused of?" she yelled.

"Murder One. You're accused of killing your sister, Pamela Foster," the male officer answered dramatically.

Big Momma threw back her head and laughed. "Obviously, there must be a mistake. Pam was my sister. I had no reason to kill her or even want her dead."

"That's for the court to decide, ma'am," the female officer stated. "Since you aren't dressed, we'll give you time to do so. Then you have a date with us at the precinct on Fifty-fifth and Wentworth.

"I'll have your heads for this. I ain't going nowhere." Big Momma stepped away from the two law enforcers.

"So you want to play hard ball, do you?" the man asked Big Momma with a snide tone of voice. "We can take you to the station as you are. He pulled a walkie-talkie from his jacket pocket and pressed a button. "We have backup outside, in case we ran into any problems. I don't have any problems calling for help."

"Okay, already," Big Momma spat. She was mad as a hornet. "Louisa, call my attorney and tell him to meet me at the precinct." She stomped toward the bathroom. "I'll be out in a minute."

Officer Sullivan nodded. He activated the walkie-talkie. "We'll be out with the suspect in approximately thirty minutes."

"Louisa, bring me something to wear," Big Momma hollered. Her body contorted as she struggled to get into her girdle.

The frightened housekeeper looked at the officers for approval. They nodded.

Louisa stepped over the clothes on the floor and rushed to the closet. She found a black dress and scurried to the bathroom. Big Momma opened the door, snatched the dress from Louisa's hands and slammed the door shut.

"Is it okay if I call Madame's lawyer," the intimidated housekeeper asked the officers.

"Go ahead," Detective Sullivan said gruffly. He then said to Detective Rice, "Let's do this one by the books. We don't want anything to come up that could bite us in the behind later.

I'm just going to my room to make the call," Louisa said, backing out of the room.

"Go with her, Sharon," Detective Sullivan instructed.

Twenty minutes later, Big Momma walked out the bathroom fully clad and turned her nose up at the officers. She walked to the closet and slipped her feet into a pair of black pumps and pulled the pink curlers from her head. She finger combed her hair. "I'm ready. My lawyer will bail me out before you can blink," Big Momma said smugly. She picked up her Yves St. Laurent purse from the bed.

Detective Sullivan cuffed her.

"Madame, I called your lawyer. He said he'd meet you at the station," Louisa said anxiously, rubbing her hands together. She couldn't believe what had just happened.

"Let's go," Detective Sullivan instructed Big Momma.

An hour later, she'd been photographed and finger printed and was cooling her heels sitting inside a holding cell.

A police officer walked to the cell, "Ms. Foster, your lawyer is here. You can speak to him now."

"It's about time," Big Momma muttered. "I pay those people too much money to sit here like a common criminal."

Dwight Smyth stood when Big Momma entered the room. "I'm sorry about the delay, Darlene. I was out when your housekeeper called."

Big Momma pointed her finger in his face. "You're here now. What have you been able to find out? Why am I being arrested for my sister's murder? How soon can you get me out of here?

"That may be a problem. The district attorney is recommending no bail be set. The police officers saw you packing at your house, and they think you might be a flight risk."

"I don't care what you have to do to get me out of here, Dwight, just do it," Big Momma roared as her face became distorted with fury. "The police don't have anything linking me to Pam's murder. I was just as shocked as anyone else when they found her body in Jernell's garage. I loved my sister. Why, I buried her myself, when the coroner finally released her remains after Jernell's trial began."

"That's all well and good, but there's a problem. Someone anonymously sent the police a gun, and it has your prints on it. It was the same gun used to kill your sister.

Darlene, did you ever own a pearl-handled twenty-two caliber weapon?"

Big Momma was so stunned by Dwight's revelation that her body sagged, and she swayed in her seat. Her mouth formed a perfect circle. "Oh, that gun. Someone broke into my house and stole that gun a long time ago. So, of course my prints would be on it."

"Darlene, they claim, and I feel it's just a scare tactic, that they have a witness who can place you at the scene during the murder." Dwight informed his client.

"That's a lie," Big Momma blustered. "I loved Pam. I would never do anything to hurt her." Her eyebrows knit together. It was obvious the woman was shaken by the turn of events. "Someone is trying to frame me, Dwight. And I want you to find out who it is."

"You know I'll do my best. But the prosecution's case against you is strong. We have a fight on our hands." Dwight looked at his client dubiously.

"I've given your firm millions of dollars over the years. I don't care what you have to do to get me out of here, but do it."

Dwight uneasily tugged at the neck of his shirt. "I'll do my best, Darlene. You might want to think about copping a plea. That is, if the district attorney will agree to it."

Big Momma thumped her finger loudly on the table. "Look here, mister. I ain't never been a snitch. And I ain't gonna take a fall for something I didn't do. Got it?" Her voice sounded threatening.

"Yes. I'll see what I can do. I'll be back here later."

"You'd better," Big Momma said ominously. She stood, walked to the door, and then turned and glowered at Dwight once more.

When the older woman returned to her cell, she sat down on the bench unceremoniously. The officer who escorted Big Momma back to the holding cell informed her that she'd probably be moved to another location within an hour or so. "It looks like you're going to be here with us for a while." He smirked as he locked the cell door. The officer whistled as he walked away.

Big Momma paced the small confines of the room. She was livid. *I knew I should have searched for the gun more thoroughly. Put some feelers out on the street. When you want to find something, money always does the trick. I should have offered a reward. I always knew that gun would come back to haunt me. Rosalee always told me to make sure I tied up loose ends, and I didn't that time.*

She snorted like a wild boar. *Anonymous tip, my butt. Someone is trying to bring me down. But whoever turned in that gun won't get away with the scheme. I'll handle this situation when I get out of here.* She punched her left fist into her right hand. Then she went and sat on the bench.

Big Momma broke out in a cold sweat as she remembered what really happened to her sister Pamela. She had lied to her lawyer. The memory of that day was always buried in the back of her mind, and it didn't take much effort for Darlene to summon up what really happened that day. The sisters were in Pam's kitchen, sitting at the table, arguing about a problem that had arisen that day about the business. Darlene was about to go home, when Pamela confessed she wasn't comfortable about heading the business, or the business period. Pamela explained that she wanted to close it down. Darlene, of course, was irate. To her way of reasoning, closing the business wasn't a viable option. The sisters' mother had drummed into their heads that nothing came before the business, not even the family.

Darlene supposed Roscoe's death had turned Pamela soft, and that drove Darlene crazy. She felt the loudmouth stump of a man, as she used to call her brother-in-law, wasn't fit to touch the hem of her sister's garment. The younger sister, Darlene, arrived at the conclusion that Roscoe had to go. His actions were jeopardizing the family business. Thus, Darlene did what she had to do. Pam's whining about how Darlene was corrupting Jernell got on Darlene's nerves. Pam wanted to take her girls and leave Chicago to start a new life. The bottom line was that Pamela couldn't leave and take the family's future.

The argument escalated as Pam walked Darlene to her car, which was parked in the garage of the gray stone, the same house that Jernell resided in. Pam laughed in Darlene's face, and told her sister that she could take her daughters wherever she pleased. Then she turned and walked back to her house. Darlene pulled her gun out of her pocket and shot Pamela. She justified her actions by telling herself that Pamela was hardheaded, and that her sister had forgotten the first rule of the business, that no one, especially the overseer, gets to leave the family.

Chapter 34

When the Foster sisters received news of Big Momma's arrest, Rochelle called an emergency meeting at her home. All the siblings were seated in the basement except for Jernell and Adrianna. The absence of their two older sisters was painfully apparent to the younger siblings.

"This family has gone to hell in a breadbasket," Rochelle observed. "I think we need to discuss who's going to step up to the plate and run the business."

Joyce rolled her eyes at her older sister. "I think you're crazy. No one in her right mind would touch the business with a ten-foot pole. Are you forgetting what happened to Jernell and Big Momma?"

"She's right," Vivian proclaimed in her squeaky voice, "ain't nobody trying to go to jail up in here. At least I ain't."

"So we're going to just turn our back on a multi-million-dollar business?" Rochelle asked.

"Was a million-dollar business, "Joyce commented. "Do you think just because Jernell and Big Momma are in jail that the Feds are going to forget about the rest of us? I know we've all stashed away a little something. So we should be all right."

"Joyce is right," Vivian chimed in. "I got money put away, a lot of it. I will be fine."

"You two are such dodos," Rochelle sneered. "Money don't last forever. We've all been living like money flowed like water, and we've got to do something to keep the cash flowing."

Vivian stood up and smoothed her oversized top over her stomach. "What you got to eat? I'm hungry!"

"Do I look like a restaurant? If the kids haven't eaten them all, there should be some snacks behind the bar."

Vivian walked to the bar. She returned with a big bag of Fritos potato chips, and a two liter bottle of Coca-Cola.

"Come on now, share the eats." Joyce looked at Vivian. Vivian took a handful out of the bag and passed it to her sister.

Joyce put a couple of chips in her mouth and made crunching noises. She swallowed and said, "I think we don't have a choice, but to let the business go. Big Momma never told us what would happen if both she and Jernell were incarcerated at the same time."

Vivian trembled. "Ooh, that sounds so ugly. I still can't get over Jernell being in prison, and Big Momma getting arrested last week for killing our mother."

Rochelle looked at her siblings incredously, like they'd lost their minds. "Big Momma wouldn't kill our mother. That's a lie. The man wants to turn us against one another. There's nothing anybody can say to convince me otherwise. Let's get back to the business at hand. Do you think Big Momma and Jernell ever had this conversation? I bet they got tons of money stashed away. Why should we suffer?"

"And there's nothing we can do about the business, for now anyway. I suggest we concentrate on keeping our own butts out of trouble. I ain't trying to go to jail. I got kids to raise," Vivian said after she took a swallow of Coke. "Joyce, what do you think happened to our mother?"

The room was hushed for a moment as the sisters pondered Vivian's question.

Joyce ventured forth tentatively at first. "I don't know for sure, but personally, I wouldn't put it past Big Momma to be involved in this."

"I told you I think it was set up," Rochelle proclaimed. Her cheeks flamed scarlet. "I went to see Big Momma last week and she told me she didn't have anything to do with Momma's death. I don't have any reason not to believe her."

"That's you," Joyce said. "Personally, I always thought Big Momma was a little nuts." She made circles around the side of her head. "Don't get me wrong, Big Momma is my aunt, and I love her, but she scares me. Anyone who does what she and Jernell have done to run the business has to be crazy. That's why I don't want any parts of that mess."

"So are you going to run out and get a job when the money runs out?" Rochelle asked Joyce derisively. "I don't think you two realize this is an emergency situation."

Vivian waved her hand in the air. "No, I think you don't realize what could happen to us. If I have to go out and get a job, then I will. Anyway, I'm married, so Darryl will support us. I'd rather be broke than in jail."

Joyce nodded in agreement. "I feel kind of sorry for Jernell. She's locked up and Morgan isn't really her child. What a low blow that must have been for her. And for the information to come out on the witness stand, that's just plain foul. Vivian, would you pass me the potato chips." Vivian passed Joyce the oversized bag of chips.

"That just goes to show you can't trust anybody. Just think what could have happened. A non-family member would have been running the business. I'm glad the truth came out about Morgan."

"Poor Adrianna," Vivian murmured, gazing at her sisters. "I went out to Tinley Park to see her the other day. Though Big Momma told us to stay away from Adrianna and Brianna, I felt bad about what's happened to her, and she's still our sister. Adrianna has really flipped out. I don't think she even knew who I was. She kept asking me when Todd was coming back."

Vivian and Joyce looked down at the floor. They felt ashamed about their treatment of Adrianna. Neither of the sisters had gone to visit her.

"Momma used to always tell us that nothing and no one should come before the family," Joyce added. "We should be doing more to help Adrianna. You know what else I think? That Big Momma had Todd killed to keep Jernell from going to prison. And her plan back-fired. We should have gone to Todd's funeral to support Brianna. She is our niece."

"Big Momma said we couldn't go to the funeral, so we didn't. I still have mixed feelings about Todd. After all, he ratted out Jernell. I'll never forgive him for that." Rochelle had a remote look in her eyes. She took a few chips out of the bag on the table and tossed them inside her mouth. She stood and asked Vivian, "Do you want a soda?"

Her sister nodded yes. "Let's order a pizza or something to eat. I'm hungry. Chelle, you know better than to invite us over and then don't feed us. That's a no-no." Vivian shook her finger in Rochelle's face.

"I just didn't want y'all to eat me out of house and home. Joyce, I have some frozen Buffalo wings in the freezer upstairs. Why don't you fix them for us. You can microwave them or put them in the oven."

Joyce stood and wiped her hands on her pants. "Okay, I'll do it." Her heels clattered as she walked up the staircase.

"I asked Joyce to fix the food because I wanted to talk to you myself, Viv. It's too much at stake for us to let the business go. I've grown accustomed to a certain lifestyle. Why should life change at our age?"

"Let it go, Rochelle," Vivian begged her sister. Her hand was outstretched. "Hasn't enough damage been done to our family already? When I walk out of my house, my neighbors are whispering about me. I'm thinking about moving away from Lake Park."

"I can't believe you and Joyce. Why, you're both wimps," Rochelle sneered curling her upper lip. "Forget y'all then, I'll just do it alone." Rochelle stood up, and began straightening up the magazines on the table.

"Then I guess we'll have to visit all of y'all in prison then; you, Jernell, and maybe Big Momma." Joyce counted on her fingers. "It's not worth it. Haven't you learned anything? Knowing Big Momma, she's been running things since Jernell got locked up anyway, and she still is. Why don't you be patient and see how things work out before you do something stupid? I ain't taking care of your kids when you get locked up, Rochelle."

Joyce returned downstairs with paper plates on top of a platter of hot wings. She heard the tail end of the conversation. "Don't tell me you're still going on about the business. Rochelle, drop it. Let it go." She put a platter of wings on the table.

"I'll hold off for now and see what happens. But if my cash flow dries up, then I'm going to do what I have to do."

The sisters greedily grabbed for the food.

Joyce wiped her hands on a napkin. "I have an idea of how we can earn money. It's legal, and I want you two to keep an open mind."

"What is it?" Vivian looked at Joyce curiously after she swallowed the meat from a chicken wing.

"Don't laugh. We could write a book, or go on television and grant interviews to magazines and the tabloids. When the trial was going on, I got lots of calls from people interested in telling our story." Her voice dropped conspiratorially. "Even *The Montell Williams Show* called."

"You're lying," Vivian said. Her eyes widened in surprise.

Rochelle's left eyebrow rose in the air. "Are you for real?"

Joyce leaned forward in her seat. "As real as a heart attack. I've heard publishing companies pay big money for them tell-all books. Everything is out in the open anyway. Why shouldn't we make some money in the process? Especially since our money might dry up." She peered at her older sister.

Rochelle stroked her chin. "That might not be a bad idea. But we'd have to split it three ways, so it might not be worth our time anyway. None of us can write a book."

"We can get a ghost writer," Joyce offered. "That's how people do it anyway."

How do you know that?" Rochelle asked curiously. She took a couple of chicken wings from the platter and put them on a napkin.

"I did some research on the Internet, that's how."

"I guess your reading all those books came in handy. Sure, we could consider it. I hope I don't look to fat on television," Rochelle said. "Maybe Oprah would have us on her show."

"Her show is taped in Chicago, and we're locals. I bet she would," Vivian said.

Joyce nodded her head as she continued to eat. When she finished, she wiped her mouth with the back of her hand. "I say we do it, and Vivian can initiate things."

"Don't you guys think Big Momma might have a problem with us spilling family secrets?" Rochelle asked cautiously.

"Big Momma is out of the picture. Now it's every family member for herself," Joyce said. She and Vivian tapped their cans of Coke together, toasting each other.

"Okay then. Joyce, see what you can find out. If it's lucrative enough, then we'll have to go for it."

"Amen," Joyce and Vivian echoed.

As the sisters discussed their future plans, Morgan was driving north on the Dan Ryan Expressway. Lucinda had invited Morgan to have lunch with her and Mabeline.

Morgan was initially adverse about the luncheon. Noah and Samuel talked Morgan into accepting Lucinda's invitation to meet and talk with her. Samuel advised the young woman that it was time for her to get on with her life. To do so, she was going to have to get closure.

Noah was scheduled for his second interview at U.S. Steel. Morgan was left at loose ends. She spent most of her days at the condo pondering everything that had gone wrong in her life.

Noah urged Morgan to look for a job in order to keep herself busy. But she didn't feel she was quite ready yet. She'd been going to church a couple of days a week to help Samuel with chores or to run errands for the older man. Noah planned to move out of Samuel's house as soon as he secured employment.

Morgan parked her BMW inside the parking lot adjacent to Mabeline's home. After she got out of the car, she looked around and pressed the button on the remote to lock the vehicle. Then she took a deep breath and walked to Mabeline's house. She knocked on the door.

"Come on in, baby," Mabeline bade the young woman. Morgan reluctantly walked inside. She sat on the couch with her arms clasped defensively across her body after Mabeline greeted her with a big hug.

Mabeline sat down next to Morgan . She pushed a strand of hair out of her face. "Cinda will be here soon. I asked you to come earlier because I wanted some time to speak with you alone."

Morgan looked at Mabeline warily. "Talk to me about what?"

"There are still some things you need to know. And I thought it would be best coming from me instead of her."

Morgan's felt the beginning of a headache. She looked at Mabeline like a doe caught in headlights. *It's always something. What now?*

"Are you hungry? Can I bring you something to eat?" Mabeline asked the young woman. It was obvious from the pained look on Morgan's face that she wished she were anyplace besides in her house.

Morgan put a blank look on her face. Then she shook her head no. She nervously picked at a loose thread on her skirt. "What is it you wanted to tell me?"

Mabeline rubbed the sides of her face anxiously. "Your other family and mine are more closely involved than you know. Since family secrets are falling like rain, there's one other thing you needed to know. Lucinda thought we should wait and tell you. But I feel we should get everything out in the open so the healing can begin."

Morgan sat upright in the chair and grabbed the handles of the seat. "That's mighty noble of you, Mrs. Brown. What if I don't want to hear any more secrets? You know what? I'm secreted out right about now. I wish you people would just leave me alone and let me live my own life." She sat against the back of the chair, clearly agitated. She chewed on her lower lip.

Mabeline looked at her granddaughter. Sympathy shone in her eyes. "I'm a lot older than you and I've learned we can't move forward until we learn to accept where we've been and with God's help you can do that child. I promise you. All I ask is that you hear me out."

Morgan poked out her lips. She nodded to Mabeline.

"I grew up in Lake Park with your grandmother, Pamela," Mabeline continued. "We were best friends and we shared secrets with one another. Pam was a good person. She'd give you the shirt off her back. She wasn't totally comfortable with the family business. I think Pam and I both knew Darlene would be better at running the business. Before we settled down and had our kids, Pam and I hung out on the streets a lot. We were both kind of fast-tailed girls. Sometimes history has a way of repeating itself." The older woman seemed to be talking to herself more so than to Morgan. She rubbed her eye.

"Your grandfather, Roscoe, was a loaded pistol. He wore his hair slicked back in a conked style. Roscoe always wore them zoot suits and a fedora hat on his head. All the girls on the South Side of Chicago loved him.

"Pam was his heart, but not the only lady in his life. He strayed from her. Though we're the same age, I had my boys before Pam had Jernell. One night the three of us were at a house party. Roscoe and Pam got into it and had a loud argument. Some floozy confronted Pam and told her she and Roscoe were messing around. Pam got mad. She left the party and went home. Me and Roscoe stayed and talked. And . . ."

"I don't want to hear this," Morgan protested. She held up her hand warningly as she shook her head from side to side. "How disgusting! Couldn't you and Lucinda get men of your own? Did you two always have to trail behind the women in my family?" Morgan's voice broke off.

"Girl, I don't know who you think you talking to," Mabeline said warningly to Morgan. "You don't know what you talking about. Roscoe got another girl pregnant. Then she up and left the baby with him. Roscoe had a place where he went to do his dirt. He asked me if would I raise the baby. I told him yes. I finally had me a daughter, Lucinda. I loved her like I gave her life."

"Okay, so what you're telling me is that Jernell is my aunt. And what is the purpose of you telling me this?" Morgan wanted to get up and run out of the house. She never thought she'd experience or heard so much sordidness in her life.

"Like I said, there are some things you need to know about the family you're choosing to cling to. If you think we was bad, then you ain't heard nothing yet. Them Fosters wasn't nobody to mess with."

Samuel's voice popped into Morgan's head. *Remember whatever obstacles you face, God is always with you* "Go on." Morgan said begrudgingly.

"Pam and Roscoe were happily married. She was happy to be carrying his seed in her belly. The only problem they had was Darlene. She was jealous of her sister and she hated Roscoe. Darlene always called him a 'little lowlife.' Pam told me all her secrets, her fears, everything. She thought Lucinda was my niece and that I adopted her. I told Pam she was a relative's child from the South.

"Even though Pam and Roscoe were running the family business, Darlene always had to add her two cents. She undercut Roscoe every chance she got. Her goal was to make him look like a fool. Darlene was the kind who always spoke her mind. Pam was quiet, and kept her feelings hid inside. I could always tell when something was bothering her, and the way Darlene treated her husband ate at Pam."

Morgan relaxed in the chair. Though she kept her face expressionless, she couldn't entirely hide her interest in the tale her grandmother spun.

"Pam had all them baby girls and she loved them something fierce, especially Jernell, her oldest. That girl was her favorite. I worked in the gray stone with her a couple of days a week, cleaning and washing. I brought Lucinda to work with me. The two girls grew up together. And except for Darlene's attitude about Roscoe, life was good. When Pam's husband was found murdered, the light in Pam's eyes went out. She was never the same. Her heart wasn't into running the business. So that's when Darlene made her move.

"I had my suspicions right off the bat about what happened to Roscoe and my husband, Melvin. He worked for the family. I had my three sons by him. My boys worked for the family too, until I found Jesus, and I tried to make them see the light and stop they wrongdoing. Well, one of them anyway. Walter, my oldest boy is in jail, Norman is still in the family, and Willie, he a Christian like me." Morgan listened, engrossed by the tale.

"Anyway," Mabeline went on, "back to what I was telling you. Before Melvin got himself killed by Darlene, he told me word on the street was that Darlene put a contract out on Roscoe and had him killed. I tried to tell Pam what I knew, but she couldn't hear me. She didn't want to believe her sister had it in her to do something like that.

"Later, she tried to talk Darlene about stopping the drug trade, but Darlene wouldn't hear of it. Then a few weeks later, Pam was gone. I always knew in my heart that Darlene killed her, just like she did Roscoe and Melvin."

"Why did you think that?" Morgan asked. Her head was spinning from the older woman's revelations.

"Pam and I had a connection that couldn't be severed." Mabeline pointed to her chest. "When Lucinda told me that Darlene pulled a gun on her, I had my oldest boy, Walter, break in Darlene's house and steal the gun. I tell you that boy could pick a lock in his sleep. I kept that gun buried in a cloth in my backyard all these years because I knew one day that I was going to have to set my family free. I was the one who sent the gun to the police. I disguised my voice and called the law about Darlene. If I had it to do over, I'd do it a million times. Darlene had to be stopped, and I was the one to do it."

Morgan covered her mouth with her hands, stunned by the words Mabeline uttered. "But, I mean Big Momma loved us. She always took care of the family. I can't believe she'd do something like that. I don't know the woman you've described." Morgan felt faint, like every ounce of blood in her body had rushed to her head.

"Now you know your legacy, Morgan Foster, and it ain't pretty is it? This was the life you'd chosen to continue. The cycle would have gone on and I don't think Pam would've wanted that for you or for her children. And neither would the Lord. The cycle had to be broken. What Jernell was doing was wrong, plain and simple," Mabeline decreed.

"I don't know what to say. Everything you told me sounds so sordid." Morgan put her hand over her rapidly beating heart.

"I can't control what Pam's girls do with their lives, but you're a part of my flesh. I couldn't let you go on living a lie, especially with the Foster family finally falling apart."

The doorbell chimed. Mabeline stood and walked over to the door. She opened it to admit her daughter.

"Am I too late? I thought you said be here at twelve o'clock?" Lucinda walked inside and looked indecisively at her daughter. "Hello, Morgan."

The young woman didn't answer. She held her head in her hands, shocked by Mabeline's revelations.

"What's wrong with Morgan? Is she all right?" Lucinda asked her mother. She walked to the sofa and sat down. She wanted to gather Morgan in her arms like she had when she was a child, but didn't for fear of rejection.

"I had to tell her about the truth about those precious Fosters, whom she chose to side with. I told her the about what happened with me, Pam, Roscoe, your daddy, and Darlene."

"Oh, Ma, why couldn't you just let that old stuff go?" Lucinda scolded her mother. "Morgan has enough to deal with without you adding to her pain." She looked at Morgan. "I'm sorry. If I had known this was going to happen, I wouldn't have invited you here today." She scowled at her mother.

"Don't look at me like that, girl," Mabeline barked. "I know you don't call yourself disrespecting me or something. You ain't so grown that I can't go upside your head if I need to. It's time that everyone see Darlene for what she really is: greedy, crazy, and a murderer. She was always using people for her own good. The Lord put it on my heart to do the right thing." Mabeline nodded.

Lucinda asked, "Ma, who appointed you judge and jury? Did you ever think maybe it wasn't your place to enlighten everyone?"

"I wasn't gonna sit by and let Darlene mess up another life, especially one of mine. Watch your mouth, girl."

Morgan stood up. "I really don't feel well. I've got to leave. Miss Mabeline, you've certainly given me a lot to think about, and I promise to reflect on all you've told me." She walked blindly to the front door, opened it, and walked out. Her destination unknown.

Chapter 35

Jernell was incarcerated in Marion Correctional Facility in downstate Illinois. She was treated like any other inmate. Harry made sure there was plenty of money in her account. Jernell was assigned to work in the laundry room. She'd just finished putting sheets into the washing machine when the matron told her she had a visitor. Jernell wiped her forehead with the back of her hand. "I wasn't expecting anyone to come here today." She frowned. "Who is it?"

The warden shrugged. "I don't know. She said it's an emergency."

When Jernell arrived at the visitor's area, she was surprised to see Morgan sitting at one of the steel tables. Morgan hadn't come to see her since Lucinda's confession on the witness stand.

Jernell smoothed her hair on her head. She walked to the table and sat down. "Morgan, what brings you here?"

"I'm not sure," Morgan stuttered. "I guess I just had an urge to see you."

Jernell smiled enigmatically. "I didn't think we had any unfinished business."

"I'm confused." Morgan rubbed her forehead. "So much has happened over these past few months."

"That's true. But what do you want from me?"

"Closure. I don't know." Morgan dropped her eyes to the table.

"I don't know that I can help you, Morgan. What do you want me to say?" Jernell sighed. "You're better off where you are. Rico and Lucinda will make sure you're taken care of."

"Did you have any suspicions about Daddy and Lucinda?" Morgan asked hesitantly.

"No. I didn't have a clue," Jernell admitted. She pulled a cigarette out of a pack and lit it.

"Did you love me when I was born and when I was growing up? Did you ever sense I wasn't your child?" Morgan asked Jernell. Her eyes begged Jernell to say yes.

"Of course I loved you, and no, I didn't have a clue that you weren't my child. I had no idea there was a baby swap. At first, I hated Big Momma for what she did, but then I realized she did it out of love. I can't fault her. Who knows? I might have done the same in her place," Jernell said candidly.

"But what she did was wrong. She hurt a lot of people, including you and me," Morgan protested. She couldn't believe Jernell was defending her aunt.

"She was like a mother to me. Big Momma was all I ever knew after my momma . . ."

Morgan looked at Jernell mistrustfully. She unconsciously moved away from her aunt. "But she killed your mother," Morgan began.

"No, she didn't, and don't you ever say that again. I don't believe it." Spittle flew from Jernell's lips. "That's not true."

"But it is," Morgan said timidly. "Big Momma's fingerprints are on the gun. Ballistic tests proved the bullet they removed from your mother was fired from Big Momma's gun. She's in prison for murdering her sister."

"Don't be so naïve," Jernell spat. "The law can do whatever they want, and that includes framing an innocent woman." Jernell squeezed her lips tightly together and her nostrils flared like a bucking bronco.

Morgan held her hands up. "Okay, I'm sorry. I won't bring it up again."

Jernell calmed down a bit, though her chest was heaving. She took a drag on the cigarette. "Have you seen my sisters?"

"Uh, no. I've tried calling them. They don't return my calls. So I gave up." Morgan folded her hands together on the table, hoping Jernell wouldn't see them trembling.

"I'll get on their cases when they come to see me. Did I tell you that they have this crazy idea to write a book?" Jernell chuckled. "They plan to do a book and hit the talk shows circuit. They hope to go on the Oprah show," Jernell giggled like a child.

Morgan looked at Jernell with a confused look on her face. She clearly didn't understand the sisters' reasoning. "What do you think about that idea?"

"Vivian has been doing some research, talking to publishing houses and fielding media requests. They even have an agent. I gave them my blessing. All of the hoopla of the trial has them on edge. This will give them a way to calm down."

Morgan shook her head, "So they're going to expose all of the family business, and you're fine with that?"

"They aren't going to reveal all of it. I have final approval on the manuscript. If Mrs. Winfrey wants to have them on her show, then who am I to stop them?"

Morgan felt like the whole world had gone crazy. Jernell was preening as if nothing was wrong. Big Momma had already been convicted of murder a few weeks ago, and would suffer the same fate as her niece. She was being moved to a correctional facility out west. Jernell was acting like she didn't have a care in the world.

"We already came up with a title for the book," Jernell announced.

"What is it?" Morgan asked dryly. She shook her head in wonder. *Was she in La-La land?* Her world had spun out of control more than a couple of times.

"Since the newspapers dubbed me, "The Queenpin of Lake Park," we thought that was a fitting title," Jernell said proudly.

"As long as you're comfortable with that, then I guess there's nothing for me to say. I wish you'd leave me out of it though," Morgan complained.

"We can't do that, Morgan. Why—you are a major character. Rochelle thinks we can even get a movie deal." Jernell boasted. "Maybe Halle Berry will play me, and Mo'nique, wearing make-up that makes her look older, could play Big Momma."

"But your sister can't write a book. I don't even remember them reading much when I was growing up," Morgan observed dubiously.

"They have it figured out. Vivian is looking for a ghost-writer. That should take care of their imaginary money problem. I take care of my own." Jernell laughed.

"What are you going to do for Brianna?" Morgan couldn't resist asking. "She's hurting, and the aunts aren't coming around her either. No one showed up for Uncle Todd's funeral, and Aunt Adrianna is a mess."

The smile on Jernell's face was erased quickly. "There is nothing to be done for Brianna and Adrianna. My sister knows that. Adrianna cast her lot with Todd and she has to live with the consequences."

Morgan felt like she didn't know the woman who sat in

the chair across the table from her. This was a side of Jernell she'd never seen. It was obvious to the young woman that Jernell was cut from the same cloth as Big Momma. Morgan realized that her mother could become ruthless and cold when she had to.

"That may be true for Aunt Adrianna, and I'm not saying I agree with you, but what about Bri? She had no control of what her parents did."

Jernell burst out laughing. "Girl, you really are soft like Big Momma always said. Who do you think would have replaced you as the head of the family if Todd's plan had seen the light of day? Brianna, that's who. If I were you, I'd keep an eye on her," Jernell advised Morgan.

You're crazy as Big Momma. Morgan bit her lips to keep the words from escaping her mouth. "Whatever you say." She pulled her purse toward her. "I guess I'd better head back to Chicago." She looked across the table at Jernell's face. "Is there anything I can do for you?"

"No, I'm good." Jernell looked down at the table. "If you want to come and see me sometimes I wouldn't have any objections."

Morgan stood up. "I can do that." She tried to smile.

Jernell stood. "See you around then." She walked away from the table.

"Momma," Morgan whispered. She wanted to run to Jernell and hug her neck and ask her to make things go back to the way they used to be. Instead, she watched Jernell's stiff, retreating back.

Back in the jail cell, Jernell lay on her bunk. She lit up a cigarette, and expelled the smoke quickly. Though she had put on a front for Morgan, pretending as if she didn't care about her fate, her heart was breaking. She realized that she had to give Morgan back to her biological parents. She owed her daughter that much. She knew all Morgan ever really wanted was a normal life, something that Jernell and Rico couldn't have. Maybe, with a little luck, Morgan would. What Jernell had never told Rico or Morgan, was that she had two markers to claim as the head of the family and not one. The second marker was restoring the three as a family, and guaranteeing that they wouldn't face any type of repercussions from the family. Morgan would finally have the love of her parents. The reason was because those three people had loved Jernell unconditionally; Morgan, Rico, and Lucinda. Jernell cleared her throat, wiped tears from her eyes and puffed on the cigarette.

Maybeline had come to visit Jernell a few weeks ago and dropped her bombshells on Jernell about Darlene's escapades. She explained to Jernell how Pamela wanted to disband the business because of the dissension it had caused in the family. At first, Jernell didn't believe the older woman, but as time elapsed and she thought hard about it, Jernell knew in her heart that there was credibility to Mabeline's story. Jernell got a message to Harry asking him to begin unloading the business. Harry was making plans to take over the business for himself.

Morgan had departed from the building and was walking to her car in the parking lot. *Miss Mabeline talked about closure, I guess that's what just happened with Momma.* She brushed a tear from the corner of her eye and walked back to her car.

When she got inside the car, Morgan's mind processed the details her meeting with Jernell. Her brow was rutted with fine lines. She dropped her gaze to her lap and turned on the CD player inside her car and lowered the volume. "Thank you, Lord for giving me strength to come here and see my mother. Lord, thank you for staying by my side," she whispered. Morgan's head dropped backward as her mind, and heart, overflowed with love and gratitude.

Morgan's heart rate hastened rapidly. Noah had made her

a CD of what he called "inspirational music." The group, Mary Mary, sang their song, "Yesterday." Then Smokie Norful sang, "I Need You Now," "Still Say Thank You," and "God Is Able." Kirk Franklin followed Smokie. He sang, "Hero," "Imagine Me," "Hosanna," and "He Reigns." Noah had also recorded Morgan's favorite songs from the gospel CD, "A Change Is Gonna Come," and "Ooh Child." As she listened to the words and musical testimonies, the words swelled inside her heart and head. Morgan closed her eyes, and lifted her hands to the sky. Her voice sounded hoarse as she said louder, over and over again, "Thank you, Lord." As she continued to chant the three words, her voice sounded resonant, overflowing with conviction and truth.

The young woman's smile widened as understanding blossomed in her eyes. She was sure that she'd had an epiphany. Samuel had told her that the day would come when she'd feel God's love for her and how His love would fill her heart and spill over. Morgan was sure that's what had just happened to her. She felt joyous. Her head tilted upward and she closed her eyes with her hands clasped together to her breast.

"Lord, this has been some journey that I've been on as I struggle to know you. It hasn't been as easy one. I felt like my body and soul has been bruised and battered from all the tragedy that had befallen my family this past year. I didn't think I'd ever feel peace of mind again. Some days I still don't. I thought I'd be devastated after I saw Momma today, especially since she acted so uncaring about me and my feelings. But you know what, Lord? It doesn't hurt so badly after all.

"Maybe it's because I've been trying to live my life according to your will. Bear with me, Lord, keep me strong. Thank you for sending Noah into my life. I swear I'll do everything in my power, with your help, to make him a wonderful wife."

Morgan sat in the car meditating on her relationship with

God when her cell phone sounded. Her face softened with love as she checked the caller ID. She clicked the phone on.

"Hey, baby. How are you doing? Are we still on for dinner tonight?" Noah asked. His grin was as wide as the one on Morgan's face.

"You'd better believe it," Morgan smiled. "Wild horses couldn't keep me away from you."

"Good, I can't wait to see you either. Did I tell you that we're celebrating tonight?"

"Let's see?" Morgan grinned at the sound of Noah's eager voice. "You've only told me that more than one hundred times. I keep asking you what are we celebrating and you haven't answered me yet."

"Come on, Ms. Foster, you know what I mean. We have so much to be thankful for because of God's mercy. My new job and new beginnings period are just a couple of things on our agenda. We have some unfinished business. Yeah, I think the time has come for us to make some major changes in our lives."

"You know what? I'm ready for new beginnings. As long as I have you, Brianna, Daddy, and Reverend Sam by my side, I think I can make it."

"You left off some other people. In time I hope you'll accept Lucinda and her family for who they are. It took a lot of courage for Miss Mabeline to go to the police and tell them what she knew. That was a sacrifice on her part. Everyone has good and bad points, and that includes you, Morgan. The hard part is trying to accept our bad traits. But with God, all things are possible."

A burst of sunshine peeked from the clouds. And suddenly, life seemed bearable to Morgan. It was like a mask had been removed from her eyes. "As usual, you're right. Give me time and I'll do better. Tell me more about these new beginnings."

"You'll just have to wait until tonight to find out," Noah teased her. "I promise you're going to love the evening I have planned."

"I'm pretty sure I will." Morgan continued talking to Noah, as she sat in the prison parking lot. She realized that she'd be just fine. Though her life had taken on a series of bumps and bruises, Morgan knew that she was going to make it out of the storm. She also knew Noah planned on proposing that evening. Reverend Sam had been smiling benevolently all week at her, like he had a secret he couldn't wait to share.

Samuel also shared a scripture with Morgan that he asked her to meditate on daily, Ephesians, fourth chapter, second and third verses. It read: *Be completely humble and gentle; be patient bearing with one another in love. Make every effort to keep the unity of spirit through the bond of peace.* The older man told her to just keep those words in mind when she dealt with everyone, especially Noah.

Morgan and Brianna had gone to the mall twice last week, and her cousin had dragged Morgan into several jewelry stores. Brianna was doing fine financially. She'd been hired by a marketing firm and started using her father's last name instead of Foster. Morgan finally told Brianna that Harry had given her a little money and she used some of it to buy Brianna a condominium in Marina City.

So, because of Samuel's secretive smiles, and Brianna dragging her to jewelry stores, Morgan figured one didn't have to be a genius to figure out Noah's plan. She couldn't stop grinning like the Cheshire cat. A rush of breath expelled from Morgan's mouth when she hung up the telephone and started the car. As she drove back to the city, Morgan couldn't help singing along with Yolanda Adams, "I Got The Victory."

She pumped her fist into the air, vowing to be a godly

woman, always spreading the Word of God to others like Reverend Sam had done for her. Morgan also promised to be the best helpmate she could be to Noah because she truly loved him. And lastly, to always remember to give God the praises. After all, He had delivered her, intact, from the storms of her life.

Discussion Questions for The Legacies

1. Do you think Morgan was cut out to be the overseer of her family business? Do you feel she really wanted to fulfill her destiny?

2. Was Noah cut out to be a minister?

3. Some people believe that people who assist us along life's journeys are angels. Who were Morgan's angels and why?

4. Was Noah correct for not going into the ministry? Do you feel he had a calling, or could he go into the ministry in the future?

5. Do you feel Morgan eventually found faith in God?

6. Did Reverend Sam and Gloria make the correct decision in not telling Noah about their backgrounds sooner?

7. Should Lucinda have told Rico about the baby swap after she had Morgan? Was her decision to remain in Morgan's life as the nanny the right decision at the time?

8. Do you feel Jernell was driven by her desire for success at the business at the expense of her child and a normal life?

9. Did Brianna seem competitive with Morgan? Would she have been a better overseer of the family business than Morgan?

10. Should Rico have done more to get custody of Morgan?

11. Did Mabeline seem vindictive toward Big Momma?

12. Can Noah and Morgan share a life happily ever after, considering their different backgrounds? Or do you think they had worked through their issues?

13. Do you think the business survived after Jernell and Big Momma were away at prison?

14. Do you feel Big Momma was a product or her environment, or was she just insane?

15. Who was your favorite character and why?

Urban Christian His Glory Book Club!

Established January 2007, *UC His Glory Book Club* is another way through which to introduce to the literary world Urban Book's much-anticipated new imprint, **Urban Christian** and its authors. We are an online book club supporting Urban Christian authors by purchasing, reading, and providing written reviews of the authors' books that are read. *UC His Glory* welcomes both men and women of the literary world who have a passion for reading Christian-based fiction.

UC His Glory is the brainchild of Joylynn Jossel, author and executive editor at Urban Christian and Kendra Norman-Bellamy, author and director of talent & operations for Urban Christian. The book club will provide support, positive feedback, encouragement, and a forum whereby members can openly discuss and review the literary works of Urban Christian authors. In the future, we anticipate broadening our spectrum of services to include online author chats, author spotlights, interviews with your favorite Urban Christian author(s), special online groups for *UC Book Club* members, ability to post reviews on the website and amazon.com, membership ID cards, *UC His Glory* Yahoo Group, and much more.

Even though there will be no fees to become a member of *UC His Glory Book Club*, we do expect our members to be active, committed, and to follow the guidelines of the Book Club.

UC His Glory members pledge to:

- Follow the guidelines of *UC His Glory Book Club*.

- Provide input, opinions, and reviews that build up rather than tear down.

- Commit to purchasing, reading, and discussing featured book(s) of the month.

- Agree not to miss more than three consecutive online monthly meetings.

- Respect the Christian beliefs of *UC His Glory Book Club*.

- Believe that Jesus is the Christ, Son of the Living God

We look forward to the online fellowship.

Many Blessings to You!

Shelia E Lipsey

President

UC His Glory Book Club

**Visit the official Urban Christian Book Club website at

www.uchisglorybookclub.net